Dark BURNING

Veracity of The Gods
Book 1

K. D. MILLER

To my husband, Dennis. I like you and I love you.

Though lovers be lost, love shall not; And death shall have no dominion.

— DYLAN THOMAS

TRIGGER WARNING

This book has several references to child abuse and neglect. The references are to memories of past experiences, not on-page actions, but if this may be triggering for you, please proceed with caution.

Sending love to any who might need it.

CONTENTS

Chapter 1	1
Chapter 2	13
Chapter 3	27
Chapter 4	35
Chapter 5	49
Chapter 6	57
Chapter 7	63
Chapter 8	75
Chapter 9	81
Chapter 10	87
Chapter 11	99
Chapter 12	103
Chapter 13	113
Chapter 14	121
Chapter 15	127
Chapter 16	135
Chapter 17	145
Chapter 18	151
Chapter 19	159
Chapter 20	173
Chapter 21	181
Chapter 22	195
Chapter 23	203
Chapter 24	211
Chapter 25	219
Chapter 26	231
Chapter 27	239
Chapter 28	253
Chapter 29	263
Chapter 30	271
Chapter 31	285
Chapter 32	303
Chapter 33	319
Chapter 34	327

Chapter 35   337
Chapter 36   345
Chapter 37   359

Acknowledgments   369
Also by K. D. Miller   371

CHAPTER

ONE

Hades lounged on the plush leather sofa he'd summoned into the throne room. He loved his throne. It sat upon a raised dais, was made of bones and black flames, and simply oozed with masculinity and raw, dark power. He loved sitting upon it and watching those brought before him cower in fear and begging for mercy.

But the damn thing was uncomfortable as hell.

He reclined on the couch, one hand propped behind his head, the other digging into a bowl of popcorn dripping with butter. He watched a projection that hovered in the air in front of him, like a large television screen. He'd sent some of his most trusted soldiers to the Mortal Plane to observe, and though they were invisible and intangible to mortals until they chose to become otherwise, he could now see through their eyes as if they were his own. He glanced towards the alcove where his famed helmet of invisibility *should* be sitting and scowled. If he still had it, he could have gone to the Mortal Plane himself, but he'd lost it to his brother in a poker game a few hundred years ago. It wouldn't even work for anyone but Hades, but Poseidon had kept it just to be a dick. He believed his brother's exact words were "go ahead and cry about it, Crybaby McCrypants." Si may be older than practically everything in existence, but he acted like a fifteen-year-old mortal most days.

Hades rolled his eyes and focused back on what was displayed in front of him. What was on his screen had become his newest obsession, his must watch show of the season.

"Bachelorette, eat your heart out."

He grinned as he shoved another handful of popcorn into his mouth. He'd told himself time and again that he was only so transfixed because he had waited thousands of years for this, for *her*. The prophecy was finally being fulfilled and soon he would win the battle for the Underworld, and that was the only reason for his interest. It definitely didn't have anything to do with the fact that she was the most beautiful and intriguing female he'd ever laid eyes on. Not at all.

The fact that he also hated her with every fiber of his being just made things all the more confusing. She was a backstabbing bitch—*literally*. In a previous life, she had driven a rare blade that could actually harm a god, coated in an even rarer toxin that could weaken him enough to be captured and controlled by his greatest enemy, right through his fucking spine.

He scowled at the memory and refocused on the screen. At the moment, the woman was wrapping a lock of auburn hair around her finger in a delicate feminine gesture, smiling coyly at a Russian diplomat while he unlocked a small black case. She was in a long, silver evening gown that hugged her sinful curves in all the right places. Her blue eyes went wide and she gasped when he showed her what was inside: an emerald the size of a baby's fist. One hand flew to her mouth as she stepped forward, the various rings she wore on her slender fingers glinting in the low lamp light. She nearly lost her balance and she gripped the man's bicep to steady herself—it must have been a *total* accident that her generous chest pushed against his as well. Hades rolled his eyes. The man stammered as he took in her new position, how close they were, all the places they touched.

He said in a heavily accented voice, "It is quite beautiful, yes? It is said to have belonged to Nicholas II and was hidden away before the family's deaths. It is priceless."

Her eyes went dreamy.

"It's *exquisite*. Can I...can I touch it?" she asked, her voice breathless. She lowered her eyes, as if embarrassed by her need to touch something so beautiful.

"Hook...line...annndddd..." Hades muttered to himself, raising his eyebrows and waiting for the Russian's response.

"I should not allow it...but, for you, my sweet..."

"Sinker!" Hades shouted as he tossed popcorn at the projection. "Cannot believe you fell for that!" He smiled, knowing exactly what was coming next. The beauty stroked the emerald reverently, sensually, then moved her attention back to the Russian, her eyes sparkling with hunger. The man swallowed hard as she leaned in to whisper in his ear, running her hand up the side of his neck.

"This once belonged to Nicholas II...but now it belongs to me." His eyes flew wide but she'd already pressed a small button hidden on the bottom of the ring she wore on her index finger. A small needle popped out and she shoved it into his neck, releasing what Hades would bet his left nut was some kind of drug to knock the man out. A second later the Russian's legs gave way and he hit the floor with a small thud. *Knew it.*

"Or, well, I guess technically it belongs to the guy paying me for this job, not to *me*." She dropped her voice a few octaves and said, "This should be in a museum!" before laughing to herself. Hades couldn't stop his smirk—he was also quite fond of Dr. Jones. She knelt and patted the Russian on the cheek. "It's been real, and it's been fun, but it ain't been real fun. Two words my friend: breath mint." She slipped the emerald into her purse as she muttered, "Longest two months of my life. *Blech*." She stuck her tongue out and shuddered.

She sauntered to the other side of the room and threw the balcony doors wide, a cold wind wiping in to blow wisps of hair across her face. She was on the top floor of a twenty-story building in the heart of a bustling mortal metropolis, the city lights sparkling against the night sky like lightning bugs. She stood for a moment, taking in the sight. Her features softened for a moment as she sighed wistfully.

A glimpse under the mask? A sign of true emotion perhaps? A soft "meow" drew her attention. Hades ground his teeth. He was going to strangle that damn cat...who really wasn't a cat at all. Conan was a friend and acted as spy when he was bored. Hades hadn't realized he'd tagged along with the other guards to watch Skylar on this escapade.

Telepathically, he said to Conan, *-what in the hell do you think you're doing?-*

-I got tired of waiting around downstairs. Someone tried to give me leftovers from the hotel's restaurant. As if I'm an animal!-

Hades rolled his eyes. *-You* are *an animal, you moron.-*

-How dare you.-

Their silent conversation was interrupted by Skylar.

"Aww hi, pretty kitty." She glanced around again with a frown. "How on earth did you get up here little guy?"

-Yeah, see, idiot. Normal cats can't climb to the twentieth fucking floor.-

-All I heard was that she thinks I'm pretty.-

Hades raised his eyes to the ceiling, wondering what he'd done for the powers that be to punish him like this. A knock at the front door of the suite drew Skylar's attention, snapping her out of her momentary lapse.

"I've gotta run." She bit her lip as she glanced around, clearly torn about leaving the cat stranded. "I guess if you found your way up here, you can find your way down again. Be good." She reached out to give the demigod-disguised-as-a-cat a quick head scratch before stepping farther out onto the balcony. She withdrew a metal hook attached to some kind of small, black box from her purse.

"Now what are we going to do with that?" Hades mused as he

rubbed his fingers across the stubble along his jaw, intrigued as always by this female. She connected the hook to the railing of the balcony, climbed on top of the ledge—*in her 6 in heels for fuck's sake*—and connected another small hook to something under her dress. She turned back to the room and blew a kiss.

"Dosvidaniya, sucker." With that, she simply stepped off the ledge into thin air. Hades shot forward, his popcorn bowl tumbling to the ground, scattering the buttery kernels across the dark stone floor. His soldier followed her down and Hades let out a relieved breath. The black box contained wire that unspooled as gravity brought her down, down, down. She was repelling off of the damn building. He barked out a surprised laugh, shaking his head. She had yet to fail to surprise him, that was for sure.

Just as she reached the sidewalk and removed the hook from under her dress, she heard shouts from above. She smiled a wicked smile and began walking down an alley next to the hotel. Not slowing her pace at all, she tugged at her gown as she walked, the bottom half tearing off completely leaving her in a short little number that showed off legs that went on for days and most certainly did *not* make Hades' mouth go dry. Not even a little bit. She tossed the extra material over her shoulder. Next, she tore the auburn wig from her head and fluffed the flowing locks of golden blonde that now cascaded down her back. She reached to her eyes and soon the blue was gone, replaced by a stunning emerald green. She tossed the contacts and the wig into a dumpster as she passed.

In mere seconds, she was a completely different person. Hades had seen this same transformation, or ones similar to it anyway, numerous times since he'd begun watching her, and each time he found himself annoyingly...mesmerized. Despite the fact that this particular skillset could make what he needed to do far more diffi-cult, he couldn't stop himself from being intrigued by it. And ok, fine, impressed too...maybe even a tad turned on. He told himself that he was mostly consumed with watching her due to the fact that he couldn't figure out what she was, which was probably at least half truth. She was a supernatural being, but he didn't know *what* she could possibly be. He'd never run into this problem in his long life, and unlike his brother, he did not enjoy puzzles. *What are you, pet?*

He heard footsteps nearing the throne room door and tensed momentarily, ready to hide the sofa and put on his *God of the Underworld* persona if necessary, though he was hardly in the mood. He relaxed when he realized who it was. Emmeralda, one of the most powerful Seers ever to exist and one of the few people he counted as a friend, strolled through the doors without a care in the world. She never seemed to have a care in the world. He guessed it was because she had already seen all the possible futures to come, so she didn't see the use in sweating much of anything. She'd insisted on being called "Emmie" for the last century because it made her seem "more normal," whatever that meant.

She could change her appearance at will and usually her form depended on her emotional state. When her mood was foul, she appeared as an old crone with white, scraggly hair and a gravelly voice, like the witch in some mortal fairytale. When she wanted something, she would appear as an innocent looking child, all big eyes and adorable lisp. Once, as a joke, she had appeared as Pennywise the Clown from the mortal movie *IT*. Hades had nearly taken her head within a second of seeing her. He may be the God of the Underworld but clowns were...he shuddered at the thought.

She nodded to the projection screen as she plopped down on the other side of the couch.

"Doing more stalking, I see." Today she was in her true form: light brown skin covered in glittering silver tattoos, silver hair to match, and eyes of deep violet with a ring of lavender around the middle. She was truly stunning, but Hades had never looked at her as more than a friend. A friend who often tried his patience, but a friend all the same.

"You call it stalking, I call it research," Hades responded as he waved his hand, dismissing the projection.

Emmie rolled her eyes. "You've been 'researching'"—she used

her fingers to make air quotes and Hades narrowed his eyes at her—"for months now. When are you going to act?"

"She's going to be...difficult. I'm learning as much as I can about her, preparing. I don't suppose you can just tell me exactly how to make this work out?"

She smiled at him sweetly.

"You know I can't. I can provide you with the prophecies and visions as I get them, and sometimes give you gentle nudges in the right direction, but for the most part, you must be the one to act on them and make the choices you deem correct, choose which road you travel down. Robert Frost that bitch." She poked him in the ribs with her foot. He glanced down and saw that said foot was currently encased in a sock covered with llamas eating tacos. His lips curled. "Plus, where would the fun be in me giving you everything on a silver platter? Bore-ing."

He rolled his eyes. You would never know by the way she spoke that she was a thousands upon thousands upon *thousands* year old oracle to the gods. She loved all things mortal and had even requested (demanded) that Hades find a way to set up mortal streaming services in the Underworld for her. He had to admit, it was a good idea: he was a secret HGTV addict, loved mortal cinema, and couldn't get enough *Schitts Creek*. He ran a hand through his hair and settled deeper into the cushions, stretching out his long legs and resting an arm along the back of the sofa.

"Are you *positive* it's her? She's so unlike Persephone, I don't see how she could possibly be her reincarnate. Could you have gotten things mixed up a bit?" It had happened a time or twenty in the past. Nothing of immense importance, more like spoiling series finales years before they aired or tipping him off to what cards his brothers held during their annual poker game, only to realize too late that she'd given him cards from a future that did not come to pass—and causing him to lose their annual game for the tenth time in a row. After all the years and all the visions, sometimes she got a little confused, which was understandable, but he *needed* her to be sure this time. His life and kingdom could very well depend on it.

"She should have Persephone's memories shouldn't she? So wouldn't she act more like her? Persephone was so..." He waved his hand around in the air, grasping for the right word.

"Weak? Fragile? Tame?" She coughed and added "snooze-fest" between the sounds, but Hades heard her just fine, as she'd intended.

"Yes, those things." He couldn't deny it. Persephone had been his wife and he had loved her, but she was sheltered and timid. Maybe that was part of what drew him to her. She needed a protector and he liked playing that role. Contrary to popular belief, he didn't actually kidnap her and drag her to the Underworld against her will. The exact opposite actually—*she* had pursued *him*, mostly to defy her mother, at least at first. He didn't blame her for that. Demeter was a bit...much as they say.

But the sexy, brooding God of the Underworld kidnapping the beautiful maiden made for a better story, so he let the mortals roll with it. Poseidon had thrown in the thing about the pomegranates as a joke and boy had that stuck. He couldn't even begin to count the number of pomegranates he'd been sent over the years in jest. He despised the damn fruit. So, no, he hadn't kidnapped her, but her being bound to the Underworld was true, and completely unintentional. Once they were married and she was queen, she *should* have been able to travel as freely as he could...but, the Underworld had a mind of its own sometimes and made its own decisions about things. He couldn't do anything about it and her irritation soon became resentment, which eventually gave way to burning hatred and a knife in the back.

"Well, until she betrayed you and tried to straight up murder you. That was literally the most exciting thing she ever did in her entire existence," Emmie pointed out, thoughtfully tapping a finger against her chin and pulling Hades back to the conversation.

"Yes, until that," he grated, clenching his fists and biting the inside of his cheek until he tasted blood. His wife's betrayal was still a sore subject. To say that he had trust issues because of her was the understatement of the millennium. Refusing to continue the lovely walk down memory lane, he brought the conversation back to the point at hand. "But this female is…"

"Strong? Cunning? Brutal? Sexy-as-hell?" Emmie supplied helpfully, wiggling her eyebrows at him.

"She is…some of those things," he hedged. Hades refused to admit he thought she was the most stunning female he'd ever laid eyes on. He was going to marry her, sure, but he refused to feel anything for her but hatred and resentment, *needed* to feel nothing else. He couldn't afford to feel for her or begin to trust her, not again. Though something about her was relentlessly pulling him towards her…*No, damnit!* "But, I still don't see how it could be her. I think you're wrong."

Emmie's perpetually happy-go-lucky façade faltered for a moment. Her eyes momentarily turned wholly silver and lightning flashed outside the castle, illuminating the throne room in white-gold light.

"Ok, ok, so you're sure, geeze." In an instant her eyes were purple once more and her easy smile had returned.

"That's what I thought you said." She shifted on the couch, tucking her feet under her. "Ok, so listen up: some reincarnates don't regain their memories until later. Sometimes being confronted with a person or object from their past does the trick, but others never get their memories back. Regardless, she could be the polar opposite of your former lovey-dovey and still be the one. No matter how much you don't want it to be true, this little Black Widow is it. Sorry, dude."

Hades snorted. Did his Seer really just call him *dude*? Then he began imagining Skylar in Black Widow's skintight black leather outfit, and he barely stifled a groan. His eyebrows drew down in frustration, but apparently it looked like confusion to Emmie. She rolled her eyes.

"Come on. *Avengers*? We've watched them all like ten times. You even cried during the last one! Your girl is *just* like Black Widow except blonde and even more badass...and I think she even has bigger boobs." *Yes, she does...*Not that he'd noticed or anything.

"I know who Black Widow is thank you very much. And I did *not* cry...much. Anyway, I was just making mental comparisons between..." He shook his head hard, needing to clear his thoughts. "You know what, nevermind." Emmie smirked and summoned an Icee. She began to slurp and when he arched an eyebrow at her, she shrugged and then summoned one for him as well. He smiled and took a long pull, brain freeze be damned.

"Ok, tell me again, witch." Though he knew the prophecy by heart and that Emmie would give him no more and no less than she had hundreds of times in the past three thousand years, he needed to hear it again.

She rolled her eyes but obliged. "The Queen of the Underworld will rise again. She is the key to winning the war. Only when it ends, will it begin. Blah blah blah. I know for a fact that you know this backwards and forwards. Why do you make me repeat it every few weeks? It's kind of creepy..."

Ignoring her, he focused on the prophecy. That last part was gibberish, but the beginning was obvious: Persephone would rise again and she was the key to winning this ridiculous war for his kingdom once and for all. He sighed. He knew deep down that Emmie was right, that this female was the one, but he also knew that she would make this as difficult as possible and he wasn't in the mood for difficult. Not to mention he would have to be on his guard 24-7 with this one and could never trust her. She was a professional liar for fucks sake. But...he needed her if he wanted to win the war, and he *would* win the war. So, difficult or not, guard up or not, it was go-time.

He took another long sip of his drink, enjoying the cool sweetness on his tongue, and then sighed.

"I collect her in two weeks."

Skylar Pembroke was thoroughly enjoying her forced vacation time in France...if "enjoying" meant gritting her teeth and baring it. She had been here for a week, and though it was beyond lovely, she needed to be back at work. They said she needed time away to deal with her father's death, but that was the exact opposite of what she needed. Time away to deal meant having to actually *think* about and *accept* the fact that the most important person in her life was gone. Forever. Just like that. She hadn't even gotten to say goodbye, hadn't even gotten to bury him. There was nothing left to bury—*nope. Will not go down that road right now.*

So, no, she did not want to "deal" with that, thank you very much. She didn't need a PhD in psychology to know that her way of dealing by *not* dealing wasn't exactly healthy.

But she had agreed to take time off anyway, away from her admittedly somewhat stressful and dangerous occupation, so they would believe that she had come to terms with his death and healed and all that other touchy feely shit they wanted her to admit to before reinstating her. The quicker she was back on the job, the better. She was going crazy here, just itching for an assignment, for an excuse to become someone else for a little while. If she got to beat the crap out of someone in the process, then even better. A broken heart calls for a broken face—someone else's of course.

She wandered along the cobblestone streets of the quaint little town she'd stumbled upon long ago while on an assignment. The kind of place she would want to come to on a romantic getaway with her boyfriend...if she had such a thing. She had what the professionals called "trust issues" and her track record with serious boyfriends was laughable at best. She wrinkled her nose as she thought about her past relationships. Her longest one had lasted a whopping seven months and that had been almost three years ago now. She had wanted things to work with Lucas, really she had (and so had her father—Lucas was his right-hand-man, trusted friend, and he already loved Lucas like a son), but she just couldn't make herself let him in no matter how much she wanted to. Not completely anyway, though he'd gotten further than most. It was like something in her brain was hardwired wrong and as soon as someone got close, security bars slammed down around her mind and heart, alarms blaring until her ears bled.

Thinking of her father had white hot pain searing through her chest, so she forced the thoughts away. She tried to focus on her surroundings instead: there was some kind of festival going on—wine, probably, but admittedly she hadn't really been paying much attention to the details—so there were people milling about, dancing in the streets to lively music, enjoying everything life had to offer. *I should join them, forget about my own shitty life for a while. That's what Z would force me to do if she were here.*

Zahara had wanted to come with her, but she was on assignment and couldn't pull out yet. As much as Skylar loved Z and a part of her wanted her best friend here to hold her hand through this so badly her chest ached, the bigger part of her just needed to be alone. Alone was her default and she was reverting to factory settings big time right now.

Skylar sighed, walking away from the crowd. She was begging

her mind not to drift to memories of her father again when she stopped dead, head cocked to the side. Her ears twitched. Her hearing was a thousand times better than any human's and the sound she heard even over the blaring music could only come from three things: pain, pain, and more pain.

Instantly on alert, she silently made her way towards the sounds. *Yes, exactly what I need: a little action!* She could swoop in and play a little Heroball, use her skills for some pro-bono do-goodering (*definitely a word*). She heard voices coming from a side street up ahead, well away from the revelers, though the music carried and would drown out the screams easy enough to any mortal.

She peeked around the edge of a building, doing a quick mental inventory of the scene: six males total. Two of them were holding an injured man on his knees. She caught whiffs of something foul, almost like a cross between sulfur and decomposing body. *Lovely.* The injured male was covered in blood, was missing one hand, one eye was swollen shut, and she was pretty sure some of the things that were supposed to be on the *inside* of his body were most definitely on the *outside*. Damn, these guys were taking "beat down" to a whole new level.

The big guy that she figured was the ring leader said, "I'm getting tired of playing nice, Athos. Tell me why he sent you here." He was tall, blonde, and oozed superiority and danger. The injured man swayed slightly but remained silent. Ring Leader rolled his eyes and almost quicker than she could track, he slashed the injured man's chest so deeply he hit bone. The man howled and bucked against the two holding him. The blood spilling out from the wound was bubbling like acid. The blade must have been laced with some kind of poison.

The injured man was panting but managed to ground out between breaths, "A girl! Damnit, Gavril. He sent us to watch a girl, but he never told us why, I swear to you."

Stalker much? Maybe he deserved what he was getting...

Ring Leader—Gavril—knelt down so he was eye level with the

injured man. He cleaned his fingernails with the tip of his blade as he said in a cruel, cold voice, "I believe you. But it's just too fun torturing his little minions, especially pathetic half-breeds like you. Now, I'm going to play with you a bit more, then I'm going to track down this girl and have some *real* fun with her before I send her to him piece. by. piece."

Alarm bells immediately went off in her head. The way he said "real fun"...she shuddered and then rage started simmering. Skylar wasn't about to let Gavril leave this street and get anywhere near this girl, whoever the hell she was. Maybe injured guy deserved what he was getting, maybe not, but she knew for sure that Gavril had just earned every bit of what she was about to dish out. Her hands weren't clean by a long shot, but she didn't *enjoy* hurting people. Well, not usually anyway—there were always exceptions. Gavril obviously got his rocks off on other people's pain and Skylar wouldn't let that slide. Call it a *very* personal pet-peeve. *The dude does not fucking abide, asshole.*

She was outnumbered, but that didn't matter. It actually just made her more excited. She did a quick inventory of her opponents, categorizing their strengths, weaknesses, and weapons, and came up with a plan of attack and a few contingencies, all within a matter of seconds. It was like her mind had been made for battle, which was one reason she was so damn good at her job.

Her patented cold calm descended over her like a second skin. With so many of them, she needed them distracted, at least at first, and when it came to distraction for six males throwing out testosterone like beads at a Mardi Gras parade, she knew just the trick. She quickly tied her white linen shirt up under her breasts, unbuttoning enough of the top buttons that her black lacy bra showed. Her shorts were short and hung loosely on her hips, the rose and flame tattoo on her right hip playing a sexy little peek-a-boo. She tossed the fedora she was wearing and fluffed out her blonde waves.

Show time.

She stumbled up the street, pretending to be drunk. All eyes turned her way as she meandered towards Gavril and his friends, flashing her Colgate smile. She donned a sweet southern accent that for some odd reason had a direct line to most men's groins. She really *did* have one, but she twanged it up more for these guys.

"Bone-joure! Ce...umm...Ce..." She scrunched her nose in what she knew was a totally adorable way and then widened her eyes as she seemingly took in the crowd, making sure to not "notice" the guy with his guts hanging out.

"Well, I sure hope y'all speak English because I would love to have a chat with you...and maybe you...and oh yeah, *definitely* you." She pinned her gaze on Gavril on the last "you" and walked directly up to him, running a hand along one of the other guy's chests along the way. They all seemed to be in a trance. Maybe she really was part Siren? *So not the time to play "what am I?" Focus.*

Gavril looked her up and down in a way that made her skin crawl and a red haze creep into the edges of her vision, but she kept her façade in place. She was a pro, nothing phased her. The job was always Priority Number One, no matter what. She made a show of eye-fucking him right back, biting lightly on her lower lip.

"Well, I was hopin' y'all could point me back in the right direction to the party they're havin' down the street, but I think there's a new party I want to RSVP to..." She leaned in closer to whisper yell "and it's the one in your pants, handsome." She giggled and ran a hand through her hair. Gavril smiled at her and it made her want to knock his teeth down his throat.

"Oh, you are most definitely on that guest list, sweetcheeks. But I'm a little busy at the moment." He nodded towards the guy on the ground, and Skylar let out a small gasp, pretending to notice the injured male for the first time, letting a flash of fear show in her eyes. "Why don't you go wait for me around the corner while I finish up here?" Skylar made a show of looking concerned, maybe even a little torn, but then shrugged and nodded. She leaned closer to him and walked her fingers up his chest.

"Promise not to take too long?" She pouted at him and while his gaze zeroed in on her lips, as she knew they would, she grabbed his wrist with her right hand and his shoulder with her left, forcing his arm to straighten. As he jerked forward, unprepared for the assault, she brought up a knee, breaking his elbow. He howled in pain and dropped his knife. He swung at her with his other arm but she hit her knees, avoiding the hit and swiping his blade off the ground. She kicked out one leg, knocking his ankles together and bringing him down to the ground with a grunt.

At the same time, she threw the knife towards the injured man. It hit its mark, as her throws always did, nailing one of the males holding him right through the left eye. He cried out, desperately clawing at the hilt to rip the blade free before he toppled over. She kicked Gavril in the face twice, breaking his nose in the process. He flung some very creative curses her way, though they were muffled from the blood now pouring down his face.

She felt her nails elongating, turning into small, black claws, and four small fangs shot longer from the top row of her teeth. She hopped to her feet and rushed toward the other male holding the injured man. He looked confused, like he couldn't actually understand what was happening—a look she'd seen on too many faces to count. She used his thigh as a stepstool, pushing her body upward to wrap her other leg around his neck. She spun, using her momentum to throw him to the ground. As soon as he hit, she unsheathed one of the blades hidden under the band of her shorts and tossed it towards one of the males lumbering towards her, nailing him in the femoral artery. Most likely not fatal seeing as how these guys were all definitely something *other* than human, but it would take him out of the fight for a while. The injured man tumbled to his hands and knees, his rattling breaths sounding wet and sticky.

"Just stay down and I don't kill you, deal?" she asked him as she stood and yanked the first knife she'd thrown out of the other man's eye socket. "Thanks, Cyclops," she muttered as she turned towards the remaining threats: two more males plus Gavril, who was now getting up and had absolute murder in his eyes. She grinned at him as he snarled at her, blood covering his face.

Bring it on, baby.

Her grin slipped and she blinked in surprise when all three of them began to change. Dark gray claws grew out of the two flunkies' hands, much longer than her own, and their skin turned into what looked like deep red scales. Horns erupted from their foreheads and down their backs, and their muscles began to bulge. They grew larger before her eyes, now topping out at close to seven feet tall. Their lower jaws extended slightly, allowing their bottom fangs to shoot upward. She had seen some shit in her twenty-seven years, but this was unlike anything she had ever encountered. What the hell were this guys? Some kind of weird dragon or lizard shifters maybe? She'd never heard of such a thing, but she had learned a long time ago that *anything* was possible in the supernatural world. Either way, this fight just got a lot more interesting. This hadn't been in any of her contingency plans, but the number two rule in her line of business: adapt.

She shifted her gaze from the dragon-lizard things to focus on Gavril. His eyes had turned a strange glassy blue color, his pupils completely gone, and what looked like electricity began sparking over his skin. He pulled a large sword from over his shoulder though she hadn't seen any sign of it a second ago and the electricity flowed from his hand over the blade. Silver wings burst from his back, but they looked like they were made from overlapping scales of a strange iridescent metal rather than feathers. She didn't have to touch them to know that the edges would be wicked sharp.

She'd definitely never seen anyone do anything like *that* before. She had no idea what he could possibly be. A warlock on steroids and meth? She was really starting to question her supernatural education right about now. This wasn't exactly the *best* development, but she still wasn't too worried.

"Nice trick. Can you make balloon animals too? I want a pony. Oh wait, no! A unicorn!" She smiled at them again and they glowered and growled back. "Now, we can do this the easy way, or the hard way. Spoiler alert: both ways end with you losing your man parts, one way just gets us there faster than the other. Gentlemen's choice." With a sound between a screech and a growl, the two dragon-lizards launched themselves towards her.

"Guess we're going with the hard way," she said as she dodged swipes of claws and snaps of teeth, slicing as she went with her remaining blade and her own claws. Her blood was absolutely singing in her veins. For unknown reasons, she had been *made* for this. She spun and ducked, kicked and punched, sliced and stabbed.

Gavril seemed content to stand back and observe for a while, a calculating look on his face, so she threw her all into taking out the dragon-lizard twins. Though they were huge and menacing, she was far faster and more agile. She danced and darted around them quicker than they could follow.

Tweedle-Dee growled in frustration and threw a punch with a little too much force. She ducked, avoiding the blow, but his momentum took him forward and once he was hunched over, she drove her blade into his side just under his ribs and sliced at his crotch with her claws.

"I warned you about losing man parts," she taunted. He howled in agony and she spun around his other side as he tried to grab her. In front of him once more, keeping his body in between her and Tweedle-Dum, she drove the blade into his other side, hoping to pierce a lung, though she had no idea if dragon-lizard-shifter-thing lungs were even in the same spot as other species'. He doubled over, clawed hands clutching at his newest wound, and she grabbed his head, driving her knee up into his nose, once, twice, three times just for good measure. He went down and didn't get up again.

Tweedle-Dum roared and rushed her. She turned and sped towards the brick wall behind her. She heard him make a chuffing sound that she assumed was supposed to be laughter. He assumed she was about to be trapped at a dead-end. She grinned as she closed in on the wall, though it faltered as a strange feeling erupted through her chest. Not painful...kind of the opposite, actually, but still very strange. She could feel Tweedle-Dum a few feet behind her, so she tried to ignore the sensation, and when she reached the wall, she didn't slow. Instead, she leaped at it, using the bricks as leverage to propel herself upwards, basically running up the wall like a ninja. She flipped backwards, arching over Tweedle-Dum's head. He couldn't slow his momentum in time and skidded into the brick with a satisfying thud as she landed behind him. She went down to one knee and slashed his Achilles tendons. He howled as he fell to his knees, black blood oozing from the wounds. She gagged at the stench.

"God, what *are* you?" She might not have a clue what she was, but at least she didn't smell like *that*.

The feeling in her chest intensified. It felt as if the iron fist that had been gripping her heart for, well, *ever*, had finally loosened its hold, a strange sense of...rightness flowing over her. A voice in the back of her mind whispered *finally*. Some unknown force pulled her eyes towards the mouth of the street where her gaze collided with the most breathtaking male to ever exist in real life or fantasy. In fact, she thought she was hallucinating for a second because he had literally stepped out of *her* every fantasy: she had dreamed of this man more times than she cared to admit.

She felt a strange connection snap into place between them, as if an invisible wire connected the two of them across the space, a wire that she wanted desperately to follow into his arms. His eyes were wide in what looked like wonder, his lips parted slightly. For a moment, everything else faded away and nothing existed but the two of them, like something straight out of one of those Hallmark Christmas movies Z loved to make her watch.

The man took a half step forward at the same time she began to turn fully towards him, but she was cried out as a searing pain laced through her stomach. She pulled her gaze away from the man to glance down, finding that Tweedle-Dum had spun on his knees to face her and had his claws embedded in her abdomen.

An unearthly roar reverberated through the space along with a surge of power that was so intense, every preternatural instinct she had went on full alert, knowing that something in this power was different, dangerous. *What the hell was that?* She gritted her teeth against the pain, frustrated. She couldn't believe she left herself get so distracted in the middle of a fight! Tweedle-Dum's lips peeled back from his fangs in what appeared to be a triumphant smile. She gave him one right back and his faded, a look of confusion spreading over his strange features.

"Mess with the bull and you get the horns, baby."

She grabbed his wrist and pulled him closer, forcing his claws even further into her stomach. Ignoring the new wave of pain, she drove her blade up through the bottom of his jaw. His eyes flew wide in disbelief before going vacant. He fell to the ground and his claws slid free.

She hissed in pain, clenching her teeth. Her skin was burning. No, her *blood* was burning. It felt as if acid was pumping through her veins and black spots began to dot her vision. She blinked hard once, twice, trying desperately to force them away. She had been injured far worse before and then run flat out for five miles. This was nothing...so why were her knees beginning to feel weak? Why were her muscles trembling?

The answer whispered through her mind: poison. The dragon-lizard things must have poison claws. *Fan-fucking-tastic.* She needed to call home ASAP. Lucas could check if they had anything in their massive records system about these creatures so she could figure out what to do to combat the toxin. If not...well, she refused to think about that right now. The fight wasn't over.

She shook her head, forcing her vision to focus on Gavril, who was now facing off with the male she had locked eyes with. She took the opportunity to really look him over. He was at least 6 and a half feet tall, with tousled black-as-night hair. His muscles bulged under his tight black shirt and she wanted nothing more than to rip it off of him. She blinked, surprised that her thoughts immediately went there. *Ok, calm down Lusty McGee.*

The man's eyes were so dark they looked almost black, though she could have sworn a minute ago they were a beautiful blue-green color, and he had dark stubble along his square chin. His lips were curled up in a sneer, absolute fury practically pulsing from him. Had that surge of power before come from *him*? What the fuck was he? And why was every being in this gods forsaken alley something completely foreign to her?

"What the fuck are you doing here, Gavril?"

"Aw what? No hug? I haven't seen you since...hmm when was it again? Oh right—when I slit your wife's throat and burned her body to ash."

Oh shit, talk about having beef. Skylar wasn't quite sure what to do and they were blocking her only exit, so she just continued to stand back and watch, putting pressure on her wound and doing her best to remain upright. Fantasy Man's lips curled upward into a cold smile.

"Shouldn't you be locked up being tortured by my brother right about now? Rumor has it you scream like a little bitch around the clock."

Whoa, torture now? What in the hell had she stepped into here? Gavril snarled. Fantasy Man smiled wider and began to close the distance between them. Skylar's breath caught as the pain somehow doubled, taking her to her knees. Fantasy Man's eyes snapped to her and his nostrils flared. Gavril looked from Fantasy Man to Skylar and back. A slow grin spread across his face.

"Oh you've got to be kidding me! *This* is the girl you had them watching? Damn, talk about a missed opportunity. Well, good to know anyway. Your brother sends his regards." He saluted Fantasy Man with his middle finger, and then turned his gaze to Skylar "And I'll be seeing you again soon, sweetcheeks."

He winked and then he just disappeared. Like there one minute, gone the next kind of disappear. Skylar knew some species had the ability to open portals from one place to another, but they couldn't just *disappear* like that. Well...*she* could...sort of. It had only happened a handful of times but she hadn't just disappeared to somewhere else, more like she kind of teleported when she was trying to run really fast, jumping between the distances in an instant. She cast off the thoughts. She might be a freak, but she wasn't like Gavril. No way. Not that it was important right now.

What was important? The fact that she was losing a lot of blood and poison was pumping through her veins. Skylar clutched at her stomach, trying to apply pressure to her wounds and remain conscious. She needed to keep her head in the game. She had no idea what Fantasy Man wanted. Sure, he didn't seem to want to hurt her, and he and Gavril didn't seem to be besties by a long shot, but did that mean that *they* were on the same team? Maybe? The enemy of my enemy is my frenemy? Or, something like that. Everything was turning pear-shaped and her thoughts were getting fuzzy.

He closed the distance between them in a few long strides, but stopped with a couple of feet still separating them. Emotions flitted across his face so quickly she could barely keep up. Awe, rage, hope, dread, hatred—lots and lots of hatred—and desire? No, that couldn't be right. But even through her muddled thoughts, desire was screaming inside her mind as well. She wanted nothing more than to strip down, wrap her legs around his waist, and have him sink his hard co—

Whoa, whoa, whoa! She was so *not* going all X-rated thoughts about a perfect stranger right now. Despite how many times she had seen said stranger in her dreams, many of which were NSFW, she couldn't possibly be wanting to jump his bones right now. Must be a side effect of the poison. That was it...*Yeah, because lusty thoughts are a totally normal symptom in a situation like this.* She told her logical brain to shut the hell up as best she could.

Again she felt that strange connection and a voice inside her willing her to go to him. She didn't understand it, had never felt anything like it before. *Could it be a spell? Was he a warlock?* Before she could begin to wrap her head around the possibilities, she started to topple forward. She didn't see or feel him move, but suddenly he was there, catching her before she hit the ground. She felt cold despite the warmth of the day and her vision was starting to tunnel, which she knew firsthand was never a good sign.

The man's face was close to hers as he cradled her in his arms, and she could see that his eyes were now that beautiful blueish green color again. She was reminded of the sea glass she had collected every summer when her father had taken her to the beach. The thought both hurt and made her smile. Or she thought she smiled. She couldn't be sure. She could hardly feel her body anymore and everything was taking on a very strange, dream-like quality.

She didn't remember making the decision to do it, but her hand reached up and caressed his cheek. She marveled at how warm his skin was, almost like he had a fever, and imaged how that stubble on his jaw would feel against her skin as he kissed every inch of her. *Ok, definitely losing my mind.*

"You're real," she said in wonder, barely a whisper. "I've always wanted you to be real."

"What *are* you?" he breathed out, dark brows drawn down in confusion. She gave him a weak smile.

"I'm a nightmare dressed as a daydream."

A moment later, she knew nothing but darkness.

THREE

Hades paced in front of his throne, wearing a track in the dark stone. Skylar had passed out in his arms after smiling a sweet smile he'd never seen in all his time watching her, and caressing his face in such a gentle, reverent way that his chest ached.

I always wanted you to be real. What the hell did that mean? He had no idea, but in the moment, he could barely even register her words. He'd been too worried about her injuries. He'd phased back to the Underworld within a heartbeat, terror gripping him like a vise. He was frantic when he'd first arrived, bellowing orders at anyone and everyone, snapping a few demon necks out of sheer frustration. Most of them would be fine after a few minutes—he only chose demons that were hard to kill as his soldiers after all—so, no harm, no foul.

Hades knew that the poison couldn't *kill* an immortal, but it could severally weaken them if nothing was done, and he wasn't even sure if Skylar hadn't transitioned to her immortality yet. If she was still mortal...he shuddered.

His mind was a swirling maelstrom of thoughts. He could barely focus to follow one train to the end of the tracks. The most pressing was obviously his worry over her injuries. A close second: Skylar was even more enthralling in person and that pissed him off...and, ok, excited him too. The combination was unwelcome to say the least. He had planned to go to the Mortal Plane and collect her later that evening, but he couldn't stop himself from turning on *Skylarvision* before that, just to see what she was up to.

Except, when he connected through Athos' eyes, something was off. Half of the screen was black, as if one of his eyes was closed, and the picture itself was turned on its side and at an oddly low angle. It hadn't taken him long to figure out that Athos was lying on the ground on a cobblestone street.

He'd been ignoring Conan's repeated requests to speak with him all morning—he'd had enough play-by-play on the cat's "mortal watching" to last a lifetime and if he heard the phrase "yas queen" one more time, he was going to lose his mind—but it had become so incessant in the past half hour or so, he finally relented.

-What do you want, Conan?! I'm a little busy.-

-I know what you're busy with and if you'd stopped ignoring me sooner, you would have been here already. Trouble afoot my great King. Get here...and if I were you, I'd hurry the fuck up about it.-

Hades was trying to make sense of the scene before him and Conan's words when he heard her voice. His heart had somehow sped up and stopped at the same time. Rage swept through him so swiftly it startled him: his woman was in trouble. Er, his woman in the sense that he was going to marry her so she could fulfill the prophecy and help him win the war for the Underworld that is. Nothing more.

He'd phased to the mouth of the side street and had been immediately entranced, momentarily frozen as he watched. She fought one demon, and had already taken out several others based on the bodies on the ground around her, and she was *glorious*. It was a lethal ballet of grace and blood and he had never seen anything so beautiful or sexy in his long life. She flipped backwards over one of the demons, landing behind him and slashing his heels with a smile on her face. Then, as if she knew he was there, her head snapped to where he stood. Their gazes collided and he'd nearly lost his breath, even stumbled backwards slightly. A connection snapped into place between them, and though he told himself it was only because she was his wife reincarnated, he knew that he and Persephone had *never* had a bond like the one he felt with Skylar in that moment.

He didn't understand how that was possible, but he didn't have time to think it through. The demon had taken advantage of her distraction. When Hades saw its claws sink deep into Skylar's stomach, marring her beautiful skin, he had nearly lost his mind.

He'd taken one step towards her when someone stepped in his path: fucking Gavril. Hades hadn't heard that Gavril had escaped the dungeon where Zeus had been holding the prick for the last three thousand years. *Will definitely be kicking my brother's ass for this one.*

Once upon a time, Gavril had been a member of Zeus' Elite Guard, a group of seven demigod warriors, created by Zeus' own blood, that guarded him with their lives. The Elite were not only his warriors, but also his children in a sense, as well as friends, so when Gavril betrayed Zeus by betraying Hades, it was a triple whammy and Zeus' legendary temper erupted.

Hades, Zeus, and Poseidon had a fourth brother who hadn't made it into the mortal stories. Maynard was...different than the rest of them. He had come out wrong somehow. There had been a blackness surrounding him since they were created, and his very soul was a dark, shriveled thing. He delighted in the pain of others, and their father, Cronus, knew that if Maynard were given the chance to rule, that kingdom would know nothing but suffering and despair. So, Maynard had been left out when Cronus had given the other three brothers their kingdoms.

Needless to say, Maynard has been a *teensy* bit upset. Hades had always been the toughest on Maynard, always begging his father to kill him outright, or at the very least lock him away or cast him to the Mortal Plane. In retaliation, Maynard set his sights upon the Underworld, his only goal in his eternal life being to overthrow Hades and become king. Plus, Maynard practically got off on the thought of torturing souls for eternity. Sure, Hades enjoyed sticking it to the filth that had earned their eternal damnation, but overall he garnered little joy from having to dispense judgment and punishment. But Maynard would have loved every second of it and Hades doubt he would reserve punishment and pain for those that actually deserved it.

Maynard recruited Gavril somehow, and the two of them had then convinced Persephone to join Team Evil, promising to free her of her bonds to the Underworld. So, yeah, his wife had betrayed him, plotted the downfall of his kingdom, worked side by side with a psychopathic god with daddy issues, and tried to murder him. Marriage counseling may have been a good idea.

Their plan had almost worked, too. Hades had been stabbed and poisoned, and bound by mythical chains even he couldn't escape. Once he had Hades where he wanted him, Maynard had ordered Gavril to kill Persephone, forcing Hades to watch, just for funsies. Hades might have been angry as hell at her, ready to throw her into the Realm of Suffering for a few hundred years, but that didn't mean he wanted to watch her die in front of him, eyes wide with disbelief and terror, the last words on her lips a soft plea for his help. He'd been unable to do more than strain against his chains as he watched Gavril slit her throat with a godsblade and then burn her to ash with mystical fire, one of the only ways to truly kill a god.

Just as the last of the flames flickered and died, Zeus and the rest of the Elite had swooped in. They captured Gavril, but Maynard got away, running away like a coward to a hellish realm he created for himself. The bastard was exceptionally powerful and had dark magic even many gods were afraid of, and no one had been able to follow him inside. Why he couldn't just be satisfied staying there for all eternity, Hades didn't know.

Hades shook his head and forced his mind back to the present. It had been two days and Skylar had yet to really wake. Upon their arrival, he had sent for the best healers and they had worked on her for hours, drawing out the poison from her blood. Being a supernatural being, she would heal quicker than a mortal from most injuries, whether she had transitioned to immortality or not, but Hades was taking no chances: they had to get the poison out as quickly as possible. A process that was...unpleasant to say the least. Even in unconsciousness, she had screamed until her throat was raw, begged for them to stop. She had jolted awake once and the undiluted terror and pain in her eyes had nearly brought him to his knees.

He knew that pain had nothing to do with her stomach wound. It was a different kind of wound, one that had been a part of her for a long, long time. He had a near irresistible urge to flay the flesh from the bones of whomever had caused it. He didn't understand where this intense protectiveness was coming from. It certainly had nothing to do with the strange connection between them that was for damn sure. That was just some weird fluke—lust on overdrive confusing his senses or something, because oh boy was he feeling some *serious* lust, despite everything else happening. He couldn't help it.

Emmie was sitting crossed-legged on the long table that sat to the left of the dais, chin resting in her upturned hands.

"Will you stop pacing, you're making me dizzy."

-Ditto- Conan added from where he lounged lazily on the throne.

Hades shot him a look that promised pain if he didn't shut his fuzzy little trap, and ran his fingers through his hair for the thousandth time.

"Conan, did you deliver the note I gave you?" Emmie asked him.

-Of course, babe-

"Note? What note?" Hades growled, momentarily distracted from his pacing.

"Just a little housekeeping, nothing to worry your pretty little head over." She waved him off and he let it go.

"It's been two days. If she doesn't wake, I'm going to throw every one of those healers into the Realm of Suffering..."

Emmie gave an exasperated exhale and Conan rolled his eyes before leaping to his feet.

-I'm out. This was entertaining at first but now it's just sad. I'm not going to stick around for the trainwreck that is sure to come. I'll be on Olympus for a while if you need me.- He swished his tail as he traipsed to the door. He stopped and turned a yellow-eyed stare on them. *–Don't* need me*-*

"I swear to the gods, Conan..." Hades growled after him. A mental middle finger was sent his way.

-Hey, if you had answered my mental call in a timely manner, none of this would have happened. That'll teach you to ignore me. Good luck, boss. You're gonna need it.-

Hades took a step towards the door to follow him out and turn him into a tiny cat-skinned rug, but Emmie snapped her fingers at him, halting his progress.

"First off, he's kind of right, Secondly, she'll wake up in approximately 37 minutes, so will you please chill now?" He glared, his smoke beginning to slowly curl around his legs in frustration.

"Gods I hate both of you sometimes, you know that?" She merely smiled in return, so he exhaled roughly and let it go. He knew that they were both right: if he hadn't ignored Conan, he would have gotten there in time to stop Skylar from being hurt in the first place, from even going into that alley at all. "Just tell me how the hell I'm supposed to convince her to marry me. Half of me still wants do her irreparable harm every time I look at her." Oh yes he did. Though part of him had screamed *mine* when he saw her, the other part had screamed *punish* even louder. Red clouded his vision. He'd been pained when Persephone had been killed in front of him, but that didn't mean his anger disappeared, and that anger had been simmering for three thousand years. It was ready to blow.

Emmie raised her eyebrows, feigning innocence, and said in a too-sweet voice, "And what, pray tell, does the other half of you want to do to her?"

He knew exactly what the other half wanted to do. He thought back to her fighting those demons. She was fluid and graceful, but deadly and fearless, and holy shit was it sexy. She'd had her top tied up under her breasts, revealing a sun-kissed belly with a piercing in her navel. Her shorts hung low on her hips and the top of a tattoo peeked out. He thought he might die if he didn't see the rest of it at some point soon. Her legs were long and toned and all he could think about was those legs wrapped around his waist. He shot from six to midnight at the mere thought and had to readjust himself. Emmie didn't even try to hide her giggle.

"You know I could take your head off before you could even blink, right?" he snapped at her.

"You wouldn't actually do it, you love me too much." She blew him a kiss and then continued. "Look, you know I can't give you too much information here, but I *can* tell you that you're going to have to let go of the whole hating-her-because-of-Persephone's-bad-deeds thing. I'm telling you right now, holding those past sins against Skylar will *not* work out for you. That one is on the house because I really want you to succeed here. Not because of your silly war, but because Skylar and I are destined to be besties, so do *not* screw this up for me. And be nice to De...er, Conan. I mean it," she added sternly, eyes shimmering silver for a quick moment. Hades furrowed his brow, wondering what she was about to say, but let it slide.

"Now, you need to go shower and get your shit together: it's almost show time!" She grinned and clapped her hands.

Hades ran a hand down his face. *Show time indeed.*

My palms are sweating as I wait in my room. My room that locks from the outside. My room where the windows are nailed shut. My room that has no toys, no books, no stuffed animals. I can hear him yelling. He's really mad about something, but I don't know what. I haven't done anything to make him mad...have I? I did all my chores, I didn't get into trouble at school, I acted happy and normal like I'm supposed to...*You never do anything yet he still takes it out on you* a small voice whispers in the back of my mind. I sit on the floor in the closet, hoping that somehow he won't find me here. It's a stupid thought. He always finds me. I hear the footsteps on the stairs and my heart starts beating faster. Sixteen steps between the stairs and my door. Dread settles as I count them down...Sixteen, fifteen, fourteen...Please let him keep walking...Ten, nine, eight...Please make it stop...Three, two, one...

I hear the lock turn and the door creak open. I hold my breath and squeeze my eyes shut. The closet door flies open a second later and I gaze up at him. He smiles his cold smile at me. It's a different smile than the one he shows to everyone else when he reads the news on the TV. He grabs my arm and yanks me from the closet. It hurts my shoulder and I scream out in pain, but he only laughs. His breath smells bad, like the brown bottles in *the trash can in the garage. I see the cigarette in his other hand and my legs begin to tremble and my heart feels like it's beating in my throat. Though I know what's going to happen, the pain still surprises me. It burns, burns...burns too much. It's never burned this much before. Something isn't right...*

Skylar bolted upright as a scream forced itself out of her too-raw throat. How long had she been crying out? Her body bowed off of the bed and she tried to lash out at the blurry figures surrounding her before strong hands forced her back down. Her vision was fuzzy, but through the haze she saw a flawless male face hover in front of her, tension etched in every line. The most gorgeous eyes she'd ever seen locked on hers, holding so much worry and pain. He gently pushed hair off of her face and told her to hold on, that everything would be ok. She didn't know exactly who he was, but she'd dreamed of him, she thought, and she somehow felt no fear, only gratitude and a sense of...home? *Odd.*

She wanted to tell him that she was burning, that something was terribly wrong, but her mouth refused to obey. She clutched at his wrists, begging him with her eyes not to leave her, to make it stop. The man barked something to someone behind him. A second later she was dragged under again into the darkness.

Hours or possibly days later, Skylar swam slowly to consciousness. Instincts combined with years of training kicked in, forcing her to keep her breathing slow and even and her eyes closed, as if she were still asleep. She reached out with her other senses to assess her surroundings. She didn't hear anyone else in the room, detected no heartbeat and heard no one else breathing. She smelled strange, though not unpleasant, spices mixed with the subtle smell of a bon fire, but the scents made her feel safe rather than on alert. Strange, but she shook it off. Ascertaining that there was no immediate threat, she slowly pried her eyes open and sat up.

Sweat beaded her brow and the back of her neck. She felt sticky and disgusting and wanted nothing more than to take a shower. Her thoughts were still a little muddled, but slowly memories started to flash through her mind, like a slideshow: the street, the fight, that guy...what was his name? Oh yeah, Gavril. Gavril transforming into something she didn't even have a name for, a...dragon-lizard-shifter-thing sinking razor sharp, poisoned-tipped claws into her gut, and a man straight out of her dreams coming to the rescue.

No, that part couldn't have been real, could it? She had lost a lot of blood and that poison packed a punch, so she must have imagined the walking billboard for tie-me-up-tie-me-down-best-sex-of-your-life. Surely.

She pulled up her shirt and saw that she was mostly healed, but still had four angry red slashes where the thing's claws had dug into her stomach. They were already scabbing over and entering that damned itchy phase of healing, but they would be gone completely in a couple of days. She'd probably have a few new scars to add to the mix, but that was a small price to pay. Though she could heal from most injuries on her own and faster than any human, those claws were unlike anything she'd ever encountered before, so she was honestly unsure how she would fare. Not to mention that she hadn't transitioned into full immortality yet, so, she *could* still be killed by poison or injuries if they were severe enough.

All species of supernatural beings transitioned at different points, but it was a little hard to determine her timetable when she had no clue whatsoever what her species *was*. Either way, she couldn't help but feel like a late bloomer when practically everyone else she knew was fully immortal already. How many times had Z teased her, calling her the twenty-seven-year-old virgin, and flaunting her own immortality just to be a dick. It was a good thing Skylar loved her like a sister. That familiar frustration began to build, so she took a deep breath in and let it out slowly. *It doesn't matter. You're fine not knowing. It doesn't matter.* She repeated her mantra

until she calmed and then focused back on her present circumstances.

She had been cleaned up and someone had changed her clothes.
Not exactly a welcome thought, but she understood the necessity,
and could feel that no one had violated her in any way. Right now
she was in tight boyshorts and a super soft long-sleeved t-shirt. Both
had Black Widow's symbol from *The Avengers* on them. Skylar
shrugged. Strange choices, but she loved the MCU and at least the
clothes were comfortable, so whatever.

Next, she examined her surroundings. She was in a large four-
poster bed carved from some sort of glittering black stone, and she
was cocooned in the most luxurious bedding she'd ever touched. It
was soft and silky, and if it were possible to marry inanimate objects,
she would take these babies to the alter right now. *I, Skylar, take thee,
Fabulous Sheets...*

The room was spacious, with high ceilings, stone floors, and a
massive fireplace that took up almost one entire wall. It was beautiful but masculine, with lots of dark wood and leather. It reminded
her of something the Property Brothers would do if they decorated a
hunting lodge man cave.

She needed to figure out where the hell she was and who had
brought her here, so she reluctantly threw the covers off and stood
on slightly shaky legs. She petted the sheets.

"I'll be back for you soon, my preciousssss," she said in her best
Gollum impression. Could she steal these things when she left? She
was sure as hell going to try.

She did a quick inventory of possible exits and weapons, just in
case, committing everything to memory within a second, and
padded to what she assumed was the bathroom. She stopped in the
large open doorway for a moment, dumbstruck. It was absolutely
huge with a shower that was bigger than her first apartment and a
bathtub that was really more of a small pool, complete with a waterfall built into the wall on one end and stone benches submerged
under the surface. Everything in the room—the floors, the shower,

the tub, the vanity—was carved from beautiful, natural stone, making it seem as if the room had just been created by nature itself. Before she could give in to the overwhelming urge to take a dip, she forced herself to turn to the sink instead. She splashed cool water on her face and the back of her neck, and found what looked like a new toothbrush and toothpaste in a drawer.

She emerged a few minutes later feeling more human—*ha*—and ready for some answers. She made her way back to the bed and found her phone on the side table. No signal, of course. She walked around the room, waving the phone all over in various positions trying to get a bar of service, even climbing halfway up one of the bed posts and hanging off like a deranged monkey. Nothing. Nada. Zilch.

"Come on!" she whisper-yelled through gritted teeth. Where the hell didn't have any cell service nowadays? Especially *her* cell. It was top-of-the-line satellite technology. This baby would have service in a submarine on the bottom of the Atlantic, so why on earth wasn't it working?

"Well, I'd never really thought about the bed frame doubling as a stripper pole, but let your creative juices flow, love."

She gasped and lost her grip on the post, toppling to the ground with a loud "oompf." The epitome of grace. She quickly righted herself, popping onto her feet and shoving her hair out of her face. She gritted her teeth in frustration, annoyed at herself for not even hearing him approach. Fantasy Man was leaning against the doorway, arms crossed over his chest, a smirk playing across his face. Everything about the pose was meant to scream *relaxed*, but it seemed a little forced and...she thought she could actually *feel* his stress? That was just about the craziest thought she'd ever had, so she quickly dismissed it as a weird side-effect of the poison.

He was wearing leather pants, which *no one* should be able to pull off, but holy hell if he didn't look damn good in them, and a tight black t-shirt. She could see the edges of a tattoo peeking out from under the collar and wondered idly what it might be. His hair was somewhere in between short and long-ish, the perfect length to be messy but incredibly sexy in that *I just ran my hands through it* way that she absolutely loved.

So...he was real. The man that had starred in her dreams over and over again was *real*. She couldn't even begin to wrap her head around how that was possible, but it was true: he was real and he was here, standing just a few feet away. And...oh God, had she really caressed his face and quoted Taylor Swift to him before she passed out? *Mortified, party of one, your table is now ready.*

His eyes roamed down her body and his nostrils flared, fists clenching. She had the strangest feeling of...was that embarrassment? No. No fucking way. She didn't do embarrassed. Basically *nothing* phased her. She could waltz through Times Square in her birthday suit and not be bothered at all, so why on earth was the thought of his eyes on her barely-clothed body doing strange things to her insides?

Oh crap. That feeling wasn't embarrassment, it was *anticipation*. As in, she was already in full on lust with this man, who may or may not be a kidnapper—time would tell—and wanted nothing more than for him to stalk over to her right now, throw her on the bed, and...

No! Get a fucking grip! He lifted his gaze back to hers and she found nothing but fury burning in those blue-green beauties. She blinked, confused. What could she have possibly done to piss him off while she'd been unconscious and almost dying? Bleed on him?

"What are you?" he snapped.

She almost snorted. That was the damn million dollar question, wasn't it? Irritated by him despite—or maybe because of?—the way her fingers itched to run through his hair and the way heat was spreading through her stomach at the mere sight of him, she decided to go smart ass with her response. She was fluent.

"Capricorn. Now, I'll see your *what are you?* and raise you a *where the hell am I and who the hell are you?*" A muscle ticked in his jaw.

"You're in my home. You're welcome by the way, for the whole saving your life thing." His voice was annoyingly attractive. Deep with the tiniest hint of an accent that she couldn't quite place, but it reminded her of British or maybe South African, but not quite either. Then his words sank in. *His home.* She should probably be freaking out to be stuck inside a stranger's home, but this wasn't the first time that had happened to her and wouldn't be the last in her line of work. But more than that...she felt like she *belonged* here. *What the hell is wrong with me?* Had to be a spell of some sort, like a love spell gone haywire or something.

She waved him off and her lips twitched at the astonished look on his face. Apparently he wasn't used to a little backtalk. Well, he was in for a real treat with her then.

"I had that totally handled. Now, I do believe my question was a two-parter there, buddy boy." He seemed to be struggling for calm which caused her to struggle not to smile. She had a knack for making even the most patient beings struggle for composure around her, and she thought it was hilarious.

"My name is Hades," he gritted out, and Skylar barked out a laugh.

"Jesus, did your parents just despise you or what?" He arched a brow. "I mean, they named you after the Roman god of the Underworld."

"Greek, actually. The Romans referred to me as Pluto," he cut in.

She ignored him and continued, "That's just plain mean, dude."

He ran his tongue along his teeth in clear irritation, and walked further into the room, trailing his finger along the top of a dark wood table carved with intricate knot patterns as he moved. She couldn't help but watch his muscles bunch and move under his tight clothing, enjoying the show far too much. She ran *her* tongue along her bottom lip, imagining it was his. Imagined lots of things she shouldn't be imaging about a perfect stranger, despite having dreamed of him for years.

Finally, he stopped and leaned back against the table, taking a deep breath. He seemed stuck somewhere between irritated and nervous.

"I wasn't named after the God of the Underworld. I *am* the God of the Underworld." Skylar laughed out loud but sighed inwardly. *Of course* her literal dream man was cuckoo for Coco Puffs. *Can't catch a break.*

"Oook, McMurphy, that's officially my cue to exit stage right. Now, I'm happy to waltz out of here in my underoos, but if you would be so kind as to throw me some pants, that might make this less awkward for all the males that will inevitably see me and die from sudden onset raging boner syndrome. It's a very real and very serious medical condition. Thousands suffer every year when I'm nearby." She wiggled here eyebrows at him.

His eyes darkened from blue-green to near black for a quick moment. So she hadn't imagined that before! How strange. Luke's eyes turned to a deep gold when he shifted, but this was different.

He took a deep breath in and let it out slowly before responding.

"I am not flying over the Cuckoo's nest, thank you very much." *Points for him getting the reference.* "I *am* Hades. This is my home. You are in the Underworld...and just as an aside," he said, leaning towards her, "no other male will *ever* be seeing you in your current state if he wishes to keep his eyeballs in their sockets."

That last bit shocked her...and, ok, kind of excited her too. He didn't want any other guys oogling her goodies, which meant he would be jealous of said guys. This sexy as all hell man would be *jealous* of someone else looking at her. Talk about the ultimate high five to the ego. But then she forced herself to focus on the actual important things he'd just said.

"Oook, I *definitely* believe you. You're Hades and this is the Underworld. Isn't there a three headed dog running around here somewhere? Oh and you're married, aren't you? Dangit, what was her name? We learned this crap in like seventh grade. It's P something...Piccadilly? Penelope?" She scrunched her nose in concentration and then snapped her fingers. "Persephone! That's it. Is she wandering around here somewhere too, eating pomegranates and umm...making Spring a thing? Ok, so I admittedly didn't pay that much attention in class, so I'm fuzzy on the details, but still."

"She is dead," he growled, his lip curling up in a sneer. "She's been dead for three thousand years." Fury practically pulsed off of him in waves, so thick she could almost feel it. Tendrils of black smoke began to curl around his ankles, and she took a small involuntary step backwards, shifting her position slightly, preparing to fight. The move was so engrained in her, so instinctual, she didn't even realized she'd done it until he seemed to notice, closing his eyes and forcing himself to calm.

He sounded so serious and upset about Persephone's death that she almost believed him. *Almost.* She knew of the supernatural world, was a part of it though no one knew exactly *what* she was. She had seen vampires and shifters, selkies and banshees, nymphs and sirens and lupin...but gods? *Actual* gods like Mt. Olympus and lightning bolts and all that? No fucking way. Mr. I-Can-Pull-Off-Leather-Pants-Like-Nobody's-Business was batshit crazy, that was the only logical explanation. *And yet*...a small part of her mind whispered, *all mortal stories are rooted somewhere in fact.* She shook her head to dispel the thought. No, just no! This couldn't be real, she could *not* be standing in front of Hades, like *the* Hades. But that damn logical, calculating part of her brain kept on hacking away at the problem, desperate to get to the solution, like a sculptor carving away bits of marble until a figure emerged.

She thought back to the fight with Gavril and the dragon-lizard things. They had looked like the typical description of...of...*damnit!* She forced herself to think the word: *demons.* They'd looked like what she pictured demons would look like, hadn't they? She had no idea what Gavril was, but she knew deep in her bones that he was more than a mere supernatural being. No, he was something entirely different. Perhaps something...godly? She was starting to see the possibilities laid out before her, the potential truth in his words, but still, she rebelled against the thoughts and focused back on what she could control.

"Well, I'm very sorry to hear that your imaginary wife died three thousand years ago. Really, condolences and all that. Now, I'll admit that you did me a solid by not leaving me in that alleyway, so thanks, but I should really be on my way now. Where did we land on that whole pants issue? Pants and a map to the nearest exit would just be awesome sauce."

His lips twitched like he was fighting a smile, but his only response was, "As much as I would love to oblige, I'm afraid I can't do that. You aren't leaving."

And there it was. Kidnapper after all. She wasn't worried though, not in the slightest. He had no idea who he was dealing with, the kind of training she had. She'd be out of here in no time flat and would make him pay for even attempting to hold her here in the first place.

"That's a good joke. Have you heard the one about the genie and the pianist?"

"I pity the man who has to ask a genie for a ten inch...*pianist.* Some of us come by that naturally." He gave her a smile full of dark and dirty promises that made her legs tremble. *No way that's true...but if it is...ooh momma.* He continued on, "But this is no joke, Skylar." The sound of her name on his lips momentarily highjacked her thoughts again. Goosebumps erupted all over her skin and a tingle shivered its way down her spine. His voice was gruff yet somehow a soft purr at the same time. Basically, it was so sexy it should be illegal. She wanted to hear him say it over and over and over, whisper it against her skin, yell it to the rafters. *Wait, no!* This guy had all but admitted he was kidnapping her and was possibly unhinged enough to believe he was a freaking Greek god. She could *not* be wanting to jump his bones right now.

She shook herself and put on her battle pants—metaphorically of course seeing as how she was still in her dang underwear. She curled her lips upward and stalked towards him, rolling her hips. His eyes widened slightly and he straightened, his entire body going tense. She saw both irritation and excitement in the blue-green pools. She was intrigued by his conflicting emotions, but she had to get the hell out of Dodge ASAP. She pulled a carved metal sun from her sleeve, hiding it in her palm. It had been attached to the front of a leather book on one of the shelves but now it was a handy dandy throwing star. *Adapt, adapt, adapt.*

Skylar didn't slow as she flicked the sun towards him with uncanny speed and accuracy. She nailed him in the shoulder. She didn't want to kill him, or even seriously injury him for reasons she didn't understand, but she needed him distracted for a few seconds so she could bolt.

He cursed as the metal embedded in his flesh with a wet *thunk*, and she took the opportunity to sprint out of the open door. She ran down a long, oversized hallway at full speed, nearly flying across the floor. She heard Fantasy Man—Hades? *Ugh no!*—make his way into the hallway as well. She flew past other doorways but never slowed. Part of her mind admired the beauty of the place as she ran. Everything was very gothic-chic and gorgeous.

"Damnit, Skylar, stop running."

"No, but thanks for asking!" she called over her shoulder. He was giving chase, but she had a feeling he wasn't trying all that hard. Did he think she couldn't escape? Ha! She could get herself out of any situation. She was one of the best agents in the company. Her father had trained her himself since practically day one, so getting out of here would be a piece of cake. She took a right and towering double doors loomed in front of her. Doors leading outside? *Worth a shot.* She careered through them but skidded to a stop about half way into the space.

It was a...a...well, hell, the only way to describe it was a throne room. It was long and rectangular, and simply screamed *masculine* and *power*. The walls were that black glittering stone, same as her bed, and a deep crimson rug with swirling black designs ran the length of the room. No, not designs, runes. She had no idea what they meant, but she could feel the power in them. Torches were set into the walls, each held by a carving of what looked like a demon. It took her a minute to realize that the flames were black, as were the flames on the fucking *throne* sitting on the raised dais in the center of the room.

The Iron Throne had nothing on this bad boy. It was huge and made out of what looked like bones. Human? *Gulp.* The flames danced along the high back and she had to admit that anyone sitting there would look pretty badass. She tilted her head slightly. The throne seemed to be...calling to her. *Mine,* her mind purred. She quickly told herself that she only wanted to sit there to take a quick selfie. That was all. A great photo-op that Z would get a kick out of, that was it. The fact that it seemed to be beckoning her, seemed to... *want* her to sit there, was just her mind playing tricks on her. After effects of the poison or something.

She stumbled backwards a step as Pretend Hades appeared on the throne. Just *poof!* and he was there. Apparently he and Gavril shared that nifty ability. He lounged in the seat and smirked at her. The flames grew higher, as if responding to his presence. Looking at him sitting there, surrounded by bones and black fire, she couldn't deny that he looked every bit the King of the Underworld he claimed to be...*and FML he looks sexy as hell.*

But no, this couldn't be real, it just couldn't! He was just a delusional warlock, that was all. She knew that the rational part of her brain was starting to gain more traction, overpowering her denials. She was pretty sure that he was telling the truth. Which meant he really was Hades...and she was in big, big trouble.

He sat up straighter and said, "There's no use in running. You cannot leave the Underworld without my help. Could have done without the stabbing too, might I add." His wound had already closed, the only evidence it had even existed was a small rip in his shirt and a few tiny dots of blood. Her mind was whirling and unease was squeezing her chest. She could hold her own, but...against a god? What the fuck? But even so, she kept her calm, sarcastic façade firmly in place. *Fake it til you make it, baby.*

"What?" Skylar asked innocently. "You don't like a little fore-play?" His eyes widened slightly but otherwise he showed no reaction. "Now, just like Luda likes em, I'm a lady in the streets but a freak in the bed, so let's move right along from foreplay into role playing: let's pretend I'm the devastatingly stunning captive who actually believes that you're Hades, God of the Underworld. Why exactly am I here?"

He shifted in the seat, leaning forward and to rest his elbows on his knees.

"That's simple enough: you're here to be my wife."

FIVE

Ok, truth bomb dropped. Hades hadn't exactly meant to do it, but his thoughts were jumbled and it just came out—word vomit, as Emmie called it. Having Persephone back here was making his blood boil and his power desperate to lash out and punish...yet having *Skylar* here was making all that blood rush to a certain appendage. Seeing her hanging off the bedpost in nothing but a t-shirt and underwear that were cut so that the delicious bottom curve of her ass cheeks peeked out had him so hard he wondered if his cock would burst through his pants. The thought of any other male seeing her in that state had the strangest sense of possessiveness roaring in his mind. He wanted to flay anyone who so much as looked her direction with lust in their eyes. *So strange.* He'd never been possessive or jealous over any female before, not even his wife the first time around.

Then she'd thrown a make-shift throwing star at him. Now, usually someone drawing his blood put a damper on his mood and that person quickly learned a new definition of pain, but when Skylar had done it, had *excited* him. He liked that she didn't cower from him, liked that she surprised him, liked that she was fierce.

Which pissed him off all the more. He didn't want to like a damn thing about her. He had to marry her—again—but he didn't need or want to actually like her.

She had him boomeranging between emotions so quickly his head was spinning. Hate, to lust, to amusement, to rage, to something dangerous he refused to name, and back to lust again. Ok, who was he kidding? The lust was there constantly, but who could blame him? She was his every fantasy made flesh. Fate seemed to have a very sick sense of humor in giving Persephone this form this time around.

"I'm never eating tacos again," she said. His brows drew down in confusion. Well, that wasn't quite the response he was expecting. "Oh, I'm sorry, are we *not* just saying the most ridiculous things we can think of? My bad."

Being his wife was ridiculous to her? The thought made him angry, and he really didn't know why. He didn't actually *want* to be married to her either, but he needed to. She had to officially become queen again if he was going to triumph in his war, so therefore they were getting hitched. Simple as that. He'd already gone down the rabbit hole of if she was Persephone reincarnated then *technically* she was already queen, but Emmie had shot him down, insisting it didn't work that way. Something about the queen title being connected to the body, not the soul. He didn't understand but learned long ago not to question Emmie.

So, he resigned himself to the fact that he had to get Skylar to agree to marry him. But it was merely a business deal, plain and simple, despite what his cock seemed to think. Why should he care if she didn't want to marry him either?

"Why on earth would I marry you?" she huffed out with an incredulous laugh, but then she tilted her head, and Hades could practically see her mind calculating the situation, all the possible angles, and it fascinated him. After a few seconds, her eyes narrowed. "Wait. Better question: why do *you* want to marry *me*?"

"Doesn't matter. It's going to happen. The sooner you accept it the better."

"You'd force me?" she gritted out, absolute rage flaring in those gorgeous green eyes, though he saw the tiniest sliver of panic as well. Damnit. No, of course he wouldn't force her. For one, for the bond between them to take root, for her truly to be queen, the marriage had to be entered into willingly. Actual *love* didn't have to be involved of course, but free will did. But more importantly, he had never—and would never—force *anything* on a female. That shit wasn't tolerated in his kingdom. The souls that made their way to him with that particular crime on their resume received extra special treatment for all of eternity, sent to the worst of the realms within the Underworld.

"I would not. But you aren't leaving here until you agree to marry me, so it's in your best interest to get on board, as they say. It's not without its perks I assure you. I'd be making you a queen after all. You'd rule at my side, have anything and everything you could possibly dream of. My power would be shared between us." She crossed her arms across her chest and jutted her chin, the epitome of stubborn. And damn him, part of him liked it. He liked a challenge. He liked being pushed. He tried to stop his thoughts from thinking of it in terms of the bedroom, grinding his teeth when he failed. Not that they'd be getting anywhere near the fucking bedroom together, but...it couldn't hurt to imagine, he supposed.

"Never gonna happen, Hay-deeze Nuts." She snorted at her own joke. His own lips tried curl into a smile, but he fought it. Laughing at her jokes was the first step into softening towards her, and that would not be happening. She eyed him critically for a long moment.

"I still don't believe you. About the whole *I'm a mythological god* thing. Can you provide any kind of actual proof?"

He did grin then. *This could be fun.* He phased, materializing in front of her, only inches separating them. She gasped and her hands flew to his chest to steady herself. He thought surely she would try to punch him or, at the very least, shove him away, but instead she flattened her palms against him. She looked to be lost for a moment, in a trance, before she began gently moving her fingertips over his chest. She bit her bottom lip and the action had a direct line to his cock. What was it she had said before? Swift onset raging boner syndrome? She was right—it was a real medical condition and he was badly, *badly* afflicted. She seemed to realize what she was doing and hastily dropped her hands to her sides, taking a small step back, looking annoyed. With herself or him, he wasn't sure.

In the next instant, Hades was on his ass. *What the...?* She had managed to kick out a leg, knocking his ankles together and bringing him down hard. His breath left him in a whoosh, which was unfortunate since in the next instant she kicked his balls into his throat and being able to breath would have been nice.

He cursed himself for getting played already. She had pretended to be lost in the feel of him to distract him. And it had worked like a fucking charm. *Damn her!* As he groaned and rolled to his side, she sprinted out onto the large balcony. He sat up and watched her stop momentarily to take in the view, then shake herself and leap up onto the railing. He had to force himself not to admire the view himself. The sun was bathing her in deep orangey-gold light, her hair was dancing around her in the breeze, and those asscheeks...*Dear gods.*

"Skylar..." he growled. She spared him a quick look over her shoulder, her eyes dancing with excitement. She blew him a kiss, flipped him off, and jumped. His heart stopped beating. Could she survive the fall? He thought she could but...he immediately phased below the balcony. He materialized just as she reached the ground. Safely, landing on one knee and immediately springing to her feet. She whirled on him, landing a punch to his chest that had him stumbling backwards a few feet. He'd known that she was stronger than she appeared, but she was stronger than he could have imagined. Her gaze swept around them, no doubt inventorying all of the possible escape routes and weapons, and coming up with a game plan.

She blew a lock of hair out of her face and said, "Maybe you didn't get the whole "I'm leaving" memo, so let me summarize it for you." She was on him so fast he thought for a moment that she had the ability to phase. She raked tiny claws across his cheek, then spun behind him to kick out his knee. "I'm outta here, dickhead."

She sped off again as he got to his feet. He could feel the skin on his cheek already beginning to knit back together. He watched her run and though he was annoyed as hell at being kneed in the jewels, punched, clawed, *and* kicked, he had to admit he was also amused. This was...fun. More fun than he'd had in years, if he was being honest with himself. Which was truly pathetic, but he pushed that thought away.

He let her make it to the edge of the lawn and into the copse of trees lining the west side of the castle before he phased again a few feet in front of her. She ran right into his chest, but before she could bounce off, he grabbed her arms to steady her. She didn't hesitate, immediately bringing both arms up and slamming her elbows down against his, breaking his hold. She tried to slash his neck, but he caught her wrist, twisting it to the side almost hard enough to snap the bone. She gritted her teeth but spun her body the same direction, putting her back to his chest, and threw an elbow out behind her into his chin. He felt the bone splinter and spit out blood. *Little witch.* She went to do it a second time and he grabbed her elbow, spinning her again, and then tossing her backwards as if she weighed nothing.

She spun in mid-air like some kind of acrobat, landing on her feet in a low crouch and skidding backwards several feet. She was grinning and he could almost sense her enjoyment, but then she seemed to catch herself, the smile turning into a scowl.

"Look, just come back to the castle and stop this nonsense, alright? You can't leave this place. Even if you get away from me and off the castle grounds, there are literal hell realms that you could stumble into if you aren't careful. You're tough, but you're out of your league here."

"Oh, right. I forgot. I'm in the 'Underworld' with 'Hades'." She did air quotes with her fingers and he ground his teeth. "I forgot to mention that I'm the Tooth Fairy, so not to worry, I can handle myself." Before he could respond, she turned and sprinted away again. He sighed but let her go. She'd tire herself out eventually. She couldn't actually leave the grounds, so he really didn't have anything to worry about.

But her piercing scream a few moments later said otherwise.

SIX

oly shit. Skylar was staring at...well she wasn't actually sure what she was staring at. She'd exited the woods and ran right into a creature that was straight out of a nightmare. It was over seven feet tall with deadly looking spikes on the end of its tail and one coming out of the top of each shoulder. Its skin was a greenish-black color and its eyes were blood red. Membranous wings flared from its back, the bony parts black and the skin in between a scaly crimson. When it huffed out a breath, small flames licked from its nose and mouth. *Holy shit, holy shit, holy shit.*

It raised a sword that was almost as long as she was and pointed it her direction, a clear sign to stop in her tracks. She could hold her own against most creatures but she had to admit that this thing might just be too much for her. Best option: turn tail and run. She was getting ready to do just that when strong arms banded around her from behind.

She stifled a gasp when Pretend Hades whispered in her ear, "Don't. Move. It can't see us if you don't move."

The creature raised an eyebrow, lowering its sword, and Pretend

Hades laughed low in her ear. The sound was warm and rich and made her skin tingle in a delicious way. *Wait…*What he'd just said sounded familiar…

She spun, putting her back to the creature—normally a dumb move, but she now knew the creature answered to Pretend Hades, so she figured she was relatively safe from an attack—and shoved him in the chest.

"*Jurassic Park*? Really?"

"What? It's a great movie!" He chuckled again when she balled her fists, ready to punch the grin off of his stupidly perfect face. He was having fun with this. "But really, you can relax. He won't harm you. He's one of my guards."

The creature nodded to her—and winked?—before walking off, sword casually resting on his enormous shoulder. She stared in wonder as he strolled off.

"What the hell was that thing?"

"That's Jeff."

She barked out a laugh, turning her gaze back to Pretend Hades. "Come again?"

His eyes blazed and his lips curled into a sexy smirk. He replied in a smooth voice, "But I haven't even come once yet, love."

Skylar swallowed hard as her insides melted. *Dirty flirting from the headliner of my own personal lady spank bank? Seriously not fair.* She rolled her eyes, hoping he couldn't tell how his words affected her. His smirk kicked up a notch and she had a bad feeling that he knew exactly what he'd done.

"He's a Rathos Demon. They can breathe fire and are obviously incredibly huge and strong and scary. Hence the guard duty."

Demon. She tried to reject the explanation, but found that she just couldn't. That's exactly what *Jeff* had to be. She had officially lost the battle within her mind. She believed him. He was…*Holy shit, he's freaking Hades.* The gods were real. She was simultaneously terrified and awed, the inquisitive part of her mind already burning up with a million questions. However, her hopes of escape crashed and burned in an instant. Sure, she could get out of pretty much any situation, but up against an actual god who wanted her to remain in his company? How the hell was she supposed to fight against *that*?

She tried desperately to remember anything she had ever read about the gods, Greek or otherwise, hoping maybe some kind of weakness would make itself known. Achilles had his heel, so maybe Hades had something too. Nothing was coming to mind, so until something did, maybe she should play nice? It was a sound strategy and one she'd used about a thousand times before. Lure them in, make them think you're sweet or innocent or dying to be their girl-friend, and then BAM!

She could play with him...couldn't she? Hades interrupted her thoughts.

"You can't escape, so you shouldn't try. You'll just end up hurting yourself or those in my kingdom."

He closed the small distance between them and pulled her against him, one arm wrapped around the small of her back. She gasped and then had to stifle a groan at the feel of his body against hers. It felt so unbelievably *right*, like a balm on a burn, soothing some pain that she hadn't even realized ailed her just by the touch of his body to hers. A heartbeat later they were standing in a bedroom. It wasn't as large as the one she'd woken up in, but would definitely still be considered huge. It was lighter than the other room, more feminine. The stone floors were white with sparkling silver threaded throughout, reminding her of the marble countertops at her father's house that served as headquarters for their company. The bed was huge, almost twice as big as a king size, she thought, with white and silver bedding and a matching sheer canopy. One entire wall was nothing but glass, opening up onto a huge balcony looking out over... the Underworld. *Cannot believe that's a thought I actually had in real life.*

Hades held her for a long second, but finally dropped his arm and backed up several steps. She was both disappointed and glad. She was far more affected by his touch than she should be or would ever admit out loud.

"This is your room," he said a little gruffly, folding his arms over his chest. "You can decorate it however you wish." As if she'd be here long enough to worry about decorating! Despite his warning and despite the fact that she weirdly felt connected to him and this place, she *would* escape sooner rather than later. She walked around, letting her fingers trail along the plush couch and pillows that sat to one side of the room in front of a large stone fireplace. She was secretly thrilled that her room had one as well. She had a weird thing for fireplaces. Well, for fires in general really. Not in a pyromaniac kind of way, but she'd just always enjoyed them. Even in the dead of summer, she would often have the urge to light one in her room back home. She would stare at the flames for hours, finding solace and calm in the way they danced and moved. She thought maybe it went back to the backyard bon fires her dad had always made when she was younger, s'mores included, of course, and assumed that the comfort she'd always found in the flames was associated with the first time she'd really felt safe and loved.

Funny that Hades' scent reminded me of those fires as well...

Though she acted unconcerned with his presence, she kept him in her peripheral. He tracked her every movement, watching her like a hawk watches as a field mouse. Little did he know, that *she* was a hunter too.

"And how long, exactly, do you expect me to stay here?"

"Indefinitely," he replied without hesitation. She grinned inwardly. *Game on then, sucker.*

Skylar stopped her perusal of the room and turned to find Hades' eyes traveling back up from where they most definitely had just been glued to her ass. She somehow kept forgetting she had no pants on and she knew damn well these undies showed him more than a little peek of ass. She was fully prepared to go toe to toe with him, regardless of the fact that he was a legit *god*, but when their eyes locked, all of that faded into the background. His darkened as she watched, turning from blue-green to an almost glittering black, and they burned with unmistakable desire.

Something began to shift around them, thickening with tension, sparking with electricity. Her breaths became quick and shallow and she licked her lips in anticipation—and invitation. His gaze followed the movement and he shifted forward, as if to move towards her. But then that blaze in his eyes shifted to one of pure *hatred*, the desire completely forgotten. She blinked at the sudden change, her entire body going rigid in response to his aggression, instincts flaring. His lip curled upward in disgust and then he just disappeared.

What in the hell had that been about? The weird hatred was one thing, but before that? The intense lusty stare down? What the fuck? In what world did Skylar fucking Pembroke want to knock boots with someone who kidnapped her?? *Apparently this one.*

Frustrated, she flung herself down on the bed, arms splayed over her head. She forced herself not to focus on the fact that it was the most comfortable thing in the universe, and instead filed through everything that had happened and everything she'd seen and learned.

She finally forced herself to accept a few key facts:

One: The gods were real.

Two: She truly was in the Underworld, apparently stuck here for the foreseeable future.

Three: Hades wanted her to be his bride.

Which brought her around to the biggest, and most important conclusion of the night.

She was completely and royally screwed.

SEVEN

ades had told her not to try to escape again. Skylar, of course, said fuck that. She'd climbed down the trellis beside her balcony—a feat that made even her heart skip a beat or two—and made a break for it as soon as she woke the next morning. She stealthily made her way towards the front of the castle, and by God, it was a legit *castle*. It was made out of that same black stone as the throne room, with towers and turrets and statues of demons perched on the numerous ledges and spires. It reminded her of the castle in *Beauty and the Beast* before the curse was lifted, or what Dracula might have lived in at some point—he preferred more of a French Countryside esthetic these days. Despite the dark, menacing look, it was also oddly beautiful and it seemed to beckon to her, just as the throne had. *What in the* hell?

She kept waiting for Hades or one of his guards to appear and try to stop her, but...nothing. She wondered why until she made it to the end of the long, statute-lined bridge that led away from the castle's massive front steps. These statues were even more sinister than the ones on the castle itself, depicting creatures in various stages of pain and torture. She couldn't believe it had been so easy to walk away, but then it hit her.

Or well, *she* hit *it*—with her face. Some kind of invisible barrier blocked the path.

"Fuck!" she yelped, rubbing her forehead. She was glad she'd only been jogging at half-speed, otherwise she probably would have knocked herself out. Irritated and slightly embarrassed, she made her way back towards the castle. She stutter-stepped when she saw that Jeff was standing at the head of the bridge, watching her. She eyed him wearily, arms at her sides and her claws out, ready to defend or attack, if necessary. He was holding the hilt of his sword with both hands, the tip resting on the ground, and he looked like he was barely suppressing a smile. She narrowed her eyes and his shoulders began to shake with silent laughter.

Skylar pursed her lips, eyeing him suspiciously, unsure what to make of him. The demon was straight out of a nightmare, but he was getting a kick out of her running into a wall? He stopped trying to hide it now and allowed his grin to spread across his broad face. The sight should have been terrifying but it was oddly...goofy and endearing. One of his fangs was slightly shorter than the other, as if it had been broken long ago. She got the distinct impression that though he was obviously a killing machine, he was really just a big old teddy bear. He reminded her of her father in that way. She decided that she liked Jeff. Simple as that.

Skylar pointed a finger at him and quirked an eyebrow.

"Not one word, Jeffrey. Not one." He chuckled again and made the gesture of locking up his lips and throwing away the key. She gave him a small, crooked smile. "I'm going to go keep trying to escape now, that cool with you?"

"Of course," he said in a deep, gravelly voice.

He stepped aside and gestured for her to have at it with his giant arm. She eyed him suspiciously. Why would he just let her wander? Her heart plummeted. He wouldn't, unless he was absolutely certain there was no way out. *Well, I've still got to try.* She shoved her shoulders back and continued on her way.

"Be careful of the bogs!" he yelled after her. She gave him a wave of acknowledgment over her shoulder as she ran towards the trees. Not too surprising, she met another barrier a few miles in.

"Damnit!" she yelled as she landed hard on her ass after bouncing off the invisible wall. "Getting real tired of running into this shit..." she grumbled as she pushed herself to her feet. She moved forward and tentatively ran a hand along the barrier, amazed when her hand met resistance though it looked as if she were touching nothing. A ray of sunlight found its way through the thick trees and made the barrier shimmer slightly. She cocked her head to the side and narrowed her eyes, realizing she could actually *see* the barrier if she focused. She spent the rest of the day walking along it, hoping maybe there was a gap somewhere, but had zero luck.

Skylar used her claws to try to cut through the barrier, but that had been a huge waste of time and she'd broken four of them in the process. They'd grow back soon enough, but it still hurt like a bitch. She'd been bitten by bugs that reminded her of overgrown mosquitos and understood Jeff's warning about the bogs too late when she'd nearly gotten sucked underground by silvery quicksand. She was beginning to panic when the bog decided she didn't taste as good as she looked and spit her back out, sending her sailing twenty feet into a tangle of vines. She could have sworn that the trees *laughed* when roots sprang up out of nowhere to trip her. She felt eyes on her several times and even thought she'd felt Hades himself somehow, though she never caught sight of him. And damn her, it was a comforting feeling, warm and welcome.

"No, *not* welcome. We do not have warm and fuzzies about our kidnappers, Pembroke," she scolded herself as she trudged back to the castle late in the afternoon, dirty, sweaty, hangry, and beyond annoyed. Once inside, she tried to find her room but kept making wrong turn after wrong turn. *Are the hallways and stairwells moving?*

"Is this freaking Hogwarts!? I just want to get to my room,

damnit!" she yelled to the ceiling. She gasped when bright green arrows began flashing on the floor in front of her. "Umm...thanks?" she murmured as she hesitantly followed the path, glancing around to see who was responsible for the handy map. Someone invisible? The castle itself? Who the fuck knew.

She finally found her room and slammed the door behind her with all her strength, then kicked it for good measure. She yanked her boots off and chucked them across the room. She grinned in very mature satisfaction when they left a trail of mud on the white stone wall as they slid to the floor. She took off her mud-caked pants next and tossed them over her shoulder, not caring where they landed. She wasn't sure who had left the clothes folded neatly on the chair near her bed when she'd woken that morning, but she hadn't questioned it and couldn't care less that she'd probably ruined them now.

"He wants to keep me here, I'll be the world's worst houseguest."

She was about to yank off her t-shirt when she froze, momentarily dazed by the view past her balcony. She had only taken a passing glance before, but now she threw open the doors and sprinted to the edge like a kid on Christmas. The sun was setting, bathing everything in deep orange-red light. It reminded her of fall back home, the way the sunlight played through the leaves. It was absolutely *stunning*.

Every tale Skylar could ever remember hearing described the Underworld as a dark, menacing, hellscape, and she assumed parts of it were—*I mean, the stories had to come from somewhere, right?*—but in reality, it was the most spectacular place she'd ever seen. Everything was lush and though the colors were deeper here, jewel tones rather than bright hues, they were much more rich and vivid than those back home. She spied a waterfall in the distance, the light hitting the water and making it look like a cascade of liquid diamonds.

She didn't know how long she stared, but the sun had completely set by the time she realized she hadn't moved. And she couldn't even think about moving now. If it was beautiful during the day, she really didn't have a word to describe it once night fell. She had never seen so many stars in all her life. They were sparkling silver and red and purple, and large groups of them moved and swirled through the sky, like living constellations, a celestial ballet that brought tears to her eyes.

Being here, staring up at this vast, breathtaking sky somehow felt so incredibly *right,* like this was exactly where she was meant to be. She put a hand to her chest, surprised at the complete ease that she suddenly felt there, as if a piece of a puzzle had clicked into place. She didn't understand it, couldn't even begin to try, but her gut was telling her that she was supposed to be here.

Rule number one of their job, the rule that her father taught her very early on: trust your gut. Tears welled in her eyes as she imagined him. Big and muscled, bald head, and amber eyes that sparkled when he smiled. He had a rough, deep voice and she could almost hear him beside her now: *your gut will never steer you wrong, Rocket. Never. Always trust it and you'll always end up on the right path.*

The need to follow her father's advice and the years of training demanding that she escape a captive situation were having an epic Battle Royale inside her mind and heart. She didn't know what the right answer was, what she should be doing. It seemed like too much of a coincidence that she had dreamed of Hades almost all her life and now felt like she belonged here with him. Maybe they were connected somehow, in some way she couldn't understand. Some species had fated mates...maybe he was hers? Did gods have such things? Was she meant to be his as well? The thought made her chest swell and ache at the same time. To finally feel whole, to feel like she belonged, to let someone in and to allow herself to feel—

A throat clearing behind her jerked her out of her thoughts. She whirled around, hastily scrubbing the tears from her eyes with the heel of her hand. Hades' eyes were blazing with anger and desire, the two emotions warring with each other for dominance. She really didn't understand why he always seemed angry with her, why he seemed to genuinely despise her half the time, yet he wanted to marry her? Demanded that she stay here with him? It didn't make any sense.

"Do you just have some strange aversion to pants that I'm unaware of?" he snapped.

She barely stopped herself from glancing down to confirm, but yep, he was right: she was sans pants once again. She quickly schooled her face into her customary mask: smug, snarky, cocky, unflinching. She tapped her chin with a bloodied, dirty fingertip in mock concentration as she made her way back inside and sat on the foot of the bed.

"I'm allergic. It's a known medical condition topside." She pointed upwards and then frowned. "Are we actually underground somehow? I mean, it's called the Underworld, but is it actually, you know, *under*?"

He backed away from the her, leaning casually against the back of the couch.

"No, the Underworld isn't actually "under" the earth as you know it. It's a different plane of existence. You are from the Mortal Plane."

"Whoa." She rolled it around in her mind for a bit. She really couldn't discount anything at this point after finding out the freaking gods existed, so other dimensions or planes of existence? Sure. Why not? "Um, ok. So, are there a lot of other planes?"

He hesitated for a moment, as if debating if he actually wanted to carry on a conversation with her, but finally said, "Within this dimension, there are four: the Mortal Plane, the Underworld, Aqueous, and Empyrean. Aqueous is the sea plane where Si—Poseidon resides, and Empyrean is the sky plane, where Mt. Olympus is along with Zeus. Within the planes there can also be realms." Her brows knitted a bit trying to keep everything straight. "Think of the dimension as a neighborhood. The planes would be the houses, and the realms would be rooms within those houses." Ok, that made sense to her. She nodded at him, conveying her understanding, and appreciation for the explanation.

"So, now you understand why you can't escape this place. There is nowhere for you to escape *to*. You are in a different plane of existence from the mortal world. The only place you'll manage to go is into a realm within the Underworld and believe me, there are ones that you do *not* want to enter."

"But there has to be a way to travel between the planes. Obviously you do it."

"Certain people have the ability to travel between them, yes. You do not." He shrugged nonchalantly and she narrowed her eyes. *Mr. cool and relaxed couldn't care less about me being stuck here.* She ground her teeth and reached for calm. She had more questions and needed to get as much information from him as she could, so she needed to attempt to play nice. Before she could speak, his own eyes narrowed.

He asked in a low voice, "What are you, Skylar?"

She shivered at the sound of her name coming from his lips again, but fought to act unaffected. Why was he so obsessed with knowing what she was? Did he plan to use her for something and her species made a difference? Then her eyes widened when realization hit her: he must not know that even *she* had no idea what she was either. Always good to have a bargaining chip up your sleeve, fake as it may be. If he wanted to know what she was badly enough, maybe she could use that against him. She filed that away for later. She arched a blonde eyebrow upwards and smirked.

"*Really* good at darts."

He rolled his eyes and ran a hand through his hair, and suddenly every rational thought flew out of her mind.

Irritation about her imprisonment? Gone.

Mind reeling over the fact that the gods were real? Couldn't care less now.

The very important need for information? No information was as important as what she was seeing at that moment.

His raised arm caused his shirt to ride up and her gaze zeroed in on the now visible strip of perfectly tanned and toned skin just above the waist of his pants. She may have actually licked her lips. His stomach was chiseled, enticing ridges and dips making her fangs sharpen. His pants hung low, revealing mouthwatering indentions beside his hip bones, and barely covering what she could only guess was a huge, thick, co—*No! Bad, Sky!*

She snapped her eyes back up and saw that his gaze was riveted where her tongue was indeed skating across her bottom lip. She couldn't stop her eyes from roaming back down where she saw evidence of his arousal straining against the fly of his pants and her mouth went dry.

Maybe that 10 inch pianist comment hadn't been a bluff...

She felt herself leaning forward as she uncurled her legs, shifting up to her knees. She didn't remember consciously making the decision to move, her body seemed to be in complete control, taking absolutely no direction from her brain. She knew she should be thinking of ways to escape or to overpower her captor, but it was as if she were under a spell. She couldn't *not* react to him like this, couldn't not react to his body. Every instinct was telling her she was supposed to, that she was *meant* to. Her heart began to beat wildly as he stalked forward, like he was in a similar trance.

He stopped just in front of her, so close she could feel the heat of his body on her skin. His eyes were dark with desire, his pulse pounding furiously at his throat, and she saw wisps of what looked like pitch black smoke out of the corner of her eye, but couldn't make herself worry too much about it. If the room was on fire, she didn't care. All she cared about was the man before her.

Without a word, he reached out and ran the pad of his thumb across her cheekbone, and she couldn't stop herself from leaning into the touch. Her skin was practically electrified where he touched her and she craved more, *needed* more. She needed his hands on every inch of her body, needed it every second of every minute of the rest of forever. Her lids slid shut and her breath hitched as his thumb moved and slid gently across her bottom lip. The tip of her tongue lapped at his finger and he made a rough moaning sound deep in his chest. Her hands slipped under the hem of his shirt, gliding over taut muscles and smooth skin. Now *she* moaned. His skin was hot to the touch and it warmed her to her core. She wanted to explore him for hours, to touch and taste and she couldn't seem to remember why that wasn't the best idea in the history of ideas.

She leaned farther into him but abruptly, he took a step back, causing her to nearly topple forward. *What the?* She swayed slightly as her eyelids fluttered open and she met his gaze. The desire was gone, replaced once again with that blistering hatred.

"Do not think you can manipulate me or seduce me like some pathetic mortal," Hades spit at her, rage flashing in his eyes.

She was confused by his sudden change of heart, then annoyed at herself for getting so lost in him. Disappointed soon followed that he thought she was faking, and then finally, anger of her own flared. Sure, she had thought about trying to seduce him, but she'd discarded the idea as soon as she'd gotten lost in that bare strip of stomach. She knew she was a goner. The whole seduction plan only works when you remain in *complete* control and use the sexy-times as a way to get the mark vulnerable, then you make your move. Skylar knew without a doubt that if she played with that fire, she would burn to ash...and love every minute of it. No way in hell would she remain in complete control with her literal walking fantasy touching her, tasting her, filling her.

But the fact that he automatically assumed she was trying to play him pissed her off...and if she were being honest with herself, kind of hurt. Well, screw him. *He wants to be a dick, I can play ball.* She gave him a cold, sultry smile.

"I don't *think* I can manipulate and seduce you." She reached forward and walked her fingers up his chest. He surprisingly let her. "I *know* I can. You'll be putty in my hands, baby." He looked both pissed and...excited at the prospect. Confusing fucking man.

"Is that so?" he said in a deep, seductive whisper. She nearly shivered from the sound. He closed the distance between them again, leaning down and rubbing her nose lightly with his. She gasped quietly as her resolve crumbled in an instant and she was once again lost in him. *What in the actual fuck?* This was so not how it usually went down. She was the seducer, not the seducee, damnit! She shouldn't be losing her mind so easily. Sure, it had been a while since she'd been touched this way, been intimate at all with anyone, but still, she couldn't believe how easily he destroyed every wall she tried to put up. It had to be a god thing, right? Anyone would crumble up against them.

Her eyes slid closed again when he leaned in even closer, his mouth mere inches from her own, his breaths warm on her lips. She took a deep breath, his scent flooding her system. She barely forced herself to keep her hands clenched firmly at her sides, but she couldn't stop goosebumps from rising on her skin or the rush of heat between her thighs. His smell was enveloping her, his lips were so close, she just needed to move forward a tiny inch...

Now he inhaled deeply and all but growled.

"Seems like maybe *I'll* be the one manipulating and seducing *you*, love. You're already wet for me. *Soaking* I'd bet."

Her eyes snapped open as realization hit. *Oh my god, he can...* smell *me?* She fucking hated him...and, ok she hated herself even more because it was true. Not only were her panties soaked, but he could absolutely seduce her in a heartbeat and she would merely beg him for more. For some reason, she was weak when she was around him, her barriers crumbling like a house of cards, and she was *not fucking weak.* Not anymore. She vowed a long time ago that she would never be weak again, so no matter how much her gut was telling her that this was right, that she belonged here with him for some reason, it was officially on like Donkey Kong. God or not, she wasn't going to let him control her or play with her or mess with her head.

Her desire transformed into fury and she shoved hard at his chest. He chuckled as he stepped away, walking backwards a few steps.

"What was that about putty?" he mocked. He smirked and she felt her claws lengthen as the rage boiled up inside her chest. He was lucky he was out of striking distance. "Now, the sooner you accept your lot, the better. Make yourself at home," he gloated, waving a hand in the air gesturing to the room.

"You can't just keep me here, you asshole!" she shrieked at him. He snorted.

"I'm the God of the Underworld. I can do anything I want." She forced herself not smile at the Chief Brody vibes he was throwing off with that line. He wiggled his fingers at her in a mocking wave and disappeared.

EIGHT

Skylar had been locked in her room for days. As if she weren't pissed enough already at being held prisoner in the fucking *Underworld* of all places, the fact that he was keeping her cooped up in this room made her so angry she could spit. Sure, the room was spacious and beautiful and she had the necessities, but still. She didn't appreciate being imprisoned, no matter how pretty the cage might be.

To her complete surprise, she'd actually passed out in that ridiculously comfortable bed almost as soon as Hades had disappeared that night, and proceeded to sleep for almost an entire day straight. She hadn't really noticed at the time, but looking back now she realized that she had only slept for a handful of hours in the entire week she'd been in France and was completely exhausted, both mentally and physically. So, she would give him a pass on day one. But the next three days? Not happening. She had a bad history with locked doors. *No, no, no. Do not go there right now. Head in the fucking game, Pembroke.*

She could have gone down the trellis again, but she wasn't in the mood. No, she was in the mood for a fight. She paced the length of the room over and over, just waiting for the prick to do his magical appear-out-of-thin-air thing. He'd popped in several times over the past few days, usually just to bark questions at her, namely asking what she was, and then scowling when she gave him the finger or told him to do unnatural things with his anatomy, and she'd begun to realize that she could *feel* him a few seconds before he appeared. A strange tingling within her chest, almost like the tickling sensation of a feather, but inside her body. She wasn't even going to begin trying to figure out what the hell *that* was about. Instead, she paced, ready to pounce the second he materialized.

"Keep me locked in this room like I'm a convict?" She paced faster, extending and retracting her claws in irritation as she moved. They'd all grown back now and were itching to slice into some godly flesh. "Except even inmates get yard time for crying out loud...and conjugal visits."

She stopped, frowning at herself. She did *not* still want him. He was holding her against her will and keeping her from contacting Z and Lucas who were probably out of their minds with worry by now. Her heart clenched at that thought. Not only did she love the two of them like family, but her just falling off the face of the Earth so soon after her dad's death? This would be putting them through the wringer and the guilt she felt over that, despite the fact that this was most definitely not her fault, began to churn in her gut, making her nauseous. Her claws flared out once more and her small fangs slid free.

No, she felt nothing but the beginnings of a burning hatred for him, one that would turn into an inferno and engulf her completely soon enough if she let it. And once she got to that point, there was no going back. She still felt that strange connection to him, the one she was constantly trying to both explain and ignore, but her hatred would sear that away in an instant if she reached the point of no return. She'd done it in the past. She would do it again. And he was getting very close to being on her shit list. The fact that she still dreamed of him every night meant nothing. Old habits and all that.

She began to pace once more but before she'd even lifted her foot, she felt it, felt *him*. She closed her eyes and let her instincts and senses take over. She felt the stirring in the air in front of her and to her left. *Eleven o'clock. Dead man walking.* Her eyes flashed open and she sped forward, moving so fast she would be a blur to most eyes. She cocked her arm back and leapt. She felt the bone of his cheek splinter beneath her fist as she made contact.

"What the fu—"

She grinned and immediately threw an uppercut to his kidney as she landed, cutting off his curse, a loud "oompf" coming out instead. She didn't let up, slashing her claws across his chest and whipping her head forward into his nose. She dropped down and threw out a leg to sweep his out from under him, but her foot hit nothing but air. He had disappeared again. *Damnit!*

"What in the actual fuck?" he grated from behind her. She whirled, springing to her feet but staying in a low crouch, ready to attack again. Blood dribbled over his lips and off his chin, but it had already stopped pouring from his broken nose. Or, well, the nose that had been broken a moment ago. *Holy shit gods heal fast.* The gashes she'd made with her claws were already knitting back together as well, faint pink lines and tears in his black shirt the only things left behind.

"I want out of this you-damned place." His brows drew down slightly and she rolled her eyes. "You're a god aren't you?" she spit, annoyed that she had to explain her joke. She thought it was a pretty good one. His lips curled up slightly on one side, the beginnings of a lopsided smirk.

"I told you already, you aren't going anywhere. You're going to marry me and you're going to remain here. The sooner that you accept it, the better," he said, and for the first time in three days, his voice wasn't laced with venom. It was tinged with...excitement? Amusement?

She straightened, seething with anger because she knew he was right. Not about her marrying him—that was obviously ludicrous—

but about her not being able to leave. She'd known attacking him wouldn't do any good today, would maybe even provoke him to do more than just lock her inside a lavish room, but she needed to lash out because that's just what she did when she was backed into a corner, both physically and emotionally. She knew that even if she made it out of this room, she couldn't get past that barrier outside. She was stuck like Chuck here for as long as he decreed. The thought made her see red. Skylar did not like having things out of her control.

"Listen up, and listen up good, buddy boy. I will *never* marry you, and I will fight you every chance I get. Today was just a little appeteaser. Some metaphorical mozzarella sticks to tide you over until the main course." She edged closer to him, sizing him up like a lioness stalking a gazelle. His eyes widened slightly but he showed no other reaction. He allowed her to get close enough that their bodies were only a foot or so apart. She leaned in, going up on her tip toes to attempt to get nose to nose with him. She made it about nose to chin. *Close enough.* "You may be a god, but you've never seen anything like me before. I'm about to fuck your world up, baby." She snapped her fangs at him and he...grinned. And *holy shit* was it a sexy one.

Before she could even really wrap her mind around how hand-some he was when he smiled, he was gone again. Her shoulders began to slump as the swagger and anger both began to leak out of her, like a deflating balloon, but then she heard it. The sound of lock tumblers turning over. She spun and found her door creaking open an inch. Her brows knitted, confusion rippling through her.

She had attacked him, told him in no uncertain terms that she wouldn't give him what he wanted and would make his life a living nightmare, and he had...rewarded her? Maybe it was a trap of some sort, but she didn't care. She needed out of this room before she went crazy, before memories of another room behind another locked door began to suffocate her. She flitted to the door, taking a deep breath before yanking it open and sauntering out into the hallway.

"You know if you want to convince her to marry you, you should probably oh I dunno...actually *try to convince her* instead of just being an asshole and keeping her locked up?" Emmie said as she lounged on the couch in Hades' suite of rooms watching his flat screen. Hades was reading— definitely *not* a romance novel about a group of supernatural beings called the "*Immortals After Dark*" that he'd disguised as some important-looking ancient tome—and studiously ignored her. He heard her sniffle though, and glanced up, confused. Sure enough, tears were leaking from the corners of her eyes leaving quicksilver trails down her delicate cheeks. He glanced from her to the screen.

"Why are you crying? I thought this was a happy children's movie?" There was a small, relatively cute blue creature and a young girl doing...whatever it was characters did in movies made for young mortals. He wasn't sure. He loved mortal cinema, but had never gotten around to trying out much this particular genre.

"It is. It's just..." More sniffles. She dragged her forearm across her eyes, smearing the silver. "It's just that he's got the book and he's looking for his family just like the ducks and then the big guy tells him he doesn't have one and he's so sad and i-it just gets me every time!" she all but wailed.

"What on earth are you even talking about right now? On second thought, I don't want to know." She sniffled once more but nodded.

"You're right. Back to important things. Like you actually attempting to make this thing work with our little hellcat." She turned the film off and leaned her elbows on the armrest of the sofa, resting her chin in her upturned hands. "You've got to step up your game here, man."

Hades sighed and tossed his book on the small table beside his worn leather chair, knowing she wasn't going to let this drop.

"I let her out of her room didn't I?"

The first few days Skylar had been here, he was overwhelmed by too many emotions to count. The one that had held top billing was hatred. Every time he looked at her all he could see was Persephone —though they physically looked nothing alike, of course—driving that dagger into his back, scheming with his great enemy to destroy his kingdom, betraying him like no other ever had. When Skylar had tried to play him, feigning being nearly blind with desire for him, it had pushed him over the edge. He'd nearly tossed her in the dungeons, but had settled for locking her in her room instead.

She'd actually slept for nearly twenty hours the first day she was there, seeming to catch-up on all the sleep she'd missed ever since her father had died. He hated how much she hurt over that loss, though he couldn't explain why. He...didn't like her in pain. He told himself it was only residual love left over from the early days with Persephone and nothing more. The jury was still out on if he believed that or not.

When he'd phased into her rooms on the fourth day, she'd attacked...and damn it, he'd *liked* it. He didn't exactly enjoy having his cheek and nose broken, but he couldn't deny that he found her ferocity oddly enticing and when she fought...gods save him, it was sexy as hell, even when he was on the receiving end of it. Her fiery nature excited him more than much had in the past three thousand years, so he'd relented and let her out of her rooms as a reward he supposed. He knew that she'd be desperate to explore and no doubt continue to attempt to escape. She couldn't, so he wasn't worried about that. Keeping her locked away had been a punishment, not a precaution.

"And she didn't immediately beg you to marry her right then and there?" Emmie gasped in mock surprise, before rolling her eyes. "That was the first *teeny tiny* step in hundreds that you need to take before you get us all on the right road. I'm nudging you as best I can here, so take my hints: you're going to have to get over the Persephone crap. Like yesterday." She got up and sauntered to the door, stopping to pat his head as she passed his chair. *Am I a fucking lapdog now?* "Work on that or you'll lose her forever. Trust me in this."

Something dark and ominous flashed behind her purple eyes, something that made the hairs on the back of his neck stand on end. If he failed in this, what future awaited them? The thought of losing Skylar, er Persephone again, he supposed, sent a shiver of cold fear through him. Because that would mean the prophecy would forever be out of his reach, dooming them to whatever bleak future Emmie had seen? Or something far more devastating...like his heart being broken?

Emmie gave him no answers, just let him to stew in his own thoughts. There was no way he would let himself fall for her again, not after everything she'd done, not after hating her for three fucking millennia. But...

"No. No fucking buts," he growled to the empty room. He would ignore all of the instincts clamoring inside him, ones that were telling him things he refused to acknowledge. There was just confusion because of the reincarnation, something going sideways in that transformation or something. He was no expert in this area, that was for sure, but he assumed that it was far from simple. So, no. He was just mixed up because this was a weird fucking situation and she was a trained temptress working her magic on him. She could be part siren or succubus for fuck's sake and could literally have powers of seduction.

Yes, that had to be it. He would accept no other alternatives.

But Hades supposed Emmie had a point. The sooner Skylar agreed to marry him, the better, and keeping up his current behavior wasn't going to help in that department. He believed Skylar completely when she said she'd never marry him and make his life a living hell instead, fighting him every step of the way. So, he had to change her mind somehow. He sighed heavily and ran his fingers through his hair.

How the fuck do I get her to do this?

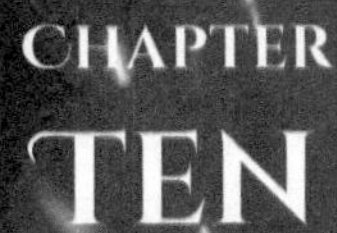

Good news: Skylar was out of her room.

Bad news: she was no closer to escaping.

She'd walked every inch of the invisible barrier, twice, with nothing to show for it except more bug bites, more mud, and more irritation. She'd wandered down hallway after hallway after hallway in the seemingly never-ending castle, peeked in what had to be at least eighty different rooms, and come away with nothing but awestruck wonder at the sheer size and opulence of the place and a burning need to ask Hades about all of the things she'd seen.

Though Hades had obviously chosen to let her out, she was still wary and on edge as she made her way through the castle and the grounds. She'd come across numerous demons, though most simply gave her an appraising look or inclined their heads deeply before continuing on their way, seeming almost...respectful of her? Others didn't do anything outright aggressive, but gave her the willies all the same. She was surprised at how quickly she'd accepted that they existed and how easily she now used the term, but she'd always had an open mind about most things, so she was just rolling with all the new knowledge.

Some of the demons looked similar to Jeff, though each had a slightly different color and arrangement to their horns. She'd run into him several more times, so she decided to just ask about it. He'd seemed initially surprised by her interest, but then happy to talk to her about it. He'd explained in his strangely accented voice that the color denoted the clan that a particular demon belonged to, and the arrangement of the horns indicated the class of warrior. His clan was the oldest and strongest of all of the Rathos demons, and of course, he was of the highest class of warrior, the Eschoms. They were highly sought after in many realms and planes by gods, demi-gods, creatures she couldn't even begin to imagine. Even some mortals employed them (though they had to cloak their appearance in the Mortal Plane obviously).

So, yeah, she got why Hades employed them as his personal guards now. And she'd confirmed that he actually *employed* them, not enslaved or anything else unscrupulous, but Jeff had assured her that he was paid handsomely.

"I'm *obscenely* rich. Even more so than the mallard who swims in his vault of coins in your world."

Skylar snorted and grinned.

"Scrooge McDuck?? How do you even know who that is?"

"I watch mortal television with Emmie," he said simply, as if that explained anything. Skylar had no idea who Emmie was—his wife or girlfriend maybe?—but the fact that they had TV here did spark her interest.

She'd seen all manner of other demons as well, and though many looked like creatures Freddy Kruger would have nightmares about, some looked basically human save a strange eye color or almost completely hidden horns beneath their hair. No matter their appearance, they all completely fascinated her. Despite being held against her will, she was excited by all of the new knowledge she was gaining, the new discoveries she was making. She'd seen animals and creatures she couldn't even describe, and had even met a demigod for crying out loud!

Or well, she'd technically already met him when she'd saved his ass in that alleyway in France. She almost didn't recognize Athos when he'd knocked on her door to thank her and vow a life-debt to her. Thankfully, he was healing, though it would take him a while. He still had the shadows of bruises over his face and the end of his wrist where his hand should be was wrapped in white bandages.

"Will it regenerate?" she'd asked, nodding to the bandage.

"It will, but it takes time and is...unpleasant." She nodded in sympathy. She'd helped Lucas get through a severed foot regeneration once and it was brutal. Thinking of Lucas made her chest ache so she did what she did best when emotional pain started: shove it way down deep and ignore it for the time being.

To distract herself, she'd asked, "Do all demons regenerate like that? Or does it just depend on the...species? Is the even the right word?"

He raised his brows. "Species is correct. And yes, some species of demons *can* regenerate but not many. I, however, am not a demon at all. I'm a demigod." Her own brows hiked upwards.

"A whatnow?"

His lips quirked slightly. "A demigod. My mother is a lesser goddess and my father was a mortal. Some gods look down on beings like me, but not the Brothers. I've been in Hades' Guard for a thousand years."

She liked the fact that Hades wasn't a judgmental douche and then scowled, not liking that she was finding more and more *to* like about him. Athos had thanked her again and promised to assist her in any way that he could. Her mind had been whirling in overdrive after he'd left and all she could think about was learning more, seeing more, experiencing *more*.

Hades still popped in to ask her what she was periodically, but he seemed to be making an effort not to be inexplicably pissed at her now and even made casual conversation some of the time. If she had known that attempting to kick his ass would make him like her, she would have done it sooner. She hadn't attacked him again, though she'd thought about it plenty of times. Every time he seemed to be enjoying himself with her, chuckling at one of her dry comments or smirking at her answers to his *what are you?* quizzes, he would flip the script and scowl, looking annoyed at himself for letting his guard down and then at her for existing apparently. She just didn't get him.

Skylar actually thought she might like him in the times he was being normal with her. He had a wicked sense of humor, loved dirty innuendo almost as much as she did, and seemed to have a real talent for handing down judgment on pieces of shit who deserved it. At least that's what she had gathered he was doing when she'd eavesdropped at the throne room door. She still didn't know if that whole *souls come to the Underworld to be tortured for eternity* thing was real or just part of the mortal stories, but it was obvious at least parts of the stories had to be true.

She hated when he went back to the broody, mad at her for no reason version of Hades. She still needed to get the hell out of this place, but she also thought that maybe, just maybe, if he would cut that shit out, she could be...content here. Which was insane, but the strange sense of belonging only strengthened with every passing hour. Hades was the man of her literal dreams, and the idea of exploring an entirely new world? *Sign me the fuck up!*

Skylar quickly abandoned the hope that she might find a hole in the barrier and shifted her focus to finding a way to travel between the planes instead. She understood that she couldn't just walk from the Underworld back home, but there had to be ways to get back and forth, even without the "ability" he claimed some people had to do so. So, started spending hours upon hours in the biggest (and most beautiful) library she'd ever seen, only pausing to sing *Beauty & the Beast* songs while gliding along the rolling ladders once or twice...ok, fine, eight times, and jumped into research mode.

Unfortunately, that was a bit slow going and Lucas had always been much better at this stuff than she was. Many of the books were in languages she'd never even seen and the rest weren't at all helpful when it came to traveling between the planes. She'd gotten lost for half a day in some of the real stories of the gods that she'd found in some kind of historical tomes though, and it was entirely fascinating. Turns out mortals had gotten only about ten percent right, but she supposed that's the way the gods wanted it.

Another book she picked up ended up being a text on what appeared to be mythological Kama Sutra. She'd spent the better part of an afternoon studying the pictures, tilting her head this way and that trying to discern what body parts a being might even need to possess in order to attempt some of the positions. There were a few though that sparked her immense interest that she knew for a fact she would be capable of...and then her mind went wild imagining trying them out with a certain God of the Underworld.

She couldn't stop her dreams of him and the images from her dreams were always resting just behind the forefront of her mind. It was only natural that she would use him as her mental model, it didn't mean she actually wanted to try any of those things. Really. Truly. One hundred percent *not* interest in him like that.

Skylar blew out a long breath and tossed the book she was reading about different demon realms onto the table. She stretched her arms over her head and decided to give research on plane-hoping a break and move on to the next order of business: finding a weapons cache. She knew there had to be one somewhere. Didn't every castle have some kind of armory? She could make a weapon out of just about anything, but nothing beat cool, forged steel. So, she began exploring the castle again, looking for rooms that were locked this time. You wouldn't leave weapons just out for anyone to find, especially a highly-trained houseguest who happened to be a supernatural mercenary.

After a few hours of wandering around, she finally found one that seemed promising. It was a huge wooden door that seemed unbreakable, even with her increased strength, and it was locked up tight. *Bingo.*

She went to work picking the lock but a few moments later, she felt someone watching her. She knew it wasn't Hades—and was annoyed at herself for knowing it, for being able to sense him on some molecular level that messed with her head—but decided to give his little minions a message. So far, they'd mostly given her a wide berth and most had been polite, but there had been some that looked at her with a little too much interest for her liking. She listened to her stalker's nearly silent breathing, ascertaining approximately how tall they were based on where the sound was originating, and determined her target.

She didn't want to kill anyone—yet—but she would make sure word spread that she was not to be fucked with. She covertly slid the toothbrush she had sharpened into a deadly point from her shirt sleeve and into her palm. Quick as lightning she spun and tossed her prison shiv. Her eyes went wide and she tried to call out a warning, but all she managed to get out was a kind of *aghh* sound. To her immense relief, the startling beauty in front of her held up a dart board—*a dart board? Who just carries around a dart board?*—and the sharpened handle of the toothbrush sailed right into the red dot dead center.

The woman smiled at her, yelling "Bullseye!" Skylar rushed forward, tucking away her make-shift picking tools.

"Shit, I'm so sorry. I thought...it doesn't matter. I'm sorry I tried to impale you." The female waved her off as if having deadly projectiles fly her way was no biggy.

"Please, this is *such* a meet cute for our friendship. People will be like "aw how did you guys become best friends?" and I'll be like "well, Poprocks here"—oh, that's going to be your nickname down the road. Trust me the story is hi-larious—"Poprocks here tried to stab me through the heart with a toothbrush!" and everyone will think it's the best story ever." Skylar's brows drew together. Confused was an understatement here. *Is this chick drunk? Or just plain crazy?* The woman smacked her forehead with her palm. "Oh, duh, sorry. All of this makes no sense to you yet. I forget sometimes. I'm Emmie, Seer to the stars!" She waved her hand in the air in a grand gesture. "Or well, the gods, but you get the idea."

"Seer? As in like...an oracle? You can see the future?" Skylar asked, eyes wide and mouth practically gaping like a fish on land.

Emmie smiled, her purple eyes sparkling, and nodded.

"Cool, huh?"

Skylar didn't know why, but she immediately liked this woman, feeling as if they'd been friends for years. *Ugh, again with the weird feeling of belonging here? Come on!* Emmie's silver-gray hair was braided in two French-braid pigtails and she was wearing an adorable red and white polka dot sundress. *I wonder if —*

"Yes, it does have pockets!" Emmie said, beaming, answering Skylar's unasked question. She tossed the dartboard over her head without a care but with surprising force, and it clattered loudly down the hallway. She shoved her hands in the slits at her hips, doing a few little half twirls. Skylar's eyes went wider and Emmie wrinkled her nose. "Ah sorry. You'll get used to it. Or maybe not, who knows. You'll stop getting that bug-eyed look about it at least after a few hundred years or so." Ok, this was so not what Skylar would have pictured when she thought *powerful oracle of the gods* but she found herself smiling, liking Emmie even more.

Emmie...she'd heard that name before, hadn't she? Her eyes lit up when it hit her.

"You know Jeff! He said he watches TV with you?"

"Of course. We have a weekly *Criminal Minds* date, which usually devolves into us arguing over whether Reid or Morgan is the best." She rolled her eyes. "I mean, the answer is clearly Morgan!"

"Ah well...I'm a Dr. Reid girl myself," Skylar said, shrugging.

"Ugh, I'm well aware! Listen, Spencer is adorable and I love him, but Derek is....*Derek*." She wiggled her eyebrows. "That smile and those arms and he's so smart and brave and ahhhh...mega swoon, amirite?"

"Oh Derek is swoon-worthy, no doubt about that," Skylar agreed.

Emmie grinned at her. "Just wait until you meet Si. He's got a total Derek Morgan thing going on. I honestly wondered if Shemar was one of Poseidon's kids running around when I first saw him. I mean, we don't know that he actually has any...but we don't know that he *doesn't* either. Shemar could absolutely pass for a demigod, don't you think?"

Skylar laughed out loud. "Absolutely. I'm still the future Mrs. Dr. Reid though, just so we're clear."

She sighed wistfully and then pouted. "I know. Jeff is going to be so thrilled that there's another misguided soul in our midst now. He's never going to shut up about it. You're getting matching "Team Reid" shirts for Christmas by the way. I bought them ages ago." Skylar laughed, simultaneously fascinated and confused by everything that was happening. The Seer shooed Skylar out of the way and made her way to the door, leaning down to peep through the keyhole.

"So, anywho, we doing a little B&E this morning then?"

"Er, well..." Skylar eyed the door guiltily. Emmie straightened and leaned a shoulder casually against the wall beside it. "Did you try just asking it to open? I mean, you do you boo, but personally I like to work smarter not harder." She hiked a slender shoulder in an elegant shrug and inspected her nails. Skylar frowned.

"Ask it to open? As in...literally *ask* the door? With words?" Skylar quirked a brow, eyeing the Seer distrustfully. "Are you for real? Is this some kind of weird Underworld mess-with-the-new-kid hazing thing?" Emmie just gave her a dry look, so Skylar took a deep breath. Fully prepared to be laughed right out of the castle, she said, "Um...door, could you please open?" She huffed out an incredulous laugh when she heard the tumblers moving. A second later the door swung inward. Skylar beamed at Emmie who gave her a knowing smile in return, like she was in on some big secret.

"You'll find that this castle will respond to almost any request you make. It...knows who's boss," Emmie said with a wink.

Skylar had no idea what that could possibly mean, but she was too stuck on this whole the-castle-actually-listened-to-me-and-obeyed thing to really think too much of it. How freaking cool was that?! She peeked her head into the room and frowned. It wasn't full of weapons at all like she'd hoped. No, it was an enormous entertainment and gaming space. There were old school arcade games along one wall, an air hockey table, a pool table, ski ball, and that basketball game where you try to make as many baskets as possible before time runs out. There were a handful of dart boards along another wall, though she noticed that one was missing from its place and she knew where Emmie's had come from, and dominating the other long wall was the most massive TV Skylar had ever seen. It seriously belonged in a movie theater it was so huge. In front of it were gorgeous leather sofas that looked comfy and inviting. She turned to Emmie.

"Why the hell was this door locked? And why is this room so... human?"

"Some of the guards can't be trusted near the bar." She shook her head and rolled her eyes as she began toying with the end of one of her braids. "And Hades fell in love with mortal arcades back in the 80s." She shrugged as if that answered the question fully when really it only gave Skylar fifty new ones. Emmie went on, "Now, I know you were looking for weapons, sooo you can either keep poking around in every room in this place until you find what you're looking for—which, be forewarned may take you a while. I don't even think I've found all the rooms yet and I've been here for almost five thousand years—*or* I can just take you where you want to go. Or we could say screw the weapons and hang out here and play Zelda. Choice is yours, my friend."

Skylar's mouth popped open. *Five thousand years!?* Emmie looked like she was 30, tops. Skylar knew that with beings of the non-human variety, the age someone *looked* was no real indication of their actual age, but *millennia?* That was hard to wrap her mind around. Then she realized what Emmie had offered.

"Wait. You'd actually *give* me weapons? On purpose? You know I could totally kill you in a heartbeat, right?" Emmie laughed and patted Skylar's head like she was an adorable toddler.

"Aw, that's so cute that you think you could kill me. Also, I know you don't—and you don't kill Hades or anyone else either, bee-tee-dubs—so, no reason not to let you play with all the sharp and pointy things your twisted little heart desires."

Indignation rose and she wanted to stomp her foot like a five year old. She would totally use whatever weapons Emmie showed her to kill Hades and escape! Probably...maybe...*Damnit!* The thought of someone hurting Hades, even herself, had strange emotions shuffling through her. Rage burned white hot and the need to punish whoever dared to harm him roared like a caged beast within her. But the stranger, far more concerning emotion was complete and utter *devastation* at the thought of losing him forever. Even the loss of her father didn't hurt as much as the mere idea of a world without Hades in it did. How messed up was that? *Shit, shit, and more shit.* Operation: Hate Hades and GTFO was *not* going well.

So, ok, fine, maybe she wouldn't actually kill him, but she would still feel better if she had some pointed-ended things around, so she held out her arm, gesturing for Emmie to lead the way.

"Weapons first. Zelda later."

They talked as they walked and Skylar tried to get as much information as she could. Deciding to go straight in for the kill instead of dancing around the subject, she asked, "Do you know why I'm here?"

"Duh: to marry Hades." Emmie pulled a Tootsie Pop out of her pocket and popped it in her mouth. Skylar smiled. Her dad used to give her those when she was younger. Their favorite were the blue, and the memories of the giant, terrifying lupin sharing suckers with her and comparing colored tongues afterward sent a bittersweet slice of pain through her.

"I used to love those things. Especially the—"

"Blue ones?" Emmie grinned and wiggled her eyebrows as she pulled a second pop out of her pocket and handed it over. Skylar's eyes widened. Having someone who could see the future around was going to take some getting used to. But her lips curled into a smile as she shook her head in astonishment and unwrapped the treat.

"Thanks. Ok, back to important things. Do you know *why* Hades wants to marry me?"

"*Ob-viously*," Emmie said in a pretty dead-on Professor Snape impression.

"Do you care to expand on that?"

"Nope," she said, popping the "p" sound on the end loudly. *Well, ok then.* Skylar was a bit disappointed but the feeling was short-lived. Emmie ushered her into Toys-R-Us for assassins and badasses and her heart leapt. She grinned and went to town.

ELEVEN

After Skylar had blazed through the weapons room like a kid in a candy store, picking up more than she could carry, Emmie helped her lug her prizes back to her room. They dumped all of the weapons on her table and Emmie turned to her expectantly. The light filtering in from the wall of glass made her silver tattoos sparkle like diamonds. They were swirling and feminine, symbols and words in a language Skylar didn't know, but they brought to mind thoughts of power and strength. In addition to that, she had to have tons of knowledge after being alive for so long and being able to see the future, right?

Skylar began to have one hell of an inner debate: *Maybe I should just ask her...or maybe not. It doesn't matter...except that it does...She might know, if anyone would know, it would be her...Will she tell Hades that I don't even know? I was going to keep that a secret...I don't think she'd tell him...Ugh, come on, stop being such a baby and just–*

"Will you just ask me already? Geeze." Emmie crossed her arms over her chest and hiked an eyebrow. Skylar squared her shoulders and took a deep breath.

"Do you know what I am?" she asked, her voice coming out softer than she'd intended. The need to know was a constant ache inside her chest despite the fact that she told herself long ago that it didn't matter. She still felt like she would never be complete until she knew, like knowing was somehow the key to something big. Emmie gave her a sad smile.

"I do, but I can't tell you, not yet. I'm sorry. You'll know when the time is right."

Skylar's shoulders slumped, though she did hang some hope on that *not yet* part and hoped that the right time was soon. She understood that Emmie couldn't reveal everything, even if she wanted to. There were apparently rules that Seers had to follow. They could drop hints every now and then, steering people towards a particular future, but couldn't flat out give everything away. Something about free will and people having to make their own decisions and blah blah blah.

Emmie leaned in and wrapped Skylar in a hug, startling her, but she quickly returned the embrace, having only realized in that moment how badly she'd needed it. After a few long moments, they parted and Emmie squeezed Skylar's upper arms before heading to the door.

She paused just inside the frame and turned back, saying casually, "Just a random friendly reminder that sometimes an *ending* is also a *beginning*. Keep that in mind." She seemed to have picked the words with great care, and Skylar knew that they were important, but had no idea what they meant. Before she could say anything in return, Emmie was gone.

TWELVE

Hades needed to get out of the castle. The situation with Skylar was driving him mad. He was trying his best to do as Emmie suggested and move past what Persephone had done, and it was surprisingly easy at times. Skylar was sharp as a tack, had a quick wit and a dirty mind, almost as filthy as his own, and he'd begun to actually look forward to her ridiculous responses to his inquiries into her species. So far she'd told him that she was:

-a Jedi like my father before me

-a joker

-a smoker

-a midnight toker

-the walrus; and his personal favorite,

-Ironman

His lips curled even now recalling the conversations. He was doing his best to speak with her about other things as well, attempting to win her over and was even able to relax and enjoy his limited time with her...until she would say something that would bring the memories rearing back or remind him that she was a queen of manipulation, and his anger would flare. He knew he must be confusing the hell out of her, but he couldn't help it. He'd seen Emmie in the hallway just before leaving this afternoon and she had simply raised an eyebrow and shaken her head at him in disappointment. He held up his palms to halt her from giving him a lecture.

"I know, I know. Save it. I'm trying my best here, ok?" He stalked past her before she could get into it with him.

"Do better," she'd called after him in a singsong voice. He'd just shaken his head and kept walking. He thought back on the past few days as he made his way down to the river. He could have phased, but he enjoyed walking through his kingdom. It was a part of him and he saw endless beauty here, and being out in it always helped to ease the turmoil that seemed to constantly be roiling around inside of him. So, he'd reflected as he'd walked: He'd watched Skylar as she'd explored the castle and grounds, spent a great deal of time examining a book on Kama Sutra that had his imagination running wild, and actually had pleasant conversations with Jeff, seeming to enjoy talking with him.

A small smile crept back across his lips. Never in a million years would Persephone have willingly gone near any of the demon guards, let alone actually been *kind* to one or form a friendship of sorts. Hades found that he quite liked all the differences he was discovering between Persephone and her reincarnate, which only made him more irritated, made him want to lash out at her with renewed viciousness. He was making his own neck hurt from these whiplashing emotions, so he could only imagine what was going through Skylar's mind.

. . .

HE'D LACED his fingers together behind his neck and leaned his head back to stare the sky. If he were being completely honest with himself, he thought he *could* get past his issues with Persephone, could forgive and move forward. The real problem was that he was... scared. He was scared of Skylar betraying him, of...hurting him. He could see a very real, very tangible future in which he fell headlong for the fiery blonde. He had to constantly remind himself that any little bit of flirting she did, those small moments he would catch where she seemed to let her guard down, those minute hints of vulnerability that sometimes slipped out from behind her mask were all an act, all carefully designed to lure him in for her to strike.

EVERY TIME he forced himself to keep that fact in mind, his irritation went off the charts...even as he found himself laughing at her jokes, felt something in his chest unclenching for the first time in thousands of years, felt like she *belonged* with him for reasons that had nothing to do with the prophecy. If he allowed himself to explore that possible future, he was setting himself to be played by a grand master. Check fucking mate if he let her.

AND HE JUST WASN'T READY for that. Persephone had broken his heart once. He wouldn't let her do it again.

TIRED OF TRYING to navigate his growing...*interest* in Skylar, he shifted his focus to a mystery that was bugging him to no end: figuring out what she was. Hades phased the rest of the way to Charon's and they lounged on the sandy beach outside of his home, staring out over the water and musing over the possibilities of what she could possibly be.

• • •

"OK, how about her fangs? Could she be vampire hybrid maybe?" Charon asked. Hades shook his head.

"I DON'T THINK SO. Her fangs aren't quite the same as a leech's—smaller, and two on either side of her front teeth. And I've never heard of a vampire hybrid that didn't share at least *some* qualities of the species, but she has none. She can walk in the sun, doesn't drink blood, can eat normal food...no, I don't think that's it."

CHARON LOOKED contemplative as he swirled the amber liquid around his glass. He was a big fan of mortal Scotch, so Hades had brought him a 62 year old Macallan that he'd...borrowed from a mortal CEO of some tech company. Ok, he'd completely stolen it, but the mortal would be making his way to stand before Hades soon enough. The tech company was also involved in far less reputable ventures. The douche deserved to have his possessions stolen. That and *so* much more. Hades couldn't wait until his time came, already having quite a few eternal punishments in mind. A soft tickling sensation brushed against Hades' mind. Conan was trying to communicate. He opened up his mind and included Charon as well.

-HMM...SHIFTER then? You said she has adorable little claws- Conan sauntered towards them along the sand before hoping up on the end of Charon's chair. Hades summoned another glass of whisky for him.

"I DID *NOT CALL THEM ADORABLE*..." Had he? They *were* quite cute...He scowled. "And why are you back so soon? Thought you were going to hang out with Zeus for a while?"

. . .

-Would you believe me if I said I just missed you too much to stay away?-

Charon snorted. "Try again, fuzzball." Conan hissed at him.

—Ok, fine. Hera may have caught me digging through her archives again for something to help my condition—

"And what else did you do? Hera wouldn't have booted you just for rifling through her personal collection of goodies," Hades said as he took another sip, eyeing the cat knowingly.

-and, ok, so maybe I also found my way into her shower...while she was also in it...-

"There it is. You're an idiot." Hades chuckled at the thought of Hera catching Conan trying to sneak a peek.

-Oh don't even start. I've been trapped as a gods forsaken feline for far too long. A man has needs, damn you, and those free websites can only help so much. Sometimes you need to see things in person-

"But can't you, you know...satisfy your needs with another cat?" Charon asked.

Conan sat up, rearing his head back in disgust.

. . .

-Of course not! I'm not an actual cat, you brute! That's...that's bestiality! Gods, why do I even bother with any of you?-

"Because you do, in fact, love us," Hades grinned.

-Keep telling yourself that. Listen, enough about me and my debauchery. Back to your little queen.-

Charon laughed but rolled with the change of subject.

"Ok, so like Conan said: what about a shifter or lupin even?"

"I thought that too, but I haven't seen her change her form at all, and she isn't compelled to change during the full moon like a lupin. Her father was one, but from what I understand he wasn't her birth father. Again, she could be a hybrid of some sort, but I can't imagine a combination that would somehow negate *all* of the most dominate traits from either of the species involved." Hades skipped a small stone across the calm water. "With the way she can completely entrance males you would think she would be part siren or nymph or succubus..."

"Are you entranced then, oh great God of the Underworld?" Charon asked in a mocking tone, grinning over the rim of his glass. Conan snorted into his own, whiskers getting wet as he dunked his nose further down. Hades flipped them both off.

. . .

"Don't you have souls to ferry or something? What do I pay you for?"

Charon chuckled. "I hate to break it to you, boss, but you've got it bad." He turned more thoughtful when he asked seriously, "Can you get past what she did though? I mean not *her* I suppose, technically, but Persephone?" Even Charon's normally jocular demeanor shifted, a rigid tension creeping across his features. A quiet, deadly anger simmered just beneath the surface and the river began to churn and bubble, reacting to his emotions.

Charon was a brother to Hades, maybe not by blood, but a brother nonetheless, and it had gutted the ferryman when Persephone's betrayal had come so close to taking him away forever. Conan sat up and his own yellow eyes darkened in anger, the demigod in him rearing up despite his current form. As always, the love and loyalty of his friends and family, love and loyalty he wasn't always sure he deserved, made his throat close for a long moment, a lump of emotion stuck there.

Forcing the lump away, Hades thought about Charon's question. Could he move past Persephone's sins? Again, he thought he...could. And though she still seemed very determined to find a way to leave the Underworld, he *thought* that maybe Skylar was beginning to soften towards him as well. Sometimes he would catch her looking at him in a way that made every fiber of his being light up with joy and awe and awareness, but he wasn't sure if it was really there, or merely wishful thinking, or perhaps even a part of her wicked plan to make him fall for her. Not that he was falling for her of course. *Not yet...*

• • •

"FUCK," he muttered as he tossed back what remained in his glass, enjoying the burn and the warmth that flooded through him. Mortal alcohol couldn't really get them drunk, but a pinch of the powder made from the poppies that grew on Mount Olympus added in did the trick. He'd caught a nice buzz, as Emmie would put it. He settled deeper into the cushioned chair, staring out over the water, calming now that Charon was as well. Hades let out a long, long breath.

"IT DOESN'T MATTER. I just need her to marry me, nothing more. She fulfills the prophecy, I win this ridiculous war once and for all, simple as that. She's a means to an end, that's all." Charon and Conan shared a skeptical look, but let it slide. Hades was just opening his mouth to change the subject, when he felt something... wrong.

HE SHOT UPRIGHT, every muscle in his body tensed and thrumming as he realized what it was: the wards around the castle had been broken.

THIRTEEN

Skylar couldn't believe it had actually worked. When Emmie told her that the castle would give her most anything she wanted, she need only ask, she got the idea to try it on the invisible barrier, not really holding her breath that it could be that easy. But when she'd simply asked the barrier to fall, it was gone in an instant. She didn't know how long she had before Hades realized it was down or that she had made a break for it, so she bolted without a second thought.

But as she ran, putting distance between herself and the castle, a feeling of utter wrongness welled up in her chest. It almost felt as if she were running away from...well, from home. Which was fucking insane. She was a prisoner, of course she should run! It was one of the many things she was trained to do. And yet...*Ugh, shut up, brain!* Though her mind was apparently having a hard time understanding that running away was the obvious right choice here, her body was thankfully obeying. The bridge let out onto a black cobblestone path, leading her into the thick trees ahead. She ran and ran until the path began to narrow, becoming packed earth instead of cobblestone.

The forest grew thicker around her, and she stopped dead,

cocking her head to the side when she heard movement. She waited a heartbeat until she heard it again and realized it was coming from ahead of her on the path, so she ducked into the trees. The road was completely hidden from view almost immediately and a sense of foreboding stole over her. Ignoring it, she made her way slowly and silently through the brush, not even remotely sure of where she was going. Hades had told her time and again that she couldn't leave, but there had to be *something* she could do, she just had to figure it out. Maybe she could hitch-hike her way off this plane with a demon or something. She had plenty of money, she could pay someone whatever they wanted for a ride out of this place.

The trees began to change, becoming black, gnarled things that looked like something out of a horror movie.

"Ok, that's probably not a good sign..." Skylar mumbled to herself. As soon as the words left her mouth, she felt something moving among the trees around her. She whipped her head around, but even her keen eyesight could make out nothing. Her gut was telling her that whatever it was didn't want to help her out, so she picked up her pace as much as she could, winding through the thick trunks, having to slow to maneuver through twisted branches in some spots. She caught sight of a small cave and had a very quick debate with herself: deal with whatever was out here without any real room to fight, or take her chances with the cave. It was a no brainer.

She moved faster, scraping and cutting her skin on the jagged bark, wincing when thorns caught up in her hair and ripped some strands from the root. She finally made it to the mouth of the cave, barely noticing the strange symbols carved in the stone before she sprinted inside.

Except, she didn't end up in an actual cave. She was back in a forest, except this one was burned-out, only smoking stumps left here and there and the ash gray sky clearly visible above her. *What the...?* Then it hit her: she'd found another realm. *Oh fuck.* Maybe those symbols had been some kind of sign...or warning. Glancing around, she found nothing but charred earth surrounding her. The air was thick with acrid smoke, making her eyes sting. Everything about this place screamed wrong and dangerous. Neon red warning signs began flashing in her mind. She needed to get out of here and fast. She turned to go back through the...door? gate? portal? whatever the hell it was, but a demon was blocking her way.

She hadn't seen anything like this one around the castle. It wasn't much taller than she was, but it was built like a barrel and must outweigh her by a good hundred pounds at least. Its skin looked like pictures she'd seen of lava as it begins to cool: a bubbled, deep gray with orange glowing from underneath. It had a tail with a ball of spikes on the end and horns flaring back from the sides of his skull. Its orange eyes studied her intently for a long moment and then it smiled, revealing large wolf-like teeth. *Maybe it'll help me?* It raised its hand and liquid fire shot towards her from its palm. *Ok, or not.* She ducked to the side, avoiding the hit, but the heat was intense enough to singe the hairs on her arm. It growled something in a language she didn't understand.

"No habala, dickweed," she murmured, glancing around the area and coming up with possible exit strategies all while keeping the demon in her sights. It narrowed its eyes and spoke again, this time in harsh, guttural English.

"Trespassers are not welcome here, girl."

"Well, you didn't put the *Do Not Disturb* sign on the doorknob, so whose fault is that? But hey, my bad. I'll just be on my way and we'll part as old friends. Savvy?" Another voice sounded from behind her. She gasped and whirled, surprised that she hadn't sensed the approach. Another one of these things was standing a few feet away.

"Perhaps she's an offering from one of the other realms? From Hades himself even," the new one said, hope in its voice. Being an offering sounded way worse than being a trespasser. Her suspicions were confirmed when she looked back to the original demon and his —she was fairly certain they were both male—eyes roved down her body in a sickening way. She swallowed back vomit. *Anatomically incompatible* didn't even begin to cover it. *Not fucking happening.* Battle calm started to settle over her, her heart pumping ice through her veins.

"I'm the furthest thing from an offering you could imagine, sweetheart. Now, you've got two choices here: you can let me leave now, with your entrails resting safely inside your bodies, or you can try to stop me, and I'll smile as I rip out said entrails and wear them like Mardi Gras beads. You decide." She pulled a knife from the sheath she'd attached to her hip and began to spin it with casual expertise. "Chop, chop, I'm in a bit of a hurry."

The one blocking the portal-gate-door thing threw his head back and laughed. More chuckles sounded from all around her and Skylar realized more of the things had joined the party, surrounding her. She quickly re-assessed the situation, coming up with game plan after game plan. She arched an eyebrow and spread her feet wider, shifting her weight and lowering her center of gravity. Preparing for the battle that was about to begin. That strange part of her that she'd never really understood but loved began to thrum with excitement. She was born for this, battle in her blood and soul.

Her lips curled upwards.

The one blocking her path, which she assumed now was the leader, said to the others, "Take her alive. We will enjoy her this eve before feasting." Her spine stiffened at his words. She had a good feeling that she would be the main course on tonight's menu as well as the pre-dinner entertainment. She clenched her jaw and took a deep, calming breath.

"Lassiez les bons temps rouler, then, fuckers."

One to her left began to move forward and she tossed the knife before its foot even hit the ground, embedding it deep in the demon's throat. It couldn't even scream before falling to the ground, only a wet garbling sound escaped its crusted lips. She quickly unsheathed and tossed two more knives, hurling one overhand at a demon who had moved in front of the leader and tossing the other sideways, nailing another demon on the right of the circle. Both blades struck true, right in the heart. Or, in theory through the heart. For all she knew, demon hearts were in their butts or something.

Knowing she needed to get out of the middle of the circle so she didn't have anyone at her back, she raced towards the first one she'd hit. Another one lunged in her path, but she easily vaulted over him, spinning as she landed to face the group once more and yanking her dagger free from the demon's throat.

"Option one is still on the table, boys..."

Another demon growled and moved towards her, swiping out with a meaty hand. She arched backwards to avoid the hit, and then stabbed him in the gut. She cried out and yanked her hand back when his blood or entrails or whatever the hell it was began to ooze out over her fist. It *burned*, as if they really did have lava inside them. The skin of her hand was bubbling and blistering in the spots that it wasn't already completely gone. She could see bone and had to bite the inside of her cheek to stop herself from crying out or vomiting. She gritted her teeth and forced herself to ignore the pain.

Skylar shifted the knife to her other hand and easily dodged the attack of another demon. She blocked his punches with almost no effort and grinned at his confused expression. She loved when people underestimated her. She kicked him in the stomach and when he doubled over, she backhanded him with enough force to send him flying back at least twenty yards. She was just turning back to face off against her next opponent when pain exploded in her left shoulder, sending her staggering backwards with a scream. One of those bastards had launched more of that liquid fire at her. The pain was so intense that her vision wavered for a moment.

She remained upright—barely—and took several steps backwards as the four remaining demons began to stalk forward. *Shit, shit, shit.* Her best option at the moment was probably to run for it, try to hide and regroup. She didn't exactly like the idea of turning tail, but she also wasn't stupid. She could probably lead them away, circle back and get to the doorway. She was ninety-nine percent sure she was faster than them. She was faster than almost anything she'd ever faced, especially if her weird random hyper-jump thing kicked in.

She glanced down: her arm was coated in blood from shoulder to wrist and she nearly gagged at the stench of her own burnt flesh. She swayed for a moment then took another step backwards preparing bolt. She stumbled over a stump and landed hard on her ass.

The creatures laughed as they loomed closer, but before they could take one more step, black swirling smoke erupted out of thin air between them and where she sat on the ground. Raw power emanated from the smoke, making every instinct she had stand up and take notice, every muscle tensing. It was unlike anything she'd ever felt before but she knew whatever this was, it was not to be fucked with. She began to scoot backwards, but when the cloud cleared somewhat she gasped and sat frozen in place, terror turning her blood to ice.

Hades stood amid the smoke.

She thought she'd seen him angry before, but that had been mild annoyance compared to this. His features were hard, more rigid and angular somehow. He looked bigger than usual, taller and as if his muscles had expanded. His beautiful blue-green eyes were now completely black and burning with rage. The smoke, darker than night, continued to swirl around him, coiling like snakes ready to strike. He pinned her with a look that was so full of contempt that she swallowed hard in real fear. *Uh oh.*

He returned his gaze to the demons and said in a cold, commanding voice, "This ends *now*."

The leader stepped forward as the others cowered back, dropping to their knees. Bowing his head, he said, "M-my Lord, she trespassed on our lands. We have every right to dispense justice and do with her what we will."

"I will compensate you for her trespass, but the girl belongs to *me*," Hades said through gritted teeth. She was embarrassed by the jolt of happiness that his claim over her sent ringing through her chest. He glanced over his shoulder towards her once more and the happiness faded to a dull echo of feeling. His nostrils flared and his black eyes blazed brighter with fury when his gaze settled on her shoulder, following the trail of blood down her arm to her mangled hand.

He turned back to the demon and added in a scarily quiet voice, "And you have *harmed* her." Black fire erupted from the smoke, the flames arching high over his back and flaring out to his sides, dancing across his fingertips. The smoke and fire began to swirl around him, churning like a cyclone out of a dark nightmare. That intense power surged with the flames, making Skylar's heart stutter and fear shiver through her. He thrust his hands out to his sides and the smoke and fire shot towards two of the demons. Their screams only lasted for half a breath before they were just *gone*, burned to ash almost instantly. *Holy. Shit.*

Skylar finally regained the ability to move and scrambled back several feet. She didn't think Hades would kill her—he wanted her to marry him, and she couldn't do that if she was dead, right?—but her most basic survival instincts yelled "run away from the insanely powerful, *extremely* angry God of the freaking Underworld," so she listened.

The remaining demons gasped and recoiled, crying and whimpering as they bowed lower, their foreheads dragging along the dirt. The leader dropped to his knees, joining the rest.

"Please, we didn't know. We would never have touched if we knew! Please my Lord, the trespass is forgotten. We didn't *know*."

Hades seemed to be struggling to reign in his temper, but slowly the flames receded, inch by inch. Finally, he merely nodded once and then turned to scoop Skylar off the ground. An instant later they were in a dank stone room.

Skylar's stomach dropped as she realized exactly what it was:

A dungeon.

FOURTEEN

Hades released her as soon as they reached the cell deep within the dungeons and immediately phased just outside the bars. He was seething with rage and wasn't even sure where it was directed. At Skylar. At the demons. At himself. He stood and watched her, breathing hard and clenching his jaw so hard the bones began to crack. Her eyes were wide...with fear, he realized. *She's afraid of me?* The thought made something inside of him recoil, but he couldn't seem to calm himself. He hadn't felt fury like this in three thousand years.

"Hades, I...I'm..." He held up a hand to halt her, unable to even speak. Thank all the gods known and unknown, she actually obeyed his silent command and clamped her mouth shut. He didn't give a fuck what she had to say at the moment, couldn't stand to hear her excuses or smart ass remarks or have her rail at him. He needed to get away from her before he...didn't know what. He realized in that instant that he couldn't *actually* hurt her, despite all the times he'd wanted to do just that. The mere thought sent a bone-deep sickness radiating through every inch of him, something in his very soul screaming *WRONG!* so loudly that it echoed through his mind over and over.

So, no, he wouldn't hurt her, but he would possibly level the entire castle around them both. He felt the flames rise around him once more and her eyes flew impossibly wider, taking a step backwards in the cell, the black fire reflecting in the green of her irises.

She raised her hand to push a golden curl from her face and hissed in a sharp breath. Fury blazed once again when he focused on her injuries. He could clearly see bone in some spots, the flesh completely burned away. *And it could have been so much worse.* Bile rose in his throat as his power pulsed outward, threatening to unleash completely. He was so close to losing control, too close. He had to calm himself and the only way to do that was to get as far away from her as possible, as quickly as possible. He summoned healers and backed away from the bars without a word. She didn't seem to even notice the healers as they began to assess her injuries, she merely stared at him as he retreated, those piercing eyes never leaving his. They were filled with pain and fear and...regret?

But he didn't stop, couldn't stop.

Emmie was waiting just inside the stairwell. He didn't slow as he passed, just glared and spit at her, "Transport the healers out once they're finished. She stays there until I say otherwise. I mean it, Seer. Do not fucking test me on this." She didn't respond and he made it halfway up the stairs before he stopped and whirled around.

"How could you let this happen?!" he roared, shaking the stones around them. He knew it wasn't her fault, but his mind couldn't think logical thoughts at the moment. Emmie didn't so much as flinch despite the smoke and fire and power radiating from him and engulfing them both.

"Are you mad that she escaped?" she asked calmly, raising a silvery eyebrow at a flame getting dangerously close to her hair, as if daring it to make contact.

"Of course I am!"

"Think about it again."

What the fuck was she going on about? Of course he was mad that Skylar had escaped! Why wouldn't he be? She was the key to the prophecy, without her he couldn't win the war for his kingdom...but as he began to *really* think about it, he realized that he was also shaken to his core...with fear. Fear of losing her. A deep, unsettling fear that had nothing to do with the war or the prophecy, had only to do with the idea of never seeing her again, never hearing her smart mouth again, never feeling the warmth of her body against his.

When he'd realized she'd broken through the wards, anger surged of course, but there had also been panic. When he'd tracked her to the Inferno Realm, he had nearly lost his mind. An unyielding cold that he didn't understand had settled in his chest, clutching at his heart, squeezing, squeezing, squeezing. Though they were far from the most peaceful or...civilized creatures, he had no problems with the demons that resided there, but they were notoriously territorial and didn't take lightly to trespassers. Of course they would have no way of knowing who she was and would have technically had leave to do whatever they wished with her...*to* her.

Vomit rose once more and he barely kept himself from retching. He'd gotten there in time, but when he saw her injuries, he'd nearly lost control of his powers and killed every demon in the entire realm without a thought. Why in the hell was he reacting so strongly to her being hurt? To the mere *thought* of her being hurt? It was ridiculous! The strange connection between them was something far more complicated and important than he'd first admitted to himself.

So, no damnit, he wasn't just angry. He was *terrified*. That was the unnamed cold constricting his heart. Not just fear, but pure terror. His heart sped up again at the thought of what could have happened if he hadn't gotten there in time. Inferno Demons ate living flesh...

Hades reared back and punched the wall over and over, pummeling the stone to dust, bellowing at the top of his lungs. Smoke and fire swirled around them dangerously.

"Calm, Hades. You need to calm..."

He heard Emmie's voice as if from a great distance. He knew she was right. He was dangerously close to losing all control. How many times had he toed the edge just this day? He hadn't even gotten in the same hemisphere as losing control in thousands of years, and now he'd apparently moved in next door. *You're a fucking god. Get it together.* He forced his body and mind under control and finally calmed enough that the fire disappeared, though tendrils of smoke still curled around his legs and shoulders.

"There we go," Emmie murmured.

Hades leaned his forehead against what was left of the cold stone and squeezed his eyes shut. He could lie to himself and say that the terror was merely for the prophecy being unfulfilled, but it was useless. Since he was already "in his feelings" as Emmie liked to say, he figured he might as well go all the way. On top of everything else, he had to admit that he was also...*hurt* that she'd fled, that the idea of staying here with him was so abhorrent to her that she would risk running headlong into the gods damned Underworld in order to avoid it.

He couldn't deny the truth any longer: he was beginning to feel for Skylar, for Persephone again, and that meant he was completely and utterly fucked. How could he be so stupid? How could he possibly have feelings for a traitorous bitch who had tried to murder him? What was wrong with him?

A fucking lot, that's what.

He pushed himself away from the wall and opened his eyes. He cut them to Emmie and found the Seer smirking, somehow knowing the exact inner turmoil he just waded through. He bared his teeth at her and stalked off without a word.

FIFTEEN

The dungeon cell was a far cry from the beautiful room upstairs, but it wasn't nearly as bad as it could be. Skylar had been in cells that made this place look like the Ritz, so all in all, she couldn't complain. At least this time she wasn't chained to the wall and the floor wasn't covered in rats. *Ah, Budapest. Good times.*

A few hours after her injuries had been tended to by several beings who identified themselves as healers, the room had changed around her. A small fireplace emerged in one corner, complete with a fire that never needed tending to stay at the perfect height and temperature. One wall pushed backwards, enlarging the space enough for a small private bath to be created. The dingy cot transformed into a small but plush bed and thick, fur rugs covered the dirty stone floors. She wasn't sure if she had Emmie to thank for the new digs or Hades himself. She doubted the latter.

He had been so terrifyingly angry when he'd found her, the power pulsing from him unlike anything she'd ever seen, ever even heard of. But she could have sworn that there was also fear there. Fear for her? Had he been afraid for her safety? Sure she knew that he needed her to marry him for reasons he'd yet to divulge, but she'd gotten the sense when their gazes had collided as he'd backed away from her that his fear wasn't merely for the foiling of some big plan. He'd looked at her like...well, like he *felt* things for her. The look in his eyes reminded her of those shared between...mates.

The thought didn't make her shudder in revulsion or laugh at the utter ridiculousness. No, it made her...hopeful? Was that what this warm tingling in her chest was? Did she *want* to be his mate? Or did she want *him* to be *hers* rather since she had no idea if gods even had such things? No. Of course not...

Maybe?

Skylar could deal with being locked up again—she couldn't really blame him or say she wouldn't do the same if the tables were turned—but this time was worse. Hades had stopped coming to see her. It had been *days* and he hadn't shown his face again. She figured he needed time to cool off because that power he was spewing was downright terrifying, but come on. *Days?* She was seething now because, well, damnit, she missed him. She knew how ridiculous and Stockholm Syndrome-y it sounded, but it was true.

Though she was still determined to leave, she had to admit that she'd been softening towards him in the days before her escape attempt. She'd also been dreaming of him for as long as she could remember. She refused to believe that that didn't mean *something*. Not to mention, that weird feeling of belonging here. It had mostly been her years of training that had kicked in and compelled her to run at the first opportunity. When she pushed past those, her gut told her that she was meant to be here, that something big was coming. *Trust your gut, Rocket.* Her father's voice whispered through her mind and she knew she needed to listen. She and Hades needed to have a long chat and get to the bottom of some shit in a big way, but she was ready to have that conversation.

"If he would ever freaking show up," she grumbled to herself.

Emmie had come to visit her every day, even making a flat screen and popcorn appear so they could binge watch *The Walking Dead*, but there was no sign of the dangerously handsome God of the Underworld.

"Just give him time. He's processing *a lot* of feelings right now," Emmie told her as they settled in to watch. "Backstabbing, betrayal, broken hearts. Tale as old as time," she said absent-mindedly. Backstabbing? Betrayal? As usual, Skylar had no idea what the Seer was talking about, so Skylar had just let it go and tried to heed her advice.

She'd now been in the dungeon for six fucking days and was starting to wonder if he planned to leave her in this cell forever. Emmie said to give him time, but come on! She'd been there long enough to bounce between wanting to have a calm, rational conversation, wanting to gouge his eyes out with a spoon, wanting to jump his bones, and back to the conversation bit again at least a hundred times. She really didn't know where she would land when—*if*—he showed again.

She was lounging on the bed with her feet propped up on the wall when she finally felt him. She immediately righted herself and hopped to her feet just before he appeared outside of the bars. Their gazes collided and neither one spoke for what seemed like hours. There was still anger burning in his eyes but there was also relief. He was relieved to see her again, just like she was relieved to see him. Her heart thudded in her chest.

His intense gaze wandered leisurely from her eyes to her lips, to her neck, her breasts, lower, lingering in every spot just long enough to make her skin heat and her breaths become soft and shallow. How could he affect her so much with only a look? He dragged his gaze upward once more and now desire had joined the emotions blazing in his blue-green eyes. Skylar swallowed hard and forced her thoughts to come back from NC-17 rating territory. They had things they needed to discuss. She couldn't get distracted by the way his black shirt hugged his chest and arms, or the fact that his hair was a tangled mess but it made him even more attractive somehow, or the way that he absentmindedly ran his tongue along his bottom lip. *Fuck me running, he's the sexiest man on the planet.*

"You ran," he rasped quietly at long last. The overwhelmingly sexy sound of his voice was overshadowed by the simmering rage and accusation in his tone. Her desire cooled in an instant like a candle snuffed out. How dare he still be mad that she tried to escape. *Alright, guess we're going with the "gouge his eyes out" option.*

She drew herself up and threw her shoulders back. She felt her claws extend and her fangs slide free. She was ready for a fight.

"I did and I won't apologize for it." His nostrils flared in irritation and light tendrils of smoke began to swirl around him. He clenched his jaw and the smoke cleared an instant later, but she got the feeling he was barely keeping a hold on himself. *Why?* Why *is he so mad? I don't understand.*

"So you enjoy staying in the dungeon then?"

"I was in a cell upstairs too, just a five-star one," she spit. He began to pace and ran a hand through his already disheveled hair.

"I should have known it was just a matter of time before the betrayal happened. It's in your fucking nature." Betrayal? Her nature? Did he mean because of her job?

"Oh my god, drama queen much? I don't think running from the dude who kidnapped you can be seen as a 'betrayal' by anyone with half a functioning brain. And you don't know a god damn thing about me *or* my nature!"

"Oh I know more than you think," he growled, "more than you could possibly imagine, and deep down, you're the *same*." He said the last through gritted teeth and his flames began dancing across his knuckles and finger tips. The same? The same as *what*? What the hell was he talking about? Gods she was getting so sick of his nonsensical responses and accusations! She knew he was close to losing it again, could feel that intense power pulsing from him, but she couldn't stop herself from lashing out.

"You know nothing, Jon Snow!" she shrieked. "But let me lay down a bit of knowledge on ya here: when Skylar is taken to another fucking *plane of existence*, finds out the gods are not only real, but one of the Big Three has decided she's supposed to be his *wife*—which bee-tee-dubs, the last chick who fell for that was stuck here for eternity, minus spring breaks in Cancun according to the stories—with no further explanation whatsoever, and held against her will, SHE WILL RUN AT THE FIRST OPPORTUNITY! Hashtag fucking facts!" Her fangs shot longer in a rush, piercing her bottom lip and drawing blood.

They were both at the bars now, both having moved towards each other without thought. They were both breathing heavily and they were staring at each other like two lions about to attack. They were fuming, the animosity around them in the air as thick as his smoke. And under that, there was a whole *other* kind of tension settling between them. The kind of tension that leads to anger banging against a dungeon cell door and possibly toppling an entire castle around them. While that thought made her stomach clench with sudden and unexpected need, the fighting wasn't want she wanted, not really. She'd decided she wanted to explore this weird, unexplainable thing with him, and raging at each other wasn't going to get them there. She needed to ease this and try to pull them both back from whatever abyss of rage they were about to topple into.

She closed her eyes and took a deep breath, held it for several seconds, and then let it out slowly. She willed her fangs and claws under control and slowly opened her eyes. His were still trained on her, burning with too many things to name. How to diffuse this bomb? Her go-to was stupid humor, but...would that work on a god? She shrugged inwardly. *Worth a shot.*

She cleared her throat softly. "So, um, did you see that new movie about you and your friends?" His brows furrowed, confusion momentarily erasing the fury. *Bingo!* "No? Well, you Odyssey it." She raised her eyebrows, waiting...*Come on. Please laugh. Please understand what I'm doing. Please...*

He laughed. A surprised bark of a laugh that seemed to catch him completely off guard, but it was enough. She felt the tension easing around them and then saw his smoke and flames slowly recede.

"That's awful. Really, really awful." But he laughed again and she smiled, relieved that her stupid plan had panned out.

"Look, I was trained basically my entire life to get out of situations like this, to defend myself and fight back and never give up. *Of course* I ran." Her voice dropped lower as she added, almost absently, "And I don't take well to being locked up." Memories began to surface. A locked room. The smell of stale beer. Burning. She fought to push them away, but he narrowed his eyes at her, and she knew that she'd let the darkness of the memories show.

She shook herself and continued, "It was mostly instinct. You get that, right?" He clenched his jaw but didn't argue, so she continued, hoping she was making progress. "Let me ask you something: did it ever occur to you to just *explain* to me why you need me to marry you? That maybe I'd be willing to play ball? You are a freaking god for crying out loud, why wouldn't I at least hear you out?"

His dark brows furrowed and she had to stifle an exasperated laugh. The thought had obviously never even crossed his mind. *Men!*

"I...hadn't thought of that as an option, no..." He looked embarrassed.

"So tell me now." She crossed her arms over her chest and waited. He took a deep breath and stared at her for a long, long moment. Finally he must have come to some kind of conclusion because he reached through the bar, settling his big hand on her hip and a second later, she was back in her room upstairs. *Her* room, like this was already home. She frowned slightly at how easily that thought had rolled off of her metaphorical tongue but didn't want to dwell on it.

"Sit," he commanded and though she thought about it for a second, she decided not to argue. Instead she made her way to the sofa in front of the fireplace and plopped down, reveling in the softness, the way the cushions hugged in around her. A fire roared to life in the hearth and a glass of something that smelled like damn good scotch appeared on the end table beside her. Another appeared in his hand and he took a long sip. He strolled to the fireplace, staring at the flames as if for answers before turning to face her, propping an elbow on the end of the mantle. Skylar took a drink from her own glass.

"Wowza," she murmured. His lips twitched but then he became all business again. She braced herself, really not sure what to expect.

Here we go...

SIXTEEN

Hades had to tread carefully here. He couldn't reveal all, but perhaps she had been right. Maybe he'd gone about this the wrong way. If he'd explained, at least somewhat, maybe she would have been willing to negotiate. He had to admit he felt foolish for not thinking of it before, but he'd been overwhelmed with three thousand years of pent-up rage at Persephone to think clearly.

So, he was going to give her way a try because...he didn't want her to feel like a prisoner here, not anymore. Sure, he'd wanted to punish Persephone at first, but now he was finding that need lessening with each day. And after the close call in the Inferno Realm? It had all but vanished. The fear of losing her had rocked him. Emmie's voice kept echoing through his head. He needed to get past his hatred of Persephone and forgive her. Could he? He was going to have to at least *try*. He took another long drink and then began.

"I've been fighting a war for the Underworld for thousands upon thousands of years, a war that's never made it into the mortal stories. It was prophesied millennia ago that you would ret...that you would be a part of it. In order to finally win the war for my kingdom, you must become my wife." *Again.*

"Me? This thousands of years' old prophecy mentioned *me,* specifically? Skylar Anne Pembroke?" she asked skeptically. He shifted slightly and took another drink before answering. This could get tricky. Emmie had warned about spilling the beans on the reincarnate situation—messing with fate and free will and all that—so he had to choose his words carefully.

"It did not mention you by name, no, but you're...her. It's you, trust me in this." She swirled the alcohol in her glass, looking contemplative.

"And you're sure it says *wife*? Not just pen pal or fuck buddy or...?" He gave her a dry look. "Ok, ok, fine. Wife it is...Now let's just pretend for argument's sake that I agreed to this: would I be trapped here forever? Like Persephone was? I mean, did the mortals get that part right?"

His gaze locked with hers, searching. Now that she was talking about Persephone and the imprisonment that was the crux of her hatred and eventual betrayal, would she remember? Did he *want* her to? He'd never thought much of it before, but now he wondered: if she did regain her memories of her past life, what would happen to Skylar? Would she remember the past, but remain herself? Or would she simply cease to be, reverting back to Persephone completely? The thought was...unwelcome. He stared for a moment longer, his eyes boring into hers, but no recognition flared in the emerald depths.

Her brows drew down slightly at his scrutiny, so he sighed and said honestly, "I'm not sure. She was bound here, that part was true, but that was an unforeseen aftereffect of our marriage. It was unexpected and even I don't know *why* it happened or why I couldn't circumvent it. I'm its king, but the Underworld has a mind of its own."

Her brows shot upwards. "A castle that takes requests, though apparently not for jailbreaks," she grumbled, "and now a realm that's basically sentient?" She shook her head. "Wow. Just...wow."

She took another small sip of her drink and stared at him over the rim of her glass as if weighing something in her mind. Finally, she took a deep breath.

"What if...what if I agreed to stay?" His eyes flew wide. She could not have said what she just said, could she? "Not indefinitely," she added quickly, "but for...I don't know, like two weeks, see how things shake out." His eyes narrowed, suspicious now.

"Why would you offer such a thing?" Her gaze flicked to the balcony doors, roaming out over the Underworld. Something sparked in her eyes: curiosity? Longing? Hope? But she merely gave a non-committal shrug and pulled her gaze back to him.

"I'm in the Underworld, might as well take advantage and explore a bit. I mean, it's like Narnia or something for fuck's sake! I could get a feel for this place, get to know you...and at the end of it, if I don't agree to marry you, you agree to let me go."

Never in a million years would he have thought she would offer such a deal. Of course he couldn't agree to let her go, but if he could get her to cooperate, to stay willingly and be open minded about this, could he...woo her? Make her *want* to marry him? *Hell, I did it once...*

"Six weeks," he countered. She narrowed her eyes and sat up straighter.

"A month." She arched an eyebrow in challenge and waited. Could he really do this? Could he put the past behind him and try to...what? Just forgive and forget? Move on? Start over with a clean slate? Was that possible for him? He'd been holding onto this rage for so long, it was a part of him now. He wasn't sure if he could function without it at this point, but he knew he had to try. He didn't like lying to her, but it had to be done. The end would justify the means, surely.

"Deal."

She looked surprised but then gave him a sharp nod and raised her glass towards him. He did the same.

"Deal."

~

"I can't believe he finally gave in and let you out. I had a whole thing planned!" Emmie threw up her hands in what appeared to be real disappointment. "I'd seen it all in perfect detail. It was epic! I was going to tattoo the layout of the dungeon on my back but all hidden within another design so it wouldn't be obvious, of course. Then I would do something to get myself thrown in a cell too, like, I dunno, mismatch all of his socks or something, *then*–"

"Wait. That's the plot of *Prison Break*," Skylar said as she pulled one arm across her chest to stretch. She repeated the motion with her other arm and rolled her neck back and forth before bouncing up and down on the balls of her feet. "Well, minus the socks part." She grinned, now dying to know if Hades was weirdly obsessed with his socks or something.

Her grin faded as Emmie frowned, brow furrowing in confusion. Skylar noticed that sometimes she seemed to get a bit discombobulated from all of her visions, sometimes having trouble keeping things straight or even telling reality from what was in her head—or in this case, television dramas. Skylar always felt a pang of sympathy for her friend when it happened, because, yes, Emmie was absolutely already a friend. When a great oracle to the gods tells you that you're destined to be besties, you just kind of accept it. Skylar couldn't imagine what it was like, trying to keep thousands upon thousands of futures straight in her mind, all the possible outcomes, changing with each and every decision anyone made. She was exhausted just thinking about it. How Emmie managed to stay sane and lucid even eighty percent of the time was astounding.

"Is it? Hmm...well no matter, you're out now." Emmie shrugged and her easy smile was back in place again. She eyed Skylar, still stretching. "You know that no amount of calisthenics can prepare you to best me in this, don't you?"

"I am a trained assassin and spy, a supernatural mercenary, a Grade-A certified badass. You don't want none of this, homeslice."

Skylar wiggled her eyebrows, looking cocky as hell. But, well, it's not cocky if it's true, right?

"And I am an oracle to the *gods*...amongst other things," Emmie added, cryptically. "Choose your weapon wisely, infant."

Skylar snorted but turned to peruse her options.

"Going with my man, Link."

"And I shall be Diddy Kong. He's such a cheeky little monkey!" Emmie squealed. Skylar laughed as they fired up Super Smash Brothers on the Wii in the game room. "So, you actually agreed to stay for a month, huh?"

"I did. It was better than being held prisoner. And..." Skylar trailed off as she started an artful attack on the game. Emmie dodged it, barely even looking at the screen. Skylar narrowed her eyes but let it slide. It was probably stupid to play any kind of game with someone who could see the future, but oh well.

"And what?" Emmie coaxed.

Skylar grunted and danced around as they played. She blew a lock of hair out of her eyes. She was a little embarrassed to admit it out loud, but she figured if there was anyone who would understand a little crazy, it would be Emmie.

"And...well, ok so this is going to sound crazy, but...I've been dreaming of Hades for almost as long as I can remember, long before I ever saw him in that alleyway."

Emmie turned to look at her, tilting her head to the side like a confused dog.

"Well, of course you have. That's how you people know, isn't it?"

"Huh? You people? Who people? Know what?"

Emmie's eyes went wide for a split second, as if she'd spilled some tea she most certainly was not supposed to spill.

"Uhhh...Oh look! A monkey!"

Skylar started to push and then realized too late that the sneaky little oracle had kicked her ass in the game. She scowled at Emmie who grinned and blew her a kiss. It was obvious that Emmie didn't want Skylar to dig, so she would let it go...for now.

"And I also have this weird feeling of belonging here, something I've never really had anywhere before. Like I'm...meant to be here. That's absolutely batshit crazy...right?"

"It is, but it isn't," Emmie said simply. *Because that makes so much sense.*

"So, anyway, my gut was telling me to explore that more. Hence the plea bargain to get out of jail."

"And you know your gut will never steer you wrong, Poprocks." Emmie winked at her. Hearing her father's words from Emmie's mouth let Skylar know that she had made the right decision. All of this meant something, and she was determined to find out what.

THINGS HAD DEFINITELY SHIFTED between Skylar and Hades. So much so that she would call them friends...friends verging on something more? She would be lying if she wasn't hoping for just that. She was falling in definite like with him the more time they spent together. He'd begun hanging around more often and they'd had actual, real conversations now, not just casual BS like before. Though she could tell he was still holding a lot of himself back, he was starting to soften, no doubt about it. He would laugh at her stupid jokes and she discovered that he had a great sense of humor himself. He'd joined her, Emmie and Jeff for dinner almost every night in an amazing courtyard dining space she'd found, though he'd never asked for the two of them to dine alone. She was only slightly disappointed by that. Really.

He'd watched her and Emmie play video games several times, but never joined in. Finally, Skylar was tired of it.

"Are you afraid of losing to a girl or what?" Skylar taunted him now. He quirked a brow and after a moment of deliberation, took the controller from Emmie with a wicked smirk. When Emmie pulled her lips in to hide her smile, Skylar's confidence faltered, and she knew she was in trouble.

He'd absolutely wiped the floor with her.

"Are you using some sort of godly mojo to cheat?!" she accused in a frustrated yell over the blaring music Emmie had put on. Hades threw her a cocky grin.

"No godly mojo needed. You just suck."

"And swallow too, if you're lucky," she retorted. She smirked with delight when he inhaled sharply, the muscle in his jaw clenching. His concentration slipped enough that she'd pulled ahead. *Yes! Almost there...No!*

"A turtle shell!? You bastard!" she shrieked when poor Yoshi spun out of control and Mario blazed by to cross the finish line, winning for the tenth time in a row. She threw her controller onto the sofa with a little too much force and snatched up a pillow. She tossed it at his stupidly perfect face and grinned when it nailed him head-on. She was just a wee bit competitive and was accustomed to being the best at practically everything. He hiked one brow at her, a smile dancing on his entirely too tempting lips.

"I believe those on the Mortal Plane would call you a sore loser." She wanted to throttle him. Her claws even grew and her fangs extended, preparing to fight. *He's a god, he'll heal...*But all thoughts of violence vanished when he smiled at her. A full on *smile*, not his cruel, mocking one and not his smartass little smirk or the little grin he let slip now and again. She'd only seen it once before and somehow hadn't fully realized the perfection of it until now. It was equal parts sexy and cute and she had never wanted to kiss anyone more than she wanted to kiss him. The need was staggering and she began to lean forward, fully intent on jumping him.

"*I wanna do bad things with youuuuu,*" Emmie sang off key with the music. It was enough to knock Skylar out of the lust-trance she'd been in thankfully, though she would bet her metaphorical left nut that Emmie's song choice was no accident. She shook herself and cleared her throat.

"Rematch, Cheater McCheaterstein."

He leaned closer and said with mischief and...something else in his eyes, "I could go all night, love." She barely—*barely*—stopped herself from asking him if he promised.

The next night he joined them for an *Indiana Jones* marathon. Emmie chuckled to herself as she passed out treats and cut the lights, apparently in on some joke. Skylar figured out what it was soon enough: sitting in a darkened room mere feet away from Hades was pure torture. She could feel the heat radiating from him though they sat several feet apart and both seemed to be making sure that distance was maintained. She completely missed the first half of Raiders because she'd been so focused on keeping her breathing even, her muscles rigid and under control, and thoughts of easing closer to him, straddling his hips, and finally knowing what it was like to kiss him out of her mind.

By the time Indy had discovered the weird aliens hours later, her claws had cut shallow grooves into her palms and her muscles were sore from how strongly she'd been clenching them.

"Now that's what I call tension!" Emmie announced as the lights came back on and she stood, stretching her hands over her head. Skylar caught sight of a wicked looking scar running up her torso and wondered idly what could have happened. She could see the future, how could she possibly have been injured like that without knowing it was coming?

To Skylar's surprise and amusement, it was Hades who stiffened as if he'd been shocked.

"T-tension?" He had to clear his throat before he could get the words out. So she hadn't been the only one feeling the strains of the strange magic that had settled around them as soon as the lights had gone off. She pressed her lips together to stop her grin.

In a too-innocent voice, Emmie said, "The movie of course...it was *so* tense wondering how it was going to end. Would they or wouldn't they...escape. *Very* tense. Don't you think?" She looked like the cat who'd found a big, juicy canary, and gave Skylar a surreptitious wink. The King of the Underworld settled a glare on the Seer that most people would run from, screaming, while possibly wetting their pants. Emmie merely smiled and raised her eyebrows in two quick arches suggestively. Hades began to stand, then thought better of it, and instead mumbled a quick good night before disappearing.

Skylar and Emmie shared a look before flopping on the couch, laughing so hard they could barely breathe.

Lucas McBride paced in his boss's—no, *his* office. He was still having trouble remembering that the office that once belonged to his boss, mentor, surrogate father, and friend, was now his. Dalton Pembroke was dead, and Lucas had taken his place as head of Willow Corp. Thinking of Dalton hurt too much, which pissed Lucas off to no end. He was no stranger to death. His family had been killed when he was a teenager, he'd lost friends and comrades-in-arms, had been the *cause* of so much death himself he'd lost track of the body count years ago...but Dalton's death was hitting him hard, harder than he thought possible.

Luke ran his hands through his hair in frustration. He knew he needed to calm down. He could feel himself starting to change, and he hated feeling so out of control that the change wasn't a conscious decision. He closed his eyes and inhaled deeply, forcing himself to calm. He needed to do better than this. He had to be on top of his game to find Skylar.

He'd forced her to take time off after Dalton died. He snorted to himself. Died? No, Dalton hadn't died, he'd been *murdered*. Burned to death in a cowardly attack with a car bomb. The strongest lupin in at least a thousand years had been taken out by a fucking car bomb. There hadn't even been enough left to bury...Bile rose in Luke's throat and he cut off the thought. His claws elongated once more, digging into his palms hard enough to draw blood. *Calm yourself, damnit. Focus. Focus on Skylar.* He shook out his hands, easing the sting from the spots where his skin had been sliced.

She hadn't wanted to take time off, of course, but she'd agreed, knowing that Lucas wouldn't let her work until she'd taken time to deal with her loss. Yeah, he was a hypocrite, so what? She'd been gone for a week, vacationing in a small town in France when she'd just disappeared. Her phone was going right to voicemail, no responses to any text messages, and her GPS locator had stopped working—which was impossible. The locators *always* worked, no matter where anyone went, they worked, yet Skylar's had just blinked out of existence, like she left the planet or something. The only way they didn't work was if you purposely disabled them, but why the hell would Skylar do that? Sure, she'd left a note but still, something didn't feel right to him.

For the umpteenth time since she vanished, his stomach twisted painfully. If something happened to her...*No.* He shook his head, refusing to let the thought even form. No. She was the best of all of them, there was no way anything had happened to her. She was just being Skylar and going off-grid for a little while. She did that some-times when things got too heavy...but every other time she'd at least given them a heads up. An actual heads up, not a damn note.

I'll be MIA for a while, but I'm five by five, promise. -Sky

The Buffy reference and atrocious handwriting let him know that the note was legit, but he still felt in his gut that something was off, and if Dalton had taught them all anything, it was to trust their guts. So, there he was, worrying.

Lucas wasn't normally a worrier. He'd never understood the need, having a firm "what happens, happens" world view. He could control what he could control and everything else wasn't up to him, so why waste time with worry?

But now worry was gnawing at his chest like a rabid animal. He still loved Skylar, despite the short duration of their official relationship, and the thought of losing her was damn near killing him. They'd known each other for over a decade and he'd loved her for nearly all that time, but they had only actually dated for about seven months. He could tell that she wanted them to work, and she loved him back in her own way, but she had issues when it came to letting people in. Given her past, he totally understood, so he never faulted her for it...but it still hurt.

Regardless of any of that, she was the closest thing to family he had, and he refused to lose her too, especially not so soon after Dalton. It would be too much, even for him. Though he had a wicked sense of humor and never seemed to take anything seriously, everyone joked that he was a robot when it came to actual emotions. That was what he liked people to believe, that he was cold and uncaring, but deep down, he felt it all. Very few people knew the truth about him. One of them was dead and now another was missing. He growled and punched the wall. Once, twice, a third time just to be sure the wall really got the message.

He felt his muscles growing larger, felt his teeth lengthening in his mouth, becoming fangs, felt his claws extending once more. *Damnit!*

"Get your shit together, McBride," he growled at himself. Slowly he felt himself reverting back to normal. Being a wolf shifter was great when it came to missions or fights, but sometimes it was a real pain in the dick.

"Yo, Teen Wolf, any news?"

Zahara sauntered into the room and hopped up on the desk, kicking her long legs back and forth. Her ridiculously short skirt rode up, reveling perfectly toned thighs. She was long and lean, with beautiful dark caramel colored skin, deep golden eyes, and long, black hair. She was basically his adolescent Princess Jasmine fantasy come to life. The fact that she was also one of the deadliest females on the planet just made her all the more appealing. He sighed. If he could have just fallen in love with Zahara instead of Skylar, life would have been much easier. He and Z had fooled around a handful of times to blow off steam, but there was never any actual feelings or chemistry between them. They were good friends, but that was it.

He plopped down in one of the chairs in front of the desk with a huff.

"Nothing. I just don't get it. I know that she needs to go to ground every now and then—"

"Like a rodent," Zahara chimed in. He arched a brow. "A cute rodent, don't get me wrong, but a little rodent all the same."

He chuckled before continuing, "Ok, yes, like a rodent. But she's always let one of us know of her plans when she needed a time out before. And not in some bullshit note left behind like an afterthought. Why not now?"

"She's never lost the single most important person in her entire life before," Z said quietly. Her humor from moments ago vanished and she became uncharacteristically somber. Lucas knew that this was killing her. Skylar was her best friend, basically her sister. Everyone in the company called them the Femme Fatale Twins, the FFTs—they'd even had shirts made. Though they physically looked nothing alike, they were two peas in a pod when it came to the job and practically everything else in the world.

The line of work they had all chosen (or stumbled into) was dangerous, so they were all always mentally prepared to lose someone...or so they thought. Telling yourself you're ready for something, and actually being ok when it happens are definitely not the same thing. Lucas felt the familiar burn of tears starting and forced them away. He knew that she was probably right, that Skylar was probably fine and just needed to get away and wasn't thinking clearly enough to tell them, but still, he felt helpless.

Helpless to find or help Skylar, helpless to ease Z's pain, helpless to do anything damn useful at all. He didn't like feeling helpless and was desperate to feel *anything* else.

His gaze skated up Z's body. He stood and stepped closer to the desk, asking her permission with his eyes. She sagged with relief and he realized that she needed to feel something else too. He finished closing the distance, wedging his hips between her thighs as she opened them in welcome. Without a word, she raised her arms and he slid her shirt off over her head, and his shirt was gone a second later. He lifted her ass off the desk with one hand long enough to pull her thong down her thighs with the other, discarding it on the floor. He leaned in and kissed her, hard and deep, his tongue dominating hers, just the way she liked it. They were both dying for something to distract them and soon it was all teeth clashing and nails scratching. She ripped open his fly as he tangled a hand through her hair, using his grip to angle her head and exposure her neck. He kissed and licked and nipped his way down her delicate flesh, making her moan and buck her hips against him. She gripped his cock hard, almost too hard, but in that moment it was exactly what he needed.

She said in a strangled whisper, "Make me forget. Just for a little bit. Please, TW."

And he did.

EIGHTEEN

With every day that passed, Skylar began to feel more and more content in the Underworld, more...damnit, more *at home*. The like she was feeling for Hades was growing stronger as well, verging on something dangerous and terrifying. They'd fallen into a nice rhythm with each other and he'd even started showing her things around the castle grounds and beyond. The barrier was no longer in place, but she wasn't stupid enough to try to run through the Underworld without a proper tour guide again, though she got the oddest sense of...welcome from the world around her as they meandered through forests and plains, villages and mountains. Maybe Hades hadn't been lying about the world itself having a mind of its own.

They'd talked as they walked and the conversation came as easy as breathing.

"So, what about the whole Underworld being hell thing?" she asked one day as they walked through a picturesque village near a sea of light pink water. The demons here were nothing like those in the Inferno Realm. They were slender and graceful, with iridescent scale-like skin and small gills on their necks. Hades had explained that they could live on land or in the water, and there were more villages far beneath the waves. She was dying to find some scuba gear and go explore.

"That's a bit hard to explain. I'll show you one day," he promised as he accepted two tankards of a sweet smelling liquid from a petite demoness, nodding his head in thanks. The demoness' cheeks deepened to a dark plum—blushing? Skylar glanced around and saw that every female was staring at Hades with expressions that were a mix of awe and lust, and the males looked at him with reverence and respect. His people truly loved him. She looked back at him as he smiled at the demoness—not a full-on make-Skylar's-panties-melt smile, but a small, genuinely kind one—and she realized that he truly loved them in return.

They strolled to the shore and sat on a bench, and she was only a tiny bit disappointed that he plopped down as far away from her as possible without falling off the end. Despite the two of them growing undoubtedly closer, he always held himself away from her physically. Never sitting too close, never brushing her hand as they walked. She tried not to take that personally. There was no way he wasn't feeling the pull between them. No fucking way. She'd seen the desire in his eyes, mirroring her own, on more than one occasion. So...why?

Skylar sipped from her cup, pushing the thoughts aside for not. The ale was sweet with just the tiniest bit of sour that bit at the back end. It was downright delicious.

"Hmm, ok. What about all the other gods and goddess?"

"What do you what to know?"

"Anything. Everything. I've read some of the real histories in the library, but I want the juicy stuff, the gossip. Come on, dish." He smiled and took a sip of his own drink as he stared out over the water.

"Hmm, ok, let's see here. Hera and Zeus were never actually married. They dated for a few hundred years, but were never really that serious—or monogamous for that matter. I think Zeus is allergic to monogamy honestly, but Hera wasn't down for it either. Anyway, someone...*maybe* me, though I'd deny it if questioned directly... spread the rumor that they'd married as a joke after Zeus had gotten blackout drunk one night." Skylar's eyes widened and Hades added hastily, "In my defense, it was Si who made sure that it was recorded in the mortal accounts. We didn't really think about what a bad rap Zeus would get as the universe's biggest cheating scumbag as a result. Not our fault." He shrugged and Skylar's lips curled into a smile.

"The mortals got her jealousy and rage right though. You do *not* want to piss her off. Let's see here...Achilles' heel is his weakness, but it was actually a curse placed upon him, not the whole being dipped in the river thing. Aphrodite hates that she's known the world over as the epitome of beauty. She's actually quite shy and doesn't like the attention that her beauty has gotten her. She routinely pays an enchantress to alter her appearance so she can go about her business without being recognized. Athena and Ares are twins and you've never met two more competitive people in your life. The first Olympic Games were actually just them competing with each other. It got way too out of hand, but we all liked the idea of the competition in general, and passed the games on to the mortals." He took another drink and Skylar shifted on the bench so she was facing him, pulling one leg up beneath her. His eyes dipped to where her dress rode up but he quickly pulled his gaze back up.

"Poseidon can't keep his dick in his pants these days and usually needs one of us to bail him out of the trouble that causes. Oh! Zeus is afraid of snakes."

"Snakes? Seriously?"

"Yep, can't stand them. I once paid Medusa to hide in his closet and he literally pissed himself when she jumped out." He laughed out loud at the memory and Skylar grinned. God she loved it when he laughed. He shook his head and took another drink.

"Speaking of Medusa: are her pubes snakes too?" Hades spit his ale out and Jeff, in his ever-present guard position a few feet away, laughed loudly but quickly tried to cover it with a cough.

"What is wrong with you?" Hades demanded.

"It's a valid question!" Skylar said defensively. "Her hair is snakes, so it stands to reason that *all* of her hair could be snakes..."

He looked torn between confusion and laughter. She smiled and raised her brows, daring him to answer. He bit his bottom lip and grinned, and damn if wasn't somehow the sexiest thing she'd ever seen. She tightened her grip around her mug in an effort to keep herself in check. He finally shook his head in defeat.

"Her serpents are only on her scalp, I assure you."

"And how, pray tell, do you know that?" she asked innocently over the rim of her cup. He shifted on the bench, his grin fading a bit.

"Um, well...it was a one-time thing...eons ago really..." She threw her head back and laughed, enjoying his discomfort as much as the conversation. She was enjoying everything far too much. He joined in and they spent the rest of the day chatting and enjoying the sound of the waves.

Skylar kept waiting for those alarm bells to go off, for her internal warning system to scream that there was danger afoot in the form of the criminally handsome King of the Underworld getting too close, but they remained eerily silent. She and Hades had developed a friendship and surprising comradery, with an intense fire burning just beneath the surface. There were still times when hatred flashed behind his eyes, but the moments were slowly becoming fewer and farther between.

When she asked about it though, he became agitated and refused to answer, which caused her to become irritated. A bickering match would begin and then one of them would storm off. They'd cool off and act like nothing happened within a few minutes usually. He also still constantly asked what she was and she still refused to answer. He was keeping his secrets, so she could keep hers, too, and he flat out refused to let her contact her friends back home. That particular argument had left her fuming for two whole days and earned him the silent treatment.

So, no, things weren't perfect. They hadn't magically fallen in love within a few hours like in those sappy romance novels, but things were good for the most part. Verging on better than good if they could just get past these few little points of consternation. She *would* wear him down on the no contact order. She needed to get in touch with Lucas and Z as soon as possible. They would be going absolutely crazy by now, assuming the worst. She owed it to them to ease their minds as best she could. She had no idea what she would actually say to them to explain any of this, but she would cross that bridge when she came to it.

Frustrated by her lack of control in this particular area, she continued to beat on the punching bag that she'd asked the castle to put in her room. Once Emmie had spilled the beans on asking the castle for favors thing, she'd discovered that she could ask for (almost) anything, and it would magically appear before her. Her room was now filled to the brim with clothes, shoes, books, movies, and a life-sized cardboard cutout of a shirtless Ryan Reynolds.

"Why don't you just go to the gym?" Emmie asked from her spot lounging across Skylar's bed reading old issues of *Cosmo*. "*36 Ways To Spice Up Your Sex Life*. This article is for you! Let's see here..." Skylar stopped and stared at her.

"Excuse me?"

"Don't you want to spice up your sex life? I mean, it has been a little...sparse lately, and by sparse I mean nonexistent and sad," Emmis replied, not looking up from the page.

Skylar pinched the bridge of her nose, praying for patience.

"My sex life is fine thank you very much." Emmie murmured what sounded like *riiiighhhttttt* under her breath and Skylar chose to ignore her. "I meant the part about the gym."

"Oh. Yeah, we've got a giant one. You would *love* it."

"Tell me you're joking!"

Emmie sat up and tossed the magazine on top of the pile of them on the floor.

"Not at all. It's got all kinds of good stuff from the Mortal Plane. Hades modeled it after The Rock's personal gym, so it's got all the bells and whistles, plus tons of weapons and other fun stuff. I tried to talk him into kidnapping Dwayne himself and "hiring" him as our permanent personal trainer, but he wouldn't go for it. I was highly disappointed. Pouted for weeks!"

"Why the hell didn't you mention it before? Ugh, you know what, just forget it. Tell me where it is please before I strangle you." She needed a good workout in the worst way. Training was like her happy place. Some girls went to the spa, she went to the gym. Not only that, but she needed to work out some *frustration*. The more time she spent around Hades, the lustier her thoughts had become. It was getting harder and harder to keep her distance from him when they were together and not beg him to do all manner of dirty things with her and to her. Emmie smiled, a mischievous glint in her eye.

"Just ask the castle, it'll show you the way. Now, go." She momentarily shifted her appearance to look like Arnold and said, "Pick things up and put them down." Shifting back, she continued, "Or whatever it is you weirdos who go to the gym like to do. Actually, wait." She sat up and headed for the closet, going through drawers without a care in the world for Skylar's privacy. She didn't actually mind though. It reminded her of something Z would do and the thought made her smile. Emmie and Z would get along great. She had a sudden clear picture of the three of them together, laughing, causing absolute chaos here in the Underworld. She wanted that future so badly she could taste it. Emmie pulled her out of her thoughts with a pile of clothes shoved in her face.

"Here, put this on instead." Skylar arched an eye brow at her, but took the offerings.

"What's wrong with what I'm wearing?" Skylar asked, glancing down at her shorts and t-shirt combo.

"There's an old saying amongst the gods: Trust the Seer...Ok, it's not an *actual* saying, but I mean, it should be. Just trust me."

Skylar shrugged and changed into the leggings and tank top.

Hades was leaving the throne room after an exceptionally satisfying sentencing of a rapist and murderer. Eternity in the Realm of Suffering, the most horrific of all of the realms was almost too good for the mortal trash. He hadn't made the conscious decision to head towards Skylar's room, yet his feet were taking him in that direction. As a rule, he didn't go to her room, not since they'd come to the agreement that she would stay for a month. He didn't trust himself to be there with her and not do something entirely stupid, so he steered clear at all costs. It was hard enough for him to control himself when they were on the sofas in the game room, if there were an actual bed anywhere near them, he was a goner. They were growing closer, but he would be damned if he let his walls fall completely.

The more time he spent with her, the more he wanted her, and dear gods did he *want*. He was barely keeping it together and had been forced to take matters into his own hands every single night in order to stave off the worst of the desire. Hell, half the time he'd even wake close to coming from the dreams he was having of her. He was going to lose his mind soon enough. Of course he could find someone to slack the worst of it, but at the mere thought of being with anyone else his mind and body both recoiled violently. What that meant, he didn't know, but what he did know: he was going to combust if he didn't find a way to touch her soon.

"If you're looking for our girl, she's in the gym," a knowing voice rang out behind him.

He changed directions and made his way to the training room instead, flipping Emmie off over his shoulder when she murmured something about him being pussy whipped without the pussy. He was simply curious as to what Skylar might be doing in the gym, that was all. Had nothing to do with the fact that he felt that if he didn't see her this minute he might die. Nope. Not at all. On top of wanting her, he found himself wanting to just be *near* her. It calmed him, made him feel at ease, and the more he was around her, the more he wanted to be. It was like she was a drug and each hit he took was getting him more and more addicted. If he kept this up, he wouldn't be able to survive without her soon enough.

He still had his moments where a flash of his rage would surface, but those moments weren't coming nearly as often as they had been even a week ago. She would get angry with him when he refused to explain the times it did happen, but that was just something they were going to have to deal with. He literally couldn't tell her that he was pissed because the former version of her betrayed him in the worst possible way and almost got him killed in the process, so she would just have to be irritated about it.

Hades stopped in the doorway of the gym and groaned under his breath while he dragged a hand down his mouth and across the stubble on his jaw. She was in tight, form-fitting pants—he believed Emmie told him they were called leggings—and a tank top that was cut wide on her sides, showing off her trim stomach. Her hair was piled high on top of her head, but a few strands had escaped and hung against her temples.

She looked mouthwatering and he had to clench his jaw as desire rocked through him so forcefully he staggered back a step. He took several deep breaths to calm himself and get his body under control.

She had obviously been here for a little while and had taken advantage of the vast set up. The room was large, with stone floors and walls, though it was a lighter stone than most of the castle. There were several different areas with mats and practice dummies, a climbing wall and ropes dominated one side of the space, and there were modern treadmills, exercise bikes, weight machines, almost anything you could think of from a high-end mortal gym, along another. Weapons of every kind imaginable hung on the back wall or sat on the long table in front of it.

Skylar was examining them, tracing her fingers lightly along the blades and handles, appreciating the collection. She loved weapons almost as much as he did and the thought made him...happy. He'd never had someone to share in his interest before. He cleared his throat and began walking towards her. She whirled and her eyes widened as she sucked in a breath. Her gaze traveled down his bare chest, lingering on his abs, and her pulse quickened.

He always trained shirtless. It had nothing to do with wanting to impress her, make her crave his body the way he craved hers. *Become addicted to me, too, love. Please...*

She swallowed hard and after a few more long moments of staring she seemed to shake herself. She met his gaze and her lips curled into a small smile.

"Go ahead and get it over with." His own lips quirked. Though he was still irritated that she wouldn't just tell me what she was, he understood why she would keep the information to herself. Every species had vulnerabilities and despite the fact that they were slowly becoming...something, he was still a potential enemy to her. He sure as hell wasn't telling her about the godsblades or the toxin that could render even him powerless for a time. Though he supposed she technically already did know about them, she just didn't *remember* it. He felt his chest burn with hatred at the thought but forced himself to push it from his mind. Bottom line was that he understood her reluctance and had even begun to enjoy their give and take each time he asked.

"Are you going to tell me the answer?"

She batted her eyelashes at him and said sweetly, "Today just may be your lucky day, darlin'." Damn her and her southern drawl. He'd found that she'd finally seemed to relax enough here to let her true self begin to shine through—no more personas, no more covers, no more masks. And her true self had a tiny little sexy twang. *Fuck me.*

He made a show of sighing heavily.

"What are you, Skylar?"

"Tired of your bullshit. Ba-dom-tiss" She did a rimshot with imaginary drums and then bowed.

He laughed out loud, and a huge smile spread across her face like it always did when he laughed. He wasn't sure why she liked it so much when he did, but if it made her smile like that, he would laugh for the rest of his eternal life. Her entire face lit up when she smiled, like heaven itself. It wasn't just her beauty that drew him, it was everything. He liked watching her mind work, calculating every detail of a situation. It reminded him a bit of someone, but he wasn't sure who. He liked her smart mouth and her quick wit, her dirty jokes and movie references. No one made him laugh the way she did, even when she wasn't trying to. He hated to admit it, but he was, in fact, catching feelings...but he was pretty sure she was as well.

He nodded towards the weapons behind her. "See anything you like?"

"They're all beautiful. I admittedly don't know much about swords though."

"The famous assassin-spy-thief-mercenary Skylar Pembroke admits to not knowing how to use a weapon?" He put a hand to his chest in mock shock. "I think the world might be ending."

She rolled her eyes but smiled. "Not much call for swords in this century, Grandpa." She arched a brow at him and crossed her arms over her chest. "How old *are* you anyway?"

"Oh, I'm ancient, but old or not, I can spank you at sword play."

She gasped, a hand flying to her mouth. "Who told you I was into that sort of thing? Was it Jeff? He's such a gossip!" He snorted and jerked his chin towards the wall.

"Pick one, smartass, and I'll teach you the basics." She couldn't hide her excitement as she turned back towards the cache.

"Does it matter which one?"

"I'd go with something on that row." He titled his head towards the line of blades to her left. He walked forward until his chest was a hairsbreadth away from her back. Goosebumps erupted along her golden, sun-kissed skin. He noticed strange circular scars peeking out from the edge of her tank top, below her right shoulder. Bullet wounds? He frowned. They looked too small, though he admittedly didn't know all the ins and outs of mortal firearms. He preferred cold steel.

Deciding he would ask about them later, he leaned around her to grab a sword of his own, all but pinning her body between the table and his own. Her breath hitched and when his arm grazed her bare shoulder, they both shuddered. It felt as if he'd touched a livewire and he wanted more, more, more. He knew he was playing with fire allowing himself to be this close to her, but gods he would gladly burn at this point.

Her breaths became shallow and slightly ragged, and she leaned ever so slightly backwards, towards him. She tilted her head subtly to the left, as if begging him to kiss the spot on her neck that she'd exposed. At the mere thought, his cock jerked to attention. *At ease, man.* He stayed behind her for a moment longer, his mouth so close to her ear that he knew each breath was tickling her skin, making her shiver. He could smell her arousal and that was enough to nearly make him lose all control. Somehow, he forced himself to step backwards, breaking the bubble of tension that surrounded them.

She took a deep, shuddering breath and then went to his indicated row, running her fingers along several swords. Her fingers stilled on one with flames carved into the hilt and etched onto the blade itself and he stiffened. She gripped the hilt, turning with a smile, but it faded and her brows drew down in confusion when she noticed his tense stance, the way his lips were pressed into a hard line.

"Is this one not good or something?"

"It's an excellent choice. It's just..." *Yours,* he wanted to say. He cleared his throat. "I gifted that sword to my wife over three thousand years ago." Her eyes blazed for a moment in what looked like... jealousy? No, surely not...

"I'm sorry, I didn't know. I can pick a different one..."

Though a week ago the fact that she had picked Persephone's blade would have infuriated him, reminded him of who Skylar really was and what she had done, now he strangely only felt glad that Skylar had picked it. As if it proved that they were connected, a connection that he couldn't explain, a connection he'd never felt before, but a connection he craved on a level so deep within his soul that it staggered him. He halted her before she could set the sword away.

"No, it's fine. Really. I want you to use it. Persephone wasn't thrilled with the gift, never once even held it. She was more of a flowers and chocolates kind of girl, apparently." He gave her a half smile. Thinking back now, he wasn't even sure why he'd gifted Persephone with the blade to begin with, but something had compelled him to have it forged.

"That's a shame. It's gorgeous."

Skylar held the blade up to the light and ran a finger down the etched flames, the fire seeming to reflect and dance in her eyes.

"Yes, it is."

Hades honestly didn't know if he was talking about the sword, or the woman holding it.

～

Skylar was going to combust. Right here and now. Poof. Flames. Explosion. Death. Hades shirtless was just plain *criminal*. That saying "built like a god" was no joke. He was lean and chiseled and she wanted to run her fingers and tongue along every muscle, every indention, every inch of skin. His tattoo covered his upper left chest and was an elegant yet masculine design of a lightning bolt with swirling waves underneath and black flames dancing behind and above, with all of the elements encircled in swirling symbols like Emmie's. She decided that it must be the language of the gods and wondered what they might mean.

Somehow she managed to tear her gaze away from his glorious body and assume a battle stance: feet apart, one slightly forward, shifting onto the balls of her feet. She was excited to learn, and being taught by Hades himself only made the excitement burn in her veins like lava.

She raised the sword she'd selected, which had apparently belonged to his late wife. She was embarrassed by the surge of jealousy that had shot through her when he told her it was a gift from him to Persephone. How ridiculous to be jealous of someone who had been dead for three thousand years! And even more embarrassing? It wasn't just that she was jealous. Oh no. Skylar wanted to rip the goddess's hair out by the roots, something deep inside her mind growling that he was *hers*. Her claws had flared, her fangs sharpening, and fire burned through her chest.

Startled by the ferocity and plain ridiculousness of the thoughts, she pushed them away and focused on what Hades was saying. She listened intently as he gave her a crash course in swordsmanship. Her mind soaked it up like a sponge and she was thrumming with anticipation to put words into action.

He grinned and stepped towards her, thrusting his sword forward slowly enough that she could move accordingly. She shifted her weight and moved her blade to block his. A bit clumsily, but her mind was already calculating and correcting, telling her body how to move next time.

"Good. Shift your grip a little bit. There you go. Now, try again." He moved again and again, letting her block his advances, giving her pointers, telling her how to attack as well, not just defend. She caught on quickly, as she always did when learning a new fighting skill or weapon, and soon they were moving at a faster pace and she was giving as good as she was getting. He was smiling as their swords clashed, as she blocked and parried and thrust. She caught him across the shoulder and she worried for a half a heartbeat if he would be pissed, but his smile grew wider.

"Good!" he said, seemingly genuinely proud. She shook her head in wonder as she watched the skin knit back together almost immediately. Supernatural species healed fast but not *instantly*. She didn't think she would ever get over how crazy cool that was. She twirled the sword, loving the feel of it in her hands, as if it had been made for her.

"I know, right?" she said, throwing him a wink. "Ok, I think I've got it now. Come on, let's play for real. Stop holding back." He raised an eyebrow but nodded. A wicked grin spread across his face.

"You're going to regret that request, love."

Her heart fluttered a bit, as it always did when he called her that. She knew it was just a stupid term of endearment that people used all the time, the way she used *darling* or *honey*, and that it didn't actually *mean* anything, but still, she couldn't deny that she liked the sound of it. She grinned back as he attacked at a faster speed, but she knew he was still holding back. She could only imagine how skilled and powerful he would be when he went full out. Even so, it was mind-boggling. To think she could ever hold her own against him, any god for that matter, was just plain stupid.

She couldn't stop admiring him as they played. His moves were fluid and graceful, though she knew they would be absolutely lethal in a real fight. He was all male and power, yet completely beautiful at the same time. She managed to block him and spin, slashing out with her own blade.

"What happened to her?" Skylar asked, a bit out of breath. He blocked her easily and eyed her with confusion. "Persephone," she clarified. "What happened to her?"

His eyes blazed and she mentally kicked herself. She didn't want them to argue or him to dip into one of his sulking, irritated moods. She shouldn't have brought it up...

"She betrayed me," he said, surprising her. "Tried to kill me—or at least, have me killed." *Clash. Clang.* They came together in a forceful meeting of metal and he stared deeply into her eyes, as if searching for something. "She stabbed me in the back, literally, and delivered me to a hated enemy. I nearly died and he nearly took my kingdom," he said through gritted teeth. Her eyes went wide.

"But...but why would she do that?" Skylar demanded, anger and rage filling her so unexpectedly that she staggered backwards. His eyes narrowed a fraction. They stood apart for a moment both breathing hard, and then he attacked again. She blocked and they continued in a dance of blocks and clashing blades.

"I told you she was trapped here. She resented me for it, began to hate me, though I had no control over it."

"What a bitch," Skylar spit before she could stop herself. How dare she? She was his wife, she was supposed to love him, protect him. And she betrayed him? Stabbed him in the back?

Rage so violent she could barely understand it exploded inside her. Her fangs flashed out, her claws flared, and fire scorched her chest. She wanted to punish Persephone, wanted to bring her back from the dead just to kill her again. *No one hurts him. No one.*

She growled, a low rumbling sound deep in her chest and Hades cocked his head, confusion plain on his face.

"This...bothers you?" he asked, somewhere between suspicious and intrigued.

"And if it does?" she countered, not wanting to admit to the insane feelings rumbling through her chest, setting her blood on fire in a need to punish. She went for him again. He blocked easily and then she spun, catching him across the left shoulder. He twisted and brought his blade up as she lunged towards him again. Their eyes met and she suddenly didn't care if what shew as feeling was insane or embarrassing.

She was tired of pretending that she wasn't feeling things for him. She was tired of pretending that he wasn't a part of her for whatever reason. Did it bother her that some bitch had nearly gotten him killed three thousand years ago? Fuck yes it did!

He spun again and put distance between them, studying her with a confused and...hopeful expression. She wiped the sweat from her brow with her forearm and shrugged.

"And if it does?" she asked again, a stubborn set to her jaw, but vulnerability leaked through her voice. *Come on. Tell me what you think. Tell me you feel something for me too.*

His lips curled upward and that small smile held the glimpse of the answer. Her heart thudded against her chest. They were getting closer to something, to where they were supposed to be. She just knew it, could feel it in her bones. She smiled back at him, not needing an actual answer for now.

"Alright, bring it on old man," she said, beckoning him forward with one hand to break the moment. He ran his tongue along his teeth before his smoke began to swirl around them. She was surprised to find that it could become solid when he wanted it to be —like when he used a tendril to tug on her hair as a distraction. When she turned to swat it away, he lunged towards her. She barely got her sword up in time.

"Not fair," she said with a laugh.

"What's the old phrase? All's fair in love and war?" The smoke churned around them and she eyed another tendril as it rose up towards her. She smacked it away and lunged for him this time, but he sidestepped, letting her momentum take her forward. He smacked her lightly on the ass with the flat of his blade and she whirled, eyes wide, and he laughed out loud. Something had shifted in him, some of the ever-present tension gone.

She narrowed her eyes, but smiled. The next time she thrust her sword forward, he reached out and grabbed her wrist, drawing her closer to him. She kicked out as his thigh and he went down on one knee, bringing her down with him. He threw her over his shoulder, spinning to land on top of her, pinning her body with his. She thrust her hips upward, knocking him off balance enough to roll on top of him, pinning *him* down. They'd both dropped their swords in the shuffle, but they'd each been hiding a small dagger. Skylar held hers against his throat, ready to easily slit him from ear to ear, and his was resting just under her ribs, poised to puncture a lung.

They were both sweaty and panting and grinning like lunatics. This had been *fun*. As if a switch had been flipped, the air around them changed, the pull between them instantly taut and burning. She realized then that she was straddling his hips and couldn't stop herself from settling in deeper on top of him. He inhaled sharply and she had to bite the inside of her cheek to keep from moaning. He was hard as stone and *oh boy* was she aware of it. He arched his hips up against her and she was suddenly struggling to catch her breath. The jolt of pleasure that shot through her at that tiny bit of contact was unbelievable. Her fangs shot longer, sharper.

"Gods..." he said in a choked whisper. His eyes darkened but not wholly black in anger this time. Oh no, there was nothing but desperate desire burning there now, and she knew she had the same look in her own eyes. He gripped the back of her neck with one strong hand and slowly pulled her downwards, towards those lips that she couldn't stop dreaming about. She dropped her blade and heard his own thud to the floor as well. The hand that had been holding the knife now gripped her hip, whether to stop her from moving against him or to encourage it, she wasn't sure. She tunneled her fingers through his hair as she leaned down, down, down...

A throat cleared and they both froze, their mouths only a few agonizing inches apart. Hades cursed under his breath and she cut her eyes to the door, irritated by the intruder and ready to do them bodily harm. She should probably be thankful—did she really need to be making out with Hades on the gym floor right now?—but all she could find was an intense annoyance. She absolutely *wanted* to be making out with Hades on the gym floor right now.

"I really hate to interrupt because *damn* you could cut this sexual tension with a knife, but I kind of need to talk to my brother."

Hades hesitated for a moment before dropping his hand from the back of her neck and releasing her hip. The losses made her want to cry out in frustration. Skylar reluctantly got up, offering her hand to him. He looked surprised, but took it and stood. She focused back on the male in the doorway and forced her thoughts away from how good Hades' body had felt under hers and how close they had been to finally *finally* kissing. She shivered with need as she glanced down to the overwhelming evidence that Hades had been just as invested in this little endeavor as she'd been.

She cut her eyes back upwards and found his trained on her. She got the distinct impression that he was very close to not giving a shit if they had an audience or not and she was very close to seconding that opinion. Oh yeah, that sexual tension could definitely be sliced and diced it was so thick. That need to murder this stranger reared up once more. This stranger that had said...

She snapped her eyes away from Hades to the towering man now standing before her. *A word with my brother.* Meaning that this was... *Holy shit, was this Zeus??* He was tall with light bronze skin and flowing golden blonde hair that fell in waves to his shoulders. He had a golden blonde mustache and beard to match, though they were trimmed short. He was heavily muscled like Hades, but he was bulkier, and he wore a tight white t-shirt and black leather pants. *What is with this family and leather pants?* He pretty much looked like Thor from *The Avengers*, which she supposed fit just fine. He was beyond gorgeous but he didn't hold a candle to Hades in her opinion.

"Are you...?"

He grinned and bowed. "Zeus, here to service you."

She busted out laughing as Hades glared daggers at his brother.

"Zeus..." he growled, warning in his tone. Zeus slapped his forehead.

"Oh, right. I meant to say: Zeus, *at your service*. My bad." He threw Skylar a wink and she laughed even harder at the way Hades was grinding his teeth.

Deciding to have a little fun at Hades' expense, she said, "You look just like Thor, all you need is your hammer." She tapped her chin thoughtfully. "Wait...I bet it's in your pants, isn't it?"

Zeus' eyes went wide and then he roared with laughter, doubling over. Hades looked between them incredulously but a small, uncertain smile began to spread across his face when she winked at him. Zeus straightened, wiping tears out of his eyes.

"Oh man, I like this one."

She did a little bow.

"Skylar," she said, holding out her hand. "Nice to meet you... Zeus. Wow, I can't believe I actually just said that." Zeus shook her hand and gave Hades a quick look, raising his eye brows slightly in question. Hades didn't respond in any way, but Zeus nodded to himself as if he'd gotten a response. *Odd...*

"Well, you said you need to talk, so I'll leave you to it. You boys behave." As she walked away, she reached out and ran a hand down Hades' bare chest, not sure why or when she'd made the decision to do it.

He caught her hand before she severed contact and said in a low, husky voice, "We'll finish this later, love."

She inhaled sharply and her muscles clenched with want, her nipples pearling at the mere thought of what they might finish later. She gave him a small nod in response and his eyes seemed to burn even more.

She needed a cold shower ASAP, so with that, she left the gods to their chitchat.

Zeus shook his head and started to speak but Hades held up a hand to silence him. Telepathically, he said to his brother:

-Hold that thought. Sky is attempting to eavesdrop.-

His lips curled into a smile at the thought and then he snapped his fingers, making the room completely soundproof. He chuckled when he heard her curse at the sudden silence. She couldn't hear *them*, but they could hear her just fine.

"Holy shit. That's her? Like *her* her?"

"That's her," Hades confirmed, letting out a long breath. He replayed everything that had just happened over again in his mind, from Skylar's outrage at Persephone's misdeeds, to the feel of her body on top of his, the want in her eyes, how close they'd come...

"So, Persephone's really back?"

Hades forced his thoughts away from all the things he'd been ready to do to Skylar on the floor and instead let images and information about Skylar flow between himself and Zeus through their telepathic link. Zeus walked to the table and grabbed some throwing knives as he took everything in. He pursed his lips.

"She doesn't seem like herself—or her old self I guess—at *all*.

They're basically opposites in every way imaginable." He twirled a blade effortlessly around his finger. "Are we even sure–" Hades held up a hand to stop him.

"I know, I know. I've asked the same thing about a thousand times, but Emmie insists that it's her."

"Well, we know better than to question Emmie I suppose."

Zeus tossed his first knife, hitting a quarter of an inch to the left of the bullseye. He was quiet for a long time as he tossed several more. Hades could feel his brother's power beginning to roil within him. A faint rumble of thunder could be heard outside and Zeus's sky blue eyes were darkening to a deep, stormy gray. Hades didn't need their telepathic link to know what was going through Zeus's head, what he was remembering.

"I know," Hades said quietly. Zeus couldn't seem to help sending memories of that day at him: Seeing Hades on the floor, bloody and broken and powerless, seeing what remained of Persephone, realizing how close they'd come to losing Hades forever. Thunder boomed now, loud enough to shake the castle and lightning flashed outside, identical forks streaking across Zeus' now wholly black eyes.

"How can you stand it?" he asked, seemingly torn between incredulity and honest curiosity. "I know she's different now, that Skylar didn't *technically* do these things, but I can't stop myself from wanting to throw her in the dungeons and exact a little revenge. A lot of revenge. A few centuries worth at the very least."

"If it makes you feel any better she did spend over a week in the dungeons here." Hades sighed and ran a hand through his hair. "I was the same as you at first. I could barely stand to look at her. Every time I did all I could see was the past and rage burned through every inch of me. But..."

"But?"

"But now when I look at her, I only see Skylar," Hades admitted out loud for the first time. "I don't see the past wrongs, not really. Instead, I'm starting to see...Well fuck, I'm starting to see the future I want. A future with her." Zeus' eyes went wide and returned to their brilliant blue once more.

"Are you falling for her—again?"

"No...maybe...I don't know," Hades said, exasperated. "It's different this time, *she's* different. Not just in the obvious ways, there's something between us this time that was never there before. I can't explain it."

"Well...I'd say you're good and fucked, brother," Zeus said, clapping him hard on the back.

"Understatement of the millennium," Hades murmured as they phased back to his chambers. Zeus flung himself down on the leather sofa while Hades made drinks.

"So, what is she? I couldn't get a clear read, which is rare. Hell, it's rarer than rare. It *never* happens." Zeus ran a hand across his jaw. "I thought maybe..." He shook his head as he discarded whatever idea he had. "Ah, nevermind."

"I have no idea and trust me, I've asked. She's playing that particular card close to the vest."

"Interesting. Well, you know how I love puzzles. I'll see what I can find out. I'm assuming Emmie knows but won't spill the beans?"

"Of course." Zeus snorted and Hades made his way towards the couch with their glasses. "Hey, so quick question, *bro*: why the fuck didn't you tell me that Gavril had escaped? And where have you been for the last few days? I've tried to reach you and you've been silent." He handed Zeus his glass and then punched him in the shoulder hard enough to dislocate the joint. He'd heal in a second, so no biggy, and he deserved it. Zeus hissed in a breath and clenched his jaw.

"That's why I'm here. We just discovered that Gavril was gone this morning and before that...Well, there was a little situation. Nothing to worry about...I don't think." Hades began to inquire about that, but Zeus waved him off. "I'll keep you posted once I know more. Anyway, they somehow managed to put someone else in the dungeon in Gavril's place, a shifting spell cast on them to look like Gavril. Fake Gavril begged, tried to convince me that he wasn't who I thought he was over and over again, but I didn't listen. I'd heard that bastard say just about everything possible over the last three thousand years, so why would I listen now, right? I...The things I did to him..."

Zeus shuddered and Hades felt a pang in his chest for his brother. He was powerful beyond measure and his wrath was literally the stuff of legend, but he was also righteous and just and kind. It's the reason their father had made him king of the all the gods. The fact that he had tortured an innocent would forever leave a dark spot on his soul.

"The spell wore off this morning. He couldn't tell us who had placed it on him or why, but you and I both know our worthless excuse for a brother was behind it. I don't know how he managed it, but I'm going to get to the bottom of it." Lightning flashed in his eyes once more, rage over another possible betrayer in his midst no doubt crossing his mind. "I came as soon as I could, I swear it. I wanted to talk to you about it in person."

Hades took a long sip of his poppy-laced whisky and sighed.

"It's ok. I don't know what's going on, but Maynard must be planning something. Maybe he found out about the prophecy some-how? Knew it was finally coming to pass?"

"That's what I'm wondering too. But how would he know? Unless..."

"Unless I have a traitor in my kingdom," Hades finished for him. Zeus gave him a sympathetic shrug. "I've thought of it, trust me. I'd like to say that no one here would dare do such a thing, but I can't, not with complete certainty. Hell, they got to my own wife last time, why would we think they couldn't sway some guards or servants?"

Zeus swirled his drink, looking thoughtful.

"Well, if Maynard knows, you need this prophecy fulfilled sooner rather than later. How are things going on the whole getting Skylar to agree to marriage front?"

Hades downed the remaining contents of his glass and rose to get another. How were things going? A week ago, he would have said that her agreeing would have been impossible, but now? Something had most definitely shifted between them and he thought that maybe, just maybe she was starting to feel something for him. He could *feel* her contentment sometimes, a feeling of belonging pulsing through her, feeling like a soft whisper against his skin. He hadn't wanted to explore the connection between them because it was so foreign, so terrifying to him, but he couldn't deny that they *were* connected somehow. He didn't know why he was feeling this with her now when he never had before with Persephone, even after they had been married and bonded, but he had to admit to himself that he liked it. He felt better anytime she was near him, better than he had since the day she'd died almost three thousand years ago. Perhaps the connection was stronger now simply because they'd been forced apart so violently. Absence makes the heart grow fonder and all that?

All of that combined with what had shifted between them today in the gym? He nearly groaned remembering how she'd straddled him and ground her hips against him, how he could feel her heat against him through the thin material of her leggings, how she'd looked so gods damned sexy that he didn't understand how it was possible. He shook himself, trying to focus back on his brother. He merely shrugged in response and Zeus joined him at the bar.

Zeus studied him for a long moment before saying, "So, you probably don't want to hear it, but you're falling for her already. Don't argue, I know you better than you know yourself. I can tell in the memories you showed me, in the way you smiled when you knew she was trying to listen into our conversation. And you calling her "love"—don't even *try* to act like that's just a meaningless pet name." He let out a long exhale, worry etched in his handsome face now.

"I want her to be different this time more than anyone. You don't know how hard it was for me to see you chained, bleeding and poisoned, betrayed by the one person who was supposed to love you more than anything else in existence...I want you to be happy, I do, and I really think Skylar is great from the very little I've seen of her, just...just be careful, ok? From what you've shown me, she's exceptionally skilled in the areas of deception and killing. And I *can't* lose you. I won't."

Hades was filled with such love for his brother in that moment that he felt the stinging of tears in his eyes. He gave Zeus a big, strong, manly hug, complete with beating on each other's backs to prove the degree of manliness.

"I will. I'm not letting my guard down, no matter what. Don't worry." Zeus nodded and changing subjects, Hades said, "So, did you hear about Si's latest sexcapades?"

Zeus groaned and then laughed.

"Oh I more than heard about it. I had to send the twins and a few others to help his dumb ass out. What kind of moron beds the wives —all *seven* of them might I add...at *once!*—of a Satyr?? Hyklon's entire army was ready to take Poseidon out until Ares showed a little muscle...and brought a whole slew of nymphs from the Mortal Plane with them as, um...peace offerings."

Hades chuckled. He loved both of his brothers, but Si was reckless and always getting himself into trouble, said trouble usually starting with him sticking his cock somewhere it didn't belong. Si had a good heart but he'd had it broken once and had sworn it would never happen again. So, he was now determined to have nothing but meaningless fun with as many people as he could— male, female, mortal, immortal, demon, vampire, you name it. Made no difference to him—and cause as much trouble as possible along the way.

Hades smiled inwardly at the thought of Skylar giving Si shit for his exploits...or hell, maybe even acting as his wingman come to think of it. He just never knew with his little firecracker, and he had to admit that he loved that about her. She kept him guessing, always surprising him. With his thoughts back in Sky territory, he decided he needed to have another conversation with his little soon-to-be queen...over dinner.

TWENTY-ONE

After giving up on trying to listen in on the conversation through the door, Skylar headed towards her room, running into Emmie along the way.

"Were you coming to ask me what you should wear to dinner? I already know what you're going to end up in—and you look hawt, trust me—but we're still going to have a full-on dressing-room-movie-montage anyway because, fun."

Skylar pursed her lips.

"Uhh, are we not having dinner in the entertainment room? Pizza and a *New Girl* marathon? I thought that was the plan?"

"Oh, right, he hasn't invited you yet—hold that thought, here comes the boom." Skylar was more confused than ever but a split second later a clap of thunder echoed around them, shaking the walls. Lighting flashed wildly for a few moments before slowly beginning to calm. Emmie continued on as if this were perfectly normal on a sunny afternoon without a storm cloud or rain drop in sight. "Anyway," she said, rolling her eyes as if annoyed by the storm, "Our mighty King of the Underworld is going to ask you to dinner and you're going to say yes." She clapped her hands and jumped up and down.

Skylar couldn't help the stupid grin that spread across her face. Hades wanted to have dinner with her? Like a date? Today in the training room had finally changed something between them. They'd been teetering, but she knew it in her bones: they'd finally fallen off the edge into something new, something more than they were. He was funny and playful and treated her like an equal despite the fact that he was a literal god.

She was seriously considering agreeing to his marriage proposal...which was insane, but the instant she formed the thought, it felt so right, so meant to be. As if her decision had been made ages ago and she only just now remembered. She knew he considered the marriage some kind of business deal, but after today...well maybe he felt differently about it. She'd agreed to a month and that was already half way gone, but she found that she didn't want it to be.

She wanted to *stay*. She wanted...damnit, she wanted him. All of him. She couldn't deny it any longer.

And just like that, her decision was made. It had always been that way with her. She would debate and fight and try to talk herself in or out of things, but once she made her decision, that was it. The deal was done and there was no going back. She knew there had to be a way around the whole being stuck here forever thing. There *had* to be. He was the God of the freaking Underworld. His brother was king of all the gods. They had to have enough mojo to figure it out.

She felt completely at ease with her choice but wasn't ready to tell him quite yet. She still had time left in her original bargain, so she would use it to get closer and explore this new shift between them. But, in her mind, it was set: she was going to marry Hades. Maybe she could secretly celebrate with him after dinner by finishing what they'd started in the gym. Practically shivering in anticipation, she hopped in the shower.

She tried and failed to keep thoughts of Hades out of her mind: the way his chest glistened with sweat; the way drops of it made their way slowly down, hugging the curves of his abs and those ridiculous indentions beside his hips before dipping into the waistband of his pants; the way his eyes had darkened with wanting; the way that though they were both pulled taught as a wire, he had been gentle when he'd pulled her down towards him.

Soon her hands were roving over her own body, wishing desperately that that they were his instead, that his fingers were the ones rubbing her sensitive clit and pumping in and out of her. As she came in a rush, she wondered if she could let go enough to do this with him. She never had before, had always been too in her head to let go enough, but she thought with Hades she just might be able to. Everything else with him eased her, made her feel right, so why not this too?

She tried to push the thoughts from her mind least she spend all night in the shower, and proceeded to play dress-up with Emmie for the next few hours. Emmie insisted that Skylar try on the most insane evening gowns though she assumed dinner was a bit less formal than that. The gowns were absolutely stunning though and made of the most luxurious materials and jewels she'd ever seen.

"Did you pick all these out for me?" Skylar called as she changed into yet another gown, this one a cerulean blue with glittering diamonds cascading down the bodice.

"Nope. Believe it or not, Hades picked out everything himself. He's strangely good when it comes to fashion—and decorating. But that second part is because he secretly watches HGTV. Well, he *thinks* it's a secret, everyone knows though." Skylar was oddly happy that Hades had picked these clothes for her, that he had taken the time, envisioned her wearing them, choosing things he would like to see on her. Why he'd thought she'd need a hundred evening gowns was beyond her, but whatever.

"What is taking you so long? I wanna see!"

Skylar laughed as she emerged. "You've already seen it, haven't you?"

Emmie whistled and then cat-called.

"Seeing it in my head and seeing it when it happens for real are very different. Now, twirl!"

They finally had enough trying on clothes for the evening and Skylar began to actually get dressed. They'd chosen a one-shouldered black number that fit her like a glove but somehow never felt constricting. The material was so soft and smooth it felt like cool water cascading over her skin when she moved. Black diamonds were woven up the sides and over the one strap, continuing down her back—in the shapes of flames of course.

Emmie plopped down on the sofa and started twirling her hands in the air above her. Skylar thought she caught sight of flashes of light dancing in between her fingers, but didn't pay it much attention as she strapped on her CFM heels.

"So, are you ever going to ask me to fix your cell so you can phone home, ET?" Emmie asked as if she were asking how the weather was. Skylar stopped dead with one foot midair.

"Come again?" she said slowly, trying to tell herself that she hadn't heard the oracle correctly and that if she *had*, she would not do bodily harm to her friend.

"I've been wondering when you were going to ask me since Hades won't do it and you seem put out about that, but I just keep waiting and waiting and waiting..."

"Since when can you fix my phone?!" Skylar yelled. Emmie sat up and looked genuinely confused.

"Umm...since always?" Skylar threw a heel at Emmie's head, knowing the Seer would duck in plenty of time. "Did I forget to mention that I have a touch of godly powers that include more than just seeing the future?" She tapped her chin and then shrugged. "Oopsie!"

"I cannot believe you, Em! Fix it now, you asshole!"

"Touchy, touchy. Geesh, Poprocks. You need to chillax." When Skylar sent her a murderous glare and snapped her fangs, Emmie held up her hands in surrender and rose from the couch. "Ok, ok, sorry. Stand back and be amazed!"

Skylar wasn't completely sure what to expect. She'd seen warlocks and enchantresses do magic before, but it was way different than the godly power she'd seen Hades use. What would Emmie's power look like? Suddenly Emmie's appearance changed, making Skylar gasp. She'd seen Emmie change her looks plenty of times, but she'd never seen her change like *this* before.

Emmie's hair turned stark white and began to flow around her head as if wind were blowing through the strands. Her eyes became wholly silver, but reflective, like mirrors, and her tattoos began to glow an unearthly green color. She began making wide, sweeping gestures with her hands, like some sorcerer in an old movie, and began chanting in an odd language. The lights flickered ominously and green mist began to rise around her. Skylar backed up a few steps, unsure what the hell was happening and not quite sure she liked whatever magic Emmie was using.

"Emmie, maybe this wasn't a good idea..." Skylar glanced around warily, her hackles raising at the unknown, strange magic. Silver lightning flashed inside the green mist.

Emmie said in a scratchy, shrill voice that seemed to echo subtly, "What insignificant being dares beseech my power?" Skylar backed further away, claws flaring.

"Emmie, stop this. Emmie are...are you still in there?" she asked. The green mist had now surrounded them completely, obscuring the rest of the room, swirling in a violent cyclone. "Emmie!?"

Suddenly everything stopped. The mist disappeared as if it'd never existed and Emmie's appearance shifted back to normal. The oracle doubled over in laughter as Skylar stared in utter confusion. Emmie finally straightened, wiping tears out of her eyes.

"Ah gods, I'm sorry, but that was just too funny not to do again. Er, well for the first time. But I've seen it in my head a few hundred times and it's never *not* hilarious! You should have seen your face!" She pointed and laughed again, so hard she was barely making any sound.

"I'm going to kill you!" Skylar shrieked, smacking Emmie in the shoulder. "What is wrong with you!? I thought you'd gone full exorcist or something! I hate you. Seriously, I hate you. Why am I friends with you?"

Emmie finally composed herself and sighed, clutching her stomach and wiping tears away.

"I'm sorry, really. And you're friends with me because you love me." Skylar pursed her lips, knowing it was true. Despite the short time they'd known each other, Emmie already had a special place in her heart, right next to Z and Lucas. Emmie smiled, blew her a kiss, and then simply snapped her fingers. "Ok, there you go. You have full bars, my friend."

"Seriously? That was it?" Emmie smiled and nodded. "There is something deeply wrong with you," Skylar said as she shook her head with a smile. "Like, *deeply* wrong."

"You aren't incorrect in that assertion. Hurry up and make your call." Emmie shooed her away as she sat back down on the couch and picked up another issue of *Cosmo* from the coffee table. "Ohh a quiz to determine if I'm 'Good Girl Hot' or 'Bad Girl Hot'! Mortals are so fun."

Skylar wandered around the room, trying to figure out what exactly she was going to say. She couldn't tell Lucas the truth, not yet anyway, but she had to talk to him. She owed it to him to set his mind at ease, Z too. She opened her Favorites screen on her phone and smiled a sad smile. Number one on the list was *Dad*. The picture beside his name was one of him smiling his huge, eye-wrinkling smile, wearing Mickey Mouse ears when they went to Disney World a few years back.

Tears stung her eyes at the memory. They had randomly talked one night at dinner about how she'd never been as a kid because of obvious reasons, and then a few days later he handed her park tickets and told her to pack her bags.

She fought the urge to select his name, just to hear his voice on the outgoing message. Instead she took a deep breath and pressed her Number Two: *Lucas.*

He answered before the first ring even finished.

"Skylar!? What the hell? Are you ok? Where are you?"

Her chest clenched. He sounded so worried. Lucas *never* worried about anything. She knew that he was still in love with her, or at least thought he was, and though she couldn't love him in the same way, she *did* love him like family, the same way she loved her dad and Zahara, and she hated that she had caused him pain.

"Luke, take a breather so I can actually answer you. I'm ok. I'm sorry I haven't been in contact—my phone took a swim and I just got it working again."

"Where the hell are you? You turned off your tracker and all we had to go on was that note–"

"Note?"

"Psst!" Emmie whisper yelled. Skylar turned to face her as Lucas continued.

"Yeah, the note you left telling us you were going off grid for a bit..." Skylar's brows drew down but Emmie pointed to herself and then mimed writing a note in the air. *Oooh.* Of course Emmie had thought to leave a note in the room for Lucas to find so he wouldn't worry. Or well, so he wouldn't worry quite as much maybe. She mouthed *OK* to the Seer and was given a big thumbs up in return.

"Skylar? Did you not leave that note? What the hell is going on??" Luke sounded even more concerned now, his voice dropping an octave and sounding more...wofly, a low growl humming just under the words.

"No, of course I left it for you, I was just worried that you hadn't gotten it, thought maybe the cleaning people tossed it or something by mistake."

"I need you to start giving me some real answers here. Right the fuck now, Pembroke." Damn. He'd last named her. Lucas always addressed all the other agents at Willow Corp by last name only, except for her and Z. He only last named her when he was *really* pissed off.

"Look, I'm really sorry Luke, but I can't tell you where I am. I...I just need to be alone right now, and that includes you guys being able to track my every move, so that's why I axed my tracker for now. I'm so sorry you were worried, but I promise you I'm ok. I'm somewhere safe."

He was silent for a long moment, clearly weighing the truth in her words.

"What should I have for dinner?"

She smiled. Their code. Depending on her answer it signaled if she were in trouble but couldn't say, or if she was all good.

"Wings from Kingly's. Seriously, I'm fine, Luke."

He blew out a long breath. "Damnit, Skylar, you've been gone for a *month*! When you said you'd be MIA for a while, I thought a couple of weeks, tops, but come on. We thought you..." He sucked in a harsh breath through his nose and her heart cracked a bit. "You had us worried sick—and I don't fucking do worry! All of your stuff was still in your hotel, you didn't check out, left a completely unhelpful note. It was like you just disappeared off the face of the planet." *Nah, just that plane of existence.* "How could you do this to us? To me?" he added softly.

"I know, I'm so *so* sorry, Luke. I just...I'm not dealing with dad's death very well. I can't explain it, I just had to get away, right that second. You know how I just get restless sometimes and right now, with dad...Well, yeah. And it's not like I'm sentimental about my junk. I figured I'd just buy new stuff when I got to where I was going, and honestly just didn't even really think about checking out of the hotel." She shrugged. Those were absolutely Skylar things to do, so he should buy it.

"I get it, I do. But you know you don't have to go through this alone. I know I told you to take time off, but let us help you. You...you aren't the only one hurting right now," he finished.

Her eyes filled up with tears. She knew that Lucas had lost a father too when Dalton died, and now for him to have thought she was missing or worse...She hated herself a little. Even though she couldn't help the circumstances, it was still her fault.

"God, I'm sorry Luke. I didn't mean for you to be worried and I know that you're hurting too. I wasn't thinking clearly. Wasn't thinking at all really. I'm just a little lost with all of this." Not a lie. She was still wholly lost when she thought about her father being gone, which is why she continued to ignore it and shove those feelings way down deep in the absolutely healthy way she always did. "But I shouldn't have let you worry like that. That was a real shit move on my part, I know."

He exhaled roughly but she could just picture him relaxing a tiny bit, leaning back against the edge of the desk and running his hand over his close-cropped hair, his hazel eyes softening. She knew he was already forgiving her.

"Where are you? I'll come get you."

"I need more time. I'm still lost and I'm not ready to be found yet. I promise to check in regularly now that my phone is working though. I just need you to trust me." He sighed heavily.

"Always have, always will. If you need more time, you've got it, but so help me if you go radio silence on me again..."

"I double pinky swear I won't. You know how serious double pinky swears are."

He huffed out a laugh.

"Z will want to kick your ass now once I tell her you're fine. No promises I can hold her back." Skylar smiled despite the tears beginning to spill down her cheeks and scrubbed her arm across her nose.

"Tell her I'd like to see her try. We can do it in a pool filled with Jello, sell tickets, and become millionaires." Lucas laughed and she felt the pain in her heart lessen just a bit. "Look, I gotta go, but just try not to worry about me, ok? Please."

"If you say you're ok, I believe you. Just...be careful alright? And don't drop your damn phone in the pool or the ocean or whatever the hell you did again."

"I'll buy one of those water-proof cases, Scout's honor. Tell Z I'm ok and I'll call her later. Love you, Luke."

"You need a damn everything-proof case," he muttered and she could practically see him rolling his eyes but an indulgent smile tugging his lips upward. Luke really was criminally handsome and just the best man she knew. Skylar hoped he found someone else to love, someone who could love him back the way he deserved soon. "I'll tell Z. Love you too, Skylar."

Skylar hung up the phone and held it to her chest for a minute. She closed her eyes and let out a long breath. She felt bad for lying to Luke, but she couldn't explain everything to him and make him understand, not when she still didn't understand everything herself. She would tell him everything as soon as she could. He knew she was safe, and that was good enough for now.

Emmie sauntered up and tsked. "You smudged your make up. Here, let me." She blew lightly on Skylar's face. Skylar felt her skin warm for the briefest of seconds and though she couldn't see herself, she knew that her makeup was now back in pristine order. Now *that* was handy! "I'm heading out. Enjoy your dinner. There's a note on your bed bee-tee-dubs. And just...don't be too mad, ok?"

Before Skylar could ask her what that meant, she was out the door, humming what sounded like the theme song from *The Office*. Skylar whirled in search of the note that had mysteriously ended up on her bed.

She picked it up and read:

Follow me to dinner.

That was it other than a drawing of a black cat on the bottom of the page. She turned it over to see if there was anything more on the back, but it was blank. Confused, she turned it back over again and gasped: the drawing of the cat was gone and a beautiful black cat with yellow eyes sat on the bed. It meowed at her and she laughed out loud.

The cat's gaze was oddly intelligent and seemed to warn her to back off as she reached out to scoop him up. However, as she nuzzled into his fur and told him what a pretty kitty he was, he began to purr so loudly she thought it could be heard for miles. She loved animals and the only part about her job that she didn't like was that it didn't afford her the luxury of being able to have pets. She was gone too often to really give them the attention they deserved. She kissed the cat's nose and scratched behind his ears and he nuzzled her neck in return. She was pretty sure she had officially made another friend.

He stiffened for a moment and cocked his head to the side as if listening to something. She would have sworn he rolled his eyes before hopping out of her arms and stalking to the door. He paused and looked over his shoulder at her and titled his head. *Oh, right, follow me to dinner.* She studied the cat as they walked. He looked familiar...though she supposed all black cats looked the same when it came down to it.

She couldn't help the smile that was now plastered on her face. She could get on board with cute note leaving, magic cat having Hades. The cat, whom she decided would be named Dean Winchester because he was handsome and a little broody, led her down hallway after hallway, eventually stopping at a door that she'd never be able to find again on her own. Dean wove between her legs and meowed as he rubbed his face against her bare calf. She laughed as she bent down to give him another scratch.

"I promise lots of catnip and pets if you come back to my room later, Dean." He nodded his head once at her, as if understanding exactly what she'd promised. She straightened and opened the door, stumbling through the doorway, laughing and watching Dean scurry down the hall.

"That was the greatest thing ever. You've got to–"

Skylar stopped short, her smile fading as she took in the scene before her. Hades was sitting at the head of a large table carved out of a dark grey stone with veins of sparkling black running through it. He looked heartbreakingly handsome with his hair tousled, his stubble at just the right length, and his shirt unbuttoned enough that she could see the edges of his tattoo and the muscles of his chest, all giving off a sexy bad-boy vibe.

But that wasn't what stopped her in her tracks. Oh no, that would be the line of half-naked female...somethings standing to the side of the table. He was looking them all over, his eyes slowly raking up and down each of them in turn. Skylar clenched her fists and willed herself not to launch across the room, end every one of them, and then scratch Hades' eyes out of his skull. The surge of jealousy and possessiveness that shot through her was staggering. She'd made the decision to stay with him. He was *hers*, damnit!

His gaze shifted past the line of girls to where Skylar stood in the doorway and though his eyes widened slightly, blazed with something sinful and dangerous, he wiped away any emotion quickly and gave her a smug, downright cruel smile. *What the hell?* This wasn't the Hades she had been with earlier this afternoon. Something had changed, but she had no idea what or why. She'd thought they were moving in a good direction, had felt so sure of it that she'd decided to agree to marry him for crying out loud, but now he was cold and closed off once more. She could *feel* it, somehow, the distance between them.

"Ah, Skylar, glad you could make it. Please sit." He gestured to the seat across from him, at the other end of the long table. Not fully understanding what was going on and not trusting herself to speak, she simply walked to the chair and sat. "I'm just choosing my... dessert for the evening," he said with a suggestive quirk of his brow. "You don't mind, right?"

His...dessert? Was he serious?? She felt her claws grow and pierce the skin on the tops of her thighs. No, he had to be kidding. This was some kind of weird joke that she didn't understand.

"You'll do nicely," he said, nodding towards one of the females in line. "The rest of you may go."

The one he'd indicated smirked at her friends—or competitors, it seemed—as they all let out huffs of disappointment and sighs of longing as they gazed at Hades before shuffling out of the room. The winning demoness was gorgeous, with black hair that flowed all the way to her waist and sparkling silver eyes. Even the small, silver horns that wound back off of her temples didn't detract from her beauty. Her generous—and that was an *understatement*—breasts were barely covered by a "top" made of strings of emeralds, and her skirt was long and sheer, leaving very little to the imagination.

Skylar felt sick, empty, as if someone had thrown a bucket of water on the flames of hope she had let begin to rise inside her heart. She had admitted before that she was in serious like with him, but she thought that maybe it was more than that. This felt wrong to her on a primal level, in a way she didn't understand. He was *hers*. A voice in her mind screamed it with such force that her fangs shot long, her claws sharpened even further, and she felt her blood begin to boil.

He had to feel the connection between them, right? She couldn't have misinterpreted everything that had been happening between them lately. There's no way. But as she watched him wink at the demoness, seemingly very excited about his choice of dessert, she thought she must have. He needed her to marry him, that was still true, but he had no feelings for her. It really was all just a business deal. He must have been just playing with her before, getting her to let down her guard. He'd seemed to hate her for so long, so he must want to punish her, enjoy her pain and humiliation. Because she was completely fucking embarrassed to have allowed herself to fall for him, to decide to stay here and marry him for fuck's sake. Thank all the gods that she hadn't actually shared that news with him yet.

Well, she wouldn't be giving him the satisfaction of seeing how much this little show hurt her. She wiped away any trace of it from her face and plastered her signature cool, cocky mask on. *Alright, asshole, time to play hardball.*

Game. Fucking. On.

TWENTY-TWO

oly hells. Skylar looked downright sinful. Hades swallowed hard, knowing he was never going to be able to make it through this. It had taken all of his considerable strength not to toss her on the table and take her hard the second she walked in the door. The black dress she wore looked like it had been painted on her, fitting her like an absolute glove, and he wanted those heels digging into his back so badly he could practically feel it. Had he ever wanted her, *anyone*, more than he did in this moment?

But then he recalled the conversation he had overheard outside of her room earlier and his desire faded as rage began to burn. She told some other male that she loved him, and the soon-to-be-dead-man had responded in kind. When they had been in the training room earlier, he thought—had let himself *hope*—that something had shifted between them. He thought she was beginning to feel for him as he had begun to feel for her. He had forgiven any past deeds done by Persephone, didn't even considered her and Skylar to be one and the same any longer, but apparently that had been a mistake. Having Skylar play him like a damn fiddle, making him believe she wanted him back when all along she was just biding her time to get back to *Luke*...Well, he was ashamed to admit that it had hurt him more than Persephone's betrayal ever had.

But now he understood and he wouldn't fall for it again. She was in love with someone else? Fine, Hades would show her that she meant nothing to him as well. He did still need her to agree to the marriage, but he couldn't stop himself from playing this little game. She needed to know that he hadn't fallen for her tricks, that he was just as unaffected as she was. And what better way to prove that than with a little dinner theater?

Skylar sat at the other end of the table, staring as his chosen demoness for the evening eased into his lap. Her face was now a blank mask of indifference, the same cold, confident one he'd seen her don time and time again, but he had seen rage flare in her eyes for a moment. Rage and...hurt? No, couldn't be. Why would she be hurt? Disappointed that her plan to seduce and attempt to kill him (that's what he assumed the plan was anyway) had failed, sure, but not hurt.

He ran his fingers up and down the demoness' bare leg as she nuzzled his neck. He had to keep himself from grimacing. He wasn't enjoying himself whatsoever, and neither was his cock. Sure, the female was beautiful, but only the blonde-haired vixen across the way held any kind of allure for him anymore. *Very fucking inconvenient.*

"So, did you have a nice afternoon?" Hades asked politely.

"De-lightful," she answered too sweetly. "And you?" She ran a finger around the edge of her wine glass and licked her lips subtly. Now *that* got his dick's attention. The demoness in his lap purred, mistaking his sudden interest as approval of her ministrations, so she began to lick and kiss his neck as well. *Ugh.*

He summoned food and the table was quickly filled with enough dishes to feed an army of demigods. Most of them were delicacies of the Underworld, but he couldn't stop himself from adding in a few items from the Mortal Plane that he knew happened to be Sky's...er, *Skylar's* favorite. *No more pet names for the little temptress.*

She looked over everything in front of her and her façade cracked the tiniest bit. He saw curiosity, excitement, and finally fondness when she spied the macaroni and cheese, a slight smile playing on her lips before she shut it down and fell back into character. The demoness "ooed" and picked up a piece of alderfruit. She fed it to Hades seductively and he had to force himself not to roll his eyes. Instead, he bit into the proffered fruit, giving the demoness a sultry look in the process, as if he would rather be biting something else instead. Her eyes sparked with arousal. He wiped a bit of juice from his lips and offered her his finger. She giggled and then moaned as she sucked the digit into her mouth. He forced himself to act as if he were enjoying every second of it, though really something deep in his chest was rebelling, his stomach roiling. Out of the corner of his eye, he saw Skylar clench her jaw so hard he could practically hear the bone cracking and flare her nostrils in irritation. Hades made a show of reluctantly tearing his gaze away from the demoness' mouth on his thumb and glanced to Skylar.

"I'm sorry, did you say something?"

Her lip curled slightly and he would have sworn he heard a small growl before she smiled sweetly and said, "I was just asking if you had a nice conversation with your brother. He really is quite hand-some...If only *he* had need of a wife for some silly prophecy." She sighed wistfully and Hades ground his teeth. He knew she was only trying to goad him, but damnit if the thought of Skylar with Zeus didn't make him want to phase to Mt. Olympus right now and burn his brother's kingdom to the ground. He could rebuild. It would be fine.

"Speaking of conversations, did you have any interesting ones today?" Hades bit out a little too harshly. Her lips parted and her eyes widened slightly before they narrowed and she pressed her lips into a thin line in irritation.

"Eavesdropping is a nasty habit, you know."

She bit into a beanstalk viciously, her teeth snapping together loud enough to be heard across the room. Hades was furious. *She* was mad he overheard her conversation with her lover? That he had foiled her plans? If anyone had the right to be mad right now, it was *him*! He turned the demoness in his lap so that her back was against his chest and didn't take his eyes of Skylar as he kissed down her neck. She moaned and undulated against him, wrapping one of her arms around the back of his neck, fingers digging through his hair. He was disgusted at doing any of this with another female, which pissed him off even more. He only wanted to be with Skylar, despite her games and lies. What was wrong with him? What kind of cruel twist of fate had decided to curse him with falling for this wretched female *twice*?

Skylar's eyes darkened—literally. He watched in confusion and fascination as the color turned from a bright emerald to a green so deep it was nearly black...and he could have sworn he saw flames rise up within the irises for a moment. They lightened again a second later and he shook himself. No, he must have imagined it...*Think about it later. Head in the game.*

The demoness spoke up then. "Mmmm, Hades, is dinner almost over? I'm dying to have you..."

Skylar grabbed her wine glass, gripping it so tightly the glass began to splinter and tossed back the liquid in one large gulp. She slammed it down again and the stem shattered. She took a deep breath and then smirked at Hades, running her tongue along her top teeth before tapping it against one of her fangs. *Why the hell is that so sexy?*

"Poor thing is *dying* to have you, Hades. You should put her out of her misery. It's just so hard when you need someone, ache for them *so* badly..." She trailed a finger lightly down the cleavage that was on display through the deep v of her dress and he shot hard again immediately, desperate to touch where she had, to lick where her finger had been.

The demoness panted in agreement, "Yes, so badly..." Hades did roll his eyes now. Nymphera Demons only cared about one thing: sex. This female had no idea what was going on around her, the game that she was a part of. Skylar's smirk turned downright evil as she leaned forward slightly in her chair.

In a breathy whisper she said, "Mmm, that's why I had to take care of myself in the shower earlier. I just wanted someone so, *so* badly, had to imagine their hands on me, in me, making me explode and shake...Can you guess who that someone was?"

Hades made a sound that was part groan and part growl. The thought of Skylar in the shower, fingers playing between her thighs, head thrown back in pleasure, was the most erotic vision he could imagine. He knew in that instant that he had to see it firsthand one day. However, the thought of her doing so while thinking of another male was enough to make his smoke begin to swirl around him. Skylar quirked a brow at the tendrils. Time to step up the game.

He whispered in the demoness' ear and she gasped and then moaned, nodding emphatically. She immediately turned in his lap, slowly lowering down his body, down, down, down, until she hit her knees in front of him under the table. Hades was silently begging Skylar to stop the game. He wouldn't actually let the demoness do what he'd asked her to do, but he didn't want Skylar to know that... *Come on...Be as jealous as I am...Stop this...Want me the way I want you... Please...*

He nearly melted with relief when Skylar screeched in outrage and stood with so much force that her chair went crashing into the wall behind her. Her claws were out and they dug into the tabletop, leaving deep grooves in the stone. He definitely didn't imagine her eyes changing this time, but he had to have imagined the shadows that sprung out behind her for a moment, looking almost like wings. *What the hell?* He was losing his mind. He stood as well, his own chair sliding backwards with a loud scraping sound. The demoness finally realized that things were not going well and sprang up, cowering at Skylar's scream and the low growl emanating from the back of her throat.

"You," she snarled at the demoness. "Out. NOW."

TWENTY-THREE

"What. The. Fuck." Skylar ground out. She was livid. Beyond livid. There wasn't a word strong enough to describe how angry she was. She felt as if her blood was literally boiling inside her, the fire that had been simmering in the hearth earlier was now blazing and the room feeling entirely too hot.

Hades had heard her conversation earlier with Lucas. *That's* what had changed. She had been momentarily relieved that it was just a misunderstanding and, ok a little happy that all of this had stemmed from Hades being jealous, but then he had that female practically giving him a lap dance at the dinner table. That was bad enough but when she sank to her knees in front of him, about to suck him off right here, Skylar had nearly lost her damn mind. *No one touches my male but me!* Except he wasn't hers. Not really. She'd thought there was a chance...but now she was mentally berating herself for being so stupid, so damn gullible. *She* was the one who did the lying and manipulating, not the other way around, but he'd been so ready to be with someone else that there's no way what she'd thought was happening between them had been real.

Hades leaned his hands on the table, digging into the stone and turning it to dust beneath his fingers.

"Who's Luke?" he growled.

"Oh, you want to know who I was on the phone with? That's rich coming from the douchebag who has sex slaves, one of which was about to give him a blowie at the dinner table for fuckssake!"

"I do *not* have sex slaves. Just because she was eager to do what I suggested doesn't mean she wasn't completely willing." Skylar screeched again and slammed a fist down on the table hard enough for the stone to splinter. "Why do you care so much anyway? You have *Luke*," Hades spit, saying the name with such dripping condescension that she barely kept herself from launching at him and digging her claws into his throat.

"God! I cannot *believe* I..." She snapped her mouth shut and balled her fists.

"What?!" he demanded. "Can't believe you *what*?"

She glared at him, remaining silent. She was desperate to beat on him, demand to know if what had been between them earlier had been real. She *had* to know and she hated that she had to know. She'd never been so disappointed in her life. It took her a moment to realize that she was also hurt. It *hurt* her to see him with someone else. This was far more than trivial jealousy. That connection with him was too strong and the voice inside of her head was screaming once more. He was *hers*. She was meant to be with him. Seeing him with someone else didn't just hurt, it killed. It was more painful than anything she'd ever experienced. He was hers, but apparently she wasn't his. She felt tears pricking the back of her eyes, but she flat out refused to cry in front of him. *Not. Happening.*

"Screw this," she muttered, damning her protective walls for crumbling around Hades in the first place, for not erecting themselves back up again now. She made it a half way to the door before Hades was in front of her, blocking her path. She bared her fangs as his smoke curled around them, tendrils snaking their way towards her, but she didn't try to move past him, didn't lash out like she'd wanted to desperately to do a moment ago. He was still glaring as he began to stalk forward, forcing her to walk backwards until her ass hit the edge of the table. He didn't stop, but instead continued to move forward until his body was pressed against hers in a way that was too much and not nearly enough at the same time.

The immediate and overwhelming need that rocked through her terrified her. Sure, she'd taken the edge off earlier in the shower, but the problem was that it hadn't taken the edge off *at all*. If anything, it had made things *worse*. She had imagined it had been his hands on her, him making her moan and shudder, and now she needed to experience it for real. Despite her irritation and hurt and everything else she was feeling, she had to have him. Here. Now. She needed to touch him, to taste him, to feel his mouth on her. She glared back at him, even as her hands flattened against his chest, her fingers dipping inside his open shirt.

"Who. The fuck. Is Luke?" he growled again as he leaned down towards her and tangled one hand in her hair.

"Why do you care?" she spit, as she unbuttoned one button of his shirt after another. She wasn't sure what was happening, but she couldn't stop herself, didn't want to stop herself. It was like her body had taken over, no longer taking commands from her brain. Her emotions were completely at odds with what her body was absolutely demanding, and her body was winning the fight.

He ran his hands down her sides, gripped her waist, and lifted her up onto the table. He tried to move forward, attempting to wedge his hips in between hers but could only get so far before the tightness of her dress wouldn't allow her to spread her legs further. She growled in frustration and ripped the material up both sides with her claws. She grabbed his hips and yanked him forward, gasping when she felt him against her. He was hard as steel and she wanted him so badly she could barely breathe.

"Who is he?" Hades asked again. He gripped her hip, pulling her against him as he flexed his forward again and again, slowly driving her mad. She bit her lip and fought a moan. Wisps of smoke snaked around them as she ripped open his shirt completely, buttons scattering across the stone floor. She shoved the material over his shoulders and down his arms, letting her fingers trail over him in the process. His skin was so soft and smooth and warm, she never wanted to stop touching him, wanted to explore every inch of him for eternity.

"Why do you care?" she asked again, softer now. The anger was seeping out of her, the need for him overriding every other thing in her mind. He met her gaze, his eyes blazing with desire and some other emotion that she wasn't quite sure of... But *something* passed between them in that moment, something she couldn't explain, but that solidified the connection she felt with him since the moment she first saw him. Even before that, when she'd dreamed of him, she'd known deep down in her soul that he was somehow the most important person in her life. He slid one hand around the back of her neck, firm but surprisingly gentle at the same time.

"I care," he bit out, "Because you're *mine*."

Her breath hitched just before his lips pressed against hers. Her eyes flew wide as something fundamental within her clicked into place. Just that single touch and she was forever changed. His lips were made for her to kiss, and hers for him. She didn't know how she knew it but she did, without question. He pulled back slightly and met her gaze, looking stunned. Had he felt it too? *Yes,* he seemed to say without actually saying a word. *Gods yes.*

Then he was kissing her again and the world around them faded away. He groaned as their tongues twined and danced and she wound her arms around his neck, thrusting her fingers in his hair. Nothing had ever tasted so good, felt so right. She was on fire, her blood becoming molten lava in her veins, like one of those demons she'd faced off with. She shoved her hips forward against him, hitching one of her legs over his hip, begging him to stay closer, demanding it.

He kissed across her jaw and ran her ear lobe through his teeth. She moaned in abandon as he kissed down her neck and across her collar bone, nipping along the way and covering the sting with laps of his tongue. She was going to absolutely *combust.* He ripped open the front of her dress and peered approvingly at the black strapless bra she'd worn.

"Like this. Sorry it has to die," he said gruffly.

She huffed out a laugh and he ripped the material in half as if were tissue paper. He made a half growl-half groan sound deep in his throat.

"Gods," he rasped before ducking his head down. He kissed the sensitive skin of her breast before twirling his tongue around her nipple, never quite making contact with the aching tip. Skylar was panting, yanking his hips forward against her again and again as he kneaded her other breast and continued to lick and tease. He shifted his attention to the other side and she held her breath, just waiting for him to make contact, but he merely hovered just above her, blowing lightly against her skin. She shivered and her head fell back. The anticipation was killing her yet it was insanely erotic.

She needed him like she'd never needed anything or anyone in her life. She felt as if he were oxygen and she were dying for breath. *So* this *is what it feels like to truly need someone.* The feeling was a little scary, but also so welcome. She'd always wanted passion and connection like this. She'd had a small glimpse of it with Lucas, but she'd held herself back, never really let him all the way in, so she couldn't ever fully experience it. But now that she was getting a real taste, she didn't think she could live without it again.

"Hades..." she growled, both begging and warning. She'd had enough teasing, she needed more, more, more, would never get enough. He chuckled against her before finally, *finally* taking mercy on her by taking one nipple between his lips. He twirled his tongue and sucked before biting down with just enough pressure. She cried out and arched into him, nails digging into the back of his head.

He pulled back slightly and asked raggedly, "Too much?"

"Not enough! Don't you *dare* stop."

She didn't have to ask him again. He went back to work with his wicked tongue while he trailed his other hand down her stomach, over her hip, and down her thigh. He pushed her leg gently, urging her to open them even wider and trailed his fingers back up her inner thigh when she obeyed eagerly. Her hips shot forward again, begging him to touch her, tease her, fill her. He trailed his fingertips lightly over her panties. He groaned in approval, and she knew damn well he could feel how wet she was already, needy and ready and desperate.

"Hades. I need you..." She could practically feel his surge of happiness at her words. With no further prompting needed, he shoved the fabric of her panties aside, his fingers making contact with her sensitive skin, though not moving inside. She groaned and he moaned, pulling back to stare at her, wide-eyed.

"You're...I mean, there's no...it's..."

"Shaved? Yep. Permanently. Is that...ok?" She was barely forming coherent thoughts anymore as his fingers brushed lightly back and forth across her bare pussy, but she managed to wonder if maybe that wasn't a thing here? Maybe females didn't shave? Well, technically she didn't either—she'd gotten laser hair removal years ago. Shaving was too much of a pain in the ass to deal with, especially when with her job she may need to be in a bikini or dress at a moment's notice to seduce a mark or act as bait.

"It's more than ok. It's fucking hot as hell."

He captured her mouth again at the same time he thrust a finger deep inside her. She nearly lost her mind.

"Gods, Sky, you're so wet. So tight..."

She whimpered as he slowly tortured her. She began moving her hips in time with his thrusts, and he eventually inserted another finger. She bit his lower lip and scratched at his back, possibly drawing blood. She had been so strung out, so on the edge and now he was driving her mad. She was losing control. She was...

Her eyes flew wide. *Holy fuck*, she was going to come.

"Hades, I...I mean, I've never..."

He stilled and pulled back, slowly removing his fingers.

"You've never?..." He arched an eyebrow in question. She rolled her eyes and grabbed his wrist, stopping his retreat.

"If you remove your hand, *I'll* remove your hand, understand?" He laughed lightly and she made a "mmmm" sound when he pressed his fingers forward again.

"No, that's not what I meant, I'm not a virgin. I mean, it *has* been a while...like a few years now..." She shook her head in exasperation. "That's not the point. I—*ohhhh* don't stop *that*." He curled his fingers in some ridiculously talented way she didn't even know was possible, hitting the most perfect spot. She closed her eyes and momentarily lost all rational thought. *Holy hell, where did he learn* that? She didn't have much longer if he kept that up. Somehow she managed to keep talking. "Look, I've done plenty, I've just never...um...crossed the finish line with anyone before, if you catch my drift."

She'd wanted to. She'd tried, *desperately*, which probably didn't help matters by putting so much pressure on herself to get there, but she just never could make it happen. She knew she physically *could*, as evidenced by her earlier activities in the shower, but when another person was involved, even Lucas, it was always a no-go. It was like she was still holding that piece of herself back, whether she meant to or not. It was one of the many reasons her and Luke would never work out. He felt like he was failing her in that department and she felt terrible for making him feel that way.

Hades' eyes went wide and he stilled, not even breathing.

"Are you saying...you're telling me that no other male has ever made you come before?"

She swallowed hard and bit her lip as she nodded. A slow, sexy smile spread across his lips that sent shivers down her spine and made her stomach flip.

"In that case..." He leaned in and kissed her deeply, before whispering against her lips, "Buckle up, love."

TWENTY-FOUR

Hades wanted to beat his chest and roar with male satisfaction. Skylar had never found release with another before. He would be her first. *Her only* a part of his mind growled. He couldn't disagree—he *wanted* to be her only. Wanted to own this part of her, wanted her to forever think of only him when she thought of pleasure. More than that, there was something happening between them, more than just the physical. It was like the connection he knew was between them had grown, strengthened, solidified into unbreakable steel.

He'd called her his and she hadn't recoiled, hadn't fought, had even seemed...happy? Relieved? He didn't want to get his hopes up, was still confused by everything going on, still pissed off about this Luke character, but he felt hope rising in his chest. If she didn't care about him, why had she been so jealous of the demoness? In fact, it had been more than jealousy. He'd seen an unmistakable possessiveness in her eyes. Did she think of him as *hers* as well?

He kissed her again, slower, deeper than before, and slowly kept up his torture with his fingers. She was so tight and wet, he was doing everything in his power not to rip his pants open and shove inside her to the hilt, right here and now. That time would come, but he needed to take this slow. Soon she was nearly mindless with desperation, clutching him closer, getting impossibly wetter. He pulled back, removing his fingers.

"What did I tell you about removing your hand!?" she screeched.

He laughed before nipping at her bottom lip, whispering, "Do you trust me?"

Her breath hitched. "Ye...yes."

He ripped the rest of her dress and her panties clean off and gently pushed her backwards to lay down on the table. He slowly kissed down her throat, across her breasts, down her stomach, biting here and there, licking. He dipped a tongue into her navel and she squirmed, throwing her hands above her head and gripping the other edge of the table. He kissed lower and then traced every line of her tattoo with his tongue. Roses and flames that were entirely too enticing. She was writhing in anticipation and making the most enticing sounds by the time he dropped to his knees. She braced her weight on her elbows, leaning up enough that she could watch what he was about to do. Her eyes were wide, blazing with excitement and desire.

He scrubbed a hand across his jaw at the sight of her, dripping and open before him. He hadn't done this in centuries—*damn, I hope I'm not rusty*—had never really taken the time to, or even cared if the females he'd been with wanted it, if he were being honest. He was more of a get in, get off, get out kind of guy, and none of the females he'd bedded over the years had complained.

But right now, with Skylar, he wanted nothing more than to devour her all. night. long. He lifted her legs, placing her thighs over his shoulders. She licked her lips as she watched him duck his head towards her, then she threw her head back and cried out as he licked her slowly. He nearly came right then and there in his pants like a mortal teenager. *Holy. Shit.* She tasted like heaven and he suddenly didn't know how he had lived without this, without her, all this time, could never live without her again. She responded to him more than any other female, and her every moan, every scratch, every hitch of her breath drove him wild. His smoke unfurled around him, snaking around his thighs and gently caressing the outsides of her thighs.

Hades pulled back and growled, "You are fucking *mouthwatering*." He leaned back in and lost himself completely, alternating between long licks and thrusting his tongue deep within her. He savored every second, relished every noise she made, every time she said his name. He added a finger and flicked his tongue over her clit.

"Fuck!" she moaned, writhing her hips. She was so damn tight he wondered if she'd be able to take him when the time came. *Can't think about that now.* He added another finger and when he sucked her clit, she began to thrash, unable to keep her hips still.

"Hades...Oh gods...Don't stop...I'm going to..."

Excitement thrummed through him. He was about to give her what no other man had, what no other man would again if he had his way. He chose to ignore that last thought and hooked his fingers forward once more as he took her clit into his mouth, flicking his tongue while he sucked lightly. She cried out and exploded. He moaned in pleasure as she writhed and shuddered, back bowing off the table, her inner walls pulsing tightly around his fingers as her climax ripped through her. He pulled his hand away and replaced his fingers with his tongue, licking every last drop of her first ever orgasm with another person. It was his prize and he'd earned it.

The room was suddenly burning hot, but he didn't care. He was completely lost in Skylar. She was shuddering and repeating his name over and over again, softly, like a prayer, and he couldn't stop himself from starting all over again, spreading her lips and licking her up and down, slowly torturing her sensitive flesh.

"Hades, I-I can't..."

She could. She would. He slowed his pace, languidly licking and sucking, nibbling, giving her a chance to recover...for a moment, at least. She moaned and writhed against his mouth.

"*Gods* that feels so good..."

She dug her heels into his back, urging him closer. He grinned to himself: he'd wanted those heels in his back the second he'd seen them and he'd gotten exactly what he'd wanted. He began to increase the speed and pressure, and soon she was on the verge once again. She bolted upright and he glanced up her body. Her gaze slammed into his. His heart thudded in his chest at the sight of her. Her eyes were wide, skin flushed, and that connection between them seemed to pulse. He didn't break his gaze as he continued to lick and she gasped as she watched, panting. She dug her fingers into his hair, holding him to her as she ground her hips against his tongue.

"Hades," she half-whispered, half-moaned as she erupted again, even more intense than the first time. Her thighs tightened around his ears as she screamed in pleasure, so loudly the windows shook.

When she finally began to calm, her shudders subsiding, he stopped his assault. He kissed her thigh softly before slowly trailing more kisses up her stomach, over her breasts, along her collarbone, up her neck. She was panting softly by the time he made it to her mouth. Her cheeks were slightly flushed, her eyes heavy lidden, and she had two small puncture marks in her lower lip where she'd bitten it, a tiny trickle of blood running down her chin. He brushed her hair back off of her face tenderly, thinking that no one had ever looked so beautiful.

"How was that, love?"

She reached up and held his cheeks in her hands, gently stroking his cheekbones with her thumbs, her eyes wide and shinning with satisfaction and some other emotion he couldn't name. Awe? Wonder?...Love? He didn't dare let himself hope for that yet, but he knew deep down he wanted it. Wanted it so badly it rocked him to his core. How could he want her love like this? After everything she'd done in the past? But he didn't care anymore, not about any of it.

Because, he realized in that moment, *I don't want Persephone's love...I want* Skylar's.

She traced her thumb lightly across his bottom lip and his eyes slid closed. She leaned in and kissed him softly. Having her hold him like this, stroking him so lovingly, was pure heaven. Could it be real? Could he really have this? Could he let himself go down this road, knowing where it could lead?

"That was...I don't have words. I'm going to need you to do that every day for the rest of forever." *Forever.* He was ok with that plan. "Did you feel...nevermind." She shook her head, clearing the thought away. "We need to talk about a few things, bucko." She thumped him in the chest and he smiled. Oh boy did they.

"I agree. I–" She put her fingers over his lips to silence him and got a wicked glint in her eyes.

"Thing is, I do my best thinking in the bathtub..."

Holy hell. He grinned, liking her way of thinking, and pulled her close to his body. Before he phased them to his bathroom, he caught a glimpse of the table. He frowned in confusion: there were dark slashes across the surface where she'd been lying. Burn marks? Had those always been there and he'd never noticed? He admittedly rarely used this room, so he had no idea. Shrugging it off, he focused back on Skylar, and a split-second later they were in front of his bathtub. It was already filled and the scent of honeysuckle—Skylar's favorite, he knew—was wafting through the space. She laughed and the sound made something in his chest clench and relax at the same time.

"I don't think I'll ever get used to that." She shook her head and stepped away from him, exploring the room, gloriously naked. He ran a hand through his hair as his eyes skated across every inch of her. Her sun-kissed skin was far from perfect, covered in scars as it was, but it was perfect for *her.* Every mark spoke to who she was and what she'd been through, made her who she was. She was a fighter, a warrior to her core, and that made her even more beautiful to him. His eyes continued to rove and when he got to her ass, he groaned. What was that mortal phrase? Bounce a quarter off her ass? *Gods have mercy on my soul.* He shifted his stance as he grew harder still. She trailed her fingers along the stone ledge of the tub, and his eyes tracked every movement.

"I've been dying to take a dip in this bad boy since that first morning." She turned towards him, leaning her back against the ledge, and arched a golden brow. Her gaze glided leisurely over his bare chest and she ran her tongue along her bottom lip. *Gods how can that tiny gesture be so damned sexy?* When her gazed moved lower, she cocked her head to the side with a sultry smile.

"I think you're entirely overdressed, babe."

He smirked a little crookedly. "My apologizes, love."

She watched raptly as he slowly unlaced the fly of his pants. She gripped the ledge tighter as his erection sprang free., eyes going wide. Her tongue darted out once more as he gripped the base and slowly stroked forward and back, once, twice. A soft growl rumbled from her chest and she shoved away from the ledge, closing the distance between them so quickly he could have almost believed that she'd phased. He hissed in a breath and his eyes slid closed when she shoved his hand away and wrapped her fingers around his shaft. She raised up on her toes to kiss him softly, stroking him slowly, running her thumb over the tip and spreading the bead of moisture that had welled there. He moaned and delved his tongue deeper into her mouth, tunneling his fingers in her hair. She sucked his bottom lip before kissing the side of his mouth and along his jaw, down his neck.

She whispered, "I know we need to talk, but first, I have to do something. Something I've been dreaming about for...a while." She slowly continued to trail kisses down his throat and across his chest, running her tongue across his tattoo before continuing down his stomach. She finally dropped to her knees in front of him and his breath left him.

Oh gods. This was another thing he hadn't experienced in centuries upon centuries. He always felt vulnerable in this position, and after Persephone had literally stabbed him in the back, he had a thing about not feeling that way. In fact, he rarely took females in any way except from behind, where he was in the most control over the situation. He had been slightly paranoid for the last three thousand years, he could admit it.

But now he wanted nothing more than to have Skylar take his cock deep in her mouth, to tangle his hands in her hair, thrust his hips forward...He bit the inside of his cheek to stop his thoughts and gain control of himself. He didn't want her to do it out of a sense of obligation, a tit for tat kind of deal as it were.

So, with truly astonishing willpower, he forced himself to say, "Sky, you don't have to..." Before he could finish she closed her lips over the crown, swirling her tongue before sucking him deep. He nearly came in an instant. "*Oh gods*, don't stop. Please, please, *please* don't stop."

TWENTY-FIVE

Skylar's lips curled upwards—as much as they could with an admittedly huge cock between them. Hades, God of the freaking Underworld, was *begging* her not to stop. She still couldn't quite believe the turn the evening had taken. She'd been so angry she'd been ready to tear the entire castle apart, ready to peel that demoness like an apple in one long slice...and then suddenly all that anger fizzled away in the wake of the fiery need that had washed over them.

I care because you're mine.

Remembering his words made her shiver in pleasure. He wanted her as badly as she wanted him. Not just to fulfil some prophecy, not just to aid his agenda. He wanted *her*, claimed her as his own. And as a cherry on top of the sundae, she had actually gotten off with another person! She'd known it would be different than when she went solo, but she never could have imagined the sheer pleasure intensity of it. She had been mindless with bliss, feeling nothing but sensation after sensation as she'd shattered into a million pieces— *twice!*—with the most mind-blowingly handsome man to ever live.

She vaguely remembered a strange urge to bite him which she'd never had before. Her fangs were more for show than anything…or so she'd always thought. Could she be part vamp after all? They'd dismissed the idea ages ago when she didn't seem to have any other traits of the species: she'd never had the desire to drink blood, ate tacos on any day that ended in Y, tanned in the sun like an Australian Gold model. None of that screams vampire…but they almost always got fangy during sex, bloodlust and lust-lust getting all mixed up together. So, maybe she was a fraction leech or something. Though she'd felt the urge to *bite* him, not *drink* from him, she realized with a frown.

She shook herself inwardly. Didn't matter. Either way, she'd denied the urge and dug her fangs into her own lip instead. She'd felt like the entire room was blazing up around them, but she hadn't cared. She'd gladly burn with Hades for the rest of eternity to feel the things she was feeling with him.

And now she was making him crazed in return. Even if he hadn't been begging her not to stop, there was no way in hell she could have. She had wanted to do this to him since before they'd even met. He had said she was mouthwatering before, but damn if she didn't crave him, needing to taste him in return. He was so big, she couldn't fit his entire length in her mouth, so she used her hand at the base, stroking gently in time with the movement of her mouth. Up, down, up down, driving him wild. She twirled her tongue around the head again, and soon his hands were tangled in her hair, thrusting his hips forward, forcing his cock deeper into her throat.

"Sorry! Sorry!" he grunted out as he stilled his hips. She pulled away and smiled up at him before running her tongue down the underside of his shaft and back up to the tip. His stomach muscles constricted and his thighs clenched.

"You thrust all you want, baby."

He groaned low, as if the words pained him, and she smirked. She took him deep again, this time stroking him harder, faster. She raked her nails across his stomach, egging him on, she knew, and he didn't seem to be able to stop himself from bucking forward again. Pride surged through her. *She* was doing this. She was making a legit god lose his ever loving mind, and she couldn't get enough, never wanted to stop. He gripped her hair in one hand and arched his hips forward, thrusting his cock down her throat. Thankfully, she'd never had a gag reflex and she moaned quietly as he did it again and again. It was so fucking hot and she was already aching for his touch, so aroused she could hardly stand it.

"Skylar, if you don't want me to...you better stop..."

"No fucking way," she growled. She dipped her tongue into the slit and then sucked him deep.

"*Ah gods...*" His head lolled back, seemingly completely lost in the moment. She dug her claws into his ass with one hand and reached down to cup his sac with the other, pulling gently. He groaned and his entire body tensed. He thrust twice more before yelling out her name and erupting in her mouth. She moaned as she drank him down, savoring every drop. She'd never really cared one way or another about swallowing before, but the taste of Hades was like a drug and she was officially addicted.

He finally finished and as she pulled away, grinning, he fell to his knees in front of her. He looked at her like...like he was *amazed*, in utter awe of her. He traced a finger along her cheekbone in a gesture so tender it made her throat tight.

"You are..."

"Perfection incarnate? The epitome of wonderful? Effing amaze-balls?" she supplied helpfully, giving him a full, unabashed smile. He laughed out loud, deep and full and she was determined to hear that sound more often.

"Yes, all of those things. Now..." He got a mischievous look in his eyes, but before she could even think about moving, he tossed her into the tub. She barely had time to squeal before she went under. It was so large, she landed with a splash, her toes barely grazing the bottom. It really was more of an indoor pool that you happened to use soap in. She sputtered as she emerged and he was bent over, laughing again, holding his sides as if that had been the funniest thing in the world. She couldn't even be mad. She loved this playful, goofy Hades. So, she merely sent water splashing into his face as he made his way into the tub.

"I give you the best blow job in your very, *very* long life, and this is how you say thanks? Nice." She rolled her eyes, feigning annoyance.

"And how do you know it was the best in my very, *very* long life?" he asked as he glided towards her through the water.

"Oh please, don't even try to pretend that it wasn't." She said it with utter confidence but inside she was dying to know if it were true...and if it weren't, her competitive nature was about to do work until there was no doubt that she was the reigning champ.

Hades circled behind her, wrapping his arms around her and pulling her against his chest before whispering in her ear, "I've never come so hard, Sky. Nearly lost my fucking mind, barely kept my power in check." She shivered as he planted a soft kiss against her ear, trailing more slowly down her neck. She lolled her head to the side, giving him better access. He slid one hand down to grip her hip, pulling her ass against him. *Oh my.* "Already hard again just thinking about it," he rasped against her skin, grazing his teeth along the sensitive spot where her neck met her shoulder. She moaned and wiggled her ass against him. "Mmmm...if you don't stop that, we're never going to have this talk." He chuckled lightly when she groaned.

"Yes...talking...about the things...and...and the stuff..." she panted, trying really hard to remember what the fuck they were supposed to be talking about. Surely it wasn't important. Surely it could wait for hours upon hours upon hours while they played some more, explored every last inch of each other, came more times than they could count...

He began lightly trailing his fingers down her thigh and back up, across her stomach...a bit lower, as he continued to lick and kiss her neck. They definitely didn't need to talk about...anything. She couldn't think about anything other than Hades and his hands, and his tongue, and...Damnit, no they *did* need to talk before things got out of hand.

She somehow regained control over herself and said, "Ok, ok. Let's talk."

Skylar reluctantly pulled away and sat on one of the submerged benches. She pointed to the other end and he arched a brow, but nodded. She didn't trust herself to sit closer to him than this for the time being without throwing all her plans of talking and taking things slow(er) out the damn window...but she also couldn't stand the thought of him being across the tub from her. He must have been feeling the same way because he did sit on the other end of the bench, but pulled her feet across his lap, lightly running his fingers up and down her legs. She closed her eyes in satisfaction. *I'll allow it.*

"Ok, first order of business: I'm going to need you to explain your little sex slave theatrics at dinner," she said, her eyes slitting in irritation.

He rolled his eyes. "I told you, they aren't sex slaves. I would never allow something like that in my kingdom. They're Nymphera demons. Your Nymphs in the Mortal Plane are a...subspecies is the best way to describe them. And, just as the Nymphs you know are driven by desire and sexual gratification, so are the Nymphera demons, except on a far more primal level. And before you ask, no, I wasn't ever planning on actually bedding her—or anything else for that matter. I was..." He let out a long breath. "I was just trying to make you jealous." He ran a hand through his wet hair and she was momentarily mesmerized by the way his bicep flexed, the way the muscles under his tattoo moved and danced. His admission softened her enough that she didn't immediately kick him in the balls, and she no longer wanted to gut the demoness...not much anyway.

"Your turn. Who is Luke?" He spit the word, like it was dirty and tasted bad in his mouth. She pressed her lips together to keep from laughing. Jealous Hades was just about the cutest thing she'd ever seen. And ok, it was also kind of hot. Don't ask her to explain it.

"He's an important person in my life."

"Do you love him?" Hades asked, clenching his jaw.

"Yes," she replied easily. It was the truth after all. She did love Luke, just not *that* way. Hades stiffened and smoke unfurled around his shoulders. She debated on drawing this out, making him suffer a bit for being an ass before, but thought better of it. "But, not in the way that you think. He's my family. I love him the way you love your brothers."

All of the tension left him in an instant, as if someone had pulled the plug and it was all sent spiraling down the drain. He let out a long breath and gave her a sheepish grin, as if embarrassed by his own stupidity and acting like an idiot mortal instead of the God of the Underworld. She just huffed out a laugh and shook her head.

"Come here," he said in low, sexy voice. He pulled her towards him and she smiled when he grabbed the honeysuckle bodywash. He gently and reverently washed her, and though he didn't do more than wash, her eyes slid closed and her belly quivered when he ran his hands over her skin. He gently turned her back to his chest once more and moved her hair over her shoulder. She tensed slightly, knowing what he would notice and hoping maybe he wouldn't ask... but she should have known better than to hope. He traced her scars gently with his fingertips.

"What are these from? I thought they were bullet holes, but they seem too small." She shivered when he placed a soft kiss where her neck met her shoulder. She could feel his smile against her skin as he kissed her again, biting gently. He'd already figured out that that particular spot made her melt. Clever man.

Skylar sighed a little, knowing that she'd have to explain the scars eventually, but she wasn't ready. Not yet.

"Let's talk about that later." He didn't press her further and she loved him for that. She moaned as he massaged the soap deep into her shoulder muscles and almost forgot what they were talking about. She wanted to steer them away from her scars, so she asked the first thing that came to mind.

"So, um...what's the deal with Dean?"

"Dean?"

"The cat. The one you sent to lead me to dinner. I named him Dean Winchester." Hades chuckled lightly behind her and kissed the top of her spine. *This conversation won't last much longer if he keeps that up.*

"His name is actually Conan. He's a demigod and an old friend. About five hundred years ago he pissed off the wrong enchantress on the Mortal Plane and she cursed him to that form. He came running back to the Underworld with his tail between his legs. Literally. Some of us can communicate with him telepathically and we've been trying to find a way to break the curse all these years, but no luck as of yet."

"Even gods can't break puny little curses?"

"It doesn't work that way, smartass." He squeezed her shoulders playfully and continued to plant kisses across her back, like now that he'd finally started touching her he couldn't stop. "We're powerful, but we can't just bend *everything* to our whim. And he didn't just piss off any enchantress, he pissed off the Queen. Very few things can counteract that kind of magic unless she wills it, and no one has seen her in centuries."

"Oh, I've actually heard of her! Well, sort of. There are stories about the enchantress Queen being captured by insert other faction of the supernatural world here—depends on who's telling the story on who the bad guys are—a really long time ago. Most clans have all but given up hope that she's alive, but there are a few that still believe it and still search. They've actually hired us a time or two in the quest, but nothing's come from it yet." She shrugged. "I have a few friends down in the New Orleans clan and mannnn, talk about party girls! You wanna have a good time on the Mortal Plane, that's who you need to find. Took me a full week to recover last time I saw them, and I still have no idea how I ended up in that fountain wearing nothing but a fake mustache and a crown that said 'Birthday King'."

Hades laughed and she sighed.

"That's got to be awful for him though, to be trapped for that long. I wonder if we have anything that could help. We have insanely immense and detailed archives of information on all supernatural species and their histories. I bet we have info on this Queen from way back when. Might be worth a shot. I mean, nothing else has been helpful, so can't hurt, right?"

"I'm sure Conan—or Dean—would appreciate that."

Skylar made a mental note to ask Z and Lucas to look into it next time they talked. Hades pulled her back against his chest, his legs closing her in, and wrapped his strong arms around her.

He whispered against her neck, "Tell me...something. Anything about your past, something no one else knows. Just...talk to me." He sounded almost desperate, like he'd been waiting for this for his entire life, needed her words like a lifeline.

She found that she...wanted to. Her internal alarm system should have been going mad, those bars slamming down into place around her heart, refusing to let Hades in, but everything was silent. If anything, she felt the need to tell him *everything*, open herself open to him entirely. She wanted nothing between them. No walls, no secrets. The thought terrified her but also made her want to jump for joy. She'd always hoped deep down that maybe, just maybe, if she ever found the one she was meant to be with, all of her barriers would crumble and she could finally let someone in. Her mind screamed that she'd found him, that Hades was her one. *He's my lobster.*

"I almost died once. A couple of years ago. I was being reckless and thought I could handle a situation on my own, trying to prove how great I was, I guess. Spoiler alert: I was mistaken. I heal from most things, even though I haven't transitioned yet, but my injuries were...bad." Hades tightened his arms around her and she smiled. "But as I was lying there, unsure if anyone would get to me in time, I...I *saw* you."

The words came out barely more than a whisper and she was

suddenly worried how he would react. Would he think she was insane? Would he go running for the hills? A lot of guys would. It was one thing to decide they wanted to try to...date, or whatever the fuck this was turning into, but to be told that the girl you just met has been dreaming of you for years? Well, she wouldn't blame him for bolting, honestly.

Hades sucked in a harsh breath and she rushed on, deciding to just rip the band aid off.

"I know that sounds insane, but I...I've dreamed of you for as long as I can remember and that day, I saw your face and though you didn't say anything, I could feel you begging me to hold on, telling me that there was something I needed to do, and I clung to that like a life raft. I...I don't know if I would have held on otherwise. There's something peaceful in knowing that you could just let go, that all of the hurt and pain and hardness of life would just drift away...but my need to hold on, for you, was more powerful than that beckoning peace."

He was quiet for a long time. Too long.

"Say something," she whispered.

"I don't know why you've dreamed of me, but I know that I've felt...connected to you since the minute I saw you, maybe even before that, without really realizing it. I think that fate put us on these paths, connected us long before now." He let out a long breath. "I've been waiting for you for a long time, Skylar...and I'm glad you're finally here."

She smiled and felt heat spread through her chest. He didn't call her crazy. He didn't run away screaming. He felt the connection between them too. She turned around to face him in the tub.

"Me too." She traced his stubble with her fingertips and he leaned into her touch. Needing to change the subject before she up and married him right here and now, she said, "So, are you ever really going to explain the whole souls coming to the Underworld thing to me?"

He relaxed slightly and she had the feeling he was grateful for the change of subject to something less declare-your-love-ish.

"Yes and no." She rolled her eyes, thinking he was just going to be vague and frustrating like he had been before, but he surprised her when he laughed and chucked her under the chin.

"As much as it pains me to utter these words...get dressed. I'll show you."

TWENTY-SIX

Hades was reeling. He had experienced some of the greatest pleasure he'd ever known and he hadn't even bedded Skylar yet. She'd been open with him, seeming to want to share. He had wanted to ask her again what she was, but didn't want to push her yet. He didn't know how everything had changed so suddenly but he didn't want to upset this tenuous, perfect balance they'd found. Being with Skylar like this had freed something inside him that he'd caged away long ago. He knew he should be careful—he'd never suspected Persephone would betray him and Skylar was literally trained to do just that—but he just felt it deep in his soul that Skylar would never hurt him.

The connection he'd been feeling between them had only strengthened and he was tired of denying its existence, denying that it meant something monumental. He'd never experienced anything like it before in all his years, even when he'd been married to her in the past. And she said she'd dreamed of him for years. Something about that tickled at the edges of his mind, but he couldn't quite grab hold of any concrete thought. Either way, it all had to mean something.

He felt like Skylar was *his*, was meant for him. There were some who believed that the Gods had a piece of their souls taken from them when they were born or created, and that piece was placed in another, the one they were destined to be with: their one true match. He'd never put much stock in it before, even when he'd fallen in love with Persephone. He hadn't felt as if there were some mythical force pulling them together, as if they were a part of the same whole. But with Skylar…

He shook his head, not ready to have that particular conversation with himself yet. Instead he focused on enjoying the view as she sauntered out of the bathroom. The girl really did have an ass that men would go to war for. Hell, he would burn the whole world to the ground for it. He really didn't know if he'd ever get over her body, over his reactions to her. This insane attraction, this desperate need to touch her had to ebb at some point, didn't it?

He finished toweling off and quickly threw on some pants and a t-shirt while she asked the castle to provide her with clothing. She shimmied into tight, low-hanging jeans and a t-shirt that had— he barked out a laugh. It was the cartoon version of himself from the Disney movie *Hercules*. Emmie had made him watch it once. Skylar grinned and made her way to him, patting his chest.

"Don't worry, babe, you're *much* more handsome than they gave you credit for."

He smiled. *Gods, I've smiled more in the last few hours than I have in the last few centuries.*

"I quite like his little friends though. They remind me of some pets I had once upon a time." He pulled her close against his body, loving the fact that she now wound her arms around his neck without hesitation, and phased them to the River.

He kissed her softly before letting her go and spinning her around to take in the view. She gasped.

"Where are we?" she breathed, hand flying gently to her mouth.

"This is the famed River Styx." He gestured to the flowing water. She looked up at him over her shoulder and frowned in confusion.

"But I thought...well, I guess I don't know what I thought. Explain."

He chuckled lightly.

"What do you see?"

She arched brow at him, but he gave her a "come on" gesture so she blew out a long breath and indulged him his little game.

"Well, it's beautiful. Beyond beautiful. The water is crystal blue and there are rocks that look like jewels under the surface and luminescent fish-like creatures swimming. The banks on either side are pure white sand and dotted with the most gorgeous flowers." She inhaled deeply. "That smell uh-mazing by the way. There are trees that kind of remind me of palm trees except the fronds are a glittering silver and it sounds like tinkling bells when they sway in the breeze. And there's a gorgeous house right over there, like this quaint little beach cottage, but bigger. Is that yours? Like a vacation house? Because, yes please!" She glanced upwards and sighed. "And the stars. My God, they're even more beautiful here than at the castle somehow, which I'd never have thought possible."

Hades couldn't help himself. He cupped her cheeks gently, brushing the ends of his fingers into her soft hair, and kissed her, soft and deep. She ran her hands up his stomach and rested her palms on his chest, just over his heart. He could kiss her for hours, but sighed and pulled away.

"This is what it truly looks like, but the souls that pass through this part of the underworld see what they *deserve* to see. Contrary to popular belief, *all* souls come to the Underworld, not just the damned. Those who lived good lives, did good deeds, tried the best they could, they see something similar to what you do and are escorted through to a joyful afterlife. Those who didn't, well, they see things like this."

Hades used his power to let her see another version of the river. She gasped and grabbed his arm to steady herself. He showed her a river of black, boiling water, thick like tar, but with blood and bone and other...*parts* floating along the surface. The sky had been replaced by dark rock that encircled the entire river, forming a tunnel that dripped putrid acid. Creatures with scales and claws and deformed wings attempted to rise from the depths, breaking the surface occasionally, their moans and cries of agony echoing off the walls. The sandy shores were gone, now replaced with ledges of jagged stone with demons and human souls alike chained to the walls, suffering for all to see. Sounds of whips meeting flesh, bones breaking, and screams of pain were a constant background soundtrack.

"Holy shit," Skylar breathed, swallowing hard and wincing as a piercing scream rang out. "This is...fuck." She shuddered. "And I'm assuming ones that see this version do *not* go to the happy afterlife?"

"Definitely not. Depending on the severity of their crimes, they're either escorted directly to a realm of punishment, or brought to me for sentencing. Any soul that requests—or really they usually *demand*, like the audacious pricks they are—an audience with me gets one. Many try to plead their case, change their fate. It usually doesn't end well."

"And you can see? Everything they've done in their lives? Bad or good?"

Hades nodded.

"Only after death though. There are others who have that ability for the living." Skylar was still staring out over the nightmareish scene before her. He'd kill to know what was running through her mind. She nodded a bit absently.

"Yeah, my best friend Zahara can. Her mother's line is descended from some of the most powerful Soul Seers in history. It's...intense sometimes for her." She glanced back up at him again. "I imagine it is for you too."

"It can be, yes. But..." He shrugged. It was part of his duties as ruler of the Underworld.

"I get it, I just—" Her words cut off as she sucked in a breath and moved suddenly, angling herself in front of Hades, as if to protect him. *How adorable.* Her claws lengthened and he would bet that her fangs were bared at the tall, skeletal figure approaching them. It wore a long, black cloak, but its hood was thrown back, revealing hollow eye sockets that glowed blood red. Great black wings rose from its back, and it held a large scythe, the blade rust-colored, stained with blood.

"Aren't you going to introduce me? I'm kind of integral to this whole process you know."

Charon crossed his arms over his chest and pouted. Hades smirked at his friend and let the vision fall away. They again stood on a white, sandy beach, beauty surrounding them, and the terrifying creature had transformed back into the big, burly ferryman of the Underworld. He had deep red curls surrounding his face like a halo and ice blue eyes. A long scar ran from the outer edge of his right eye down to his cheek, though Hades didn't think that it distracted from his features. In fact, most females seemed to find him quite attractive, despite—or maybe even because of?—the scar. Skylar relaxed her stance immediately, straightening.

"Holy shit. *Please* tell me you own a kilt and can do a Scottish accent."

Charon smiled wide and Hades rolled his eyes. Emmie was addicted to the mortal show *Outlander*, so Hades and Charon both knew exactly what Skylar was inferring to. Charon *may* have looked a little bit like Jamie Fraser. And Hades *may* know in far greater detail than he would ever wish to know about the times that Charon and Emmie had role played as Jamie and Claire. Emmie insisted on kissing and telling no matter how many times Hades begged her to stop.

"Oh aye, lass." Charon winked and Skylar fanned herself.

"Alright you two, knock it off. Skylar, this is Charon. Charon, Skylar."

"Dude, you can look wicked scary sometimes." Skylar grinned as she extended her hand. A strange sense of pride surged up in Hades' chest at the way Skylar handled herself with everything that came her way.

"I know, right? You should see some of these big baddies quake in their boots when I'm currying them across the water. Eight out of ten piss themselves."

"They can still piss themselves?" Skylar asked with a grin.

"Ehh, it's kind of complicated. They're souls but they still have bodies. No use in punishing something that doesn't have a body to feel it, right?"

"Good point. So what happens—ohmygods!"

Before Hades could even figure out what was going on, Skylar was off, running full speed towards the cottage, practically flying over the sand. He saw what she was after and mentally told Cerberus not to attack, but soon realized he hadn't needed to waste his time. Skylar slid to her knees in the sand in front of the three headed mutt and immediately started petting and nuzzling and scratching behind his numerous ears. The famed guard dog of the Underworld that was supposed to instill fear in the hearts of men began to lick her face enthusiastically and wag his tail like a golden retriever before plopping to the ground and rolling over for belly scratches. Hades raised an eyebrow at Charon who just smiled and shrugged.

"You're such a good puppy aren't you? Yes, you are! Er, puppies? All of you. Such good puppers, keeping all the bad souls scared and crying. Who's a good guard dog?" She rubbed his belly until his foot started kicking in the air a mile a minute. Hades and Charon couldn't help but laugh.

Charon said quietly, "So, that's her, huh?" Hades nodded and Charon looked thoughtful. "Well, I already like her much better than the last version." He clapped Hades on the back and strode forward to pet one of Cerberus' heads.

Me too, Hades thought to himself. *Me too.*

TWENTY-SEVEN

The next week was one of the best of Skylar's life. Things with Hades continued to get better and better...verging on damn near perfect. The animosity she felt from him at the beginning was completely gone. Now he only gazed at her with adoration...and blazing hot desire that melted her panties. They hadn't had sex yet and he had surprisingly agreed to her idea to take things slow as far as that final step went. She was still confident in her decision to stay and marry him, but she was still holding that piece of herself back. If she slept with him, she knew she would be a complete goner. Right now, if something went south, it would hurt like hell but she would survive. Maybe. Once they took that last step, there was no way.

They'd been getting to know each other, playing, flirting, spending as much time as possible together, all the fun "new relationship" things. He'd told her amazing stories about his ridiculously long life, and gave her the real stories behind some of the most famous myths. She'd told him about her work, her friendships with Lucas and Zahara, though she still hadn't worked up the courage to tell him about her past, and couldn't force herself to deal the pain of talking about her dad, so those topics were still on the "to be discussed" list.

She'd spilled the beans to Z and Lucas about where she really was and who she was really with a few days after the infamous dinner date. Lucas had been quiet and Z hadn't seemed 100% convinced, but she didn't outright call Skylar crazy, so that was a good sign. Z always told it like it was. No sugarcoating, no bullshit. Some people called it crass or blunt, but Skylar called it refreshing and it was one of the things she loved most about her best friend.

"Gods. Like...*gods*, gods?" Lucas had demanded, incredulous.

"Yep, the real deal. I know it sounds insane, but it's all true. Well, I mean, kind of. Most of the mythology we know is a bit skewed, but yeah, overall, it's all true."

"And you're with...Hades. *The* Hades?" Z had asked. "Isn't he like...blue with fire for hair?" Skylar had snorted.

"He looks nothing like the cartoon, believe me."

"Oohh I know that tone. Full on panty melter then? I want all the deets! I need size, both length and girth, and–" Lucas had interrupted with a very obvious clearing of his throat.

"Listen, I'm not saying I believe this, but whoever you're with... you're ok? You trust this guy?" Luke had sounded skeptical, but Skylar knew it all came from a place of total love and caring and she just wanted to squeeze him.

"Yes, I promise I'm ok. I trust him, and you know how I am with trust. I know it's a lot to take in, so just let it all stew for a bit and then we'll talk more ok?"

They'd both promised they would, but she knew they were both going to dig into it in their own way: Lucas was going to the archives because deep down he was a big nerd, and Z would most likely hit all of the supernatural Shadow Clubs: places where anything dark, illegal, or unusual could be found in the supernatural world. Skylar tried not to worry, knowing that Zahara could take care of herself, but she also wondered if she'd *actually* find anything. None of them had ever thought to ask about anyone with information on gods before, so who knows what she might uncover.

Though overall everything was amazing, Skylar had begun having odd dreams that were making her a little uneasy. They weren't bad or scary necessarily, but they weren't full of rainbows and butterflies either. She dreamt of fire. Every night, she was surrounded by it, could see Hades through it, and knew she had to get to him somehow, but she felt as if she had to let go of him to do that and she couldn't, *wouldn't* lose him. She wasn't afraid of the flames in her dreams, but she couldn't get past them. They pinned her in on all sides and she knew she had to walk directly into them if she wanted out and Dream Skylar couldn't ever take that step.

She had no idea what the dreams meant, but if her previous dreams of Hades had taught it her anything, it was that dreams could be important. The dreams seemed to be becoming more *insistent* as the days wore on, as if begging her to understand the meaning before it was too late. She tried not to let them invade on her happiness during the days, and instead focused on her budding romance with Hades.

One afternoon, they'd explored the lake and waterfall she could spy from her window and it was a memory she'd cherish until the day she died...and not only because of the wicked things Hades had done with his tongue beside those falls as she laid in the softest, most lush bed of flowers.

She smiled at the memory, a soft shuddering rolling through her entire body. She was back at those same falls now, alone. Hades had God of the Underworld business to attend to, so she was exploring on her own. He'd explained what areas to avoid and how to sense the entrances to other realms, so she wasn't worried about ending up somewhere she shouldn't again.

The lake had become her second favorite place, the first being her balcony at night. She was lounging on a large stone that extended over the water, her feet dangling in the cool liquid. She watched as creatures that looked like seahorses but with tails like mermaids danced and played in the water. They were deep greens and reds and teals, but their scales changed colors as they moved and she was mesmerized by the constantly shifting rainbow before her.

Suddenly, the hairs on the back of her neck stood on end and that strange sensation of being watched rushed over her. All of her preternatural instincts went on full alert as she tensed and wheeled around. She leapt into a low crouch on the stone, unsheathing a dagger she had strapped to her thigh under her sundress.

A man stood fifty yards away in front of a portal, its green and gold light shimmering behind him. His head was shaved and strange symbols were tattooed down one side of his scalp and neck, disappearing under his shirt. They were like those tattooed on Emmie and Hades, but these seemed wrong somehow, though she couldn't really explain why. Just a gut feeling. He was tall and broad, though not as tall as Hades nor as broad as Zeus, but similarly built. His eyes were a deep shade of purple, much darker than Emmie's beautiful violet, but she caught flecks of gold when the light hit them. His nose was straight, his lips full, and he was smiling, showing off a killer smile and dimples.

All of the features together should have made him handsome, extremely so, but there was something...off. Something dark and unnatural radiated from him, detracting from the beauty, turning the features into something sinister instead. He cocked his head to the side and a half a breath later, he was before her, not ten feet away. She inhaled sharply in shock though she forced her body to remain in place and ready. She still wasn't used to people "phasing" as Hades had called it. The man studied her intently, letting his eyes roam over every inch of her from head to toe. When his gaze met hers once more, she raised her chin and flashed some fang.

"I'm usually a stab first, ask questions never kind of girl, so I'm only going to give you one chance here: who are you and what do you want?"

His smile widened. "Well, you're quite a bit feistier than the last version. I like it. My brother has always had good taste, I'll give him that."

Brother? Though she hadn't met him yet, she knew without a doubt that this wasn't Poseidon. This was Maynard. Hades had told her all about their fourth, psycho-black-sheep-of-the-family brother, about their ongoing war for the Underworld, and how Persephone had joined Team Evil way back when (which totally explained Hades' trust issues and the complicated feelings he seemed to have about wives and love and marriage).

"You're Maynard," Skylar said, not a question.

He smirked and inclined his head. "My reputation no doubt precedes me." He continued to smile, but there was a bite to his words making her body tense, readying for an attack. Hades had explained that Maynard had crazy dark power—not quite to the level of *actual* dark gods that existed and sounded fucking terrifying, but definitely not anything to turn your nose up at—and Skylar could feel it pulsing from him. She didn't know what would happen if he unleashed it. Did he come there to kill her? The thought left her a little uneasy because she knew damn well if he wanted to, he could do it easily. Even so, she would fight to the bitter end if that's what it came to. *Need to distract him.*

"If you can phase, what's with the portal?" She jutted her chin over his shoulder.

"Sadly, my darling brother has blocked me from phasing directly into the Underworld. I can phase once here, but to enter, I have to go with other means of transportation." He waved a hand negligently behind him towards the glowing portal. "I don't have much time, he'll know I'm here soon, so I'm just going to lay this out there: I want you to help me. I want the Underworld. It should be *mine*," he growled and his eyes darkened, turning completely black. Skylar took a small step backwards as a surge of that dark power swelled around him. Not smoke or flames like Hades. This was more like a cloud of dark gray sparking energy. She eyed it wearily. He noticed and took a deep breath as if to calm himself. His eyes returned to their deep purple and the energy dissipated around him.

He cleared his throat before he said again, calmly, "It should be mine, and I want you to help me win it, once and for all."

"And why the hell would I do that, pray tell?"

"I can only imagine what Hades has told you about me, but he's a liar. I guarantee he's lying to you even now. You don't know him as you think you do." Skylar pressed her lips into a thin, letting him know that she didn't believe a word he was saying. He shook his head. "Let me guess, you agreed to stay for an allotted period of time so he could convince you to marry him, and at the end of such time, he agreed to let you go if that's what you wanted." She raised her chin, refusing to answer and he grinned in response, figuring it out all the same. "I thought as much. Well, I hate to break this to you... Skylar is it?" There was something in his voice that made it seem like that was some kind of joke she didn't get. Her fangs sharpened in irritation. "But he was lying. He has no intention of letting you go— ever. He will do anything, say anything, be anything to get what he wants."

No, she refused to believe it. Hades hadn't lied to her. He wouldn't...would he? *No, no, no.* He was falling head of heels in love with her, she knew it, could practically feel it through the weird connection they shared. But a small voice in the back of her head reminded her that he'd made that promise long before they'd begun to get as close as they were now.

"Has he even told you about the prophecy?" She narrowed her eyes, surprised that he knew about it. Hades had made it seem like only a handful of people did and Maynard was definitely not on that list.

"I know about it," she answered defensively.

"A relief, but just how much about it do you really know?" She sensed truth in his words and uncertainty floated through her mind, just a quick, soft breeze, but it was enough. Maynard's eyes sparkled and she knew that he knew that he'd gotten a foot in the door. *Damn it.* Skylar gritted her teeth and clenched her hands into fists.

"Ask him what the prophecy says *exactly*."

Skylar thought back to the times they'd discussed it and realized he'd never told her the exact language, just a general explanation: a war for the Underworld; she was the chosen one for whatever reason; her and Hades had to get hitched so he could win it. That was it. Was there more to it? Was he hiding something from her? The doubts began to blow harder now, no longer a gentle breeze, but big, sweeping gusts battering her mind and heart, determined to break the trust she'd allowed herself to build up in Hades.

Maynard smiled a sharp, unkind smile. *No.* This was a trick, some of his dark power seeping in and planting doubts in her mind, that was all. She wasn't going to listen to this prick, play his games and let him get in her head. He was just trying to sow discord between her and Hades so that she wouldn't fulfill the prophecy. *Of course.* She arched an eyebrow at him in response.

"I'm not stupid. I know what you're doing and it won't work. I'll never help you." He cocked his head to the side as if listening to something far off.

"Almost out of time. I can tell you're starting to feel all the feels for him as the mortals say, but when you decide that you can't trust him—and believe me, you *can't*—all you need to do is call and I'll get you out of here. Don't forget: if you marry him, you're stuck here for good. If I recall properly, that was a hard limit last time." He smiled that weird inside-joke smile again and Skylar wanted to smack it off of him. "You help me beat him and I'll let you go back to your life. Simple as that." He tossed a small silver ring at her. "When the time comes, just put that on, come to this spot, and twist it counterclockwise three times."

Before she could say anything, he grinned once more and phased back just in front of the portal. A heartbeat later Hades was in front of her, shoving her behind him, glaring at his brother across the distance. Black smoke swirled around them and midnight flames licked down his arms and over his hands. Hades moved forward as if to attack Maynard, but then seemed to think better of it, reaching behind him to lay a protective hand on her arm instead, the flames retreating so that she wasn't burned.

"Miss me, brother?" Maynard mocked.

"If you come near her again, they will never find all of the pieces of your pathetic carcass, Maynard." Tendrils of smoke slithered around Skylar protectively and though the air was tense with the potential danger, she relaxed a fraction. The power within the smoke was still terrifying in its strength and intensity, but she now felt safe within them. She could never fear them again.

Maynard merely arched a brow.

"I wouldn't be so sure...I got her before, I can do it again." Hades stiffened at the words but before he could do anything further, Maynard blew him a kiss and stepped within the portal. As the edges began to close in on themselves, sealing the doorway, he met Skylar's gaze. He nodded to her, almost imperceptibly, and then he was gone. Hades whirled and took her face gently in his hands.

"Are you hurt? Did he touch you?" Something inside cautioned her not to tell Hades what Maynard had said or about the ring, so she casually slid it into her pocket before grabbing his wrists lightly.

"I'm fine, I promise. He didn't even get near me, just watched me for a second from across the way and then you were here." She shrugged. She didn't like lying to him, but her gut told her that it was the right thing, so she listened.

Hades nodded hard. "I'm taking you back to the castle and I want you to stay there. Please. I'm going to make a sweep, make sure that prick didn't do anything else while he was here, didn't hurt anyone. I don't think he has the balls to come back but..." He glanced over his shoulder to where the portal had faded, muscles tense in worry. She didn't like that he was so concerned for her, but she understood. If anything threatened him, she would burn the whole world down to protect him.

She nodded. "Yes, of course." A second later they were on the front steps and Hades was handing her off to Jeff.

"Take her inside and stay close. If anyone other than me or Emmie comes near her, they lose a head, no questions asked. Got it?"

"You don't want me with you, boss? What if it's some kind of trap?" Jeff was already scanning the area, alert and ready. Hades shifted his gaze to Skylar and what she saw in his eyes made her heart thud against her ribs. He was looking at her like she was the only thing in existence, the only thing that mattered...looking at her the way she knew she was looking right back.

"I need you here," Hades said simply, never taking his eyes from hers. He brushed hair away from her forehead. "I have to go. You're safe here, I promise you. I doubt he'd be stupid enough to try to come here himself, but...well, I don't know who I can trust inside now other than Emmie and Jeff and a small handful of others." His brows furrowed and she hated that he didn't even know who he could trust within the walls of his own home. This war had to end sooner rather than later.

"If anyone tries anything, they're as good as dead. I'm kind of a badass, remember?" Skylar said, trying to lighten the mood. She smiled at him and he gave her the tiniest one in return.

"I'll be back soon." He kissed her forehead and was gone.

Jeff gave her his elbow and said in his low, raspy voice, "Shall we?"

Skylar spent the afternoon playing half-hearted Mortal Kombat with Emmie while Jeff stood guard at the door. As the hours grew longer, even Emmie changing her appearance and doing impressions couldn't keep a knot of worry from lodging in Skylar's stomach. She made her way back to her room with her Jeff-shaped shadow and tried to calm her nerves. There was a reason that this war for the Underworld hadn't ended already, prophecy aside. Maynard was dangerously powerful. Did he come back? Did he ambush Hades somehow? Was Hades ok?

The thought of anything happening to him, of possibly losing him, made her stomach clench painfully and she could barely breathe. She didn't *think* Maynard would come after Hades so directly, especially not after he'd just asked for her help, but still, the worry wouldn't ebb. To distract herself, she began replaying her earlier conversation with Maynard. She tried desperately to keep the doubts from surfacing again, telling herself that Maynard was just trying to manipulate her...but she couldn't stop them completely.

Was Hades lying to her? He'd promised she could leave after her month, but would he let her? That lie was a bit moot now that she was planning to stay, but still...if he lied so blatantly about that, would he lie about whatever else Maynard had hinted at? Were there things about the prophecy that she didn't know? Probably...but what? Why did it matter? She was ending up with more questions than answers and began to pace out on the balcony in frustration.

Sklyar searched out over the Underworld, straining her eyes, desperate for a glimpse of Hades. It was stupid of course, but still she searched. It had been hours and the worry was beginning to feel like claws ripping through her chest from the inside. When she was just about to say fuck it and set off to search for him, she felt his presence.

She whirled to find him standing in the center of her bedroom. Her heart stopped and then started beating double time. The claws finally stopped tearing her to shreds and she could actually breathe again. She sprinted forward and leapt into his arms, kissing him fiercely, her lips hard and demanding against his. She hadn't wanted to truly admit how afraid she'd been and now that he was here and safe, she never wanted him gone from her arms again. She pulled back and after he reluctantly set her on her feet, she reared back and punched him in the arm–*hard.*

"Ouch!" He rubbed the spot. "Well, that's a funny way to say *welcome home.*" She punched him again in the other arm.

"I was worried about you! What took you so long? Are you ok? Is everything ok?"

His lips curled into a brilliant, breathtaking smile. "Say that first part again. The part about you being worried sick for your man."

She scrunched her nose up trying to fight a smile of her own. "Oh shut up and tell me what happened."

He pulled her close to him again and brushed the hair out of her face. She wrapped her arms around his waist without a second thought. It was so effortless, so natural.

"Everything is fine now. Maynard let some of his more monstrous lackey demons run lose through some of the villages. They caused a lot of damage and...a good many lives were lost." He clenched his jaw and Skylar hated that his people had been hurt.

"Why do you think he came?" she asked, feeling a little guilty because she already knew the answer. He'd come here for her.

"I think that he knows about the prophecy somehow, which means that someone within these walls is feeding him information, and he came here to take you. Thank all the gods he didn't have time," he added, looking at her so reverently that guilt turned sour in her stomach.

Maynard had had time, plenty of it, but he didn't want to kidnap her. For whatever reason, he wanted her to come to him willingly. She wondered if it was all just a sick game to hurt Hades, trying to turn her against him the way Persephone had all those years ago. Well, like hell that would be happening! A small voice in the back of her mind reminded her about Maynard's accusations, that Hades was hiding things from her and that he'd lied...but she told that voice to shove it. He was allowed to have his secrets, just as she had hers. He would tell her everything when he was ready to, she was sure. But still, she couldn't stop herself from asking the question.

"Hades, is there anything in the prophecy that you didn't tell me about?" He tensed for a fraction of a second before relaxing, but she'd noticed nonetheless.

"No, of course not. Why?" She studied him, trying to gauge if he was lying. The way he'd tensed at the question...well, she couldn't be positive. She wanted to believe that if he *was* lying, he had a good reason. She would give him the benefit of the doubt because that's what you did when you loved someone. Her heartrate sped up, thrumming in her chest like a hummingbird. Yes, she was finally admitting it: she was in love with Hades.

"Just wondering if there was something that we missed that Maynard might be trying to use to his advantage or something." She shrugged and ran a hand down his chest, letting her palm rest over his heart, letting the reassuring, steady beat settle her. "Well, I'm glad that everything was relatively fine out there after his visit, all things considered. I'm sorry for the loss of life though."

"Me too, I..." He took his eyes off her for the first time since he'd arrived and surveyed her room. His eyes flew wide and he looked an adorable mix of astonished and horrified. "What in the hell happened in here?!" She glanced around. It wasn't *that* bad...though she could admit that to a normal person, it might look just a tad bit messy. There were clothes and shoes strewn all over the floor, couch, and coffee table, even hanging off the bedposts and lamps. The cardboard cutout of Ryan Reynolds had become a perfect place to hang her bras. Empty soda cans, water bottles, and food wrappers littered the table and floor. Books and magazines were lying in haphazard stacks throughout the space, and of course weapons were in piles all around them.

His mouth hung open and he looked like he wanted to respond, but honestly didn't know what to say. His gaze roamed over the bed and he frowned in confusion. He glanced around the room again and found what he was looking for on the balcony.

"Why on earth are your covers out on the balcony?" She flushed slightly.

"I, uh, kind of sort of sleep out there?"

She'd reluctantly enforced a no sleepovers rule in addition to the no sex rule, so they'd been sleeping apart every night. She honestly just didn't trust herself enough to sleep beside Hades all night, tucked into his warmth, feeling his hard muscles cradling her, and *not* beg him to fuck her six ways from Sunday. She had a nice little nest out on the balcony where she hunkered down most nights.

"What? Why?"

"It's...it's just so beautiful under the stars here. I feel...complete when I lay under them, like I..." She trailed off, and he traced his thumb lightly over her bottom lip.

"Like you what, love?" he asked quietly.

She closed her eyes and sighed.

"Like I'm home."

She heard him swallow and felt hope pulse from him. As soon as she said the words out loud, she knew. She knew deep in her bones that they were true. This was her home. *Hades* was her home. They were connected in a way she couldn't understand, but couldn't live without. He leaned his forehead against hers and she took a deep, somewhat ragged breath. She'd admitted to herself that she was in love with him. Now it was time to admit it out loud to the God of the Underworld himself.

Here goes nothin'.

TWENTY-EIGHT

Hades met her gaze, her words echoing in his mind. She felt at home here, like she belonged. A part of his mind assumed it was only because she was Persephone reincarnated, that she felt at home here because she had once been bound to this place in another life, but the bigger part was screaming that this had nothing to do with Persephone at all.

Skylar was feeling at home here all on her own, because *she* was connected to this kingdom and to him. He almost laughed at the one-eighty he'd done: when she first arrived he couldn't separate Skylar from Persephone and barely stopped himself from punishing her for past deeds, but now, he could hardly reconcile them as one and the same. He had to admit that he didn't *want* them to be one and the same. He knew what he wanted meant absolutely jack shit and they *were* the same person, that one day Skylar may remember her past life, but he hoped...

Skylar reached up and gently ran her fingers through the hair at the back of his neck, pulling him from his thoughts.

"Hades," she said softly. "I have a very important question."

"And what's that, love?"

She kissed him softly, gently biting on his lower lip. His eyes slid closed and he tightened his grip on her waist, pulling her more firmly against his body. He was barely keeping to their agreement of no sex. If she kept that up, all bets would be off. Hell, he was already hard, just from that tiny nip, just from the feel of her in his arms. He knew that holding off on sleeping together had been the right call. If they had taken that step, he knew he would be lost for her completely, no hope of keeping himself—and his heart—closed off from her any longer. She would have him completely, would have the power to destroy him once again.

But after seeing Maynard anywhere near her today, after thinking about how differently the day could have gone and how easily Maynard could have just ended her with hardly a thought... well, he was done for anyway. He'd known it for a while now, but hadn't fully admitted it until today: he was in love with Skylar. That should terrify him, but all he felt was relief and a sense of rightness. The fist around his heart finally released its grip completely and seemed to whisper *finally* as it dissolved into nothingness. He realized now that he wanted her to marry him, not to fulfill the prophecy, but because he wanted her. He wanted her to be his wife, to be bound to him and belong to him—*with* him—more than he wanted his next breath. He knew it then, deep down on the most basic level of his being: she was his. His one true match. A part of his soul rested in Sky.

Why he'd never felt the pull before with Persephone, he couldn't understand, but he was done questioning it and worrying about it. To be quite honest, he was done even thinking about the past. Skylar was meant to be with him, regardless of the prophecy, regardless of the fact that she was Persephone reincarnated. She didn't *feel* like Persephone to him, she felt only like Sky, his beautiful, perfect Sky. The question was, did she love him in return? Even if she didn't, the love he felt for her was too strong. She had him, had his heart, hook, line, and sinker. He was hers.

She whispered softly against his lips, "Are you sure you want a total slob for a wife?"

He stilled and his eyes flashed open. She pulled back to stare up at him and smiled a gorgeous, mischievous smile. Had he heard her right? Had she just...no, couldn't have...but...

He cleared his throat. "Are you saying what I think you're saying?"

"I'm saying that I would make a pretty badass Queen of the Underworld, dontcha think?" She grinned and his heart nearly burst. He kissed her with almost too much force in his excitement, their teeth clashing together. They both laughed and when he pulled away she said, "I want to do it now. Before. I mean, I want to be your wife the first time we're...I mean the first time that we..." She trailed off and Hades smiled. She was flustered and it was adorable. His cool, confident Black Widow was *nervous*. His heart softened...as other things did the opposite. The thought of finally being with her fully, of stripping her down, sinking deep inside her tight, wet— *Stop! Almost time, but not yet. Focus.*

Hades leaned in and kissed her softly and said in a low, husky whisper, "So, now you're saying that I'm getting lucky tonight?" He wiggled his eyebrows and she laughed, slapping his chest.

"Not if you don't marry me already. Unless it's like a big huge thing? I mean, I doubt we have to go down to the courthouse and get a marriage license, right?"

He chuckled lightly. "No, it's actually a very simple ceremony and it can be just between us. But, I want you to be absolutely certain, Sky. You'll be bound to the Underworld, maybe not able to leave it— you remember that, right?" She shrugged.

"Something is telling me that this is right and that we'll figure out the being bound here thing." He began to protest. He didn't want her holding on to false hope and have history repeat itself again. She put her fingers over his lips to stop him. "So, yes, I'm one thousand percent sure. Just trust me." He nodded and she gave him a quick kiss in reward. "Now, let's get this show on the road. I'm ready to get hitched!"

He laughed lightly but nodded. He reluctantly stepped away from her for a moment and summoned a dagger. The blade was made of a glowing gold and was etched in black runes. Hades sliced his palm and then unbuttoned his shirt enough to reveal the top of his chest before making another small slice there, just over his heart. The wounds didn't immediately heal and Skylar arched a brow.

"Methinks that's no ordinary blade."

"You would be correct. Now, your turn." He held the hilt to her and she took it. Her eyes widened when she felt the power from the weapon surge into her. No ordinary blade indeed. This was a gods-blade. Only a few existed, made by Hephaestus himself before he stopped smithing and began letting his apprentices do all the work (while he retained all the credit of course). There were drops of Cronus' own blood mixed in with the metal, giving each blade a small fraction of his own godly power. They were some of the only weapons that could truly injure a god. Persephone had shoved this very one into his spine all those years ago. Hades gritted his teeth and forced the memories from his mind. Tonight, this blade would be washed clean of its tainted past. It would be used to forge a new future.

"Cut your hand and chest, just as I did."

She nodded and repeated his movements. She didn't even flinch, seeming to not even feel the sting of the blade as it sliced into her skin. He couldn't tear his gaze away from hers and he felt as if the entire world had fallen away around them, that they were the only two beings in existence and that this was the most important moment of his long life. How could it feel so different this time? They'd been here before, but at the same time, this was completely new. He didn't understand, but all he cared about what making the beautiful, perfectly imperfect creature before him his wife. He took one deep breath before he began to speak.

"Blood by blood, heart by heart, soul by soul, I am bound to you. I am yours as you are mine. We are one, now and always. My power is yours. My kingdom is yours. My heart is yours. Protect them forevermore as I will protect yours."

He nodded to her, dying to hear the words from her mouth. She took a deep breath and stared deeply into his eyes for a long moment. He worried that maybe she was having second thoughts, but then she began to speak.

"Blood by blood, heart by heart, soul by soul, I am bound to you. I am yours as you are mine. We are one, now and always. My power is yours. My kingdom is yours. My heart is yours. Protect them forevermore as I will protect yours."

The words were laced in power, more than any magic Skylar had ever encountered. She didn't know if it was because of any actual mythical power they possessed, tying them together, or simply because of what they meant to her. She'd finally found someone that crashed through every wall she'd ever put around herself, even when she hadn't meant to. She meant the words in every inch of her soul. Everything she had, everything she was, everything she would ever be, belonged to Hades. She was his.

Once she finished, he pressed his cut palm to her chest, directly over her wound. She did the same to him, and gasped when the bond between them suddenly flared like fire before snapping into place around them like an iron cuff. A blue-white light seeped from the places where their hands touched each other's chests and black smoke and flames swirled around them like a tiny cyclone.

She closed her eyes and gasped quietly as she felt Hades' power flow through her, mold around every cell in her body and become a part of her. She could feel the Underworld itself, as it were a part of her as well, could feel its energy, its strength, feel the stars and the water and the plants and the beings within it. It...welcomed her? She felt as if it had been waiting for her, the same way she had been waiting for it without even knowing. She knew she was bound to it now, but she didn't feel trapped. No, she felt *free*. For the first time in her life, she truly felt free and if she were right where she was meant to be.

She cracked her eyes open and let the new sensations settle over her. It was strange and a bit overwhelming, but nothing she couldn't handle. Again, it felt too *right* to be too much. She'd been made for this, to share this power and this world, to protect it and the man standing before her. This was her purpose.

Slowly the light faded until finally disappearing. Neither one of them moved for what could have minutes or hours, she had no idea. Finally thoughts started pouring through her mind.

Holy shit. I'm married. I'm married to Hades. I'm the Queen of the Underworld. I'm Mrs. Hades Underworld.

A giggle escaped her lips and she clamped her hand over her mouth. Hades gave her the most devastating, heartbreakingly beautiful smile that had ever existed. She could feel the unmistakable happiness flowing from him now through their connection. She'd caught glimpses of his emotions before, but where that had felt like a sea mist lightly kissing her skin, this was solid wave, crashing against her again and again.

"What's so funny, *wife*?"

She slid her eyes closed. "Mmmm, say that again."

He leaned in and kissed her lightly, whispering the word against her lips. He did the same thing over and over again as he kissed down her jaw, licked in that perfect spot just below her ear, and kissed down her neck. She was shivering and digging her hands into his hair, her self-control slipping with every whisper, every touch.

"Hades..."

He finally made his way back to her mouth, kissing her slow and deep. It began slow and sensual, but it quickly began to spiral out of control, turning into something primal. They both needed this too much, had been waiting too long. He ran his hands down her back, over her ass, and he lifted her up. She wound her legs around his waist and they both moaned when he pressed hard against her. She was still in the sundress she'd been wearing earlier in the day, so all that was between them were his pants and a thin strip of lace. But she wanted *nothing* between them and nearly growled at the audacity of the material to still be in the way. She clawed at his back as their tongues dueled and twined, as teeth clashed, grazing lips and skin.

He walked them backwards to the bed and sank down on the edge. She straddled him, grinding her hips against him, feeling how hard he was beneath her, and yanked the hem of his shirt upwards. He released her long enough to reach back over his head and pull the material off in that sexy way guys do, tossing it behind her somewhere. She ran her hands down his chest, over every rippling muscle on his stomach, across those ridiculous indentions that made her forget her own name. In the next instant he ripped the front of her dress clean in two and groaned when her breasts sprang free. Her nipples were already hard and aching, begging for attention. He immediately took one into his mouth, sucking, biting, twirling his tongue. He reached down and ran his fingers lightly over the lace, teasing and torturous. She shuddered and he made a deep rumpling sound in his chest.

"You're *soaked*," he rumbled against her sensitive skin.

"Only for you, always for you," she panted, grinding her hips, desperate for him to do more, touch more, more, more, more.

He kissed her again and ripped her panties to shreds in one easy movement before thrusting two fingers deep inside her. She cried out against his mouth, digging her hands into his shoulders. She bucked her hips as he moved his fingers, desperate for more. She was riding his hand, begging him to go harder, faster, to never stop.

"Don't stop, please..." He bent his head and traced his tongue around one of her nipples again, teasing, before sucking it hard into his mouth at the same time he pressed his thumb to her clit. She made some kind of semi-embarrassing animalistic sound that she'd never heard before.

"Holy shit...*holyshitholyshitholyshit*, don't stop."

He curled his fingers forward so the tips hit just the right spot, and took her nipple between his teeth, just hard enough to get her attention. The pleasure-pain sensation sent her right over the edge. She cried out and dug her fingers into his scalp, holding him to her breast and shuddering from the orgasm ripping through her. She felt hot, too hot, as if her every nerve ending were on fire, but she'd gladly go up in flames right now, burning forever for Hades and the things he made her feel.

Before she had even stopped spasming, he rolled them over, moving further up onto the bed, pressing his body over hers and bracing his weight on his hands on either side of her head. She moaned, hands digging into his lower back, holding his hips against her as her own rocked forward against him again and again, desperate for more, missing his touch. She had just come but it hadn't even seemed like a release, it had only increased her need to staggering heights. She had to have him tonight, now, this very instant.

Skylar shoved her hand into the front of his pants and gripped him hard, stroking as she yanked his head down to kiss her again. He groaned and arched his hips into her hand.

"Hades, I need you. *Please.*"

"You're sure?"

"Yes, yes, yesyesyes."

He chuckled and grabbed her wrist to stay her hand. She pouted. He began to remove it from his pants and she flashed fang at him in irritation. He merely gave her a sexy smirk and moved her hand upward, trapping them both above her head in one of his big hands, pinning them lightly to the bed. *Ohh I like.*

He kissed her again, sucking and biting on her lower lip until she was squirming against his grip, desperately bucking her hips, needing him so badly she thought she might combust.

"Hades..." she growled.

He laughed again and said a bit hoarsely, "Have an idea."

A second later the entire bed, sans canopy, was outside on the balcony. She gasped and laughed lightly when she gazed past his head and saw an endless midnight sky, the stars dancing above them in their rainbow ballet. They seemed even brighter now, more in focus, and she could *feel* them, like they were a part of her.

She stared into Hades' eyes, seeing so much more than ever before, feeling as if she could see down to his very soul and getting completely lost. She wanted to memorize every single detail of this moment. The way the moonlight reflected off of his raven hair, making some strands appear almost blue, the way the starlight sparkled against his skin as they moved and they danced through the sky, the look of absolute bliss on his face.

He was hers, and she was his.

Forever.

TWENTY-NINE

Skylar was looking at him in such a reverent way, he nearly swept with joy. He was still reeling from the marriage ceremony. The things he'd felt...Well, he could hardly even put them into proper thoughts. He knew now that his entire life had led him here, to this moment. To this perfect female looking up at him like he hung the very stars that soared above them.

To his wife. *His*. Forever.

Hades dipped his head and kissed her softly but deeply, hoping to communicate everything he was feeling without a word. As before, the kiss quickly turned into something hot and wild, dangerous. His control was already completely frayed, hanging on by the tiniest thread. *Must go slow, must stay in control, can't hurt her...*

He kissed down her neck, over her breasts, down her stomach, stopping to dabble in her navel. He kissed her tattoo and lower, but forced himself to move on. If not, he would spend all night worshiping her, devouring her, and he had other plans for now. He would just save the worshipping and devouring plan for tomorrow. He took a deep breath, inhaling her scent. *Ok, maybe later tonight.*

He kissed down her thighs and legs, until he slid off the end of the bed and stood. She pushed up on her elbows to watch him as he unlaced his pants and slid them off. He was so hard it was painful. He'd never been this hard in his very long life, never wanted anyone so badly. He gripped his erection as she watched, a look of absolute hunger on her face, as he rubbed up and down his shaft. Her tongue darted out over her lips and the sight of it made him impossibly harder. He remembered how that tongue felt on him, how hot and wet it had been as she'd licked his cock, how she'd taken him deep in her throat...He groaned as he stroked again, harder.

He inhaled deeply at the sight of her: sprawled, completely bare before him, starlight dancing across her flushed skin. Her nipples were pearled, begging for attention, her lips swollen from their kisses. Her eyes were burning with too many things to name, her fangs glinting in the moonlight, her blonde curls fanned out around her in a halo. He scrubbed a hand across his mouth. *Perfect. She is absolutely fucking* perfect.

He crawled up her body, settling himself over here again. He forced himself to wait though the need to bury himself in his wife was nearly unstoppable. Sweat was beginning to bead on his temples from the force of restraining himself, from the heat radiating from her. He gritted his teeth.

He kissed her again, thrusting his tongue against hers, demanding. She arched her hips upward, doing some demanding of her own. He finally pulled back and pushed up onto his knees. He gripped his cock and positioned it in the right spot, so tantalizing close to heaven that he bit the inside of his cheek until he tasted blood to keep his thoughts and body under control. He didn't move, waiting for her final permission.

"Oh...umm, what about protection?" she asked, breathless, still rocking her hips nearly mindlessly, begging for what he wanted so badly to give her.

"No need. I can't get you pregnant right now...I'll explain later," he said, shaking his head, thoughts so muddled with need that he could barely think straight, let alone explain godly reproductive processes. "And I can't get sick or catch any diseases if that's what you're worried about."

"Oh, well in that case..."

Her gaze turned downright evil and she held his stare. She trailed her hand downward between their bodies and gripped his cock, guiding him forward until the head kissed wet heat that sent a shudder through his entire body, so forceful he had to gnash his teeth.

"Fuck, Sky..." She stared up at him with those beautiful eyes... eyes that had darkened again, he realized. *What the...?*

"I need you, Hades. *Now.*"

"Yes. Now. Going to go slow, don't want to hurt you."

She looked like she wanted to protest, but when she wrapped her hand around his length again, she seemed to realize that slow was probably smart. She bit her lip, her tiny fangs digging into the tender flesh, and swallowed hard. She nodded and when he shifted his hips forward ever so slightly, the first inch of his cock sliding inside his wife, his world nearly exploded.

Fuck. Me.

So fucking hot. So fucking tight. So fucking mine.

She moaned and gripped his hips, but he stilled, forcing himself to stay completely immobile.

"Ok?" he gritted out, sweat rolling down his temples, his chest. His muscles strained as he held himself over her, forcing himself not to thrust into her with all his might, forcing himself not to move a godsdamned *inch* until she told him to.

"*Yes.* More. Please please please."

He smiled and eased forward again, giving her more. He groaned. *Going to be the death of me.*

"You're so fucking tight, love." His fingers clenched on her hip, holding her steady.

"*More.*" She was panting, writhing under him. He wanted to surge forward, give her everything, but he somehow refrained. He knew she was strong, far stronger than she looked, but he could hurt her so easily...

He slid forward another inch, another, another. Slowly, so agonizingly slowly. What seemed like hours later he was as far as she could take him. He stopped, letting her get used to his size. She was so tight around him, tighter than a fist, and he had never felt anything so right, so good. She shifted her hips a bit and he pulled back an inch, then pushed forward again. Another surge of wet heat surrounded him and he was able to thrust even deeper.

"*Fuckkkk*," he groaned through gritted teeth when he was suddenly seated inside her to the hilt. She gasped and dug her nails into his lower back. "Fuck, are you ok? Did I hurt you?"

"I won't be unless you move again. NOW!" He laughed and pulled back again, then shoved forward, still slowly. "Oh god, yes, Hades. Faster. Harder. *Pleasepleaseplease*."

That last remaining thread snapped, his control completely gone. He pulled back, almost completely out of her, before slamming his hips forward once more. She cried out and dug her claws into his back, so deep he felt blood trickling down his sides, but he didn't care. He fucking loved it, would never get enough. He began pounding into her with abandon, hooking his arms under her knees, spreading her legs wider and allowing him to get deeper with each thrust. His smoke began to coil around them, small black flames dancing within them.

"Gods, look at you," he rasped, eyes locked where their bodies met, watching as he sank so deep inside her. "Look take me so fucking well, love."

She whimpered, bucking her hips up to meet his thrusts, digging her claws into the sheets beneath her and shredding them apart.

"Right there...oh gods...going to come...Hades!"

She screamed his name so loudly as she came he thought that it could be heard clear across the Underworld. He had to admit, he kind of liked the idea of every being on the plane hearing his name on her lips like this. The flames in the sconces surrounding the balcony erupted, blazing higher and higher and his own flames mirrored them. He felt as if he were on fire, burning from the inside out. She was burning him to ash and rebuilding him. He was no longer the same man he'd been. He was now hers, body and soul and everything in between. Her husband, her king, her anything and everything.

"Fuck, can feel you coming..."

Her muscles spasmed around him, and he nearly followed her over the edge, but he force himself to hold on. He was determined to draw another orgasm from his wife first. *My fucking* wife. He'd never grow tired of saying that. He pulled her up and into his arms, resting his weight back on his knees, so that she was sitting on his cock. She wrapped her legs around his waist and her arms around his neck. He gripped her ass and wrenched her down as he thrust his ups upward, pounding into her so hard he worried that he must be hurting her, but she only begged for more, clawed at his back, kissed him so deeply that he thought he might die from the pleasure of it all.

He wrapped her hair around one fist and yanked lightly back, forcing her to expose her throat. He kissed and bit, hard enough to leave small bruises, but she demanded more, more, more. She rode him hard as he thrust upwards, pulling his hair, biting his lower lip. He couldn't believe she was meeting him thrust for thrust, wasn't afraid of him, of the...savagery of it. He tried to stop his mind from making comparisons, but it did it anyway. Persephone would have been beside herself if he'd tried to take her this way, would have been terrified, would never have let him near her again. Being able to be with Sky this way was...freeing. She was truly his match, his perfect counterpart in every way.

She leaned in, pressing her forehead against his, and said in a breathless whisper, "I love you." His chest clenched, joy searing every inch of him. He wanted to roar, to beat his chest, to fall to his knees and worship at her feet.

"Again," he commanded. He felt her lips curl upwards against his own.

"I love you."

He reached between their bodies.

"Again."

He rested his fingers just over her clit and waited until she answered before moving them.

"I love you. I love you, I love you."

Gods, he would never tire of hearing it, could barely believe it was real. He pressed down then, putting just the right amount of pressure on the sensitive spot...

She cried out as she came in a rush, the orgasm splintering through her like wildfire. She turned her head so quickly he had barely even realized she'd moved before she bit down on the spot where his neck met his shoulder, drawing blood with her small fangs. The sensation was unlike anything he'd ever experienced and he immediately began to come, taken completely by surprise.

He yelled her name as he came apart, coming inside of her hard and fast as she held her bite, moaning around the spot where her fangs were embedded in his flesh. His flames shot higher within the smoke, swirling and flickering all around them. He had the faintest thought cross his mind that the bite meant something, but it was gone before he could really even acknowledge it.

They collapsed down on the bed, both panting, their bodies slick with sweat. Though he hated the thought of being separated from her, he gently pulled away. She pouted and he laughed. He laid beside her propped up on one elbow. She was practically glowing with satisfaction and love, and no one had ever looked so beautiful. Aphrodite paled in comparison next to his Sky.

His Sky. His wife. His queen.

His.

THIRTY

Skylar was dead. Must be. She must have died and gone to heaven because there's no way that this could be real life, that anything could be this perfect. Sex with Hades had been...cataclysmic? Mind-blowing? Uh-Fucking-Mazing? No word in any known language was good enough to describe it properly. It was more than sex it was...she didn't know how to explain it without sounding like a crazy person or like the biggest sap in the world, but, well, it felt as if their *souls* were joining, not just their bodies. She had felt a part of herself join Hades and a part of him join her during the marriage ceremony, but what she'd felt while he was inside her was something even more fundamental. The voice inside her head had demanded that she bite him, that she mark him as her own, and when she'd slid her fangs into his neck, everything had become clear.

There wasn't Skylar or Hades, there was just them, together, as one. He was *hers*. Whatever she was, she understood that he was her mate, her one and only, her forever.

Her eyes skated to his neck now and she frowned, jerking upright. She'd seen him heal almost instantaneously from injuries.

not a single mark remaining...and yet two small circular scars now marred his perfect skin. She reached out and grazed her finger across them. They felt warm to the touch.

"What's wrong, love?" he asked in a husky voice, brow furrowed.

"Where I bit you...there are scars." He blinked in surprise. "How could I scar you?" He ran his fingers over the marks then, and pursed his lips. Did they feel warm to him as well? What in the hell was going on? He shrugged, as if unconcerned about it.

"Maybe us being bonded now has something to do with it. We'll worry about it later."

She glanced down at him and decided that was an excellent idea. She would much rather stare are her literal dream man in his post-climax perfection. Hair mussed, muscles still glistening with sweat, a self-satisfied grin resting perfectly on his face.

She settled back down, but flipped onto her stomach and rested her chin in upturned hands. He reached out and gently pushed a lock of hair behind her ear. She leaned into his touch like a cat. He hadn't said he loved her back, but she knew he did. She could feel it through their connection, in the way he touched her, the way he breathed her name. She wouldn't push him on saying the words though. Given his past, she understood why he may be scared to admit to falling again. She could wait.

She slowly traced the lines of his tattoo lightly with her finger as he leaned back against the pillows, an arm tucked behind his head. He looked so at ease, so content, she wanted to see him this way every day for the rest of eternity. *If I ever freaking transition into immortality that is.*

"So, what's the story with the tattoo anyway? Drunk on spring break?" she teased.

"No, that's the story behind the tattoo on my ass," he said with a wink and she sniggered. "*This* one," he nodded towards his chest, "is one my brothers and I all have."

"Ah, so a brotherly bonding thing then." He chuckled, the sound sending shivers down her spine and heat through her belly. Could she already be wanting more? She gazed down at his chest, letting her eyes wander to his stomach, watched the sheen of sweat catch the starlight...oh yeah. She could definitely be wanting more already, but she forced herself to behave...for now.

"Sort of. We like having the matching mark, that's true, and chose the design to represent all of us, but these symbols around the outside, they bind us together, allow us to pull from each other's power and communicate telepathically, even across great distances."

"That's pretty cool actually."

He raised an eyebrow and gave her a light smack on the ass. She yelped and his lips curled upward.

"Your turn." He trailed his fingers lightly up and down her back, goosebumps erupting across her skin. *If he keeps doing that, there won't be any more talking.*

Forcing herself to focus, she said, "I don't really know exactly. The rose goes back to my dad. He used to leave a single rose for me in my room every time I came home from a mission. I kept every single one, dried them in between books. They're all in this old shoebox in the back of my closet."

She huffed out a small laugh and then a slice of pain speared her chest. She hadn't thought of the roses in a while, and then she realized that she'd never get another one, that one hadn't been waiting for her when she got home from the job with the Russian. He'd already been gone by then. She felt tears burn the back of her eyes and scrunched her nose to try to stem them. She cleared her throat before continuing.

"So, I wanted the rose, but it felt like something was missing when it was just the flower. For whatever reason, I kept coming back to fire, so I added that to it."

He leaned up and kissed her softly. "It's perfect. Beautiful but deadly, just like you." He lingered, the kiss slowly starting to deepen. He pulled back and ran his thumb along her cheekbone, making her melt. He was gazing at her in what looked like wonder. "What are you, Sky?"

She stiffened, immediately feeling defensive. She didn't know why. It wasn't like she needed to keep her secret anymore, didn't *want* to, but...well, she was a little embarrassed. She hated not knowing who she was—*what* she was—being a freak even within the world of freaks. She knew Hades wouldn't see it that way, wouldn't judge her, but she wasn't used to this whole letting people in thing. She wanted to be though, wanted to break down any wall that could possibly remain between them, so she took a deep breath and let it out slowly.

"I...I don't actually know. No one does." His brows furrowed in confusion.

"What do you mean no one knows?"

She sat up on her knees beside him, resting a palm on his chest, just over his heart, not seeming to be able to go two seconds without touching him. The steady beating calmed her and gave her strength. *Here we go.*

"They found me wandering around the street when I was about five, that's what they guessed anyway. I was covered in blood—not my own—and babbling nonsense. I knew nothing of the supernatural world until much later, but even once I started exhibiting my preternatural traits, we still didn't know what exactly I was. I have traits similar to multiple species: speed, strength, claws, fangs, maybe even my looks and voice. But I don't fit into any one of them quite right, even hybrids. I accepted a long time ago that I would never know. I can't tell you how much research we've all done trying to figure it out and we've never gotten anywhere close to an answer. But even so, I still feel...incomplete, like I can't ever be whole without knowing the truth of what I am, where I came from."

He placed one hand over hers and squeezed reassuringly.

"We'll figure it out, Sky. I promise you. You've got the King of the Gods looking into it now and when Zeus finds a puzzle, he's like a dog with a bone. Plus, Emmie knows, she's just not spilling the beans. I'm not above torture if need be." He gave her a reassuring smile and she blew out a long breath, relaxing and laughing lightly. She had forgotten that Emmie knew, so she felt better knowing at least *someone* in the world did and one day she would find out the answer as well.

She tensed when he asked, "How soon after they found you did your dad adopt you then?"

She looked down at where their hands touched over his heart. *You can do this, you can do this, you can do this.* She'd never shared her full history with anyone before, not even Zahara or Luke. They each knew bits and pieces, knew she had a shitty childhood before Dalton found her, but not the details, *never* the details. But...she found herself wanting to share everything with Hades, wanting him to know everything about her, the good, the bad, and the ugly. *Well, here comes the ugly, baby.* She swallowed hard and met his gaze.

"Are you sure you want to hear this? There are parts that aren't exactly...pleasant."

He immediately became serious and pushed himself up, resting his back against the headboard. He seemed to know instantly that he wasn't going to like this story and he was on edge. She could feel his apprehension pulsing between them through their bond. It was still a little strange to be able to feel someone else's emotions, but it felt like such a fundamental part of her, of them together, already, that she knew she'd get used to it soon enough.

"Tell me. Now," he demanded in a rough voice, but added softly, "Please, Sky. I need to know."

She loved when he called her that. So, she steeled her nerves, squeezed his hand for dear life, and dove into the story that she'd never shared with anyone else in her life.

"Ok here goes: I spent three years in foster care before landing a permanent home...but that home wasn't with my dad. Another couple adopted me first, when I was eight. On the outside, they were perfect. Perfect big, white house with blue shutters and flower boxes under the windows, and a white picket fence around the front yard.

Perfect blonde, member of the PTA, former beauty queen, cookie-baking wife. Perfect handsome, former football star turned local newscaster husband. So, they needed the perfect little blonde, obviously absolutely *adorable*, adopted daughter because unfortunately the happy couple weren't blessed with the ability to conceive."

She swallowed hard before continuing, and Hades interlaced their fingers, pushing his strength into her, giving her all that she needed.

"But on the inside, it was a nightmare. They were terrible people, truly awful. My "mom" drank all day when she wasn't screwing the guy who cleaned the pool—I mean, how cliché right?—and usually forgot to feed me breakfast or lunch if I wasn't in school...usually forgot I existed at all unless I disturbed her, which I learned after being locked in a closet for two days *not* to do. And *him...*"

Skylar inhaled deeply and cleared her throat once...twice. It was too dry, she couldn't get anything past it. Her heart beginning to hammer in her chest, her palms and brow beginning to sweat. *A locked door, the stench of stale beer, that terrible look in his eyes...*She squeezed her eyes shut against the memories. Hades must have felt her rising panic either through the connection or just because he seemed to understand her better than anyone ever had before.

"Hey," he whispered quietly as he pulled her into his lap, wrapping one arm protectively around her while sliding the other gently across her cheek. "Hey, it's ok, you don't have to..."

Her heart rate began to slow and her panic began to recede. She sighed. *You can do this. With him by your side, you can do anything.* She opened her eyes and met his gaze. His eyes were worried and fearful, and she leaned in and kissed him softly before pulling away and letting out a long breath.

"Well, he was an asshole. Took out his frustrations about his lackluster stardom and whore of a wife on me." She nodded over her shoulder. "Those marks are burns. He put out cigarettes on my back, where no one could see, of course." Hades stiffened, his entire body going taut, but she continued on because if she didn't, she'd never get it all out. "He dislocated my shoulder once, told the doctor I fell climbing a tree. A broken finger was me "slamming my hand in the car door"...you get the idea. It was always spread out enough that the doctors never questioned it, just normal kids being kids kind of accidents, you know? And it wasn't always like that, only when he got in his moods and got drunk, but it was never good, never happy. My room was locked from the outside, the windows were nailed shut. I didn't have any toys or books or anything like that. Wasn't allowed to have friends over or go to birthday parties. It was...well, it was just bad. Really fucking bad."

Hades was breathing hard through his nose, his jaw clenched so tightly she thought the bones might crack. He was so coiled so tight it looked like his muscles might burst through his skin. Absolute rage was rolling off him in waves. His smoke was coiling around them again, but this time it wasn't in a loving, protective cocoon like when they were having sex. No, this was a storm of simmering anger, a viper ready to strike out against the ones who'd hurt her. She could *feel* his hatred and his...helplessness? That one tore at her heart and she wanted to erase his hurt and pain more than she'd ever wanted anything before. She knew in that moment that she would do anything to protect this man, go to the ends of the earth, or the dimension, or whatever, if it meant keeping him from pain and keeping him safe. All over again, incredulity and rage boiled inside her chest at Persephone, at the fact that she'd fucking dared to hurt him, almost gotten him killed.

She tamped that away, knowing now was not the time to lash out at a ghost. Hades was quiet for a long minute, but she could tell he was working up to something, so she gave him time.

He finally asked in a deadly quiet voice, "Did he ever...touch you?" Flames shot within the smoke around them and danced across his knuckles. She eyed them from her peripheral. She wasn't afraid of them, but she understood the power they held.

"No, never," she reassured him. Hades let out a long breath and she continued, needing to get the rest of the story out. "He started looking at me differently when I turned eleven, in a way I knew even then meant something bad. He came into my bedroom late one night and I just *knew* he planned to...that he planned to..." She tried to swallow past the lump her in her throat. "Well it doesn't matter. I guess that's when something inside me finally kicked into gear. My nails grew into claws and my fangs shot out. He tried to grab me and I sliced at his chest, cutting so deep I hit bone, and then shoved him as hard as I could. He flew clear across the room and slammed into the wall, like he was nothing more than a ragdoll. I didn't know what was happening, how I was doing any of it, but when he hit the wall, it jarred the door open. I knew I wasn't going to get the chance to run again, so I bolted. I was so fast, I practically flew down the hallway and stairs, so fast that I thought for a minute that I teleported from one place to another. I grabbed the bitch's purse on my way out the front door. That was it. I had no shoes on, no jacket, only pajamas with ducks on them and eighty bucks cash that I fished out of her wallet before tossing the purse in the yard.

I had no idea where to go or what to do, but I just kept running. I ran and ran and ran, until I couldn't anymore. I ended up downtown in this really nice little park by the river. We'd had pictures taken there once to keep up appearances as the perfect, happy family. It had actually been a pretty good day—they'd both been in good moods, they'd let me play with other kids on the playground after the pictures, we had a picnic by the water and they'd let me have cheesecake. Maybe my mind decided that I had actually felt somewhat safe at that park once upon a time, surrounded by other people who saw us as a normal family, so there's where I ended up. I curled up in the little tunnel thing on the playset, exhausted and terrified. I don't know if I was more afraid that they would find me and take me back to that house, or that someone would see my claws or my teeth and take me away somewhere. I was too keyed up I guess because they wouldn't retract, so I was walking around looking like something out of a horror movie. I mean, something had to be wrong with me, right? I had claws and fangs for crying out loud, I was a freak."

She spit the word, irritated that she still felt that way, after all these years. "Anyway, I had been on my own for about a week when my dad found me."

Skylar smiled fondly now and Hades squeezed her closer to him.

"I was digging through a dumpster outside of a swanky club when he came out the back door. He spotted me and I froze. I still remember how impossibly huge he seemed. I mean, he is—*was*." She closed her eyes against the pain in her chest and Hades rubbed her back in soothing circles. "He *was* a big man, but to me in that moment I would have sworn he was ten feet tall. I can't imagine what he thought when he saw me. I was dirty and bloody, no shoes, torn pajamas, a little runt of a thing digging through a damn dumpster. But he noticed my nails and fangs, noticed how terrified I was, though I didn't cower from him despite the fact that danger practically pulsed from him. I vowed when I left that house that I'd *never* cower to anyone ever again," Skylar said fiercely.

"After a long moment, he nodded his head and said simply 'you're scared, but strong, and no one will ever hurt you again. I promise you. Now, come with me and let's get you a cheeseburger.' That was it. No questions, no trying to take me back where I came from. He just *knew*, knew that I had escaped something terrible and that he was meant to be my dad, that I was meant to be his daughter. He took me with him back to Virginia and within a few days had all the paperwork in place—a perk of working for people that weren't always necessarily above-board was getting forged paperwork was easy peasy." She gave Hades a small smile.

"After that, I was officially Skylar Pembroke, officially his daughter, and that was the day my life really began. He explained about the supernatural world and eventually taught me everything he knew. I learned to fight, use weapons, scheme and lie and disappear. I became a thief, a spy, an assassin, a mercenary, a ghost, a distraction —anything and anyone. I joined the company as soon as I was old enough. Something about fighting and battle and danger just...called to me, like I was built for it. It all came so naturally. We always try to be on the right side of things when it comes to jobs, but sometimes there is no right side and we just do the best we can. My hands are far from clean...but I don't think you mind that." She quirked a brow at him, a flirty, challenging look in her eyes and he tried to smile back but couldn't seem to manage it. She let out a long breath.

"I don't know what I would have done if he hadn't found me."

Hades continued rubbing her back but seemed lost in his own thoughts. He was still tense and she wondered what kinds of thoughts must be flying through his mind, but he only said softly, "Tell me about him." She knew it was going to hurt, but she wanted to tell Hades about her dad, wanted him to know Dalton as best as he could through her words since they would never have the chance to meet.

"He was amazing. He was this huge, terrifying man—a born lupin, so you know how they are—but really he was the biggest teddy bear. I mean, don't get me wrong, he was lethal and brutal and had more blood on his hands than I even know, but that was only part of who he was. With me, with the people he cared about, he was a big softie with a huge heart. He had the best laugh, and when he really got going, he would do this weird wheezing chuffing sound, like that dog from the old *Hanna Barbara* cartoons...you probably have no idea what that is, but there's this cartoon dog who does this crazy laugh." She chuckled and shook her head. Tears began to pool in her eyes, but she didn't fight them, not now. The time had come to finally face this. She realized it wasn't fair to her father to keep pushing all her memories of him away, keeping them behind a wall. He deserved better than that from her. He deserved to be remembered, to be in her thoughts.

"He lost his pack when he was younger, and when word spread of how he'd tracked down and...*handled* those responsible, other people in the supernatural world took note and started hiring him for jobs. His clientele and jobs kept growing and growing, the demand for his talents becoming too much for just him. He started recruiting friends and even a few rivals and it all eventually became

Willow Corp." She was quiet for a moment and then continued on as tears slipped slowly down her cheeks. "He called me Rocket, like Rocket Raccoon, because he found me digging in the trash can. He loved scotch and *The Rolling Stones*, and he insisted on eating cake for breakfast on anyone's birthday. He secretly loved chick-flicks, though he would make a big show out of being "forced" to watch them. He cried like a baby when we watched *The Notebook*. He was a pool shark, spoke fourteen languages, loved dad jokes, could kill a man in about a thousand different ways, and made the absolute *best* chocolate chip pancakes. He –" Her voice broke but she managed to push out. "He saved me, in so many ways. And I miss him. God, I miss him so much. It's not fair. He was just gone! I came home and they told me he was dead and I didn't even get to say goodbye. Didn't even have a body to bury. I just...I should have been there, I should have gotten to say goodbye."

She sobbed then, great big ones that racked her entire body, her face buried in Hades' chest, fingers gripping him so hard, she knew she would be leaving bruises on anyone else. She thought she might cry forever, thought she could physically feel her heart breaking, and Hades held her through it all, letting her shatter. As her tears finally began to slow and the shudders finally subsided, she felt Hades somehow putting the pieces back together again, without a single word. Eventually she pushed off of him, sniffling, knowing she looked like a hot mess. Hades gently wiped the remaining tears from her cheeks.

"Thank you. I...I needed that. I've been super mature about this and basically refused to think about it or accept it."

"No thanks necessary. I understand. When you live as long as I have, you lose people along the way. It never gets easier, I won't lie to you, but you learn to keep living, allowing each loss to leave its mark on you, for better or for worse. They make you who you are, and as long as you keep their memories alive, they're never truly gone." He brushed her hair out of her face and kissed her on the forehead, then the tip of her nose, and finally her lips.

She melted into him, moving to straddle his hips. He tensed for a moment, but then relaxed and settled his hands on her hips. They took things slow this time, each savoring every touch, every moment, every breath, learning every inch of each other.

Hours upon hours later, they were finally sated and dozing off as the sun began to rise, and Skylar didn't think that a more perfect moment had ever existed.

THIRTY-ONE

Zahara Massoud was dressed to kill—literally—in skintight black jeans, a leather corset top, thigh-high leather high heeled boots and so many weapons hidden on her that she'd lost count. She sauntered up to the front doors of Wayward, an upscale club in the heart of D.C. that also happened to be a Shadow Club: the choice haunt of the supernatural world's less than reputable crowd. If you needed information, weapons, poison, anything you could think of that was out of the ordinary or not quite above board, you went to a Shadow Club. There were several spread out in supernatural-rich areas across the world.

Of all of them, Wayward was by far Zahara's favorite and she'd been there a time or twenty over the years, sometimes on jobs, sometimes just for funsies. She liked the atmosphere, liked the non-mainstream information that floated around, liked a few of the regulars. It was through one of those regulars that she'd managed to track down someone who supposedly knew some information about the gods. She still felt a little weird thinking the words, like they could *actually* be real, but she had always had an open mind and wouldn't discount the possibility yet. Lucas didn't want her to go down this road, but she was prepared to do anything to make sure Skylar was ok. And if she wasn't, well, Zahara would also do anything to fix that, even pick a fight with the gods.

She made her way through the club. The lights were low, the furnishings lush and high-end, in shades of deep blues and golds. There were shady alcoves with velvet sofas, and booths set at intervals along the walls. Music thumped in the background, not loud enough to be over powering like a dance club, but loud enough that conversations couldn't easily be overheard. She sauntered to the bar where she spied Maxwell, a half vampire, half incubus, whole lot of yum, who had found this contact for her. He was on the tall side and though he was lean, he was all sculpted muscle. He had startling golden eyes, sandy brown hair, and the kind of lips that made girls to do stupid things...had made Zahara do stupid things on more than one occasion.

"Hiya, handsome." She kissed him on the cheek and slid into the chair next to him.

"Zahara." His eyes traveled up and down her body. "Mmm, mmm, mmmmm. You're trying to kill me in this outfit tonight, girl." He ran his tongue along one of his fangs and she smiled. He could do wondrous things with those fangs...She shook herself. *Not the time, Z.*

"So, where's my guy?" she asked, signaling to the bartender for a drink.

Maxwell held a hand to his heart, pretending to be wounded. "And here I was thinking that *I* was your guy, darlin'." He'd been around for centuries and had spent almost all of that time in the deep south for unknown reasons. Z secretly dug his cute little southern twang.

"Oh, always, you know that. Let me rephrase: where is the guy I'm supposed to be meeting tonight?"

He nodded in satisfaction. "Better. What's your sudden fascination with mythology anyway?"

Zahara took a long sip of her Old Fashioned and shrugged. "Call it a pet project."

He gave her a skeptical look before his attention was snagged by a nymph in a sparkling silver mini-dress. Oh, Maxwell was on the hunt tonight, that was for sure. Zahara shook her head and smiled. Maxwell had very few interests that didn't involve his cock, but it's not like he could help it. The incubus side of him literally fed off of sexual gratification, and vampires were known for their lusty natures as well. Somehow biting and fangs and drinking blood got all tied up together in their brains with sexy fun times. She shivered at the thought of the times she'd spent with Maxwell, how she'd benefited from that crazed lust-lust meets blood-lust moment at the height of passion. *Don't knock it til you've tried it, friends.* The nymph caught his stare, gave him a devilish smile, and crooked her finger at him.

He drained his drink, kissed Zahara on the cheek, and said, "That is definitely my cue to leave. God I love nymphs...mmm mmm mmm. Always a pleasure, darlin'. I'll be around when you're done if you want company." He winked and then gestured over her right shoulder to a booth in the far corner, hidden in the shadows. "He's over there. Be careful, beautiful."

"Always am," she said before he swept the nymph up into his arms and carried her into the darkness.

Z drained her glass and made her way to the booth. A male with deep bronze skin, eyes the color of warm honey, and strange silvery symbols tattooed along his neck lounged across one seat. She plopped down on the other side, sizing him up. Something was most definitely different about him. She was a Soul Seer, or part Soul Seer anyway on her mother's side, and could see flashes of any person or creature's past deeds, good and bad, and the color of their soul. It could be overwhelming sometimes, with all the shitty people in the world who did even shittier things, but the flashes didn't last long and then they were gone. A true Soul Seer could call up the memories anytime they wanted, not just get a slideshow thrown at them the first time they met a person, but she could rarely pull that off. A point her sister *loved* to throw in her face. She barely stopped herself from rolling her eyes. She and her sister were...complicated.

This guy was unlike anyone she'd ever met before though. She caught glimpses of battles in worlds she'd never seen, among creatures she had no names for. Tender moments and laughter, fights and heartbreak. Pain. Lots of pain. There were too many images, too many flashes. That could only mean he had been alive for a long, *long* time. Not only that, but his soul didn't look...normal. The color of someone's soul hung around them like a very faint, hazy outline and she usually had to concentrate to see it, but his was a bright silver that outlined his body perfectly. It was just there, no concentration required. *What the hell?* She'd never seen silver before, so she didn't know exactly what it meant, but it didn't speak of ill-will or an overly sinister nature, so she decided to just go with it. She'd promised herself she'd keep an open mind with all this gods stuff, so she was going to have to live up to that promise it seemed.

"So, you know about..." She felt a little silly saying it, but if there was one place she could say it without someone thinking she was bonkers, it was here. "About the gods?"

"That I do." His voice was low and husky. He leaned forward, resting his elbows on the table, and popped a toothpick in his mouth. "Why are you interested?"

"None of your concern. I want to contact them. Is that possible?" He studied her for a long time. She didn't flinch, didn't fidget, just stared at him straight in the eye. She wouldn't be cowed or intimidated. She arched a dark brow at him after a few moments and he finally let out a long breath.

"Yeah, it is. It'll cost you though."

She hid her excitement behind a bored façade. "Name your price."

He huffed out a laugh. "*My* price is two grand, but there's another that you'll have to pay to the one you summon. Seven days. You'll be bound to whoever you summon, or whoever answers the call I should say, for seven days. They'll be free to do with you what they will, ask of you what they will. You won't be able to deny them much of anything. Are you prepared for that?"

She didn't have to debate. She was strong and deadly and a certified badass. She could handle anyone and anything for a week. Plus, this was for Skylar, her sister not by blood, but by choice. Skylar had saved her life too many times to count, in more ways than Sky could ever know. She was worth any price.

"I am." She shoved a wad of cash across the table to him. "So, how do I do this?"

He took a long drink and then said, "*You* don't do anything, not without me. I have to open the lines of communication first, then you can take it from there. You just tell me when and where—probably somewhere with a little privacy, if you want my advice. The gods can be...intense. And unpredictable."

She studied him critically as he ran his finger along the rim of his glass.

"How do you know this anyway?" Zahara asked.

"I spent time with some of the folks you're interested in. That's all you need to know."

"Spent time? With the *gods*? What does that even mean?"

"What part of 'that's all you need to know' did you not understand?" he asked as he drained his glass.

Zahara smirked and shrugged. Who was she to pry into people's secrets? Well, more than she already did without meaning to anyway.

"Fair enough. Can we do it now?"

"What's the rush?" he asked, eyeing her.

"Yes or no?"

He sighed. "Well, I have a date, but I can cancel...for an extra thousand." Z rolled her eyes and tossed another wad of cash across the table.

"Ok, let's go. I've got a place where we won't be disturbed." She had no idea what contacting gods would entail, but he'd said privacy was ideal. She slid out of the booth and as he shifted to exit as well, she placed her hands flat on the table. She leaned down so they were eye to eye, only a few inches separating them. "If this turns out to be some kind of trap, or you tricked me into summoning Bloody Mary or Candyman or some shit, I will end you—*slowly*. Understood?" The man's lips curled into an attractive smile.

"I like you. I think whoever gets stuck with you for a week will have their hands full. May I recommend Zeus himself? He could stand to get knocked down a few pegs."

She led the way out of the club towards her Astin Martin DB11. She'd liberated it from a douchebag CEO that had embezzled millions from his company, leaving his employees jobless and penniless, and fled to Italy to live a life of luxury. When her team was done with him, he didn't need the car anymore, and it needed a new home. It was a rescue car, so to speak, just like a puppy. She gave it a loving stroke as she walked down the length of the hood towards the driver's door. The man let out a long whistle.

"Hot damn. What exactly do you do for a living?"

Zahara flashed him a smile. "You don't wanna know…just know that I'm very, *very* good at it."

When he slid into the passenger seat, she started the car, loving the purr of the engine. She whipped away from the curb at a speed that was not exactly "safe" according to mortals, but she was more than mortal, her reflexes keener. Plus, even if they did crash there was a 99.98% chance that she'd survive unless she got decapitated or burned to a crisp. Perks of immortality. She rubbed the steering wheel soothingly. *Not that I'd ever wreck you, baby. Don't worry.*

"So, what's your name anyway?" Zahara called over the sound of the wind wiping through the windows she'd rolled down. She sped through the streets, weaving in and out of traffic, drawing plenty of attention, but she didn't care. They had enough clients in high places around here that if she were to be stopped, it wouldn't matter. She had this thing about going fast, getting her adrenaline pumping. Call her a junkie if you wanted, but she couldn't get enough. And she'd be lying if she said that the adrenaline junkie part of her wasn't excited about the possibility of speaking to actual gods…and ok, fine, even of being saddled with one for a week. What the hell kind of shenanigans would a god get into? She was dying to find out. Zahara was what you might call a little wild. She had her reasons, but she rarely missed a chance to experience anything—good, bad, exciting, painful. She soaked up every single thing she could.

"Allister. You?" She debated lying for half a second but decided it wasn't worth her time or energy. Maxwell probably already told him anyway and he'd either forgotten or was using as an opportunity to test her, see if she would lie. So, she hit him with the truth.

"I'm Zahara."

She drove them to one of her safe houses in a secluded area on a lake in Maryland. It was normally about an hour drive from the club, but when speed limits don't apply to you, you can make it in half that time.

"So this seven days thing, does that start as soon as someone picks up our call, or is it later, or what?"

Allister shrugged. "It can be whenever they decide. It can be seven days all at once, it can be spread out over the rest of your life. It can be tomorrow or an eternity from now."

As they made their way inside, she cleared her schedule for the next week, just in case, texting Lucas that she doing recon on a potential job offer and she'd be in touch. He didn't question her, just told her to be safe. She sighed. She wished she could love Lucas as something more than a friend or brother, but no dice. They were close and they sometimes relieved stress together—and boy oh boy was Lucas McBride good at relieving some stress—but there was nothing deeper between them. Life probably would have been easier if they could be more, but it just wasn't in the cards.

She wondered sometimes if it were in the cards for her at all. Relationships were hard when you could see every misdeed your significant other had done, could see if their soul was a piece of shit hiding behind a pretty face. Whatever, it didn't matter. She had plenty of fun and didn't need all the flowers and cuddles and other girly bullshit afterwards. Really. She didn't want it at all. *Keep telling yourself that.*

Once inside the cabin, they pushed the living room furniture up against the walls to give Allister space to do whatever the hell it was he was going to do. A thought hit her then.

"Wait, this doesn't call for like a human sacrifice or something, right?"

He rolled his eyes and threw his arms wide. "And where, pray tell, do you think I'm hiding a human sacrifice on my person?" Her lips curled upwards and she decided that she liked Allister already. She held up her hands in surrender.

"No, the whole sacrifice thing was never something the gods demanded or wanted. I think Ares said it as a joke at one point, like 'bring me the blood of my enemies at least if you're going to summon me!" you know? And somehow that got around but lost in translation and then mortals were offing each other left and right to catch a god's attention. It was a messy few centuries." He shook his head and went about clearing the rest of the furniture out of the way, but Z tilted her head as she watched him. He talked about it...as if he'd *been* there. *What the...*

She expected him to maybe draw some symbols on the floor and say some crazy sounding incantation or something, but all he did was stand in the middle of the floor and close his eyes in concentration. The symbols on his neck began to glow and when he opened his eyes, they had had turned silver. The air in front of them began to shimmer slightly.

He looked to her and said, "Ok, now you need to call forth your chosen victim...I mean, god." He winked at her then told her what she needed to do.

She gave Allister a skeptical look, but nodded and reasoned through what she should do. Skylar said she was with Hades, but if that were true and she summoned him, would that put Skylar at risk somehow? She claimed she was safe and happy, but Hades had a bad rap. *I mean he's basically the devil right?* No, better not risk that. She decided if she was going to do this, she might as well swing for the fences. She was going straight to the top.

"I humbly beseech an audience with Zeus, God of...Thunder? I think...or is that Thor?...Shit. Umm Zeus, King of the Gods." She glanced at Allister who looked to be trying desperately to hold in his laughter, his shoulders shaking slightly. She threw her hands up in exasperation. "The guy with the lightning bolts and fidelity issues that lives on Mount Olympus, ok? I call Zeus forth...and you better fucking show," she added in a huff.

Allister didn't try to hide his laughter now, shaking his head. "Well, that's one way to do it I guess."

"Shut it. It's not like I summon gods on a daily basis, ok? I improvised." She shrugged and waited, holding her breath. "If they don't answer, do I leave a voicemail or something?" she whispered, bouncing from foot to foot as anticipation and excitement and a little bit of a fear swirled inside her chest.

"Just give it a second," Allister said, cocking his head to the side as if he could hear something. "Someone is answering..." The shimmering area in front of them began to glow with bluish white light, so bright she had to avert her eyes for a moment. The light faded and she looked back again with a gasp, stumbling backwards a few steps.

Possibly the most perfect man she'd ever seen or imagined stood before her. He was tall, with golden skin, golden blonde hair that hung to his shoulders, a golden blonde stache and beard—dude was all about the golden apparently—and piercing sky-blue eyes. He was broad and built, his arm and chest muscles seeming cut from stone and fully on display in the flowing white toga he wore. It was as if he stepped right out of painting. A crown of golden lightning bolts sat atop his head. He was the exact image that the name Zeus called forth in her mind.

Suddenly, images began to assault her, thousands of them, maybe more. Full scale battles unlike anything she'd ever seen or could imagine. One-on-one fights, both real ones meant to inflict real damage and playful ones with what she could only assume were friends or family. Beautiful places she could barely comprehend. Terrifying places she wanted to forget. Family, lovers, friends.

Torture, vengeance, pain. She couldn't keep them all straight and there were more than just images, there was an intense, unmistakable power coming with them. It wasn't painful exactly, but it wasn't pleasant either.

Her hands flew to her temples and she squeezed her eyes shut, but that didn't stop the images. She ground her teeth and finally, *finally* they began to subside. She knew only a few seconds had passed though it had felt like hours to her. She felt sweat beading along her forehead and on the back of her neck and willed her heartbeat to slow.

She opened her eyes and blinked as the images burning on the backs of her eye lids began to fade. His light was even more bizarre than Allister's was. Zeus's light was a bright, you guessed it, faintly glittering gold, radiating out from him like the halo of a lightbulb. *Whoa.*

He looked her up and down, taking his time, and she felt it like a caress against her skin. Somehow she forced herself not to shiver. His eyes met hers and *fuck me*, she was suddenly drowning, lost in a sea of need and connection and things she couldn't even explain. This man, this god, was...She swallowed hard. *Couldn't be. No fucking way.* She sucked in a quick breath, trying to calm her thoughts and find her center. She'd been trained by the best and knew how to handle any situation. Tension seemed to shoot through him for a moment, but it was gone so quickly that she thought she'd imagined it.

His lips curled into a smile, revealing straight, white teeth. She finally understood why people said that someone who was attractive was built like a Greek God: he was *magnificent.* He crossed his arms over his massive chest and she most definitely did not bite her lip at the way his biceps bulged even more with the movement. *You aren't here to bone Zeus, you're here on a mission. Head in the game!*

Zeus' gaze shifted to the right and his brows shot up.

"Allister? Well, hell, if I had known it was you, I wouldn't have bothered with the whole–" he gestured up and down his body–"thing." A second later he was in leather pants and a...David

Bowie t-shirt? Zahara almost snorted. "It's been a while since anyone has used the old ways to summon me, I figured I should come in all God of Thunder and Lightning, ya know? Don the whole persona." Allister laughed and glanced towards Zahara.

"I think you had the desired effect." Zeus slid his gaze to Zahara once more, lips shifting upward into a sexy little smirk, which reminded her to shut her still-gaping trap. He focused back on Allister.

"It's been too long, old friend. How are things here on the Mortal Plane?"

"I can't complain too much."

"You could come home you know. We miss you." He paused for a moment before continuing a little softer, "Hermes would love to see you...to apologize..." Allister clenched his jaw and a look of both pain and longing passed over his face before he cleared his throat and wiped the emotions away. He eyes met Zahara's and she arched a brow in question.

"Bad breakup. I'll tell you about it over some very strong vodka one day."

She nodded. She had a feeling that she and Allister would indeed become friends, and her feelings were rarely wrong. They weren't quite premonitions, but in that neighborhood she supposed. She didn't have clear cut visions of the future or anything like that, but sometimes she was just struck with a feeling in her gut that told her things and those things were almost always correct. Allister turned his attention back to Zeus.

"Maybe I'll come visit soon...but look, that isn't why I'm here. She needed you." He stepped back and leaned against the wall, arms crossed. He jutted his chin at her, telling her in no uncertain terms that she was up.

Ok, just going to talk to a god. A real god. Not just any god, but the big man. No big deal. Zahara cleared her throat and stepped forward.

"Um, yeah, so...you're really Zeus? Like, *the* Zeus?" She didn't really have to ask. There was no denying it while standing in his presence. There was just something completely otherworldly and powerful about him. Zeus spread his arms wide.

"The one and only." He flashed her another smile that would make every dentist in a five mile radius faint, and she forced herself not to return it. Instead, she lifted her chin and pulled herself up to her full height, which was pretty impressive when you included the six inch heels.

"I need information. A friend told me that she's...well, that she's in the Underworld with your brother, I guess, and I need you to confirm that for me."

"You're friends with Skylar?" Her heart fluttered at the mention of Skylar, at the casual way he said her name, as if they were old friends. Surely that had to mean she wasn't in trouble or danger, right? "Oh yeah, she's with Hades. She's fine." Z wanted to believe his words, but she needed more.

"Can you prove it to me? I need to know she's safe, that she's ok. I need to see it with my own eyes."

Zeus studied her for a long minute, something sparking behind his blue eyes. Mischief mixed with interest and something else, something hotter, something dangerous. Finally, he said, "I can...but you owe me an additional three days on top of the seven for summoning me."

She shrugged. "Fine." What was three more days anyway when you were immortal? He waved her forward but she paused.

"Do my seven, er, ten, days start now?"

"Eager to spend so much time with me already?" He gave her a weirdly adorable crooked smile. How can he be the epitome of sexy and adorable at the same time? "No, not yet. I've got to take care of some business first. This is just a show and tell trip to get your proof."

She nodded and continued towards him. When she was close enough, he reached out and tugged her close to him. She inhaled sharply, trying to ignore his scent, like that delicious smell of rain in the air just before the sky opens up, and the way his light seemed to burn brighter when she neared. She definitely needed to ignore the way she was so close that she could almost feel the hard planes of his stomach touching hers. He kept one hand resting lightly on her hip, not in an overtly sexual way, but damn her if her body didn't react as if he were palming other things...and damn if she didn't want him to be.

He grinned as if he knew what she were thinking and whispered, "hold on tight" so close to her ear, goosebumps sprung up along her skin, the fine hairs on her neck standing on end. She had better get herself under control before he came back to collect on his ten days or she was in big fucking trouble...or maybe not, she decided, imagining all the ways that time could go.

A second later they were standing in a large room overlooking a lush garden and pool. She gasped at the strange sensation that rippled through her. Tingles almost like her entire body had fallen asleep and a slight hint of freefalling. She'd traveled through a portal before but it was nothing like this. She was at the safe house one minute and here the next, a sharp rush of adrenaline accompanying the journey. She grinned. It was the perfect mode of travel for someone like her.

She glanced around, momentarily distracted enough to forgot that not only was Zeus' hand still on her hip, but she had moved closer to him on the short trip, their bodies now touching, just barely, but enough that she could feel his heat against her, the hard planes of his chest and stomach.

There were no doors separating the outside from the inside, only white columns set at intervals, ivy and golden flowers climbing along the stone. The floors looked like white marble with veins of glittering gold weaving throughout. Everything in the space seemed to have at least a touch of gold: the sconces in the walls, the rugs, the large table in the middle of the space. Normally it would have been gaudy, but here it was understated somehow, perfect. Zeus released her and stepped away, putting a bit of space between them. She couldn't decide if she liked that or not. She continued to glance around and sucked in a gasp, quickly palming two daggers from hidden sheaths in the back of her corset. In between one breathe and the next, six ridiculously large men with silver *wings* stood in between the columns.

"What the..."

Zeus smiled and nodded to the nearest man. "All good, Dante. She's with me." The angel-man-thing, Dante, inclined his head, though he eyed her blades with interest, and then they were all gone. Just like that. Poof.

She glanced up at Zeus in question.

"Those are The Elite, my personal guards."

She arched a brow. "The King of the gods needs bodyguards?"

"Just call me Whitney, baby," he said with a grin. *Ok, so the gods are real...and they watch 80s movies?* She had *so* many questions, but knew they had to wait. Zeus waved her towards the table. He snapped his fingers and a large section of the table was replaced with glass, swirling gray and blue smoke floating under the surface.

Zahara braced her hands on the table in front of her and felt Zeus' body heat as he came to stand just behind her, not touching, but close. She closed her eyes, surprised by how much his presence affected her, how badly she wanted to rip his t-shirt off, run her hands along his muscles, maybe replace her hands with her tongue... *Stop it!* What in the hell was wrong with her? Zeus chuckled behind her, again as if he could read her mind and she wondered if maybe he actually could. She shrugged inwardly. Oh well, nothing she could do to stop the torrent of dirty thoughts running around in there, so he would just be getting a good show if he could get a peek inside. He waved a hand over the top of the glass and the smoke began to swirl faster before dissipating to reveal–

Zahara gasped. It was Skylar! She was sword fighting with a gorgeous man. *Since when does Skylar know how to fucking sword fight? And talk about tall, dark, and handsome.* Skylar had lied when she'd said that Hades was a panty melter. This man was a panty *liquefier.*

They were a blur of movement, blades clanging together, bodies spinning and ducking. Without taking her eyes off of the scene before her, Z demanded, "Take me there, now. I have to help her. You said she was fine, you dick!" she added accusingly.

Zeus laughed. "She *is* fine, just watch for a second...and pretty bold to call the King of the gods a dick, you know," he added in a low voice. It wasn't threatening exactly, but it was laced with authority and power, reminding her of exactly who he was. Something about the tone made her shudder with want when a normal person probably would have had fear skittering down their spine. She couldn't help it: she had a thing for BDE guys and Zeus was the absolute *king* of BDE in addition to being king of the gods. She somehow forced herself to focus back on the visual in front of her.

She watched as Skylar did some fancy maneuver that looked like it was straight out of *Game of Thrones*, twirling her blade and using the motion to flick the sword out of Hades' hands. *Attagirl! Gut the bastard!* Skylar grinned...but then tossed her own sword to the ground.

"What is she doing!?"

Skylar leapt on him, wrapping her legs around his waist. He gripped her ass with one hand, bringing her face down to his with the other, kissing her fiercely yet somehow tenderly. Hades slowly dropped to his knees, then leaned forward until Skylar was lying under him, kissing down her neck. The look on Skylar's face could only be described as euphoric. Zahara had never seen her look like that before, not even with Lucas. Hades made his way down Skylar's neck and to the top of her chest before ripping her shirt clean off. Zeus cleared his throat and waved his hand again, the smoke returning.

"As much as I love free porn, that's my brother and sister-in-law, so that's just weird."

Zahara spun to face him, her hands flying up to steady herself on his chest. She hadn't realized just how close he was. She couldn't ignore the hard lines of muscle that she could feel under the fabric of his shirt, couldn't ignore the way his eyes darkened to a deep, stormy blue, the way he inhaled sharply, as if the touch felt as good to him as it did to her. She dropped her hands and he took a step sideways, separating them.

"Did you say sister-in-law?"

Zeus nodded as he leaned casually back against the table, any trace of whatever had just passed between them completely gone. Had she imagined it? Or was he just really, really good at playing things off?

"Yep, they tied the knot. I sent a blender."

"Holy shit. Married. To Hades. Holy shit, holy shit, holy shit. Ok... ok, focus, Z. She's safe...and married...and the gods are real...and... *holy shit*." She was babbling, trying to organize her thoughts, but her mind was pretty much blown. She rubbed the back of her neck and shook her head in pure astonishment.

"I'm sure this is a lot to take in, but I promise your friend has never been safer, or happier I'd be willing to bet."

Zahara glanced where the screen had been. It was just a table again, but she replayed what she'd seen. She couldn't argue with the fact that her best friend seemed lighter than Z had ever seen her, as if some huge weight had been lifted from her shoulders. She was going to wring Skylar's neck for not telling her about the whole being married thing as soon as the deed had been done, but if Skylar was happy, then so was she. Skylar had had a pretty rough life at the beginning, she deserved a happy ending. And if that happy ending involved being married to the God of the fucking Underworld, so be it.

Zeus smiled at her. "I'm sure you have plenty of questions...but you have ten whole days to ask me anything you wish. I'm an open book—mostly."

"Why ten anyway?"

He hiked a shoulder in response.

"I like round numbers and ten sounded better than eight." Zahara narrowed her eyes at him, but before she could say anything, he moved closer, making the words die in her throat. "We'll get to know each other *very* well during that time, I imagine." The dirty promises held in that sentence had Zahara shivering and clenching her fists at the sudden need clawing inside her like a rabid beast. Was it just because he was a god? Was this some sort of godly super power? Making everyone around you instantly aroused?

He winked and she felt her stomach flip.

Ohhh yeah. She was most definitely in big fucking trouble.

THIRTY-TWO

Perfect. That was the only way to describe life with Hades. Absolute perfection. They had made love and fucked and everything in between, in every way imaginable—and some she hadn't until she was in the middle of it—and were somehow still barely able to keep their hands off of each other. Emmie had declared them "disgustingly happy" and complained that all their playtime was interfering with *Criminal Minds* night. Emmie was right, so Skylar made a point to stop shirking her friendly duties and part from Hades long enough to swoon over Dr. Reid once a week.

They'd shared more of their pasts and talked about the future. Turns out Hades had the nifty ability to basically turn on and off his godly baby making abilities as he wanted, so she didn't have to worry about getting pregnant right now, but she'd be lying if she didn't imagine a future that included children with him. What would they be like? Half god, half...whatever the hell she was. She could see little troublemakers with her blonde hair and his blue-green eyes running around the castle, starting black-flamed fires and biting the guards with their little fangs. The vision made her smile and suddenly want it so badly she could taste it.

She was laying on her stomach on Hades' bed now as he traced shapes along her spine, nearly boneless with bliss. She'd ridden him like a bull at the rodeo until they both couldn't take anymore and had collapsed in a multiple-orgasmed heap on the silk sheets moments ago. She grinned at the memory, still a bit awed by the staggering need that was constantly simmering just below the surface. How could they still want each other this badly and this often? This had to wane at some point, didn't it?

He stiffened for a moment and then leaned down to kiss every one of her scars softly. He made his way to her shoulder and said quietly, "So, I kind of did a thing. I don't want to upset you and you don't have to...partake, but the right is yours if you want it."

She wasn't sure what this could be about, but she sat up, turning to face him and eyeing him suspiciously.

"You didn't invite those Nymphera Demons to have an orgy did you?" He barked out a laugh and tapped her on the nose with an index finger.

"For one, you're the only one I want in my bed, love, and for two, I know for a fact you would slice and dice every single one of them if they so much as glanced at me or my cock."

She grinned. "True story. You're mine...*all* of you." She leaned in and kissed him softly, sucking lightly on his lower lip while she gently gripped his cock in her palm. He groaned and she smiled against his mouth, but her curiosity was too keyed up now, so she reluctantly pulled away, releasing her prize. "Ok, so what's this thing you did?"

He looked a little uncomfortable which made tiny alarm bells start to ring in the back of her mind. She sat up straighter, more alert.

"It'll be better to show you. Get dressed. I picked something for you, if you'll wear it..."

Well, she was intrigued, that was for sure. Hades waved a hand and the most gorgeous gown she'd ever seen appeared, hanging from one of the bed posts. It was black, with glittering black jewels sewn into the shape of flames on the bodice. An overlay containing more of the same jewels covered the skirt, flowing out into a small train in the back. The front dipped down into V, the point landing just between her breasts, with sheer cap sleeves. The material of the sleeves cascaded down the back of the dress, almost like wings, but the middle was open, leaving her back completely exposed. It was beautiful but far from dainty. Whoever wore it would look fierce, like a complete and total badass.

*It's...*she smiled as the realization hit her. *It's a dress for the Queen of the Underworld.*

She ran her fingers lovingly over the flames and he held out a large, intricately carved box. She opened it and gasped at the crown that she found nestled within. It was delicate yet screamed *power*, and was made from the same glittering black stone as the jewels on her dress. The edges curved up to look like a cross between flames and horns. She ran her fingers along it.

"It's beautiful," she breathed. He leaned down and kissed her.

"It's *yours*, my queen."

She got dressed and pulled her hair into a loose updo low on her neck, leaving her back completely exposed. Hades placed the crown reverently on her head and then stepped back, sucking in a breath.

"You are...gods, Skylar, I don't have words." She ran her eyes up and down his body.

"Back at ya, baby."

He'd changed while she dressed and he looked equal parts fearsome and delicious. He was in black leather pants and a tight black shirt, with thick leather bands strapped on each wrist. A deadly looking blade hung from his waist and large rings adorned most of his fingers. Though that could possibly look feminine, it only added to the masculine danger radiating from him.

He phased them to the throne room and she grinned when she saw that there was now a second throne beside the one that belonged to Hades. He led her up the stairs and they both sat. He squeezed her hand reassuringly.

"Remember, you don't have to do this. If you want to leave, just say the word." Apprehension began to bloom in her belly. Something was going on, something she wasn't sure she was going to like.

"Hades, what's going on?"

"I don't usually get involved with mortal lives, none of us do. When we do it too often or overstep, the powers that be don't appreciate it and things can get messy. We often end up doing more harm than good. Pompeii? Yeah, that was our bad. But sometimes, it's warranted and we *do* step in..."

"What are you trying to say?"

"I..." His nostrils flared and smoke curled around the edges of his throne, the flames along the back dancing higher. "I couldn't let them live," he said firmly, coldly. "Not after what you told me. I won't apologize for it because I'm not sorry, even in the slightest. But they haven't been sentenced yet. As the Queen of the Underworld, you have the right to hand down punishment, same as I do. And as the victim of their crimes, you have the right to decide their fate—if you want it."

Her next breath got caught in her throat as she realized what he was saying, realized what he'd done. He had killed her adoptive parents, or had them killed anyway, and was now offering her the chance for retribution. She was scared to see them again, even after all this time, but as she stared into his eyes, eyes that held nothing but worry and love for her, the fear ebbed. He had done this for her, couldn't stand the thought of people who had hurt her walking the earth a second longer. She honestly couldn't say she would have done anything less had the roles been reversed. Hell, she wished she could gut Persephone herself for what she'd done to Hades all those years ago.

So, call her crazy, but she was touched by what he'd done. She leaned forward and put a hand against his heart. It was racing. She kissed him softly, deeply, somehow falling even more in love with him in that moment.

"Thank you. I..." She took a deep breath and the memories of her time in that house come to the forefront of her mind. She clenched her jaw and nodded. "I want to do this. I *need* to do this. When my father took me away that night, I never looked back. Never tried to find them, never tried to have them punished. I actually made my dad swear that he wouldn't even try to track them down or go back to that place. I just wanted it to be over. I wanted to just forget, but I couldn't, no matter how hard I tried. I never got closure, never got to demand that they answer for what they did, what he *planned* to do."

Hades ground his teeth and a low growl emanated from his chest and the flames on the back of the throne arched even higher, sparks flying and smoke swirling. She caressed his cheek and he seemed to calm slightly. He gave her a sharp nod.

"Are you ready then?"

She squared her shoulders and sat up straighter in her throne. She inclined her head and a moment later Jeff and Athos escorted her "parents" into the room. Athos met her gaze and gave her a deep nod. He'd sworn her a life debt for saving his, and though she was sure that this wouldn't make them square in his mind, she appreciated his hand in it. She'd told herself that she wouldn't be afraid, that they were nothing, but her heart began to pound in her chest as soon as she saw them. She quickly shifted her gaze downward, too scared to even look at them for more than a moment.

The familiar tickle of Dean's request to speak with her brushed against her mind. She was thrilled that her marriage to Hades and the sharing of his power had included the ability to speak with the man-in-cat's-clothing, and had been secretly delighted that he'd decided to keep the new moniker.

-You are a Queen, pet. You do not cower. You do not avert your eyes. You meet their gaze head on and fuck. Their. World. Up.-

He didn't know the full story, but she assumed that he had assisted in this little mission. Though he was stuck in his feline form, he was cunning and vicious and still retained some of his demigod strength and abilities. So, she assumed he knew enough. She blew out a slow breath. *He's right. I'm not that scared little girl anymore. I'm a fucking Queen.*

-Thank you- she told him, more grateful than he would ever actually know.

-Anytime. You've got this-

She caught the black blur of movement out of the corner of her eye as the cat leapt from his perch on top of one of the statues and moved to stand on the arm of her throne instead. She gave him a quick head scratch and saw Hades incline his head subtly to Dean, thanking him for the pep talk. Skylar took a deep breath and then pulled her gaze back to her former parents.

They glanced around the room, looking afraid and confused, but when their eyes landed on the dais, they looked downright terrified and tried to stop in their tracks. Skylar glanced to her right and had to stifle gasp. She wasn't looking at Hades, her sweet, goofball husband who had played *Guitar Hero* with her and Emmie the previous night, who loved dirty jokes and made the most adorable sound when she nibbled on his earlobe, who loved watching *The Property Brothers*.

Oh no. She was looking at Hades, God of the fucking Underworld. All humor was erased from his face. His features had somehow hardened and his eyes had darkened to full black. The black flames on the back of his throne surged upwards, causing her "mother" to shriek and his smoke began to swirl around him. Slow. Sinister. Black flames danced lightly across his knuckles as he stared down the people before him. A dark crown, similar to her own, sat gracefully among his tousled locks. Hades looked terrifying...and perfect...and ok, sexy as hell, though she was probably the only one in the room who had *that* particular thought.

-No, you're right. He's sexy as fuck- Dean confirmed. She pulled her lips inward to stop her smile.

She returned her gaze to the pathetic excuses for human beings before her. She forced herself to remember who she was now and the fear subsided once more, her heart slowing to a steady thrum. She knew she was drawing strength and calm from Hades and would never be able to thank him enough for that.

She titled her head to the side, really studying them for the first time as an adult, not as a scared, broken child. They looked small and weak.

Dan, her "father" dropped to his knees, immediately followed by Donna. She was crying and trembling and it may have made her a terrible person, but Skylar felt no sympathy for the woman, even *enjoyed* her fear.

"Please, please there's been a mistake. We don't belong here. We lived good lives," Dan said, eyes wild. Skylar knew what he must have seen as Charon ferried them down the river. The black water, the bodies and creatures rising from the depths, the screams of agony. *Good.* She hoped that Charon had gone extra terrifying reaper on their asses for the journey.

Donna sobbed. "P-please, we're good people! We haven't done anything wrong, we don't deserve...whatever this is."

Anger flared inside Skylar's chest. How dare they kneel there and lie? How dare they claim to be good people? Flames erupted from the back of her own throne and she caught the surprised flicker in Hades' eyes before he again donned his hard, cold expression.

"I don't believe that you are good people. I think you are some of the most despicable people to ever come before this throne and I think you deserve far worse than any punishment I could hand down." Even his voice had changed. It was icy and rang with an unmistakable note of authority and power. He shifted his gaze to Skylar, asking her silently if she was ready. She gave one small nod. "But, this decision isn't up to me. My wife, the Queen of the Under-world, and of your fate, will have that honor."

That was her cue. Skylar took a deep breath and stood, stalking down the stairs towards them. Their eyes went wide and she could see the fear in them. *Good. You should be afraid. You should know how it feels.* She could feel pride surging from Hades and it gave her the final bit of confidence she needed.

Her voice was strong and sure when she said, "You claim you're good people, but do good people abuse children? Do good people lock them in closets for disturbing them while they fuck the pool boy? Do they grab them so hard they dislocate their shoulders? Do they break their fingers?" Her voice was rising, her anger building and building within her. "Do they put out cigarettes on a child and laugh when the child cries, begs them to stop, screams that it *burns*? Do they plan to do unspeakable things to an eleven-year-old girl at night in her bedroom?!" she roared, the sound reverberating through the throne room.

The flames in the sconces along the wall flared upward. She saw Jeff tighten his grip on his massive sword out of the corner of her eye, his muscles tensing and smoke curling from his mouth and nose. Athos clenched his fists and anger flared in his now nearly-black eyes. The fact that they all felt such anger on her behalf, after only knowing her for such a short time made her heart swell. These were her people. This was her home.

"I...we...I..." Dan sputtered, eyes wide. Donna sobbed, her entire body shuddering under the force of her cries.

Skylar leaned in close to them and asked in a quiet voice, "You don't recognize me, do you?"

Dan's brows drew down in confusion. "What are you talking..." He trailed off and sucked in a breath as Skylar turned her back to him, showing him her scars. She heard Jeff growl deep in his throat.

Donna gasped. "*Lindsay?*"

"My name," she said with lethal venom in her voice, "is Skylar." She'd abandoned the name Lindsay when she fled that night. When her father had found her and asked her name, she'd hesitated, not wanting to be that girl anymore. *Skylar* had flitted through her mind in a soft whisper, like something from a memory or a dream, but she couldn't grasp on to any more than that, just the single word. Her name. She knew it without knowing how, that it was her true name.

"No...that's not possible...I..." Dan stammered, not able to finish a sentence. She whirled back around, her fangs now fully out, her claws extended. For a moment she felt a strange sensation at her back, as if something soft had caressed her skin, but she wasn't sure what it was and it was gone as quickly as it came. Donna screamed and tried to scramble backwards. Hades was behind her in an instant blocking her retreat. Donna peered up and screamed again as the smoke curled around her, locking around her waist and pinning her in place. Tendrils of smoke wound around Dan for good measure, holding him upright on his knees before Skylar. He strained against the hold, but it was no use.

Hades gritted out through clenched teeth, "You do not move until my wife allows it. Do you understand?" His eyes burned with rage and black flames blazed up around him. "Answer me!"

"Ye...yes," Donna whimpered, turning her gaze back to Skylar. Dan couldn't seem to speak, but nodded jerkily. Donna went to her knees and held her hands in front of her, as if praying. "Please. I tried to stop him. I never wanted him to hurt you. I loved you, Linds—" Skylar curled her lips back from her fangs. "Skylar. I loved you, Skylar. I wanted to protect you." Skylar huffed out a humorless laugh.

"You never tried to stop him. You couldn't have cared less about protecting me. And don't for one second try to pretend that you cared for me at all." She turned her icy gaze back to Dan. His mouth was gaping like a fish. "Anything to say for yourself now?"

"You..." He licked his lips, eyes darting around like a trapped animal. "You misunderstood. You were just a kid, you don't know what you're remembering. I didn't do those things to you, it must have been someone in the foster home. Yes, that's it. We loved you. We were devastated when you ran away." Hades growled behind him and Dan cowered at the sound.

"No. More. Lies!" he commanded. "Admit it. Tell the truth for once in your life—the *entire* truth—and I'll spare you from the Realm of Tortures." Both of their eyes lit up with a mix of terror and hope. They exchanged glances, weighing their options. Finally, Donna nodded and Dan cleared his throat.

"I...yes, I did those things. I hurt you. I...wanted to do more. I came into your room that night, the night you ran away, planning to do more. But I'm sick, don't you see? I needed help, but I couldn't reach out to anyone, not in my position in the public eye, we would have lost everything!"

A cold thought entered Skylar's mind and she narrowed her eyes.

"Were there others? Before me? After?" He met her gaze and swallowed hard, and she knew. She knew without him having to answer, knew that though she had escaped, the monster had not been defeated at all. She felt sick.

"Y-yes. There were others," he admitted quietly. "I'm sorry. I'm so sorry. I...I beg your forgiveness. All of their forgiveness." *All of them.* Her stomach churned and her claws ached to tear him to pieces. She refrained, but couldn't stop herself from backhanding him. He toppled to the ground and Donna screamed out. Dan pushed himself up once more and met her gaze. "Please. Please have mercy on me."

Skylar met Hades' gaze over their heads. He nodded to her, reassuring her that he was behind her no matter what she decided. She bent down so that she was eye to eye with the pathetic excuse for a man, for a father.

"You will suffer for all of eternity. Things will be done to you that you can't even begin to fathom. And when you think you can't possibly endure a moment longer, the pain will *double.*"

"B-but you said! You s-said you would spare us from the Realm of T-T-Torture!" Donna wailed. Skylar straightened and shrugged.

"I am. We never said anything about the Realm of Suffering. And that is precisely what you will do. You will suffer for as long as I demand it. You are pathetic and weak and sad. Both of you. Now, *go.*"

Hades grabbed each of them by the scruff of their necks and disappeared, their screams of denial echoing off of the walls. Skylar let out a long shaky breath, almost doubling over, and wrapped her arms around her middle, staring at the spot where they'd been a moment before. She searched within herself for a shred of remorse for what she'd just done and she found none. She didn't know what that said about her and frankly, she didn't care.

"Skylar?" Jeff asked quietly from the door. She raised her face and met his gaze. His eyes held concern and anger and pride.

"I should have gone back," she said quietly. "After I escaped, I just thought if I ignored the past, pretended they didn't exist, everything would be fine. I even begged my dad not to track them down. I wanted to pretend that they were just a bad dream. But...oh gods, he went after other girls...I should have gone back and stopped him! I should have..."

She covered her mouth with her hand and felt tears spring to her eyes. Her stomach churned, her chest ached. Jeff was there then, towering over here but griping her shoulders with a surprising gentleness.

"Skylar. Skylar, look at me." She obeyed a bit numbly. "Nothing that man did was your fault, do you understand? To you or to anyone else. He is filth and you aren't responsible for his actions."

She let his words sink in. She knew he was right but she would still struggle with this for a time. Still, she felt better. She gave him a small nod. He stepped back beside Athos, who had silently approached as well.

"You did well, my Queen," Athos said. He and Jeff both bowed to her, a bow worthy of a true Queen. It made her stand straighter, made pride flow through her. She inclined her head to them both in return. A moment later, Hades returned, hands empty. He immediately grabbed her face gently in both hands and held her gaze.

"Are you alright, love?"

She grabbed his wrists, squeezing reassuringly, and nodded. She was. She still felt guilt, but not over what she'd done to them, for the sentence she'd passed down. Maybe it was wrong, maybe she should have been merciful, but she couldn't find it in her. She didn't know how many others had been hurt by them, by *him*, but she sent out a silent message to all of them, wherever they may be: *It's over. I'm sorry.* She felt as if that chapter of her life was finally finished, the book closed forever. She was ready to start a new one, one full of love instead of pain. She leaned in and kissed Hades fiercely, communicating with him in the best way she could that she was ok.

"I'm proud of you."

"Thank you. For this, for being proud, for...everything," she breathed against his lips. As suddenly as a switch being flipped, a fire scorched through her chest, the air around them heavy and tense with need, every other emotion and thought forgotten.

A second later they were back in his room and she was tugging his shirt off. She was on fire for him, needed him so badly she couldn't wait a moment longer.

"I like you as Hades, God of the Underworld. All Mr. Commanding Badass. It's sexy. Apparently Dean thinks so too." She laughed before she bit his bottom lip and he growled in appreciation. She tugged at the fly of his pants, shoving the material out of the way and wrapping her hand around his cock. He was already rock hard for her. She stroked once, twice, her mouth watering for a taste. The things she planned to do to this man tonight...She smiled against his lips and stepped back, reluctantly letting go of him. She reached up to remove the crown but his hand shot out, grabbing her wrist.

"The crown stays on...the crown, and the heels." His voice was low and husky, making her shiver. He quickly got her out of her dress and she stood there, completely naked save her strappy six-inch heels and the crown resting on her head, just as he'd wanted. He took in the sight of her with absolute hunger in his eyes. He licked his bottom lip before biting down. Her nipples hardened at the sight, something so intensely arousing about the action that she couldn't stop her body from reacting. He let his eyes travel slowly down her body, lingering over his favorite spots and making her begin to tremble with need and anticipation. The way he looked at her made her feel like the most beautiful creature in the universe, made her feel sexy and powerful in a way she'd never felt before. Sure, she had always been a femme fatale for her job, but this was different. The way Hades made her feel because of the way he felt *for* her was staggering, empowering.

"You want God of the Underworld, you've got him, baby." He backed her up slowly until she hit the bed. His smoke flared out, moving and writhing around them in a sensual dance.

"Grab the bedpost above your head and do not remove your hands, no matter what," he commanded in that cold, authoritative voice he'd used in the throne room. The one that sent heat through her body and made her breaths come swift and shallow. She liked where this was going. She did as he asked, grasping the post with both hands just above her head. He gripped both of her wrists in one hand, holding them in place as he kissed her fiercely, his tongue dominating hers, before making his way down her neck and breasts, biting and licking as he went. She kept her hands above her head, fingers clenching around the post as she moaned and shook. He dropped to his knees in front of her and trailed his tongue along the lines of her tattoo.

"Spread your legs," he commanded once more, a little more gruffly this time.

She obeyed immediately and he kissed lightly up the inside of one thigh and then the other. Her legs were shaking with anticipation when he finally leaned in to kiss where she needed him...but the bastard only blew lightly against her instead. She closed her eyes and moaned at the sensation. She arched her hips forward, begging him. He chuckled lightly before leaning in again and lightly trailing his tongue just above her clit. *Gods that feels good*...but it wasn't enough. He was killing her.

"Hades!" she groaned. He laughed again and stared up at her with a wicked glint in his eyes.

"What does my Queen want?"

"You." He trailed a finger oh so lightly between her lips and she shuddered, hips bucking wildly.

"Tell me what you want." He leaned in again and she held her breath, hoping maybe he was going to give her what she so desperately wanted, needed. Instead he ran his nose along the skin just above her pussy, and whispered, "*Command* me."

His breath once again lightly caressed her and she writhed against the bed post. She began to move one hand off of the post, to steer him where she wanted, but he glanced up and narrowed his eyes.

"Uh, uh, uh. Hands on the post. *Now*." She was dying for him but damnit if she wasn't loving this little game. She obeyed and then tendrils of smoke wrapped around her wrists, binding them to the post. *Holy hell if this isn't the most erotic, sexy thing that's ever happened.*

"*Good girl,*" he rasped.

"Oh gods," she whispered at his words, her entire body shuddering. He ran his fingers lightly up her thighs, making her legs tremble.

"Now: *Tell me*." Another breath against her. "*What*." Another lick so close yet so far away. "*You want*."

Now she understood: she wanted the King of the Underworld, and he wanted the Queen. He wanted her to play the part, he wanted her to command him, to rule him. *Fuck, it was hot.*

She met his gaze and said "I want you to lick my pussy until I scream your name to the rafters. I want you to make me come so hard my legs shake. And you will not stop until I'm *begging* you."

His eyes blazed and his lips curled up into the sexiest smirk she'd ever seen.

"As my Queen commands."

Turns out, Hades was *very* good at following commands.

THIRTY-THREE

Another week passed in utter bliss. Skylar had never been so happy in all her life and she got the feeling that neither had Hades. He was finishing up some things in the throne room, so she was headed that way to meet him, grinning to herself as she replayed their morning. She'd woken him up in a particularly naughty way that involved his cock in her mouth. He'd come full awake with a throaty moan of pleasure that sent shivers down her spine and tangled his hands in her hair, thrusting his hips and fucking her mouth. Gods she loved when he did that. Too soon he'd stopped and she had begun to pout, but he'd spun her so that his mouth was on her as well.

She closed her eyes and "mmmed" quietly to herself remembering them both climaxing on each other's tongues, wanting a repeat so badly she began walking faster, practically sprinting. *Will this ever ebb? Will we ever get enough of each other?* She really didn't think so.

When she got close, she heard Zeus' booming voice and grinned. She loved her new brother-in-law. She was about to barrel through the doors, but she paused, deciding to give them a moment before she interrupted...and, ok eavesdropping was a hard habit to break, ok?

"So, how are the newlyweds? Wanting to kill each other yet?" Zeus asked. Hades let out a half laugh, half sigh. She imagined him running his hand through his hair, leaving it in that sexy disarray she loved.

"Things are...perfect. *She's* perfect. It's so different than last time, I can't make sense of it."

"Have you told her yet?"

A sense of foreboding slithered up her spine, like that feeling on a theme park ride when you're sitting way up in the air, just waiting for the drop. You don't know when it's coming, but you know it's going to and, if you're Skylar Pembroke who cannot stand big drop rides of any kind but goes on them because her best friend is an adrenaline junkie, you white knuckle the armrests waiting for the dreaded moment you fall. Something told her this wasn't a conversation she wanted to hear, but she couldn't force herself to walk away. *Told me what?*

"No, not yet. I'm going to, I just...not yet. I know what she's going to think and I just need more time to figure out how to handle this." *Handle what, damnit?*

"Uhh, I'm no expert here, but I think the longer you wait, the worse it's going to be. There is never going to be a good time to drop the bomb on her. 'Hey honey, how was your day? Oh by the way, you're the reincarnate of my dead, betrayer, bitch of a former wife and that's the whole reason you're here and I needed to marry you. So, what's for dinner?' Yeah, not good, man."

Skylar couldn't breathe. She tried, but air was refusing to enter her lungs. She felt cold and hot at the same time, not understanding the conflicting sensations. She was...she was *Persephone?* Reincarnated? *That* was the only reason he'd wanted her? That was why she felt connected to him and to this place? No. No, she couldn't accept this. She felt these things because *she* felt them...right? If it was true then...she swallowed hard against the bile rising up in her throat.

Then he never really wanted *her*, he just wanted his ex back. *No, no, no.* She knew how he felt about her. He loved her, even though he hadn't said the words yet for whatever reason...*Maybe he hasn't said them because he's waiting for you to remember who you were...are... fucking hell.* She ground her teeth at the whirling thoughts, her head already throbbing trying to make sense of it.

She thought back to that day at the gym, the first day things really shifted between them and...*oh gods, I'm going to puke.* They had been talking about *Persephone* right before they had gotten physical, nearly kissing for the first time. He'd been hard as a rock for someone else while she straddled him, been thinking of someone else as he grabbed her nape and tugged her down, eyes heavy with want and need.

She dug her claws into her palms and blood quickly began to well, spilling down her hands. Her mind was reeling. Was everything she felt from him actually just from his former wife who was apparently squatting like a fucking toad inside of her somehow? She couldn't quite organize her thoughts. It was too much. She couldn't make it all make sense, but one thing she did know: he'd lied to her from the start. He wanted her because of who she used to be to him. Maybe he'd grown to want her for who she was now somewhere along the way too, but she didn't know for sure—or even if it mattered if it was true.

She felt her heart begin to crack and she willed her feelings to stay within her, commanded them not to be felt by him through their bond. She didn't know if that was even possible, but the longer they were married, the more she felt that she understood the power that connected them, his power that had flowed through her during their marriage ceremony, and hoped that she was able to block him from feeling this.

Skylar felt numb, felt like her knees may give out at any moment, but she somehow managed to stay upright as she backed away from the door. Her vision began to blur with unshed tears as she turned and ran towards her room. Her heart was pounding so hard in her chest she worried it might explode. She couldn't make her mind slow enough to process this, everything just racing within her head a mile a minute.

She was...Persephone. She was the key to this whole prophecy thing only because she was the former Queen reincarnated. She didn't *feel* like a reincarnate though. Wouldn't she know if she'd lived another life before this one? Wouldn't she have some sort of memory of it? She felt like herself, like the same old Skylar she'd always been... only royally pissed off and hurt beyond repair.

The biggest question of all resounded through her mind: Could she forgive him? Could they ever possibly move forward? Would she ever be able to fucking breathe again? Every time she tried, it felt like a knife being driven into her chest.

You knew this was too good to be true, a voice whispered inside her mind. *Things were too perfect. You let your guard down, let him in, and look where it got you.* Skylar ground her teeth and felt her fangs digging into her lip.

She entered her room and Emmie was sitting in the middle of the bed. Skylar just held her hand up, silencing the Seer before she could even begin to speak. Of course, she didn't listen.

"What's wrong? You look upset." She furrowed her brow and stared off into space for a moment, seeing something Skylar couldn't. Then she focused again and snapped her fingers. "Oh! You found out you're part phoenix, right? That's no reason to be so upset, Poprocks," Emmie scolded her. "It's actually pretty incredible."

Skylar stutter-stepped before freezing completely, the reincarnate business somehow completely forgotten for a moment. A phoenix? Like...like Fawkes from *Harry Potter*? *I'm a fucking bird? Like feathers and a beak and shit? What the hell?* She turned back to face Emmie, brows arched and eyes wide and giving the Seer a look that clearly said *fucking explain yourself right now.*

"Hmm, ok so not that apparently. I must be getting my visions mixed up." She tapped her chin and then her eyes lit up. "Oh! Did you find out that you're also part god? Is *that* what's wrong? Again, nothing to be upset about. It's almost equally as incredible."

Skylar shook her head like a dog. She must be losing her hearing...or going crazy...or having an aneurism. *Yeah, definitely all of the above.*

"Wha...what did you just say?"

Emmie blew a lock of silver hair out of her face.

"Well, shit. I wasn't exactly supposed to spill those beans, but Pandora's Box is open now...literally," she added in a soft voice, staring off into space again. "That's going to be interesting..." She shook her head and focused back on Skylar again, a calculated look in her eyes. Skylar suspected she'd done this on purpose, that this was no "oops I got my visions mixed up" moment, but she was past caring about that right now. She needed answers. She made an inpatient hand gesture to get Emmie moving.

"Oh, right. So, yeah, your mom was a phoenix," she held one hand up, "And your dad is Ares." She held the other hand up and then mashed them together, interlacing her fingers. "A little bow-chicka-wow-wow, and the adorable little creature to emerge from that union was the crazy powerful phoenix-demigod hybrid currently known as Skylar Pembroke, Queen of the Underworld."

Skylar's brain was officially broken. "Ares...Ares as in..."

Emmie smiled and nodded. "As in, God of War? Yeppers."

Her brain kickstarted and went into overdrive, so many thoughts bouncing around that she closed her eyes and put her hands to her temples to steady herself against the onslaught. Things began to shift inside her mind, inside her heart, understanding forming without her having any idea of how exactly that was happening. It was like finally hearing the truth of her origins somehow flipped the switch for some of her instincts, and she suddenly understood more about herself and her abilities, more than she ever had before. That strange need to bite him? It had been an instinctual need to *mark* him. To mark him as her mate for all to see. *Her mate.* Her eyes flashed open.

"The dreams. The dreams about Hades. You said before "isn't that how you people know." You meant a phoenix, didn't you?" She began to pace in front of the bed, her mind reeling.

"Yep. Your kind—or your mom's kind anyway—dream of their mates before meeting them, sometimes for *centuries*." Skylar knew the dreams meant something but never would have guessed this. All her life, they'd been leading her to him...or leading Persephone back to her ex-husband apparently. Gods, she was so hurt she wanted to die...and so mad she wanted to claw his eyes out.

"Umm...I'm assuming you found out about the whole Persephone thing then, since the parentage seemed to be a complete shocker?" Emmie said, wincing a bit. Skyler nodded dumbly. "That's a very complicated story...but in the end, *you* are the key to the prophecy, no matter how you slice it."

The prophecy. Maynard. *When you decide that you can't trust him —and believe me, you can't— all you need to do is call and I'll get you out of here.*

Skylar began to wade through memories of her time since coming here. Hades had seemed to hate her so much in the beginning, even as he desired her, and now she understood why: he was angry at *Persephone*. The prick had punished Skylar for his ex's bad deeds. She wanted to scream, but took several deep breaths through her nose and began to pace, forcing her mind to go through everything in a semi-calm, calculating way. She'd relied on this part of her mind so many times in the past, so she gratefully let it take over, let emotion take a step back out of the equation.

Images shuffled through her mind like a movie. She let them all crash into her, studying each one from different angles and catching the nuances that she'd missed the first time around, nuances that she couldn't fully understand without this new knowledge. She saw things she hadn't before, understood things she hadn't before, noticed things that made all the difference. Everything began to become clear, and soon, her eyes flashed wide.

Her path was set out before her in perfect clarity, the only path that made sense now. She knew what she had to do. Emmie sighed in relief, as if she'd been waiting for the decision Skylar had just made, as if it solidified some version of the future that had been in flux.

She stopped pacing and whirled around. Emmie was already standing, ready and waiting for her orders. *Of course she would already know what I'm going to ask.* Skylar raced to the hidden drawer she'd asked the room to create for her in the nightstand and retrieved the ring that Maynard had given her. She had tears streaming down her face as she hugged Emmie fiercely and kissed her cheek.

"I love you, no matter what happens."

Emmie wiped a tear off of Skylar's cheek and she saw tears swimming in Emmie's own eyes. What future had she seen? Didn't matter now, her decision had been made. Skylar forced herself to turn and walk out of the room. No matter how much it was going to hurt, she knew what had to be done. She left the castle, left the love of her life who had destroyed her heart, and the only place that had ever truly felt like home to her behind. *But*, she reminded herself, *it had only felt like home because it was* Persephone's *home first*.

She sucked in a ragged breath, and with her heart shattering in her chest, she ran and didn't look back.

THIRTY-FOUR

Hades dropped into his throne and put his head in his hands, groaning.

"I know, ok? I know I should have told her sooner and that the longer I wait the worse it's going to be. I'm up shit creek without a paddle right now, I get it. Trust me."

"Understatement of the millennium. But I absolutely want a front-row seat to watch Skylar kick your ass over this because it's going to be EPIC." Zeus laughed and clapped a hand down on Hades' shoulder, giving him a reassuring squeeze. "It will all work out. You two are sickeningly in love. She'll forgive you...just be prepared to be in the dog house for a while, and to give her lots and lots of gifts—and orgasms! Gifts and orgasms are the way to a woman's heart, I'm telling you."

Hades lifted his head to glare daggers at his brother, who only laughed harder. Hades' lips twitched at the corners as he fought a smile, despite feeling awful. He let out a long breath. Zeus was right. He needed to tell Skylar the truth about everything and he needed to do it soon. *Tonight. I'll do it tonight.* She would be pissed as hell and probably hurt and confused too, but they would get through it. They had to. He would do anything and everything to make this right with her.

"Ok, change of subject. You said you had news about her? You figured something out?"

"Yes! Oh man, you aren't going to believe this: she's part *phoenix*!" Hades moved quick as lightning and punched his brother in the stomach. Zeus doubled over and let out a string of curses. "Hey! What the hell was that for?"

"I thought you had real news, dickwad. You really came all this way to fuck with me?"

"I'm serious! Absolutely, completely, one thousand percent serious. She's half phoenix."

"But that's impossible. The phoenix are practically myths, even to us. They've been gone for millennia, if they ever really even existed. You know there are plenty who think they didn't."

"Well, they *did* exist and a few have survived all this time, remained hidden. You know the stories, how valuable their blood was and the absolute lethal warriors they were. They gave even the gods and the Titans a run for their money in their heyday. They were hunted to extinction out of lust for their blood or out of fear—or so we thought anyway. But, I have it on absolute authority that her mother was a phoenix, one of the very last ones."

A phoenix. Hades could scarcely believe it. *Leave it to Sky to be the stuff of legends even among the gods.* His lips curled into a small smile. His girl had to keep things interesting, that was for sure. But as he thought back on the stories of the fierce race, he could see parts of them in Sky perfectly. It was crazy, but he could see it.

"This is insane...but ok, let's put the phoenix thing aside for now. What's the other half then?"

"So, remember when Ares went missing for a few centuries a while back? Well, uh, you kinda gotta call him daddy now. He's Skylar's father. She's half *god*." *Holy. Shit.*

"What!? No fucking way. That's...that's..."

"I know right? It's true though. I guess it makes sense that

Persephone would come back as at least part god again. Anyway, Ares came upon the phoenix hiding out in the Mortal Plane, completely by chance. He had no idea what she was, but immediately fell for her—hard. Can you imagine Ares head over heels? Man, I would pay good money to see that. She tried to keep him at arm's length for a while, ran from him, but you know how he can be. He chased her clear across the world, and she finally couldn't deny it anymore: she fell for him too. She eventually told him what she was and he knew that she would always be in danger. They went into hiding for a couple hundred years, had a good life, and eventually, had a child. But apparently someone found out—he still has no idea how—and came after them. They both fought like the lethal warriors they were but they were outnumbered, and Lana—that was her name—ended up being gravely injured trying to protect Skylar. Ares managed to kill most of the ones who remained, but several fled...and he couldn't save Lana. He knew Skylar would never be safe in our world. Anyone who knew the legends and thought there was the slightest chance her blood would be as valuable as a full blooded phoenix's, or had an inclination of how powerful she could become given who her parents were, would never stop coming after her.

The only thing he could think to do was send her to the Mortal Plane. Lana had hidden there for thousands of years undetected, so he'd hoped that his daughter could do the same. He planned to make arrangements for her after he made sure to completely neutralize the threat and destroy the ones who'd fled. He assumed she'd be safe in the Mortal Plane. I mean, she was just a child, someone would help her, right? But that's when he was captured by those sirens. He was only with them for a few weeks, but time passes differently in their realm, you know that. So, by the time he made it out, it had been *years* in the Mortal Plane and he'd lost track of Skylar. He's beside himself right now, knowing that she's alive and ok, that she's *here*. He's not exactly thrilled that you married her, but not much we can do about that now. He wanted to come, but I convinced him to give everyone a bit of time to navigate this first before we have a big family reunion."

"Holy. Shit," Hades muttered as he ran his hand through his hair. His mind was blown, but the more he thought about it, the more her parentage explained everything. The scorch marks on the table and the way fire seemed to respond to her. He'd thought it was just because of the connection they shared, that somehow his power over the fire had transferred to her even before they were married, but now he knew that that was all Skylar. Other things too: the way her eyes darkened (the same way all gods' or demigods' did when they were experiencing great emotion or using their power); the shadow of wings he thought he saw spring from her back at dinner and again in the throne room when she was passing down judgment on her adoptive parents; the way she seemed made for warfare and fighting; even the dreams she had of him. Now he remembered stories about phoenix dreaming of their mates. Though this was in no way what he'd expected to discover about who and what she was, he was thrilled. He knew how badly she wanted to know, how she felt incomplete without the knowledge. To be able to give her this piece of herself...well, it may earn him a few brownie points to cash in when he dropped the rest of the news on her about Persephone.

"I'll go find her now so we can tell her, she'll be so–" He stilled and titled his head to the side. Someone had just opened a portal into the Underworld. "Fucking Maynard," he growled. Zeus became serious in an instant, the goofball brother gone, King of the Gods now standing in his place.

"Here? Now?" Anger and hatred were rolling off of him. The symbols around their tattoos glowed bright enough to be seen through their clothing as they fed off of each other's power, preparing to fight. Thunder boomed outside and lightning streaked across the clear sky.

-Si, if you can pull your dick out of whatever orifice it's currently stuck in, we could use some help over here.-

Hades didn't wait for a response as he and Zeus stormed from the throne room.

-*What's going on? And my cock is tucked neatly in my pants at the moment, thank you very much. I'm not* constantly *fucking, you know*-

Hades could practically feel his brother's eyes roll through the telepathic connection.

-*Maynard is here again. We're going to end this. Now*-

Suddenly, Poseidon was there.

"Where is that piece of shit?" Poseidon asked as he fell into step beside them. Zeus clapped him on the back and Hades gave him a nod in greeting as they rushed down the hall. Hades glanced sidelong at his brother, thinking that though he had the same cocky swagger as always, looking like someone who stepped off the front of a mortal romance novel cover with his light brown skin and amber eyes, something seemed off, like he was putting up a front. Hades promised himself that he would talk with him later, but right now, he needed to be sure that Skylar was safe.

"He opened a portal by the lake. I have to find Sky."

"Ah yes, the little missus. Been dying to meet her...or well, meet her again, I suppose. How weird is this whole reincarnate thing anyway?"

"Totally weird," Zeus said as the rounded a corner. Hades wasn't sure where she might be at the moment, so he was about to start phasing to her favorite places when he caught sight of her out of one of the windows, eating ice cream with Jeff by the front steps. He let out a sigh of relief, the weight on his chest gone now that he knew she was here and safe. Fury quickly replaced his worry, boiling hot and deep in his soul. He was so sick of this shit with his brother. Now that Skylar was his wife, that meant he would finally win the war, right? So, it would end today. He was done playing games.

"Weapons," Hades grated. They all phased to the armory and each strapped on swords, knives, throwing stars, anything that could inflict some pain. Hades closed his eyes and reached out with his mind, letting the Underworld speak to him. *Show me where he is. Tell me where that bastard went.* He frowned. The portal had already closed. Why would Maynard portal in just to stay for a few seconds? He knew better than to get caught here when a portal closed: he could open one *into* the Underworld, but not out of it, so if the one he created closed, he was stuck here. Something was off, but Hades wasn't sure what. Then he felt the small tickle in his mind that meant Conan—er, *Dean.* It was going to take him a while to get used to that—was trying to communicate with him. He opened up, letting the voice in.

-*Uh, H, you need to get to Skylar's room.* Now.-

Something in Dean's tone made Hades' stomach plummet. Something was very, very wrong. He phased to Skylar's room, Zeus and Si arriving a second later. Dean was sitting on the bed. He inclined his head towards the comforter beside him where a note sat, Skylar's crown beside it. Hades stormed to the bed, acid churning in the back of his throat. He snatched up the note and read the simple words she'd written:

You should have told me. I deserved to know the truth before you made me love you.

X – Skylar...or is it Persephone?

She'd also drawn a picture of a hand flipping him the bird. A small part of him wanted to laugh at that, but the majority of him wanted to drop to his knees and sob. He felt as if his chest were on fire, his heart literally breaking apart. *No. No, no, no.* This wasn't how it was supposed to go. She must have overheard him and Zeus talking earlier. She knew who she was and why he had originally brought her here, but she didn't understand! He had to talk to her, had to explain that none of that mattered to him. He didn't care that she was Persephone, not at all, didn't even think of them as the same person. She had to let him explain, right? He could fix this. Not like she could leave, and he had just seen her on the front steps with Jeff, so he really didn't understand the note...

His blood went cold as realization hit him like a sucker punch. He threw back his head and roared at the ceiling.

Zeus laid a big hand on his shoulder. "What? What the hell is going on?"

"She's gone. Maynard has her. She went to him somehow, I think. Maybe even summoned him here herself. But either way, she's gone." Zeus frowned in confusion.

"But she's on the front steps with Jeff, we just saw her two seconds ago, man."

"No, we didn't," he growled.

"Uh oh..." Si said, knowing how close Hades was to losing his shit. Smoke and flames were swirling around him already, his power a bow string strung almost too tight. He phased to the steps and Skylar-that-wasn't-Skylar leapt up, backing away. Her looks shifted and then Emmie was standing before him instead.

"What the fuck?!" he yelled.

"She asked me to and I agreed. She didn't tell me what she was planning."

"SHE DIDN'T HAVE TO TELL YOU, GODS DAMNIT!" He stormed toward her, fire erupting along his arms, engulfing him, smoke swirling like hissing snakes. "You knew! You *knew* what she was doing! How could you let this happen!?" They were nose to nose and he was barely stopping himself from ending her here and now. She showed the smallest flicker of fear and uncertainty. She didn't know how this would play out any more than he did. He knew that the only fate she couldn't see was her own. So, she had no idea if he would actually snap and kill her or not, but she'd still agreed to help Skylar run off to Maynard. Gods, history was repeating itself all over again. Except this time, he'd driven her away by lying to her. This was *his* fault.

Hades dropped to his knees and put his head in his hands, pulling at his hair so forcefully he felt strands pull free from his scalp. He didn't know what Maynard had promised her, but whatever it was, it wouldn't end the way Skylar imagined. Maynard would use

Skylar, use Hades' obvious feelings for her to get what he wanted once and for all. His stomach churned at the thought of what Maynard would do to her. He bowed his head and his shoulders slumped in defeat, lost in a way he'd never been before.

"H, we'll get her back. It'll be ok." Si placed a hand on his shoulder. "We'll fix this, I swear to you we will." *Yes, we will.* Hades knew what he had to do. He would do anything to get her back, to protect her, even...even give up his kingdom. He stood on shaky legs and glanced up, taking in the dark beauty of his home. *Not mine anymore.* He looked around at the small group gathered. He met each of their gazes, silently telling them what he planned...telling them goodbye.

"It's time to go see my brother."

THIRTY-FIVE

Skylar was sitting on a small throne in Maynard's stronghold. His realm was truly nightmarish, like the vision Hades had showed her of how the River Styx looked to the truly damned, but worse. The room was large and though he was going for opulent, it came across as desperate. Like someone who had never seen wealth before trying to decorate the way they *thought* a wealthy person would. Everything was gaudy and garish, and the fact that there were blood stains and...*parts* littering the floor didn't help matters. Screams of agony constantly echoed from outside, as if torture was a non-stop activity. She forced herself to remain calm and keep her emotions in check. The last thing she needed was Maynard knowing how on edge she was, how upset, though she didn't think even all her considerable training could hide that right now.

"What's the plan?" she asked, hating the small tremble in her voice.

"You just need to sit there and look pretty, darling. I'll take care of the rest."

"You won't hurt him. Once he hands over the Underworld, you'll let him leave and you'll send me back to the Mortal Plane. That was the deal." Part of her rebelled at the idea of leaving Hades, of leaving the Underworld. It fought back against it so violently that she felt it like a physical blow inside her mind, like someone was body slamming against the walls, desperate to change the course of events. Maynard smiled at her, flashing a dimple, though it did nothing to make her feel better.

"Of course. You have my word." Her instincts were screaming that he was a liar, that his word meant less than jack shit, but she had no choice. This was the only way. She had to do this. He considered her for a long moment and she tried not to stir under the scrutiny. "Why the change of heart?"

She tried and failed to hide her anger. "He lied to me, kept things from me. Important fucking things." She growled and clenched her fists, her claws digging into her palms. She cleared her throat, shaking her head and trying to calm herself. "It doesn't matter. I just want to go home and forget any of this ever happened. Whatever godly shit you all need to hash out, leave me the hell out of it."

Maynard inclined his head slightly. "Fair enough. He should be here soon. He'll have figured it out by now. My brother might be a complete ass, but he's not stupid. I'm sure he'll come riding in like a knight hell bent on saving his damsel in distress." She narrowed her eyes and curled a lip, showing a fang. He held his hands up in surrender, laughing. "No offense intended."

As if summoned by their words, Hades was shoved through the large doors on the other end of the room by two hulking, disgusting demons. They were scaly and *gooey*, some kind of puss leaking out of their skin. Skylar could barely hold back a gag at the stench rolling off of them. When Hades met her gaze, her breath hitched and she braced her hands on the arms of the chair, beginning to rise, the instinct to go to him almost overwhelming, but Maynard placed a hand on her shoulder, forcing her to sit back down. Hades looked angrier and more...heartbroken than she'd ever seen him. *Don't cry, don't cry, don't cry. This has to be done.*

The demons forced Hades further into the room, then flanked his sides, holding his arms. He shoved them off and they hissed at him, but Maynard waved them away.

"Ah, Hades, so glad you could join us. I even took down those pesky wards so you could waltz right in. I really am a very gracious host. Now, let's get right down to business: *kneel*." Maynard smiled the most evil smile Skylar had ever seen. Hades clenched his jaw, but dropped slowly to his knees. The sight nearly killed her. Her proud, strong king shouldn't be kneeling before a piece of shit like Maynard. Chains appeared from nowhere, connected to the floor on either side of Hades, clamping around his wrists and holding his arms out at his sides.

The doors opened once more and Gavril strolled in. He blew Skylar a kiss, nodded at Maynard, and then went right to Hades, greeting him with a punch to the jaw hard enough that Skylar could hear the crack of the bone from across the room. Blood flew from Hades' mouth and Gavril kicked him in the ribs, before punching him again, and again, and again. Skylar screamed and leapt to her feet, rushing forward, but Maynard grabbed her around the waist, holding her still. Hades could have fought back, even chained, but he didn't. He took the beating with little more than a few grunts of pain. She whirled around on Maynard and bared her fangs.

"Stop it. Stop this now. This wasn't part of the plan," she hissed. "I want to be free from him, but I don't want him hurt."

She returned her gaze to Hades and when their eyes met, she could practically see the last flame of hope he had been holding onto that maybe she wasn't here by her own free will, that she hadn't betrayed him (again), die, the light fading from his eyes. He hung his head and his shoulders slumped. Gavril stopped his assault and stepped to the side, leaning against the wall and grinning. Skylar wanted nothing more than to wipe it off of his face...by removing his lips from his face completely. She still owed him for the alleyway outside of Paris, she reminded herself.

Blood leaked from Hades' eyebrow, his lip, his side. A bruise was already forming on his cheek. Her brow furrowed. *What the hell? Why isn't he healing?* Her every instinct was screaming at her to protect what was hers, to fight for him, despite how badly he'd hurt her. Claws and fangs sharpened, heat flooding her chest.

"Why isn't he healing?" she demanded. "What is this?"

Maynard laughed. "A nifty little trick I added to this realm specifically for this purpose. His godly healing is slowed here. Makes the torture much more fun when the results last for more than a few seconds." He threw her a wink and her stomach churned. Hades couldn't heal? Would Maynard truly torture him? Was Maynard's healing slowed here as well then? This plan had all seemed to make perfect sense before but now...

He clapped his hands together, drawing her out of her thoughts.

"Alright, now that we've had a little bit of fun—and we'll have much more later, brother, I promise you—let's get this show on the road, shall we? You know what I want. Hand it over and we can be done here."

Skylar felt him shift beside her, but she couldn't tear her gaze away from Hades. It was then that she felt the kiss of cold metal against her throat and realized exactly how Maynard planned to use her. Hades strained against his chains.

"Leave her alone, Maynard. *Now*," Hades growled and bared his teeth at Maynard, looking like he'd never wanted to tear someone limb from limb more than he did at that moment. Maynard pressed the blade harder against her skin, and she felt blood begin to trickle down her neck.

"Maynard!" Hades bellowed. "Just fucking stop! She hasn't transitioned yet. Stop this! Please. You can have it, ok? You can have it all." He held her gaze as he added softly, "I don't want any of it without her anyway." Her already broken heart somehow splintered even more, the tiny shards piercing her chest like a thousand tiny pinpricks. Hades slid his gaze back to Maynard. "Just leave her alone. Let her go, and it's yours."

She could hear the smile in Maynard's voice when he replied, the triumph practically pulsing from him.

"Say it. Say the words."

"Hades..." Skylar didn't know what she wanted to say exactly, just that she had to say *something*. He clenched his jaw, refusing to meet her eyes again.

"I give up my kingdom. I relinquish the rights and power bestowed upon me and am no longer ruler of the Underworld. I give the rights and power to you, Maynard. You are now the King of the Underworld." A strange light flashed around them and Hades' back bowed, as if in pain. He sucked in harsh breaths through clenched teeth as she felt some of his power pulling out of him, trying to shift to Maynard. *No!* No, this was wrong. She couldn't let this happen... but it was too late.

Maynard removed the blade from her throat and she breathed a small sigh of relief. She reached up to wipe the blood from her neck, surprised that the cut was deeper than she initially thought. He walked around her, towards Hades, but stopped before he made it very far. Skylar knew something was wrong when the color drained from Hades' face. His eyes went wide—with terror.

"Maynard no, please. *Please*, I'm begging you, damnit! I'll do anything. *Please!*" Hades struggled against his chains, desperate.

Maynard spun to face her and slammed a short sword he had pulled from nowhere straight through her heart. Her eyes flew wide, her mouth forming a small surprised "O." The pain was unimaginable, worse than anything else she'd ever experienced. There was something different about this blade, something *wrong*. It felt dark and sinister inside her body, like it was turning her insides to ash as it sliced, filling her with darkness. Maynard smiled at her and jerked the blade out again. She felt it scrape against bone as he pulled. Her legs gave out and she fell to her knees.

She watched the blood—*her* blood—drip off of the black blade onto the floor, adding yet another stain to the grey stones. She tilted her head to the side as she watched the droplets fall. The way the red shimmered slightly in the light from the fireplace and sconces, she saw a faint hint of gold mixed in that she'd never noticed before. It was oddly beautiful, her blood. Beautiful and...powerful? She had no idea where the thought had come from, but things were starting to get fuzzy.

"But you said..." She coughed and felt blood spill over her chin when she did. Probably not a good sign, but she forced herself to continue. "You said...if I helped you get the Underworld...you'd send me back..."

Maynard knelt down and chucked her under the chin.

"Aw, that's just precious."

Precious that she was so naïve, so blind in her anger and hurt about Hades and what he had kept from her, that she believed the words of a psychopath. *Yep, just adorable.* She heard Hades screaming behind Maynard and never had she heard cries so agonized. Maynard stood again and moved to the side so that she could see Hades. He was straining so hard against the chains that his wrists were bleeding, cut down to the bone. She wanted to tell him to stop hurting himself, that it was ok, but she couldn't form the words.

"Sky! Look at me. Sky, stay with me. Just stay with me, love. You'll be ok, I promise." Tears were running down his cheeks. She wanted nothing more than to go to him, kiss them away and make sure he never had any reason to cry ever again, but she couldn't move, could barely remain upright. She didn't care that he'd kept things from her, didn't care that he'd only wanted her because of who she used to be. None of that mattered now. She could feel her life slipping away, but she had to hold on, just a few seconds more.

"Skylar, I love you. I've loved you since the moment I saw you. I don't know why I didn't say it until now, I was scared I guess. But I don't love you because of who you *were*, I love you because of who you *are*. Do you hear me? I love *you*, Skylar, no one else. You're my heart, my soul, my everything. Please. Please don't leave me." His voice broke at the end and so did her heart, one final punch and it was dust inside her chest.

She felt herself going, her vision going black and hazy around the edges, that peaceful nothingness beckoning her, but she held on to Hades with all her strength. He was her lifeline, always had been. She forced the words from her throat.

"Love...you. Will be...ok..." She knew she didn't have much longer. She was barely aware enough to see Maynard step in front of her once more.

"Sorry to have to do this, darling. He claims you haven't transitioned, but have to be sure. You understand." Did she? She could barely remember what was happening, what she needed to hold on for. Maynard raised his hands and she heard Hades bellow once more. She realized what was happening a second before the flames erupted around her, engulfing her.

Ah, yes.

She did understand.

She closed her eyes, smiled, and finally let go.

*N*o! The word echoed through Hades' mind over and over and over. Though history was repeating itself, this was new, so unlike what he'd experienced before. He had hated seeing Persephone killed and burned before him, despite what she had done, but seeing it happen to Skylar was literally ripping him apart. He felt...wrong, like a part of himself were burning with her. He had never felt this kind of pain before and wasn't sure he could survive it, wasn't sure he wanted to. A life without Skylar wasn't a life he cared to have.

He felt as if he were split into two people. One of them was numb, silent, unmoving. The other was raging, roaring, pulling so tightly against the chains that, despite the fact that they were mythically fortified to hold any being, began to give way. He watched in horror as the flames consumed her. His wife, his love, a part of his soul, his home. Yes, Skylar was his home and with her gone, he had nothing, *was* nothing.

The only thing that kept him from just giving up completely was the white hot rage roiling inside him. It was like a living thing, close ing, scratching, digging into his flesh from the inside out, demanding to be set free to seek vengeance. He'd never felt something so raw, so all-consuming before. A thought tickled the back of his mind, but he couldn't even try to grasp onto it. He decided he would met out retribution against Maynard and every being in this gods forsaken realm, and then he would be done. He wouldn't live in a world without her in it.

"I'm going to fucking kill you!" Hades shouted at Maynard. His voice was ragged, his throat raw and bleeding from his screams. Gavril laughed from his spot on the wall, the demon henchmen joining in.

"Anyone else having the strangest feeling of déjà vu?" Maynard smirked, rubbing his jaw with two fingers in mock concentration. He nodded to the demons. "Gather the army. We move to the Underworld soon."

They left the room without a word, but Hades could feel their excitement over the carnage to come. He felt a pang for his people, but it barely reached him. He couldn't accept what had happened, though he knew it was real.

He wanted to stop staring at the flames, but he couldn't force his eyes away. Everything had taken on a dreamlike quality, everything moving in slow motion. Gavril was still laughing as Maynard made his way back towards his throne. Hades flicked his gaze towards his brother for a moment, and when he looked back to the fire he saw... No, it couldn't be...but...yes. The fire was climbing higher instead of dying down, and now flames of black joined the licks of red and orange. Maynard couldn't conjure the black fire, only *he* could do that...So, how were black flames now erupting from the pyre?

Hades' heart began to beat wildly against his chest as a shape began to take form within the flames. *No...there's no way...*The flames reached a crescendo before disappearing in an instant, as if drawn inside the perfect creature now standing on the scorched stone. It was Skylar, but...different. Her skin had a slight golden luminescent quality to it, shimmering in the firelight. Her hair had subtle streaks of red now woven throughout the golden blonde and though her eyes were still her beautiful deep green, when she met his gaze, they darkened, turning nearly black with small flames burning in the irises. She smiled, displaying those adorable fangs, and winked at him. Her claws were out but now they looked more like talons. She was gloriously naked but a heartbeat later, she looked like a warrior goddess in the flesh: a short leather pleated skirt, thigh-high leather boots, and a leather halter top. Blades were anchored to holsters on both thighs, on the sides of her boots, and on the leather cuffs that stretched from her wrists halfway up her forearms. *Way wrong time, but damnit if she isn't the sexiest thing I've ever seen.*

He thought maybe he was hallucinating at first, the loss of Skylar breaking his mind once and for all, but that wink...only his Sky had that mischievous glint in her eyes. And that smile, the one that could tear him apart and put him together again, that was all Sky. She was here. She was back. Against all odds, somehow, she'd come back to him. His heart seemed to heal itself in an instant. He still didn't quite understand what was happening, but he knew that she was back and that was all that mattered for now. Only a few seconds had passed, but it felt like an eternity to him. The most precious eternity.

Gavril pushed off the wall, eyes wide, and began to speak when Skylar turned her gaze to him and cocked her head to the side. He froze in place, mouth gaping like a fish, no sound coming out. Hades could feel the power emanating from her. A mix of his power that they shared, and something else that was entirely her own. Something new and tantalizing and wholly *Skylar*. His own mouth fell open when wings erupted from her back. Real, honest to gods *wings*. They were a mix of red and orange feathers, tipped with black, and flames danced along them, black and orange. Hades' mind suddenly cleared enough for him to understand, for the thought from earlier to crystalize in his mind:

She was part god and part *phoenix*. So, while fire was most assuredly one of the only ways to kill a god or an immortal, it only *strengthened* a phoenix. He wanted to laugh out loud. *Joke's on you, Maynard.*

Maynard seemed to sense something amiss and spun to face them, eyes going wide in disbelief and confusion.

"What the..."

"Cool, right?" Skylar said, waggling her eyebrows as she unsheathed a sword from her back. The sword that Hades had originally given to Persephone all those years ago, the one that he realized now he hadn't had forged for her at all. It had been made for Skylar all along, was hers from the start. She attacked then, a blur of orange and red and black streaking at Maynard almost too quickly to follow. Hades wasn't sure if it was due to surprise or the fact that Skylar was actually better than him, but Maynard could only manage to defend himself, never gaining the edge to go on the offensive as Skylar lashed out with her sword over and over, spinning to use her wings as weapons as well—those black tips were apparently wickedly sharp.

Though she was landing plenty of blows, Hades got the feeling that she was just playing with Maynard. The thought staggered him. She leapt back eventually, giving Maynard a break, and they slowly circled each other. She smiled and ran her tongue along one fang as Maynard glared, eyes black and burning with anger.

"What the fuck are you? How is this possible?" Maynard barked, wiping blood from his forehead with the back of his hand.

"Part god, part phoenix, one hundred percent awesome." She twirled her sword, the picture of relaxed confidence. "Alright, kiddies, gather round: time for the part of the movie where the supervillain starts monologuing and reveals all the scheming, though I don't think I'm *technically* the supervillain here." She shrugged. "So, check it: I needed you to believe that I was so mad and hurt that I was really willing to betray Hades. I knew you'd never keep your end of the bargain, so I just had to wait for you to slice and dice me, then light me up like a bon fire, which I had no doubt you would do. Can we say predictable?" She *tsked* at Maynard in mock disapproval. "It would be just too tempting to make Hades relive the past again. Thanks for that by the way. I needed to die and burn to fully transition, and for all of my abilities to finally manifest. Death by fire is the catalyst for us, you know, so I totally owe you one."

Maynard's eyes were blazing with fury and hatred and disbelief. He wasn't used to being the one getting manipulated and played. Hades smirked. *Shouldn't have messed with my girl then, you prick.* The muscle in Maynard's jaw was working as he fought to remain in control of himself.

"You could have gotten anyone to kill and burn you then, why come here? Why the whole dog and pony show?" Hades could tell that Maynard was livid, but he was also intrigued by Skylar. It was hard not to be. He himself was still trying to figure out the reason behind all of this, so he hoped she would answer and put all the pieces of the puzzle together for them both.

"Because I am the key to the prophecy. It said that the only way to end this war was with me, but it didn't mean that Hades would finally win by marrying me. It meant that *I* was the one who was going to end it. Right here. Right now. I just needed to get the whole gang together for the finale."

Maynard laughed, a deranged, desperate sound.

"As if you could! You may be a demigod, but you're no match for me, girl. Even full gods cower before my power."

Skylar tapped a claw against her chin. "Hmm...are you sure about that?" She leaned forward to stage whisper, "By the way, you've still got a little blood right here, sweetie." She pointed to her own cheek and Maynard growled. Hades saw Maynard's hand twitch as if to wipe the blood away, but refused to give Skylar the satisfaction. Skylar merely smirked, clearly enjoying herself. She'd once told Hades that she could try the patience of even the most serene creatures, and he could tell now how much fun she had while doing it.

"Enough!" Maynard yelled. "It doesn't matter. The Underworld is *mine*, he relinquished it to me. The war is already over. It's *done!* Whether you died then or you die now makes no difference." He sneered, maniacal glee dancing his eyes, blood staining his teeth from the elbow Skylar had thrown into his jaw.

"Act-u-alllllyyyyyy," she taunted in a sing-song voice and Maynard's nostrils flared in irritation. "It wasn't his to give." She snapped her fingers and her crown appeared on her head. "Marriage comes with that pesky 'what's yours is mine' clause. I am the *Queen* of the Underworld. It belongs to me as much as to him—I'm pretty sure it even likes me best, actually—and I don't relinquish shit to you, Kick-in-the-May-Nards." Hades barked out a laugh. She glanced towards him and hiked a shoulder, grinning. "I know it's not as good as Hay-deeze Nuts, but I work with what I'm given."

Maynard roared, the sound unearthly and so full of rage, even Hades flinched. He flew at Skylar and Hades inhaled sharply...but she phased out of the way, landing behind him and kicking his back hard enough to send him sprawling forward. He spun and landed in a low crouch.

She'd *phased*. Like it was nothing. It had taken him months and months of practice when he was young to really perfect it. He was so full of pride for his wife that he felt like his chest may burst.

The symbols tattooed on Maynard's body began to glow and strange red mist began to seep from his palms. He thrust his hands forward and the mist shot towards Skylar, hitting her in the chest and propelling her backwards. She spun in midair and landed on one knee, claws digging into the stone floor, leaving deep grooves. Blood dripped from her lip, but she merely smiled and stood. Maynard kept throwing his mist towards her, but she was somehow able to block it each time now, the mist making impact with an invisible barrier and crackling like lightning. Smoke began to curl around Skylar's legs, just likes Hades' own smoke, but a light grey color instead of his deep black. The light in the sconces around them flickered and dimmed, and it felt as if a storm cloud had settled over them, the air heavy and thick. Skylar threw her hands at Maynard and the smoke and her own fire surged forward, hitting Maynard in the chest. He flew backwards, but quickly put up his own barrier as she struck again.

Maynard's tattoos glowed brighter and he smiled before thrusting his hand into Skylar's smoke. Something exploded within it and she screamed out in pain, stumbling backwards. Hades called out, straining against his chains, but Skylar was already up and snarling at Maynard. She stalked forward and when his mist came at her again, she merely flicked her wrist, as if shooing a fly, and it shot into the wall, crumbling the stone. Maynard's eyes flew wide as he realized the full expanse of her power. He slowly began to back away from her approach.

"You can't win this, Maynard. Maybe if you beg, I'll have mercy on you...though I haven't exactly been known for my merciful side in the past." She gave a mock wince.

"Beg you? I am a *god*! I do not beg, especially not to disgusting half-breeds!" He flew at her, his rage making him lose all control. He began lashing out with blades Hades hadn't seen him pull, but Skylar was prepared and blocked him with her own sword, over and over. Hades had never been more thankful that she'd allowed him to train her, that she'd had such natural skill with the blade. It was if it were an extension of her arm, a part of her from the start.

The sounds of metal clashing echoed through the space, the scent of blood filling the area. Smoke and flames and red mist circled around them as they fought. They came together once more, blades poised at each other's throats but each of them managing to block the other. Maynard bared his teeth and Skylar curled her lip.

"Just remember, I gave you a chance."

With that she pushed away from him, leaping into the air and flipping backwards. She hovered in the air, her wings beating behind her. She wiped blood from a cut on her cheekbone and cocked her head to the side.

"In the words of the great Willow Rosenberg, 'bored now.'"

Skylar held out her palms, causing Maynard to freeze, the same way Gavril had. His mist vanished and his eyes grew wide with absolute terror. Hades had never seen his brother terrified in all of their years, but he was out of his mind with fear of Skylar. Hades realized then that she really had merely been toying with Maynard before, getting some payback for all the pain he had caused. Her new power was staggering, and he had a feeling he'd only seen the merest glimpse of what she was capable of. The legends of the phoenix were vast and awesome. Who know which ones could possibly be true. That combined with the godly abilities she'd inherited from her father, plus the power she shared with Hades...

Well, to put it mildly, Skylar was a creature that was not to be fucked with.

Maynard suddenly fell to his knees as if shoved by an unseen hand. Skylar's chest and shoulders glowed and symbols of her own appeared on her skin. She closed her eyes and threw her head back as a surge of power rushed through her. It flowed through Hades as well, strong enough that the chains broke away from his wrists. He felt it then, wrapping itself around his chest, his soul—he'd shared his power with her and now she shared hers with him.

My power is yours. My kingdom is yours. My heart is yours.

They were one. Now. Forever. He leapt up and though he felt like he needed to hold Sky in his arms more than he needed oxygen, he forced himself to remain where he was. He had to let her finish this on her own. She lowered her head and opened her eyes. The flames within them were now blazing out of control, bright orange flickering within the black. She pinned them on Maynard as he gaped from the floor.

"No..." he whispered.

"Actually, it was *technically* Willow's evil vampire doppelgänger from that other reality where Buffy had never come to Sunnydale that said it, but you know what I mean. Now," she turned to look at Hades, letting her eyes roam over his injuries before snapping her fiery gaze back to Maynard. "You caused my husband great pain, physically and otherwise, and that is something I will not tolerate."

Her grey smoke billowed around her and black and orange

flames formed in her palms. She raised them and the fire shot forward towards Maynard. He was engulfed within an instant, his screams echoing through the room. It only lasted a second before they disappeared and there was nothing left of his brother but a pile of ash.

She lowered softly to the ground and Hades phased to her, both hands flying to hold her face. He stared at her in utter awe. She was glorious and deadly and terrifying and perfect and *his*. She pushed a lock of his hair off of his forehead and smiled. A second later, he landed hard on his back, pinned to the stone by an unseen hand. *What the...?*

Skylar stood above him, one leg on either side of his hips. She crouched down and punched him square across the jaw. His head rocked to the side, cheek splitting. *Ok, deserved that.*

"That was for lying to me about who I was." He started to speak but she gripped his shirt and pulled him to her, slamming her lips to his in a soul-shattering kiss that made everything else in all of the planes of existence fade away. She dropped to her knees to straddle his waist and his hands gripped her hips tightly, pulling her against him. He was lost in the feel of her, reveling in the fact that she was here and whole and his. By some miracle she was still his.

When she finally pulled away, she said a little breathlessly, "And that was for loving me for *me*, not because of who was." He brushed her hair back from her face, marveling at the way her skin shimmered now, like a faint dusting of diamond powder sat atop it.

"I'm so sorry, love. I just...I didn't know how to tell you. That's why I was so angry at you when you first arrived. All I could see or think about every time I looked at you was Persephone's betrayal and I just wanted to punish you for it over and over...even as my mind screamed that you were mine and the connection between us was unlike anything I'd ever felt. It had never been that way with Persephone, and that just made me even angrier. Wanting you that way...it terrified me. But as time went on, I completely forgot about you being Persephone's reincarnate, I just...I just saw you, only you.

You are the person I fell in love with. Not a reincarnate, *you*. You have to believe me, Sky. Please."

She studied him for a long moment, running her thumb along his bottom lip.

"I do. I looked back over our time together and I could see it. I could see the shift and the way that you looked at me, not as if you were looking at your former wife come back, but at *me*. And I understand why you didn't tell me. It was a screwed up situation and you didn't expect to fall in love with my awesomeness." She smiled and he huffed out a choked laugh. He couldn't believe she was here, in his arms, making jokes. What had he done to deserve this? Her smile faded and a tear slid down her cheek as she gingerly touched the cut along his cheek from Gavril's attack.

"I'm so sorry, Hades. I didn't want you to experience any of that, but I knew if he didn't believe your reactions, it wouldn't work. I didn't want you to be hurt." She took a deep, shuddering breath. "I...I wasn't *positive* it was going to work out the way I planned. The thought of it not working, of being taken away from you forever...I've never been that scared in my life," she whispered.

"How did you even...?"

"Emmie spilled the tea about my parents and what I am, and it was like something just slid into place inside me and I understood, like some instinct was finally woken up after a lifetime of hibernation. I just understood deep in my bones that I had to die and burn, and rise from the ashes. And something Emmie said to me weeks ago kept echoing through my mind, too. She said that sometimes an ending is also a beginning: I had to end to begin. I was ninety-nine percent sure I was doing the right thing but that one percent..." She shivered. "I love you. I'm still going to need you to grovel a bit and provide me with lots and lots of gifts—and orgasms—to make all this up to me though."

Hades laughed. "Gods, you sound exactly like Zeus. Like literally, exactly."

"Then he's smarter than he looks," she smiled but turned a bit more somber. "I never want to be parted from you again. Even those few moments was way too long for me." He smiled and leaned his forehead against hers.

"I agree, never again, even for a second. I love you, Skylar. More than my life, more than my kingdom, more than anything."

She exhaled and her lips curled upward. "Mmmm I don't think I'll ever get tired of hearing that. Oh! Speaking of kingdoms..." She closed her eyes and he felt his connection to the Underworld re-solidify in his soul. "That belongs to you. Don't try to give it away ever again, jackass."

He smiled and traced his fingertips along her cheek bones, her neck, her shoulders. He couldn't stop touching her, reassuring himself that she was really here. Her skin was warm to the touch, as if an eternal fire now burned within her. He guessed it kind of did.

"Yes ma'am. But there's no way the Underworld likes you better than me."

She laughed and gave him a quick kiss.

"We'll just see about that." Skylar nodded to where Gavril was still frozen. *Damn, her magic is* strong. "What do you wanna do with him? I did promise him once that our encounter would end with him losing his man-parts, but if you have other plans..."

"Please," Gavril gasped out, finally able to speak again.

"I think my brother would like a few words with you," Hades said.

Gavril paled but before he could protest, Hades mentally told Zeus *incoming* and snapped his fingers. Gavril disappeared, sent directly to Zeus where he and the others were waiting for news in the Underworld. Hades had refused to let them come with him, knowing that Maynard wouldn't have even *thought* about leaving Skylar alive if they'd all come. He knew it was a slim chance anyway, and judging by how things had played out, Maynard had planned to kill her all along, but still, he couldn't risk it. Hades had been determined to do anything in his power to try to save Skylar. His bothers had seen the crazed resolve in his eyes and had agreed to wait—for a time anyway.

"Let Zeus handle him, I've got other things I need to attend to." He wrapped his arms around his wife, pulling her hard against his body once more. She inhaled sharply and he gave her a wicked smile.

"Let's go home."

THIRTY-SEVEN

It had been a few weeks since the showdown with Maynard. Skylar had met her birth father...who, holy shit, really was Ares. She knew Emmie had told her the truth, but hearing it and actually meeting the man, er, god...well, they were two *completely* different things. She understood why fighting and battle had always come so naturally to her now. He told her of her mother and everything he knew of her phoenix heritage. From what he understood, her mother had been one of the very last full-blooded phoenix alive, but they were planning on researching and exploring different realms, hoping to track down more, or even more hybrids like herself.

She'd learned that she could, in fact, leave the Underworld whenever she wished. They weren't sure why, but she had a suspicion that the reason was that the Underworld really did like her best, far better than it ever liked Persephone anyway. Call her immature, but she liked that idea way too much. She wanted to be seen as her own person, not just a reincarnate of some long-dead (bitch) goddess. She wondered why she hadn't regained any of Persephone's memories, but Hades had told her that it didn't always work that way and they had no idea why.

She was a little nervous but looking forward to spending time with Ares. He reminded her a little bit of her dad and the similarities made her smile. He was tough and terrifying and exuded masculinity and danger, but he had a fantastically dry sense of humor and a healthy handle of the use of sarcasm. They got along just fine.

She'd finally plucked up the courage to ask Hades the question she'd been dreading: where had her father's soul gone after he'd died. He was far from a saint, but if he were suffering somewhere, she couldn't deal with that. She would use every ounce of her new queenly juice to set that to rights, but Hades and Charon scoured through the records and their own recollections and only came away with disturbing, but hopeful, news: he wasn't here. He wasn't in any realm, had never come to the Underworld...which meant, he wasn't dead. Her knees had buckled when Hades had explained it to her. Dalton Pembroke was alive somewhere.

She'd phased to headquarters immediately, scaring the absolute shit out of Lucas when she appeared in his new office, which had been about the funniest thing she'd ever seen in his life. She chuckled now as she recalled the afternoon:

"What the fuck, Skylar!?" Lucas gasped, a hand rubbing his chest. She laughed and threw herself at him with probably too much force. She still wasn't completely used to all the new strength and power she'd come into with her transition. He staggered backwards, but quickly recovered and returned her embrace. They each clung so tightly she was pretty sure they'd both have bruises afterwards, but she didn't care. She was at home in the Underworld, but Lucas was part of her family, another version of home that she'd missed desperately.

"How...why...what..." He shook himself to focus. "You look different," he said, brow furrowed. "Good, but...different. Your hair and—dude your skin is kind of shimmery like that pale dude from Twilight. Jesus, I have so many questions."

"I'll answer all of them, I promise, I'll stay and talk all night, but I have news first: he's alive, Luke. Dad's *alive*."

His brows had drawn down. "No...that...that isn't possible. What are you talking about?" She gestured to the bottle of scotch and glasses sitting on the shelf behind the desk. Luke grabbed them before heading to the couch on the other side of the room. "Ok, explain."

She did her best to explain how every soul came through the Underworld, damned or not, and that Dalton had never passed through, which could only mean one thing.

"I was too in my own grief—or avoiding it anyway—to really ask many questions before, but I need to know now. What exactly happened that night, Luke? Tell me every detail, everything leading up to the night too. Everything you can remember." He blew out a long breath and took a large gulp of his drink.

"He'd been working on something that was completely Tier One Classified for months. Even I wasn't in the know on it. He said he would bring me in when he could, but he had to figure out more first. I trusted that he would tell me when he was ready, so I didn't think much of it. I mean, he'd had plenty of jobs like that over the years, you know? Anyway, he had been gone for a couple of days doing who knows what, recon maybe, but he called me at 3:00 a.m. the morning of...well, the morning it happened. He said he had to tell me something crazy and that it was big. Like end of the world kind of big. He seemed worried, Skylar, really worried. And you know how he was, nothing phased him when it came to the job, so I knew something major had to have happened. He said something..." His brows drew down trying to remember the conversation. "Something about 'it's real. The box is real. And it isn't what we thought.' I have no idea what he was talking about and never got the chance to ask him."

Skylar held up a finger, telling him she needed a minute. She took a long drink, closed her eyes against the burn, and then opened them again. She'd nodded to Lucas that she was ready. Luke blew out a long breath and reached out for her hand. She slid hers into it and squeezed, holding on tight.

"I got an alert a few hours later that he was...that his car had exploded. I raced to the scene. I swear I've never run that fast, even in wolf form and you know how fast I am then." He cleared his through roughly. "I was too late. Two other agents got there first and said they saw...they saw him try to get out of the car right before it exploded. It went so fast, they couldn't do anything." Tears stung her eyes, but she knew that he was ok, or alive at least, so that was something.

"Who were they? The two?"

"Hatcher and a newer guy...Realto maybe? I don't know him well."

"What are they?"

"Hatcher's a shifter—panther. I don't know about Realto off the top of my head, but I'll check the file."

"So, we assumed a car bomb of some sort?" Lucas nodded. "And you haven't found anything here that could help us understand what he was working on? Notes or a flashdrive or anything?"

"No, nothing, but I'll look again." She nodded, thinking through the whole situation and definitely getting the feeling that something was off.

"I want to talk to them. Hatcher and Realto. Something isn't adding up here, Luke. How'd he get out of the car if they saw him struggling before it went up? And then there was nothing left in the car afterwards. He couldn't just disappear."

She'd nearly gasped out loud. Maybe *he* couldn't, but she knew plenty of beings who could...most of them of the godly variety. No way her father was mixed up in something having to do with the gods...right? She would have to talk to Hades and the others about that later. Luke had gotten up and keyed in a few things on his computer.

"Both out on jobs, but I'll send messages to have them back ASAP."

"Ok good. So, until then, let's get the grand inquisition over with."

He'd grinned and refilled their glasses before launching into so many questions she did, in fact, talk all night.

THINGS BEGAN to look really sketch when the two agents who had "seen" Dalton die magically disappeared. Could they have been involved? Working for whoever set the whole thing up? Or had they merely been taken out by the same people for seeing too much? Lucas was on the trail, ready to rip someone apart piece by piece if it turned out they were part of this, and Skylar was anxious to get in on that action. She needed more information to complete the disjointed puzzle in her mind.

What had her dad been working on? Who had he been working *for*? He was out there somewhere and someone had gone to great lengths to make them think that he had died. Why? Who? She had far more questions than answers and it was driving her crazy. Whatever the reason, it wasn't good, and he was in danger. Knowing that she couldn't do anything about it today, she forced herself to relax and enjoy the party.

She looked around the room now at the small(ish) wedding celebration they'd decided to throw. Zeus was talking to Zahara and both of them were trying and failing to hide the fact that they were eye-fucking the hell out of each other. Z had told her about summoning Zeus and the price she'd agreed to pay. Skylar offered to try to get her out of it, but Z had given her some line about paying her debts. Skylar suspected that Z just wanted to spend ten days oogling the King of the Gods. Poseidon was there with *three* dates: a siren, a Nymphera Demon, and some creature Skylar had no name for but that was devastatingly beautiful, so beautiful that it almost hurt to look at her, like looking directly into the sun.

All three were trying desperately to vie for his full attention and though Si was giving them his panty-eviscerating smile and flirting at all the right times, his heart didn't really seem to be in it. She didn't know him well yet, but he seemed distracted to her. He looked towards them then and grinned, tapping the ridiculous helmet he'd worn for some strange reason, and winked while doing finger guns at Hades.

"Fucking prick," Hades grumbled beside her. She cocked an eyebrow at him, but he just shook his head, letting her know that he'd explain later. She let it go and continued surveying the room. Ares and a handful of other gods and goddesses were lounging in a sitting area playing some sort of drinking game with Jeff, Athos, and a few other demons. Lucas was chatting with Emmie and Charon while they all played darts. She'd caught Lucas staring at the Seer more than once during the course of the evening. She knew Luke well enough to know when he was infatuated. She smiled into her drink. Luke was in for a real ride with that one. Dean lounged on the back of a sofa, eyeing the whole scene with that aloofness only a cat can pull off. It was still a bit hard to believe that this was her life.

Skylar was sitting on Hades' lap, playing with his hair, when Emmie sauntered up to them. She flopped down in the chair to their right, and hooked her hands behind her head, the picture of relaxed satisfaction.

"Man, am I good, or am I good? You wouldn't *believe* all the work it took to get us here. Thousands of years' worth. Feeding Maynard information about the prophecy through his idiot minions, dropping subtle hints that would only make sense later on, making sure to "accidentally" spill the beans on your heritage at the exact right time. Honestly, I'm exhausted and deserve a raise."

Hades rolled his eyes and Skylar laughed, but the sound slowly faded as she began to worry yet again.

"I know that look," Hades said as he gave her hip a squeeze.

"Me too," Emmie said. "That's worry face. Why do you have on worry face?"

"It's just...I'm wigged out by the Persephone thing. It's weird having this other person or soul or whatever just...*in* there. What if I do finally regain memories of my past life and then I just disappear? Is that possible? Could I just...become Persephone again?"

Emmie looked at her like she was the kid in class eating the paste.

"Well, that's a dumb thing to worry about since you aren't Persephone in any way, shape, or form, silly."

Hades and Skylar both stiffened.

"Umm...of course she is," Hades said slowly. "She fulfilled the prophecy. Plus you *told* me she was Persephone, *many* times, despite me insisting that she couldn't be."

"Ah, ah, ah. I only ever said that Poprocks here was "the one." I never actually said she was *Persephone*. Persephone wasn't ever part of this. You assumed it and I didn't correct you. You needed to believe it in order to move on. You were still too jaded to be able to really be with Skylar, to let her in. You wouldn't be ready until you faced your past. And you wouldn't face the past unless you thought you were quite literally *facing your past* with Persephone's reincarnate." Hades gave her a skeptical look. "Think about the prophecy, bucko."

They ran the words through their minds: *The Queen of the Underworld will rise again. She is the key. Only she will have the power to end the war. Only when it ends, will it begin.*

Skylar sucked in a sharp breath.

"*Holy shit,*" she whispered, and Emmie smiled.

"You are the true Queen of the underworld. When the prophecy said that the Queen would rise again, it meant you rising from the ashes like the cheeky little half-phoenix you are. You had the power to end the war, not by giving Hades the power, but by defeating Maynard yourself—which you figured out on your own. I'm so proud. When your previous life ended with your death, your new life and the end of the war began. Get it?" Hades opened his mouth to speak then shut it, then opened it again.

"But...I...you..."

Skylar giggled at his incredulity, feeling so relieved that she was just *her*, that she would never have to worry about losing herself again. She felt a little lightheaded. Hades let out a long exhale but then his eyes grew wide.

"That's why I felt the connection with Skylar but never with Persephone, why the marriage ceremony was different, why *everything* was different this time." He turned and gently caressed Skylar's cheek with the backs of his knuckles and she shivered at the contact. "It's always been *you*, love. I told you."

Skylar smiled, fighting back tears. Emmie patted her on the head, gave Hades a peck on the cheek, and flounced off back towards her dart game. She stutter stepped though, her eyes going vacant for a moment. Skylar knew that meant she was seeing something that the rest of them weren't. Suddenly she gasped, her hand flying to her chest. Skylar frowned, getting the feeling that something was wrong. She began to rise to go to her friend, but before she could really move Emmie's gazed focused once more. She looked from Dean to Lucas. She tilted her head to the side and looked concerned, verging on afraid. Skylar's blood went cold.

What had Emmie seen and what the fuck did it have to do with Luke?

"What is it?" Hades asked, rubbing small circles on her thigh with his thumb. Skylar watched as Emmie shook herself and plastered a grin on her face. She decided to let it go for now, but she'd bring it up soon. She had that feeling in her gut and she absolutely knew better than to not trust it.

"Nothing, everything's fine."

She glanced around the room, still unbelieving that everything had somehow worked out so perfectly. Her heart had never felt so full and she'd never felt so whole, so completely and utterly *right*. She had never been happier and, now that she had transitioned, she had an eternity to experience the feeling. An eternity with Hades. She turned her gaze back to the man who had gone full on Miley and come into her life like a wrecking ball, knocking down every wall and barrier she'd ever put up. She ran her thumb lightly across Hades' bottom lip and his eyelids lowered.

"Ask me again," she said softly.

He opened his eyes again, brows drawn down slightly. He knew what she was asking and though he looked confused, he decided to play along.

"What are you, Sky?"

She leaned in and kissed him softly. She pulled back and whispered the most beautiful word he'd ever heard, the most beautiful word she'd ever spoken.

"*Yours.*"

Acknowledgments

As usual, this book wouldn't have been possible without a whole host of people, so I need to thank:

- My husband, for always supporting me in this crazy hobby.
- Lexie, the best bestie who has ever bestied.
- Kayleigh and Kala, for being my nonstop cheerleaders.
- My amazing PA, Nancy, who I couldn't survive without and who never bats an eye, even when I say "Hey, what if we completely re-did all of the Gods novels..."
- All of my readers, past and present. I wouldn't have been able to breathe a little new life into Hades and the gang without all the love you showed these characters and this story.

ALSO BY K. D. MILLER

Adult Contemporary Romance

- Carpe F*cking Diem
- Wrong Place. Wrong Time. Right Viscount.
- Puck the Holidays (Vipers Sin Bin - Book 1)
- Puck of the Irish (Vipers Sin Bin - Book 2)
- The Pieces You Kept

Adult Paranormal Romance

- Red
- Dark Burning (Veracity of the Gods - Book 1)
- Sweet Tempest (Veracity of the Gods - Book 2)
- Vows Forged in Blood

Young Adult Sci-Fi/Fantasy

- Titan Rising (Outliers Series - Book 1)
- Titan Unleashed (Outliers Series - Book 2)
- Titan Reckoning (Outliers Series - Book 3)
- Evansfire

www.ingramcontent.com/pod-product-compliance
Lightning Source LLC
Chambersburg PA
CBHW022302310726
48973CB00001B/183